MURDER IN A Moonlit MASON JAR

MURDER IN A Moonlit MASON JAR

CORINNE F. GERWE

ink swift

Murder in a Moonlit Mason Jar

ISBN: 978-1-62020-554-9
eISBN: 978-1-62020-478-8

Cover Design and Page Layout by Hannah Nichols

INKSWIFT
Greenville, SC

Dedicated to my dear mother,
Dorothy Diebold Helton

'Twas the noontide of summer,
And mid-time of night,
And stars, in their orbits,
Shone pale, thro' the light
Of the brighter, cold moon,
'Mid planets her slaves,
Herself in the Heavens,
Her beam on the waves.
I gazed awhile
On her cold smile,
Too cold — too cold for me . . .

~ Edgar Allan Poe, *Evening Star*

CHAPTER ONE

The wailing owl
Screams solitary to the mournful moon.
~ Scottish Dramatist, David Mallet

IT WAS CLOSE TO MIDNIGHT, and the mountaintop was alive with sound. A legion of tree frogs croaked loud and urgent from a nearby stream, drowning out all the other noises in the forest. It was a disturbing, constant reminder to him that time was running out. Clouds had swept across the waning gibbous moon like they were in a hurry to get somewhere. He was in a hurry too, and getting impatient.

"Drink up, Caleb. It's Purvis McCabe's best batch. We can't let it go to waste. Besides, we've got some important things to talk over."

Caleb appeared reluctant for a minute, then took a long sip from the Mason jar. The smooth white liquor would slide down his throat like silken honey, leaving in its wake a burning sensation. Suddenly, his head jerked backwards. He gasped and then croaked in a raspy voice, "Whew! That has one heck of a kick!" He leaned forward, almost falling off the log he was sitting on, and put his left hand down to steady himself. "I'd best be gettin' back now, or I won't be fit for anything tomorrow. We can talk later. I'm feeling way too woozy to think straight."

But when he attempted to stand, his body listed to the right. The jar in his hand tilted, spilling the remainder of his drink onto the spongy moss growing at the base of the log. He stared down at the ground as if in disbelief.

"Just as well," he slurred. "I don't seem to be able to hold my liquor anymore."

It appeared to be true as he swayed back and forth, to and fro, and then slid from the log. A soft thump sounded when his body hit the ground. Lying on his back, he clutched his constricting throat with one hand while loosening his grip on the empty jar with the other. It rolled away, stopping near the foot of the man who stood silently watching, a grim expression on his face.

Caleb continued gasping for air and reached up toward his trusted companion as if appealing for help. In sympathy, a large horned-owl screeched outrage from a high limb above them as furry creatures scattered into hiding. The trembling hand shifted direction away from the man and toward the witnessing face of the misshapen moon. The owl screeched again when a gurgling last breath brought a merciful end to Caleb's struggle. It was a June summer night, the last summer of Caleb Thompson's life.

The one who had watched him die sighed with relief. Picking up the pine branch he'd cut for this purpose, he swept away the print of his boots and checked the well-used clearing for signs he had been there. Satisfied, he went on his way down the worn path through the forest, stopping at an edge where the view opened before him. From there he could see the lights of the small mountain town of Serena, which was nestled below in a shallow-bowl valley; a gap cut through the mountaintop, surrounded by ridges like the one from which he was descending.

He looked beyond the lights of town and those dotting its perimeter toward the southeastern ridge where its peak rose prominent, barely visible in the muted moonlight. His gaze moved downward, searching through the darkness for the dreaded sign. A chill ran through his veins like a runaway train, pulsating blood he had only moments before believed to be ice-cold. He stood there watching a steady stream of smoke curl upward into the night sky, rising from a chimney he could not see but knew was there.

He said aloud, with a mixture of fear and venom, “So the old witch is busy tonight.” Incredulous, he continued to stare, and then closed his eyes and mumbled, “As sure as I’m standing here, she knows. I don’t know how she does, but she knows.”

CHAPTER TWO

The moon gazed on my midnight labours,
while, with unrelaxed and breathless eagerness,
I pursued nature to her hiding-places.
~ Mary Shelley, *Frankenstein*

THE ANCIENT STONEWORK CHIMNEY WAS attached to an isolated cabin, hidden from view by a canopy of dark green forest blanketing most of the landscape. The source of the smoke was a potent concoction being brewed in a black cast iron pot hanging at the center of the chimney's fireplace. The pungent fragrance of herbal-scented vapors filled the air. The eerie, endless rolling-call of a Chuck-will's-widow issued warning to the forest creatures nearby, alerting them to the powerful happenings going on inside and outside of the cabin.

The rapid movement of darkening clouds shadowed the pale yellow moon as signals and stirrings and sacred portents were set into motion by the old woman who lived there. The roots she had gathered bubbled and boiled into a broth of intent. The herbs had been dried and mixed carefully in accordance with her ancient rituals and recipes. She attended to each step with deliberation, adding ingredients not designed for ingestion; hair and bone and the deadly fragrant *Flower of Death*. She was making this potion in preparation for the time it would be needed. It was a time soon coming. She'd had the premonition sent to her in a dream. It would be her final act—an honorable one—making her ready to meet with her maternal African ancestors, the women from whom she'd inherited *the Gift*.

CHAPTER THREE

The moon has a face like the clock in the hall;
She shines on thieves on the garden wall,
On streets and fields and harbour quays,
And birdies asleep in the forks of trees,
The squalling cat and the squeaking mouse,
The howling dog by the door of the house,
The bat that lies in bed at noon,
All love to be out by the light of the moon.

~ Robert Louis Stevenson, *The Moon*

"COCK-A-DOODLE-DO!" CRIED THE MAGNIFICENT DOMINICKER rooster at the top of his ample lungs. Disoriented, with feathers ruffled and appalled at his situation, he marched around the unfamiliar fenced-in yard like a captured king in an unknown country. He had been abducted, mishandled, and almost smothered to death inside a rough-textured burlap sack tied at the top with cord. He'd then been transported in the back of a battered pickup truck before being unceremoniously thrown across a fence into these strange new surroundings. He was incensed rather than frightened, and everyone within earshot was going to hear about it. His crow increased in volume several decimals as he strutted back and forth, cocking his head upward toward the hillside above him and the high church bell tower that overshadowed him.

Kate sat upright in bed, awakened by a rooster's relentless crowing, which was accompanied by the loud cooing of her white pet dove, Dewey. Dewey had recently become a widower, having lost his mate, Penelope. Although still grieving, he remained protective of his domain, regaining a spark of his old self to let the rooster know who was in charge of the hilltop and the old church house where he resided. He was also in charge of a family of tiny zebra finches. Their aviary was situated off the breakfast room near his cage by the window. The large casement window overlooked the hillside and the expansive yard below where the rooster ranted on. The finches were rhythmically chirping like a frenzied backup group to a lead singer competing with a contending performer.

Upon awakening, Kate had thought it part of a dream she'd been having, something to do with a farm, like the one she'd lived on for a while during her childhood. When the rooster continued to crow after she opened her eyes, a perplexed expression replaced her sleepy one. She yawned and rubbed her eyes in an effort to wipe the sleep from them so she could see the clock on her nightstand. It was almost 5:30 a.m.

"Good grief," she grumbled. "Surely the Morgans haven't decided to keep chickens."

She threw back the bedspread and reached for her robe. When she came into the kitchen, the dawn light had just begun to break, but it did not obscure the odd-looking moon still visible through the high horizontal front window. She thought of it as a sign, a reminder of night mingled with morning, the moon holding sentry until sunrise. Yes, a reminder of crimes and misdemeanors done in the hours before dawn, the hours when most people are asleep, blissfully unaware of "*things that go bump in the night.*" She shook her head to rid herself of morbid thoughts. The noise coming from the breakfast room helped, the feathered flock demanding her attention.

Dewey cooed louder when Kate entered the kitchen. The finches followed his cue, emphasizing their role in the major high alert. The manic crowing coming from outside reached a fevered pitch. Kate went to the window by Dewey's cage and tried to see down to her neighbor's yard, but it was too foggy and dim. Her view was also blocked by a row of boxwood bushes and occasional white pines planted along the top of the retaining wall that separated the properties. The ivy-covered wall dropped down several feet to the lower yard.

Like many of the homes built along the ridges within the city limits, the Morgans' house sat only one block from the main street of Serena, but on a higher level. The old church house, Kate's renovated private residence, was situated two blocks up on an even higher level of the ridge, overlooking her neighbor and the town below. Both homes were accessed by Church Street, which rose from Main Street to the top of the hill, curving in front of Kate's home and leading away from it along the ridge to Columbine Street, which led back to town.

There was an old-time saying in Serena:

Up, down, and round and round
Weaving in and out of town
Nothing straight and nothing wide
Hills to climb and hills to slide
Curving left and curving right
Destination out of sight
Walking to and walking fro
Knowing not which way to go
Turning right when going round
Always leads you back to town.

Kate slipped on her nearly worn-out garden shoes and ventured out the front side porch door into the cool morning air, stepping carefully down steps, damp with dew, to a path leading to her lengthy side yard. Squeezing between two thick-branched boxwoods, Kate peered down from the top of the wall, spotting the rooster immediately. He looked up at her at the same time, cocked his head quizzically, and ceased crowing. She was as astounded as he seemed to be, seeing her appear above him out of the morning mist.

He was a creature of enormous size and striking colors: brilliant shades of bronze, black, and red. He raised his head a bit higher, stretched his neck forward, looked up at her for a second more, and then raced toward her with long jerky strides. He covered the terrain between them so swiftly, she was taken aback to find him in such close proximity. There was a strange moment of quiet as they stared at one another, both seeming to understand the absurdity of his predicament.

Suddenly, the silence was broken by a gruff voice bellowing from the back door of the Morgans' big frame house. "Get the gun, Dottie! I'm going to shoot that bird before it sees daylight. Whoever threw him in here is going to pay for this."

A door slammed, and the tall burly frame of her neighbor, Joe Morgan, appeared. His furious expression said it all, and so did his double-barreled shotgun. He was a crack shot, and he too had been awakened by the rooster. Kate knew from experience there would be no reasoning with him, but she tried.

"Oh no, Joe," Kate pleaded, not thinking. "I'll take him. I'll catch him and take him. Please don't shoot him, Joe. Please!"

"Well, you better catch him quick, or that bird will be dead before sun-up. I'll guarantee you that!"

CHAPTER FOUR

I count my time by times that I meet thee;
These are my yesterdays, my morrows, noons
And nights; these my old moons and my new moons.
~ Gerard Manley Hopkins, *The New Day*

DEAREST DEV,

I seem to be the only person on the planet who writes e-mails so formally. I could start off with Hey Dev, a proper mountain greet ing, or Hi Dev, more common these days, or "Hello Darlin'," like the old Conway Twitty song. But I'll stick to my old fashioned approach, it seems more romantic to me, *and* I miss you very much.

I hope the final stages of the sale transactions are going well. I'm glad I traveled to Denver with you last Christmas to help you begin the process. I can now envision your surroundings, and the psychological services practice you established there, such a fine accomplishment. Thanks again for having convinced me to join you for the holidays in the aftermath of our near-fatal Halloween night. I hadn't expected to be snowbound with you during that phase of your recovery, but it turned out to be a blessing in disguise. It gave me a chance to nurse your wounded body, instead of remaining behind in Serena with nothing better to do than worry about you, fend off reporters, and try to analyze in hindsight the mind of the man who almost killed us.

Besides, it was a healthy change for me, and one made more agreeable by such a compliant and lovable patient. The traveling you've done back and forth to Serena since then has made me realize I cannot do without you. So please take care, darling. You've tried very hard to convince me you're completely recovered, but selling your practice and your other real estate holdings has to be exhausting. Although I must admit, your stamina *had* returned in full force long before your injury healed—a subject best saved for our phone conversation tonight.

This separation had been a busy time for me, too. Even though I've taken the summer off, I've had several meetings with my department head to work out a less demanding schedule for the fall semester. Since your investments are enabling you to retire to a life of leisure, take up fly-fishing, and spend endless days wading in the mountain streams around here, I'd better become more adept at frying fish and making hush puppies. I might even tag along with you, Coleman stove and frying pan in tow.

Thankfully, things have quieted down in Serena regarding the news media. The reporters have gone, the TV documentary is finished, the curiosity seekers are fewer, and the warm summer weather has most everyone enjoying the outdoors again. People still talk about what happened and shake their heads in disbelief. The old-timers are more resilient. They've lived through calamity, misfortune, and several wars, and move on as they've always done, setting an example for the rest of us. They know how to let nature take its course and relegate the past to the ancient art of storytelling. They don't attempt to explain a sick mind in any way other than a happening of nature, like a mad dog gone rabid or a hungry wolf gone mean.

Maybe their way *is* better. We've made little progress in preventing, identifying, and curing the most severe psychotic conditions, with all our knowledge and well-funded studies. The old-timers understand human nature through generations of knowing passed down. They see the treachery of humans much like the treachery of weather. When the mighty winds of destruction blow through to destroy their best efforts, they take it as it comes, relying on God's grace and mercy, sadness and death being part of life, suffering and hardship accepted as God's will.

On a lighter note, I *have* had some excitement this week. I saved a gigantic rooster from almost certain death, with the help of Chief Farley, who sent Deputy Purdy up here to help me catch him. I've never seen such an enormous rooster. Would you believe a canine cage was needed for this fine fellow? The poor creature was quite distraught and for good reason. Apparently, there is an old custom around here of dumping a rooster on someone's property to exact revenge for a wrongdoing. It's a noisy and noticeable sign of retaliation and creates havoc for the target; in this case, my neighbor, who was going to shoot him! It might be an effective way to retaliate, but one with little concern for the innocent bird at the brunt of the payback.

I also learned how difficult it can be to catch a rooster when he is unwilling to be captured again. It took over an hour of strategic maneuvering before Deputy Purdy and I finally trapped him behind a garden-shed, and it was no mean feat to get him into the cage. I tried to make his time in captivity less traumatic by feeding him Dewey's seed treats and making a fuss over him, but he was not happy, nor was Dewey, and they both let me know it. The finches are always happy, so that was a bright spot.

Fortunately, after putting up a notice on the bulletin board at the post office, I had a response the next day and found a placement for him. He was adopted by a woman who lives in one of the most beautiful summer homes in Serena. Her name is Charlotte Reed, and she lives up near Warrior Mountain Ridge. Do you remember, Dev? We drove up there one day to look at the gorgeous view.

Charlotte is the wife of Congressman Jordon Reed and had been living full-time in Charleston for the past twenty years. She's returned to Serena for the summer and indicated she might be staying longer. We talked only briefly while waiting for Deputy Purdy to come and transport the rooster, but I did learn that she summered here throughout her childhood and adolescence. She is a bit dramatic and somewhat erratic in behavior, but also charming in manner, and there is a whimsical, childlike quality about her. I had the impression she wanted to confide in me but was afraid to. She hinted at an issue in her marriage and then quickly changed the subject. However, she seemed genuinely thrilled about Henry—the rooster. Yes, Dev, she named him after *Henry the Eighth*. She said he deserved a name "fit for a king."

She thanked me profusely when leaving and assured me Henry would thrive in his new habitat, roaming up and down her glorious banked gardens. Of course, I felt better knowing he'd be in a caring environment—an understatement if there ever was one. And Dewey is certainly relieved after having his territory invaded, feeling out-sized and out-crowed or out-cooed, whatever. Between the crowing, cooing, and chirping that went on until Henry's adoption, it was a blessing to get back to normal again.

My darling Dev, I miss you more than you know as I find my life evolving in many new ways. I feel as though I've come out of the fog into a world that keeps me continually amused and excited. Maybe that's what facing death did to me, made me realize the important things in life: love, laughter, friendship, and yes, even catching roosters.

Awaiting your return,

Kate

Devlin McManus read Kate's message and smiled. Short phone calls and long e-mails—her suggestion—no update information interrupting the warmth of their conversations late in the evening. It was the longest period they'd been apart since he'd come to her aid the previous autumn. The fact their lives had almost been cut short by a maniacal serial killer was only part of the drama cementing their long-distance friendship and turning it into a deepening, passionate love.

Initially, he'd had concerns. After all, he was ten years older than Kate, and his life before meeting her had been marked by tragedy and failure, followed by a miraculous transformation. He'd left the priesthood, which he'd been encouraged to believe was his calling as a young boy in Ireland, for a solid professional life as a clinical psychologist with a thriving practice. His real estate investments had proved more lucrative than he'd imagined when purchasing his outdated office building and additional acreage on the outskirts of Denver. The deal he was about to close would afford him a geographical change and comfortable early retirement.

He marveled at this miraculous event in his life, attributing it to either God's grace or the luck of the Irish, or maybe a little bit of both. After leaving the church, he had retained a desire to help his fellow man, but in a profession more suited to him than the priesthood. He'd met Kate at his first conference in the field of psychology, and they'd formed an enduring friendship.

Over the next thirteen years, he realized his ambition, developed a successful practice, and began traveling to Ireland regularly with thoughts of moving back to the place of his birth. But he had found nothing there to ground him, no person with whom he felt a deep connection. During that time, Kate not only suffered the loss of her beloved husband but had subsequently become embroiled in a series of mysterious events that were almost her undoing. Responding to her plea for help, he'd come to Serena in her time of need and helped her solve a decades old mystery that would have cost them their lives had it not been for the heroic actions of the Serena Chief of Police, Jeff Farley, now a close friend.

Dev re-read Kate's letter. With each line, the force of his personality gathered steam, radiating enough heat to spark a glint of steely determination in his eyes. He was a man to be reckoned with, like an embattled warrior confident in his abilities, empowered with love for another, and equipped with the survival instinct of one who has faced unimaginable demons and come away victorious. Upon his return to Serena, he planned to ask Kate to marry him.

CHAPTER FIVE

There are three things all wise men fear:
the sea in a storm, a night with no moon,
and the anger of a gentle man.
~ Patrick Rothfuss, *The Wise Man's Fear*

THERE WAS NEVER ENOUGH ROOM for his long legs. The opening under his desk was far too low and narrow, requiring him to stretch them out to the side whenever he tried to do his paperwork. Everything in the Serena Police Department was antique, including the century-old building that housed it. The news media had made a big deal about Serena's quaintness, particularly this office. Their condescending articles had irked him, and it took a lot to rankle Chief Jeff Farley. They had failed to note the advanced technology and state-of-the-art law enforcement equipment he had introduced into the police station and its vehicles. Nothing was reported about the grants he'd been awarded for improvements not afforded by the city budget with its limited tax base. This was quite an accomplishment, considering Serena was the smallest town in the county. He thought it typical of outsiders to underestimate the intelligence of a police chief who works out of an outdated storefront office with a screen door and old furniture and a one-secretary office staff. One reporter suggested the remarkable outcome of last year's murder case was a result of pure luck on his part instead of exceptional police work.

Lately, Serena couldn't have seemed more peaceful—except for the usual traffic violations, a public dispute erupting over a new sign ordinance, and one arrest for vagrancy, the vagrant being Serena's one and only homeless person, Sherman Wilkes, who normally camped in the forest by the old quarry but on occasion found refuge in the Presbyterian church basement. Attending to crimes once again on a small scale *was* a bit humbling. None more so than the call he'd received earlier this week reporting the attempted murder of a giant rooster.

If it hadn't been made by his close friend, Kate Delaney, he might have dismissed it as a prank call. Fortunately, Deputy Purdy had just come off night patrol, so he'd sent him up to the old church house with the portable canine cage. Purdy had acted with dispatch, helping Kate capture the rooster and warning her neighbor, Joe Morgan, to put away his shotgun and provide him with a list of possible culprits.

He and Kate had talked later that day and laughed about it. She'd asked if she could use the cage until finding a home for the rooster. He'd agreed, as the cage was seldom needed. She also recommended that he commend Deputy Purdy for his capable handling of the situation. In light of her suggestion and Purdy's recent completion of a police investigative procedures course, Farley had ordered him to further investigate the incident, although rooster retaliation cases were seldom given this much attention, and Joe Morgan was always feuding with someone. Even so, Purdy was delighted with his assignment and took it seriously.

Farley thought he'd heard the last of it. Then the phone rang. He was pleased to hear Kate's cheerful voice. She apologized before asking for Purdy's assistance again.

"I've found a home for the rooster, Jeff! But I need help moving him to his new location. Dev won't be back until Friday, or I wouldn't be calling again. It shouldn't take more than a half hour of Deputy Purdy's time. Incredibly, after posting a notice, I got a response from Charlotte Reed, the congressman's wife. She's staying here for the summer. Do you know her? She said she'd always wanted a Dominicker rooster. How lucky is that?"

Not waiting for an answer, she enthusiastically went on to tell him about the adoption. However, after hearing Charlotte's name, Kate's words faded into the background as Farley remembered a long-ago summertime and autumn under the ever-changing Carolina moon. *She's back,* he thought in reverie. *Charlotte's come home to Serena.*

After the phone call and contacting Purdy, Farley needed some air but would wait till Aura Lee, his secretary, returned. He got up from his chair and walked over to the large plate-glass window facing the maple tree-shaded sidewalk and Main Street.

There wasn't a parking spot empty. Cars and pickup trucks filled every slant-angled space facing Serena's one-street business district. The pedestrians walking by were a mixture of locals and tourists. A steady stream of mountain bikers pedaled along the street, hugging the side of the road as they cycled toward the Serena Grade, the steepest mainline railroad grade east of the Rockies. A pickup truck went by with a sorrowful-looking bloodhound riding in the truck-bed, followed by a Subaru loaded with kayaks and camping gear.

Serena was encircled by a paradise of wilderness that drew people into it for adventures such as fishing, camping, whitewater rafting, hunting, hiking, and for some, escape from city life. The mountains of Western North Carolina held within them the history of an untamed land where Cherokees had once ruled and fearless frontiersmen had once roamed.

Jeff Farley identified with such men, having the tall, rawboned look of a mountaineer of days gone by. His respect for nature was inborn, nurtured by his love of the highlands and its people. When he looked beyond the street, past the railroad tracks, and up toward the misty blue ridges, he knew they also held secrets, past and present, hidden from view and from the long arm of the law. He thought about the sacred rituals performed, customs once depended upon for survival, created from folklore and superstition, old ways and ancient knowledge, handed down and sometimes forgotten, but ever-present and underlying the culture he understood. It was perhaps why he valued Aura Lee and her way of collecting information: through observation, over-hearing, and word-of-mouth, and then translating all of it into a rapid-fire report he had come to expect on a daily basis.

She had been a welcome addition to his staff since the maelstrom of attention brought about by the press had created the need for a secretary. Aura Lee, a veritable unlimited source of information from the incidental to the outlandish, was unable to distinguish one from the other. He'd learned from experience to listen to her. Because of her, he knew more about what was happening in Serena than he had before hiring her. With that knowledge, he no longer took the peaceful appearance of his town for granted. Not anymore.

Farley could see her out of the corner of his eye, a whirlwind of energy coming down the sidewalk with a look of anticipation on her face, eager to tell him something newsworthy. He opened the screen door for her.

Aura Lee Bloom came bounding through the door full of news.

"Oh, Chief, you'll never guess what happened! Caleb Thompson's gone missing, and it's feared he's met with an accident. You know how he's always traveling about, sizing up properties for Rodney Granger. According to Willa Mae Parsons, her father stopped by Caleb's place, and it looked as though he hadn't been there for several days. He's searching for him now, up on Piney Ridge where he'd seen him last. Frank sent Willa Mae to tell you about it. I ran into her in front of the market when I was coming out of the Grill. I told her I'd let you know, but she's in the market now, if you want to talk to her. Judy Ward hired her for the summer to help run the cash register, now that school is out. Have you seen her lately, Chief? She's gotten to be the prettiest thing you've ever seen, always was such a sweet child. It's a shame she had to lose her mother at such a young age. But Frank's done a good job raising her since, she's so polite and all. I also heard—"

"Slow down a minute, Aura Lee. Let's get back to Caleb. Did Willa say anything about Frank needing my help? Maybe I should take a run out there. I know he doesn't carry a phone, but I might be able to locate him."

"She didn't say, Chief. Maybe you *should* talk to her."

Aura Lee paused for a moment and said, admonishing him for the interruption, "Now you've gone and made me forget what I was going to tell you. Well, I guess it wasn't important. I've got to get back to work at my desk anyway."

Farley ducked out the door and walked a short distance to the recently renovated market, which maintained the charm of an old country store and was connected by a wall to the Serena Grill, where patrons enjoyed a fifties theme with Coca-Cola memorabilia. When Farley entered the market, the fair-haired head of Willa Mae Parsons was bent down as she scribbled some figures on a tally sheet by the cash register. When she looked up, Farley caught his breath. Her cornflower blue eyes met his, and she smiled in recognition.

Willa Mae was as pretty as a wildflower, her beauty as natural as the blossoms of springtime. She appeared hesitant and shy, yet open and sincere, her voice full of concern as she repeated her father's message about Caleb Thompson. "I would have brought you Daddy's message myself, Chief Farley, but Miss Aura Lee said she'd give it to you. I hope that was okay. This is my first week working here in the store, and I didn't want to be late."

"I got the message fine, Willa Mae, but I thought he might want some help. Did he say anything about when he might return?"

"Oh yes, I should have remembered. He said he'd come into town by mid-afternoon, one way or the other. I guess he figured he'd either find Caleb or know more by then. He was awful worried though, Chief Farley. He said it wasn't like Caleb to be gone like that, him being regular in his habits. Daddy said he knew that to be true 'cause he and Caleb's been friends since they was boys and they do a lot together, mostly fishin' and huntin' since Mamma died."

Farley thanked Willa Mae and left the market just in time to see Frank Parsons pull into the parking space designated for police vehicles in front of the police station. Farley knew right away there was trouble.

CHAPTER SIX

At midnight, in the month of June,

I stand beneath the mystic moon.

An opiate vapor, dewey, dim,

Exhales from out her golden rim,

And, softly dripping, drop by drop,

Upon the quiet mountain top,

Steals drowsily and musically

Into the universal valley . . .

~ Edgar Allan Poe, *The Sleeper*

THE OLD WOMAN IN THE cabin had finished her work and could finally rest. It wouldn't be long now before she could go to her *final* rest and glory in the spiritual world of her ancestors. She slept soundly, the sleep of the peaceful heart, her dreams floating like memories along a winding stream, taking her back to another time, the long-ago time of her beginning, and an even earlier time that formed the place of her birth.

It was a time when the mountain ridges, peaks, and valleys surrounding her had evolved from chaos and natural eruption into a landscape touched by the artistic mastery of her creator. The source of her power sprang from the ancient slopes of the Appalachians, a mountain range that extended from northern Alabama to Canada; the oldest mountains in North America, created long before the Rocky Mountains. A product of nature's violence, through mighty earthquakes and colossal upheavals, they formed over the centuries into majestic peaks of startling beauty and treacherous terrain.

The peak from which her sparkling waters flowed, shadowed her land like a protective cloak, while still allowing the warming rays of sunshine and the magical beams of moonlight to nurture her plantings, nourish her spirit, and enhance her special gifts.

Shadow Peak was the highest point of the southeastern ridge, connected to a mountain range that extended north for more than a thousand miles, encompassing a variety of trees richer than all of Europe: stands of virgin spruce and balsam fir, primeval pine and poplar, walnut, oak, hickory, chestnut, and maple. The cold rippling waters that sprang from each mountainside fed thousands of steady streams, each with unique formulations of minerals and elements. They were the heart and the blood of the forest, flowing hither and yon, spurning a multitude of cascading waterfalls, some of amazing height and velocity, but none more beautiful and vibrant than the falls spewing from the mouth of Shadow Peak, none with waters made up of such singular quality, and few as geographically protected.

The dense and difficult terrain of the southeastern ridge inhibited exploration into the region for centuries. As such, the wonders it held remained, for the most part, undiscovered, except by the native Cherokees. Only the heartiest of explorers would have ventured into Cherokee territory. Most who had traveled the old trading routes to this part of the Appalachian range had gathered collectively to create settlements and trading establishments in places more conducive to survival. The nearby town of Serena grew from such a settlement, but only after the defeat of the Cherokee Nation and the construction of the railroad up the steep grade rising from South Carolina and crossing through the gap in the mountaintop. Unlike other railroad towns in the mountains, Serena remained small due to its location, bordered by an escarpment dropping over two thousand feet to South Carolina, and rugged terrain extending north, west, and particularly to the southeast, where the ridges sloped down precariously into the southern region.

Yet long before the town had been established, two large parcels of land were acquired at the base of Shadow Peak, the properties divided by a stream flowing from the falls. These parcels were purchased by two extraordinary men, each of whom left a legacy of family ownership, one of whom was her ancestor.

Back then, the land she'd inherited could be accessed only by Indian trails. There were no paved roads winding throughout the mountainsides, like the one ascending from Serena, which curved past the road leading to her cabin. A "Private Road" sign at the entry of the road deterred people from turning there. Those who ignored the sign entered at their own risk on an uneven rocky road with deep ruts and stony edges and an eventual fork in the road, where a sign was posted forbidding trespassers. At the fork, the road split into two rougher dirt roads that separated away from each other like the top of the letter Y. The right side of the Y led to her cabin.

Those who came to her for help took a different route to get there—a shortcut from the outskirts of town that weaved through the forest and intersected with the road on the right side of the Y. The path was well-worn, the trail-head almost hidden. No one wanted to be seen entering or coming out. But over the years, many had trekked the earth-packed trail out of desperation, seeking her aid, her healing touch, or other things never discussed within the community. They came to her with a purpose, sometimes reluctantly, often as a last resort. They made the journey in secret and almost always alone. They came to her with respect and faith in her abilities, and when they approached, they invariably saw smoke rising softly from the chimney and inhaled the welcome scent of heather and dried herbs. No one in need had ever been turned away, but visitors were fewer these days. Times had changed, and many of the old-timers had passed. She had lived a long life and had stayed true to her calling. She'd grown tired and physically weakened by age, her work almost done. Nevertheless, her greatest challenge lay ahead.

There were no trails from town leading to the driveway on the left side of the Y. It was a known fact that anyone who turned in this direction, without invitation, would be shot on sight. The dusty, dirt-packed drive led to a compound built at the base of the ridge made up of a ramshackle homestead constructed with a combination of ragged pinewood and rusted tin roofing. Makeshift outbuildings with haphazardly attached additions spread out randomly from the main structure.

In the distance farther up on leveled area of the ridge above the compound, a tiny secluded cabin sat hidden from view, protected by and nestled into a naturally carved-out hollow. The cabin could be accessed from the compound by a rocky, overgrown path. A much older Indian trail led away from the back of the hollow, crossing over the high ridge toward Shadow Peak and then graduating down until it reached the lavish swirling pool of sparkling blue water at the base of the falls. The properties divided by the stream flowing from the pool were made up of hundreds of acres of forestland that formed a protective boundary around open areas of field and pasture.

Few would have chosen the land below Shadow Peak to claim and settle, as her ancestor had done. Accessibility to the southeastern ridge during the eighteenth century was extremely dangerous because the Cherokees dominated the area and the terrain was a formidable challenge. Yet during that time, the forest-enclosed parcels of land divided by the stream were acquired by two men, both of whom traded with the Cherokees but otherwise had little in common. One was a Scotch-Irish immigrant by the name of Jacob McCabe; the other, a frontiersman named Jackson Runyon.

Men like Jacob McCabe came to this country during the time of the Revolutionary War, escaping the Scottish rebellion in which the fathers and sons of Highland clans were sentenced to death by the British monarchy. Because they didn't trust the monarchy there and were reluctant to be conscripted into the Revolutionary War here, they found a haven in the mountains where they could avoid being ruled by anyone. They settled in family clans, which were like small closed communities, inviting no interference unless it was welcomed.

In the beginning, they traded with the Cherokees and bartered for land with rich soil, plentiful wood and water, and good hunting grounds. It was a bountiful land with mist-shrouded mountains as awe-inspiring as the mystic highlands of Scotland. Jacob McCabe was a whiskey-maker by trade, savvy and unscrupulous, but he also traded in other goods. It was illegal to sell or barter whiskey to Native Americans. Nonetheless, he established a trading relationship with them and began acquiring land in exchange for much-needed goods. It was a devastating time for the Cherokees as invading forces supported by the government posed a threat to their survival.

McCabe learned about a large parcel of land adjacent to another large parcel owned by a man named Jackson Runyon, a friend of the tribal chief with whom he traded. He took advantage of his position during a particularly harsh winter, when supplies were in great demand, and offered a trade for the land he coveted. Runyon was away on a hunting expedition for enough game to help his friend through the winter. He returned home to find the land across the stream from his in the hands of Jacob McCabe, and the tribal chief in a state of despair.

Jackson Runyon came from a long line of hunters and explorers. He made his own rifle-guns and was known for creating weapons of precision and accuracy. He was an excellent marksman, stoic and self-reliant, who ventured into the tangled depths of the forest and climbed up precipitous terrains to hunt in territory that required him to have an instinct for survival and an ability to use his weapons with exceptional skill. All seasons were hunting seasons then, and a hunter's limit was how much he could bag and carry home.

Typically clad in buckskin, he hunted through the gaps and hollows and ridges where smooth-running streams could become treacherous waterfalls, hidden by thick mazes of twisted laurel and interlocking vines. He plunged through bramble thickets and underbrush, climbing the rocky ridges upward to summits and peaks that overlooked vast acres of un-trailed forest. In some areas, Indian trails presented another form of danger, the possibility of ambush, the potential for an attack. On he would trek through streams and gorges, where gigantic boulders could dislodge and slide and crush a man in an instant.

He had a keen understanding of his prey and stalked it in areas inhabited by black bear and panthers, wolves, cougar and bobcats: predators that could tear a man to shreds in seconds. Rawboned and daring, he thrived in the most remote areas and challenged prodigious barriers and obstacles in exchange for his freedom and independence. He was a backwoodsman and a rugged individualist. It was the land that bred men such as Davey Crockett. Jackson Runyon was such a man.

For over a hundred years after the first settlements, there existed a way of life in the mountains governed by a sense of justice that grew in isolation, while a united country and federal government formed around them. Mountain people were protected by an Appalachian fortress that made intrusion into their lives nearly impossible. Initial attempts to open the area to the rest of the world were met with a multitude of geographical setbacks and failures. Those who thrived in this wilderness were guided by their own instincts rather than external governing dictates. They were territorial and defiant, understandable when each plot of ground and each settlement was hard won, costing many their lives.

Jackson Runyon was a man governed by his own code of ethics. In his younger days he had won the respect of the Cherokees and hunted freely among them, sharing meat and hides when the weather turned severe. He was gifted the land beneath Shadow Peak when he became a blood-brother of the tribal chief. The ceremony was held at the base of the falls and sanctified by the waters that flowed from them. Shadow Peak was considered a sacred place by the Cherokees, a place where they had performed ancient rituals and rites of passage. But it was also a place they feared because of the unusual blue-black rock formations that made up the Shadow Peak rock-face; its craggy jutting configurations continually showered and altered by the powerful rushing waterfall. They named the rock-face Demon Rock because of the evil features sometimes seen in its changing structure and composition, and named the waterfall after the symbolic Black Raven, as an omen. The stream below became known as Raven Brook, and the waterfall, Raven Brook Falls.

They believed Raven Brook waters represented light and goodness and the blessings of their gods; the blue-black-rock represented evil and darkness, the shadow spirits, the deadly ones. They also believed the water held the forces of life and death because of its sapphire blue color, which combined light and darkness, and gave it the power to choose between the two. But they kept their knowledge a secret, even in their gift to Jackson Runyon. It would be his to discover and one day to share. They held onto the land on the other side of the stream as long as they could. But a cruel destiny would take most of them away to other lands and a different way of life.

Runyon built a fine and sturdy cabin on the land he was given, made with the best hickory pine he could fell. He lived in it only when he wasn't hunting for bear and roaming the vast mountain range and valleys for months at a time. In the years that passed, he became more of a loner as a steady stream of white settlers moved into the area. He ventured deeper and deeper into the forest and into himself, closing off from a new society and its norms. He'd been powerless to change the tide of destruction that had defeated a race of people he admired, and came to detest his own race for their relentless intrusion. A man of few words, he spoke to few and frightened those he came across with his intimidating presence.

His only neighbor, Jacob McCabe, had started his clan and a tradition dependent on the waters, having made his own discovery of its unique quality. The two men rarely saw one another or communicated. Their homesteads were separated by miles of acreage, but they shared the Raven Brook stream in deeded agreement and for generations to come would be irrevocably linked by it. Had it not been for a strange twist of fate, Jackson Runyon's family line might have ended with him.

Runyon was forty-eight years old the day he found her. He was at the end of a month-long hunt that had taken him into the southern foothills region of South Carolina. He had stopped to set up camp and was gathering wood for a fire when he noticed a young woman lying near a laurel thicket. She lay dying on a bed of pine needles, her threadbare clothing ragged and torn, her fragile limbs scratched and bleeding, her unprotected legs streaked with ropey burns from unyielding vines and thorny branches. She had other bruises, too, yellowish, older, and visible beneath the purplish-black swellings, welts, and lacerations. Her body was bone thin, her skin hickory-nut brown, and her breathing imperceptible from where he was standing.

He loosened his heavy pack from his shoulders and placed it on the ground, resting his long-rifle aside it. He knelt down to examine her, placing his ear to her mouth and his hand to her chest, feeling a slight indication of breathing and heartbeat. Leaning back and staring down at her, he fell into a trance until the snort of his pack mule brought him to his senses. He raised himself slowly, backing away from her, not wanting to turn away.

When he reached his mule, he unstrapped a bear hide and brought it to her, wrapping her inside of it. He quickly made camp and started a fire, then moved her next to it. He brought a small container of molasses from his pack and forced some of the thick syrup, mixed with water, into her mouth. She responded by moving her lips and trying to swallow, as though willing herself to live. He found himself wanting her to live and felt confused by his feelings.

It took days to carry her back to the cabin, but she was no burden to him. She felt weightless in his strong arms, like carrying a child. In the course of their journey, he studied her delicate bone structure and fine form and wondered at the strength of her spirit. When conscious, there was no sign of fear in her eyes, but something more akin to knowing, as though she knew all about him, all his worth and all his pain—not hers, but his—and he desperately wanted to save her. He suspected she was a runaway slave, but that didn't matter to him. He had no desire to *own* her, nor did he plan to send her away. The thought of her living in captivity stirred a desire in him to protect her and allow her to live freely in his home and on his land, where she would be safe.

Her full recovery took many months. She told him her name was Jemmy. She said she had no other. She stayed on with no agreement spoken between them. Over time, she began venturing outside on her own, gathering wild plants and herbs, harvesting seeds from them and planting them, then making strange brews and concoctions from her harvest. She cooked wild game into delicious stews, made in her special way, and minded the cabin whenever he was away. She felt safe there and content to remain.

During spring and summertime, when the plants and flowering bushes and wildflowers erupted in an explosion of color and the flaming wood azaleas burned orange and crimson, she flourished in their midst. She was drawn to the waters of Raven Brook, where the intertwining rhododendrons and mountain laurel bloomed in shades of pink and lavender, blanketing the slopes of the falls and the stream below in glorious profusion.

Jemmy felt safe under Jackson Runyon's protection. No one dared to trespass on his property, not even Jacob McCabe. McCabe respected Runyon's fearsome reputation as a crack shot and, like him, valued privacy and ruthlessly defended his domain. Territorialism and property lines were a matter of life and death in the settled parts of the Appalachians. The Native Americans, who had lived there for centuries, had also been territorial but had no concept of land ownership and had therefore been defeated by an invasion of human forces beyond their understanding or control.

Jemmy had been *raised* in an environment she could not control, victimized by a type of ownership she understood all *too* well. Born the child of a plantation slave in the low country area down the coast from Charleston, she'd been taken from her mother at the age of eight and sold to a wealthy landowner who lived in the northern region of South Carolina. She was never to see her mother again but held her teachings in memory and practice—even at her young age—in the fundamental art of folk magic, known as root-work or simply "roots."

Roots, known to the slaves as *hoodoo,* was the practice of mixing herbs, minerals, and other items into potions for healing and for other reasons known within the black slave communities as "African Survivals." The beliefs and customs brought to America by African slaves mingled with the beliefs, customs, and botanical knowledge of each region. These ancient rituals were handed down by a people sold and scattered and displaced without ceremony or determination on their part.

African hoodoo traditions often incorporated methods from other religions and cultures, depending upon the placements of the practitioners. However, there remained traditional consistencies that were adhered to with an emphasis on personal magical power. Whether seen as witchcraft, mysticism, religion, or magic, the hoodoo practitioner was held in high esteem by those who came to him or her for a particular need.

Jemmy witnessed firsthand the respect given to her mother and learned at her knee by observing and helping mix the potions and conjures. She learned about foot-track or footprint magic, crossroad magic, laying down tricks, how to use ritual candles and incense, how to mix formulas for hoodoo oils, sachet powders, methods for "fixing up" a *mojo* bag or conjure bag filled with roots, herbs, minerals—especially the lodestone—and other curios to stop evil conditions, combining such rituals as floor sweeping and washes and spiritual baths.

She observed her mother diagnosing problems with skill—as a recognized conjure doctor —and counter them with preventive conjurations, sometimes using good luck *mojo* or trick sacks or *mojo* hand after "casting the bones," a method of reading chicken, rooster, or possum bones and divining the meaning. She could also divine dreams and watch the moon for signs or portents of evil. When necessary, she could generate a curse that could scare the living daylights out of the person it was focused upon.

The most powerful curses involved making a mojo bag with the blood, bone, and flesh of a sacrificed rooster—a last resort, as the chosen fowl was prized and rarely used for this purpose. Antidotes were performed to forgive or save a person from untold misery and even death. They included finding and destroying the buried bottle spell, setting out salt to kill the roots, performing ritual baths, sweeping and floor washing to remove powders, and wearing protective amulets, such as a silver dime or nine devil's shoestring twigs in the shoes or around the ankles. Belief in these rituals gave exceptional power to their magic.

Jemmy had developed a natural understanding of this power and had seen her mother use it judiciously. She carried this knowledge into her new surroundings and continued to learn from older slave practitioners, although none were as proficient as her mother. She was a quick learner, and her remarkable gifts were recognized by the elders. She was quiet and modest, performing her duties without calling attention to herself, while also observing her world with intense curiosity. Her intuitive relationship with nature fed her spirit, despite the harsh reality of a life bound in slavery.

However, the strength of her spirit would be tested almost beyond endurance when she began to physically mature. Her lissome bearing and comely appearance brought unwelcome attention from the slave-owner's unruly sons. There was no avoiding the youngest of the three, who took her virginity before her thirteenth year and shared his success with his older brothers, who followed suit at their pleasure.

After four years of relentless abuse, she retaliated with a potion, which rendered each of them violently ill in turn. Suspicion grew around her when hints of her reputation reached the ears of the landowner. She was severely beaten to force an admission of guilt, but she refused. Thrown into slave quarters separate from the others and left alone to suffer from her injuries, she pulled upon her last reserve of strength to flee into the night, facing a death she preferred to the one she would have surely met had she stayed.

Yet when she finally collapsed and closed her eyes in final surrender, she was awakened to an unexpected fate held in the strong arms of Jackson Runyon, and her life thereafter began. For it was with him, after many years of devotion, she bore a child. After his death, she remained on the land he'd bequeathed to her, raising her daughter alone, teaching her as she had been taught, passing on her skills and the knowledge of her discoveries. From mother to eldest daughter, her legacy continued for generations to come. Some of them married men of African ancestry, others men of Cherokee blood, but never again a white man, and their bond with the land and its waters was never broken.

The old woman fell asleep recalling her history, and there slept the wise and gifted hoodoo doctor known as Mamma Phoebe.

CHAPTER SEVEN

O, swear not by the moon, th' inconstant moon,
That monthly changes in her circle orb,
Lest that thy love prove likewise variable.
~ William Shakespeare, *Romeo and Juliet*

COCK-A-DOODLE-DOO!

The resonant refrain echoing repeatedly across Warrior Mountain Ridge slowly awakened Charlotte Reed with comforting reassurance. Her neighbor, Bradford Johnson, had been awake since the first booming crow. He was not a morning person by nature and was neither comforted nor reassured by a noise he found intrusive and irritating. He thought it just his luck, which had been rotten for years. A history of financial instability and poor coping skills had resulted in the loss of one job after another, causing him to suffer a mental breakdown, after which he'd been approved for disability payments. His sister Eunice had taken pity on him and created a basement apartment in her home. His recovery there over the past two years had been a slow process, despite the fresh mountain air, the peaceful environment, and the loving care his sister provided. A gentle soul at heart, she was one of the few people who could tolerate his difficult personality.

Her modest home was located down the lane from Charlotte's sprawling three-storied summer home. From the small window of his bedroom, Bradford had a clear view of Charlotte's multi-tiered garden, where row upon row of low rock-work walls supported masses of flowering perennials, occasional climbing-rose trellises, and ornamental Japanese maples.

White-graveled paths skirted the garden with flat-rock steps placed where needed. The floral displays were accented with an array of statuary and sprinkling fountains, all splendidly arranged to set off the grandeur of the finest summer home in Serena. A statue of St. Francis of Assisi, holding a bird in his hand, gave a benevolent touch to the scene.

Bradford Johnson was not impressed. He reached for the pair of binoculars he kept handy by the window. He'd taken to using them more frequently as a distraction from restlessness and boredom, rationalizing a need for peace and tranquility that required vigilance. He adjusted the lenses into focus, zeroing in on the culprit who'd been disturbing his sleep. The infuriating bird was parading around the garden, strutting as if the morning sun had risen just for him. Bradford grumbled his frustration. He went over to his bed, sat down on the edge of it, and began to devise a plan.

Oblivious to Bradford's scrutiny, Charlotte looked out her bedroom window that overlooked her garden and smiled down at her new feathered companion. His glorious tribute to sunrise had inspired her to rise with the dawn each day and begin her new life in Serena in accordance with his schedule. He had also readily adapted to his new territory, and she appreciated his protective guardianship. He was supremely independent and yet fiercely loyal; she'd named him well. Henry made her feel courageous by knowing she could count on him; she believed their spirits had communed. Besides, he fit into the scheme of things on Warrior Mountain and gave flourish to the landscape, most particularly her garden. In return for his allegiance, he would be treated like a king, a symbolic replacement of her husband, a position Jordon no longer held in her mind or her heart.

In her estimation, Jordon deserved the loss of her love and esteem, had in fact drained them from her in a series of betrayals and abuses over the twenty years they'd been married. While it was true he'd given her credit for contributing to his success, she'd expected his love and loyalty in return. After all, she'd been the perfect political wife and partner, her inherited wealth funding his campaigns and her prestigious family connections providing him with influential friends and allies. She'd even given him the perfect son, Taylor, a replica of himself in many ways, perhaps not as ruthless, not as calculating or cruel, but there were definite similarities—startling at times—and it made her shudder to think of them.

She felt saddened by the thought of Taylor and how much he'd changed. They once had a seemingly unbreakable bond, she and her darling son. She and Jordon had been married less than a year when she'd become pregnant. It was the same year Jordon began his obsessive climb up the political ladder and declared his need for a campaign "think tank" retreat, requesting the use of the summer home in Serena from her father, who was in poor health at the time.

Her father's health had been declining since the death of her mother several years before. He died six months after Taylor's birth, leaving everything to her in a protected trust that excluded Jordon and transferred, upon the event of her death, to his only grandchild, Taylor. Jordon had been enraged at being bypassed. He retaliated by spending more time away from home, often retreating to the summer home he'd taken over.

In a sense, Jordon had taken over the only place Charlotte thought of as home, the place where all her happy memories were stored away for safekeeping. It was the mystical green mountain of her childhood imaginings, fanciful dreams, and fairy-tale wishes. She'd spent her summers there from the time of her birth until her seventeenth year, creating a history of fond recollections of her genteel parents and the graciousness of life then, nurtured under the protective wing of her beloved Nanny Pen. The secrets they'd shared were locked away there too, and along with them, the precious memory of her first love.

For twenty years, she'd longed to return but couldn't bring herself to do it, afraid that returning to Serena would be too much to bear compared to the reality of her life in Charleston. But she belonged there, not Jordon Reed. There were no sentimental attachments for him; it was just a place to use. But then Jordon used lots of places . . . *and people*. They were always around him, running his errands, making his calls, setting up meetings, exploring possibilities, attracting donors, and catering to his every whim, both professional and personal. Jordon operated as a moveable feast, the people and places changing as they were needed or discarded, like the summer house in Serena he'd abruptly stopped using after only one year.

She'd carried on her social obligations in Charleston, creating a fantasy world in which she played hostess to Charleston society for the benefit of her husband, and devoted mother to her only child.

"I will always have *your* love, darling. And you will always have mine."

The words became a ritual, a mantra she repeated over and over to diminish the loneliness and dispel her growing disappointment and despair. Taylor became the center of her world, the core of her stability, the foundation upon which she performed the endless social duties vital to Jordon's political career, thinking only of Taylor's future instead of her frequently absent husband. She entertained lavishly in the magnificent home she'd inherited, and always included her son whenever possible, doting on him in private to an obsessive degree.

By the age of twelve, Taylor had become mature for his age, and accustomed to attention and praise, not only from his mother, but from the scores of people invited into their home. He'd grown tired of it, wondering if all the fawning over him was just a ploy to gain access to his father. It started with something his mother had said after one of her parties, a comment about the hidden agendas of people. He hadn't understood at the time, but it triggered in him a curiosity, which grew into suspicion. He hadn't trusted words of praise since that night, suspecting a motive for each act of friendship.

His mother's possessiveness had also become tiresome. He felt suffocated by her, and wondered about her motives too, and why his father was away so much. He yearned to spend time with the one unattainable person in his life;

Taylor believed him to be trustworthy. After all, wasn't his father trusted and admired by a multitude of voters and supporters?

As if suddenly granting Taylor's wish, Jordon began spending more time in Charleston. He was running for Congress and needed to project a solid family image and background. His attentions turned toward Taylor rather than Charlotte, and as he and his son grew closer, Charlotte felt increasingly excluded. Within a very short period of time, a bond formed between them she found difficult to comprehend, considering Jordon's lack of parental interest during Taylor's childhood. She attributed some of this bond to Jordon's need to have an ally in their home. Their marriage had deteriorated to one of convenience and polite civility. Divorce was out of the question, in view of Jordon's probable election to Congress and his continual need for campaign funds.

After he'd been elected, the years passed quickly in a haze of public duty and demands. During his high school years and first year of college, Taylor spent time with his father in Washington whenever Congress was in session, while Charlotte remained behind in Charleston. It became evident to Charlotte that he was being groomed for some future role in his father's life that didn't include her. Concerned her son was growing more distant, she bargained with Jordon to have Taylor spend part of the summer with her in Serena, where she had impulsively decided to relocate for an undetermined period of time.

In previous years, Jordon would have been appalled at her decision to return to Serena and bullied her into staying in Charleston. But things had changed, and he was no longer concerned about his public image. He thought it fortuitous that her presence in Serena fit nicely into his plans. He agreed under the condition that Taylor take a summer job working for a local realtor and supporter, Rodney Granger, with whom he'd remained in contact since his early days in politics. He assured her that Taylor would gain valuable experience in real estate investment and land development by taking this summer job. He said he'd been thinking of making some land investments and wanted Taylor to be knowledgeable on the subject.

Charlotte didn't know Rodney Granger and wondered what he and Jordon could possibly have in common. She also thought it strange that a job for Taylor had been so quickly arranged. She assumed it was Jordon's way of keeping Taylor in his clutches. She could not have imagined the extent of his ruthless scheme.

It seemed to Charlotte that her marriage had become a sham and their son a pawn. Throughout the years of Jordon's political rise, she had gradually lost her sense of identity and self-esteem, while Jordon had gained his egotistical air of entitlement. She needed a break from everything involving him. Taylor was eighteen years old, and Charlotte desperately wanted a chance to restore their relationship in a different setting, away from Charleston society and Washington politics. Returning to the place of her youth, there might be a chance for renewal. Therefore, she was pleasantly surprised when, after talking to his father, Taylor agreed to take the job with Rodney Granger and spend the summer with her in Serena. What she did not realize was how well her request fit into her husband's agenda.

Charlotte arrived in Serena in early May, before Taylor's semester ended. She wanted plenty of time to settle in and prepare. The grand summer home on Warrior Mountain Ridge had been built by her great-grandfather, who had left a legacy of wealth and property for his heirs. Charlotte would have been the last of his line had she not given birth to Taylor, who would eventually inherit everything from her. She had only recently begun to suspect Jordon's motives for monopolizing her son.

She had to fight back in the only way she could: by reaching into the past to find the strength she needed, and by trying to remember everything Nanny Pen had taught her. She would not be defeated by a man who had used her for her money and who was now using his son. Here in the mountains, she would find her courage, her center, her equilibrium. She was part of the old Serena gentry and knew the old ways—and who to go to as a last resort.

CHAPTER EIGHT

The devil's in the moon for mischief;
they who called her chaste, methinks began too soon
Their nomenclature; there is not a day,
the longest not the 21st of June,
Sees half the business in a wicked way,
On which three single hours of moonshine smile—
And then she looks modest all the while.

~ Lord Byron, *Don Juan*

ERNIE DAVIS REACHED THE Y fork in the road before sundown. His nerves were shot, and his shirt was soaked with sweat, partly from exertion, partly from fear. He wasn't sure he could go through with it. He started going over everything in his mind, recriminating himself with every step, thinking out loud in mumbled whispers.

"I should have refused, but I got myself in a bind. Doing this job *is* the only way out. That's what happens when you get in too deep with Rodney. He lets you take the line out so far, you get to thinkin' you're on your own. Next thing you know, you're sellin' a little extra on the side and takin' more for yourself. Then he reels you in like a wily old fisherman, like he know'd all along you'd been takin' from him. Look what happened to Caleb. Caleb tried to get out from under him. He even threatened to go to Chief Farley.

"Just keep thinkin' about what happened to Caleb and keep movin', Ernie. Better yet, quit thinkin', period, and pay attention to what you're doin'."

He planned to stay off the long driveway toward the compound, using patches of woodland and underbrush for cover. A map marked the spot where he could cross the pasture toward the stream without being seen. From the stream, he'd climb the ridge to the hiding place indicated on the map that showed where Purvis McCabe kept his still. It would be dark by then. After doing the job, he'd have to rely on the light of the moon to find his way back out, if he wasn't shot first. He was already exhausted and had at least another mile to cover before dark. If McCabe spotted him, it would be the end of everything. Everybody knew the old man had the instincts and nose of a bloodhound.

Dense forest bordered McCabe's property on every side except for the bottomland extending out from the Raven Brook stream. The Shadow Peak Ridge rose above the fields and pastures like a protective fortress of greenery camouflaging an internal system of ledges, hollows, caves, and crevices, a natural masterful design as tricky as an intricate maze. Purvis McCabe was the great trickster who had been master of the moonshine trade for decades. The ancestral skill of whiskey-making had been passed down to him through the genes of Jacob McCabe and his predecessors in Scotland. Ernie had heard stories about Jacob McCabe and tried to remember some of them to keep his mind off the dangerous property upon which he was trespassing.

The legend of Jacob McCabe began with his questionable trade with the Cherokees for the land adjacent to Jackson Runyon's property. A tale was also told of his trade with the Cherokee chief for one of the tribe's youngest maidens. At that time it was illegal for a white man to marry a person of Native American or African descent. But the mountain people intermarried at their own discretion and without interference from outside authority. Legal enforcement in these matters would not come until much later, and by then the mountain culture had become a rich mixture of race and culture, the Scotts-Irish/Cherokee combination quite prevalent.

McCabe and his wife produced numerous children and turned his whiskey-making trade into a profitable, albeit illegal, family business. He'd been taught every nuance of his craft as a boy in Scotland and had inherited the talent necessary to make an exceptional product. His experience as a trader gave him a network upon which to build as his moonshine gained a widespread reputation for fine quality. He trusted no one outside the family and depended on his children for product distribution, setting a precedent for future generations. His property was off-limits to customers or anyone else who dared to trespass.

Through the Civil War, Prohibition, and the Great Depression, McCabe's large family dwindled in size but continued their trade, the property handed down from father to eldest son to the present day. They were a fearsome bunch who lived in a world within a world as a law unto themselves. Nevertheless, the eldest son of each generation carried on the tradition with steely determination and authoritarian rule.

Ernie remembered Purvis McCabe from younger days, when his two brothers were still living on the compound, before the death of his wife and then the tragic death of his daughter, Evangeline. He'd been in his early teens when he began delivering moonshine for Purvis. He'd been trusted with the job because of his uncle, who had run liquor for Purvis for many years. He'd known all the pick-up points back then and had been slick as a fox, never getting caught, even when revenuers were sniffing around. He'd heard about one revenuer who had sneaked onto McCabe land and never been heard of again. But that was before the feud broke out between Purvis and his brothers. After they took off, Purvis cut back on production and distribution, becoming a one-man operation with only two trusted carriers and pick-up places known only to them. That was right around the time Purvis had a falling out with Evangeline. Talk was, she'd moved out of the main house up to the old cabin above the compound, keeping mostly to herself. She was never seen in town again.

Then one morning, that old healer woman, Mamma Phoebe, found Evangeline lying dead in the Raven Brook stream. Seemed she'd slipped, hit her head, and dragged herself to the edge of the water. The old woman had to cross the stream—the first time ever she'd crossed the property line—to tell Purvis the bad news. He was never the same after that, and he became even more reclusive and paranoid about trespassers.

It was getting dark now, and Ernie's attention turned in the direction of the stream, which he could hear in the distance. When he reached it, he followed alongside against the flow of the current toward the falls. The moon was reflected in the rippling waters, lighting his way and producing a hypnotic effect on him. Darkness fell when he diverted away from the stream through a tangle of laurel to begin his climb toward the ledge where the moonshine still was hidden. He no longer had to check his map, remembering the way and the one time Purvis had allowed him to see it. No other runner had been given this privilege, and he'd felt proud to have won his trust. It happened right before he went into the Army and was the last job he'd done for the old man.

He'd never told anyone about its location. To do so would break a mountain code of silence he'd been taught since birth. No, he'd never told anyone until that long fateful night of drinking with Rodney Granger. Now he was being forced to do a terrible deed because he'd allowed himself to be manipulated into talking too much and bragging about knowing the whereabouts of the still.

It was a dirty thing he'd done, and a dirty thing he was about to do. Riddled with shame and guilt, he reached his destination like a man walking in his sleep, driven by a force greater than himself. After adding the mixture he'd been ordered to pour into the distiller, he looked up through the trees at the pale cold moon staring back at him and cried.

Later that night, close to midnight, caught in the callous stare of eyes much colder than the moon, it was almost a relief to slip into the deep blackness of death as atonement for his betrayal.

CHAPTER NINE

We're both looking at the same moon, in the same world.

We're connected to reality by the same line

All I have to do is quietly draw it towards me.

~ Haruki Murakami

DEAREST DEV,

I can hardly believe I will see you on Friday. How wonderful! It must be a relief to have your transactions completed and the closing set up for tomorrow. I hope the transition was made easier knowing the fine psychological practice you established will be in good hands. Are you feeling a sense of freedom yet? I suppose I should wait until tomorrow to congratulate you, when the signatures are on the dotted line.

I am certainly relieved to have things worked out with the university and the whole summer off to enjoy time with you. I've been doing lots of sprucing up around here. The old church house has a fresh new look, and the flowering bushes in my front garden are in bloom. The lavender pink and lilac rhododendrons, crimson camellias, and spring roses are so pretty, and the Rose of Sharon bushes I transplanted have taken hold. Roving sweet peas cover the hillside, and large pots of red geraniums sit on the front side porch. I think the old church reflects the happiness inside and out after so much sadness and sorrow. How lovely for the month of June.

However, (don't be worried) there have been a few strange events happening, but nothing to do with the house. The first concerns the woman, Charlotte Reed, I wrote to you about who adopted the rooster. I think she now considers me a friend. The friendship began with a lovely note she sent, thanking me for Henry, the rooster. I thought no more about it until I received another note with a poem she had written about him that she wanted to share with me. Yes, Dev, a poem, entitled *Reigning over Warrior Mountain*. Here it is:

Each day I break the peaceful calm,
My trumpet peals a mighty cry.
It is my fate to greet the dawn,
If one should ask, I know not why.
I stand upon my trusty perch,
In regal stance, as I survey
The quiet vista, sleeping sound,
The message clear I must relay.
Awake! Awake! The time is now,
The day is new, it's time to rise.
My noble task seems never done
And some resist my urgent cries.
Why must it be that those who rule
Must rise above in every way?
I greet each dawn with firm resolve
To help my subjects start the day.

~ Henry the Eighth

At first, I thought she had written it as a joke. I tried to compose a note in reply, but wasn't quite sure how to word it. The problem was solved when she phoned and invited me to lunch. That is when things really got weird.

Of course I was delighted to have a chance to see the inside of her home and thought it kind of her to invite me. She was very gracious when I arrived and immediately gave me a tour. She'd recently had the entire house redecorated, and it was like something featured in *House Beautiful*. She had dressed casually, for which I was grateful, but on her, casual looks chic. I looked shabby in comparison. Charlotte is very attractive, slim and fine-boned, and projects a tense combination of frailty and strength. Again, I felt quite sympathetic toward her; there was something odd in her behavior, she seemed troubled, acted nervous, her movements erratic, her mood changeable. I found myself trying to put her at ease.

After the inside tour, she led me outside to her magnificent garden so I could, as she put it, reunite with her pride and joy, Henry. The rooster was perched on the edge of a fountain, dipping his beak into the water. As we approached, he calmly looked up at us and cocked his head back as though questioning our right to be there. It was very comical, but then became absurd when Charlotte proceeded to introduce me to him.

"Please don't be offended by our intrusion, Henry dear. Don't you remember your kind and brave savior, Miss Kate? She's come for a visit."

Henry (yes, Dev, I know he is a rooster) ruffled his feathers and looked at both of us as if we were insane, or maybe it was my imagination.

Charlotte dramatically made his excuses. "Please forgive him, Kate. He's just had his lunch, and it's time for his afternoon nap. Maybe he'll be more charming when you come out to say goodbye after we've had *our* lunch."

Turning to Henry, she asked, "Do you think you could be more attentive, darling, after your nap?"

No answer, haughty expression.

Lunch was served on the veranda and, much to my surprise, Charlotte had prepared everything herself: chicken salad with grapes and walnuts, iced tea, and a light strawberry frappe dessert. She told me she'd learned to cook as a child from a family servant, "Nanny Pen," who had served as both nanny and cook for her family when they'd summered here. She went on to talk about her with great affection, and I learned that Nanny Pen, who may still be in this vicinity, is the younger sister of a woman named Mamma Phoebe, who lives out on the southeastern ridge. According to Charlotte, Mamma Phoebe was a renowned healer who taught her younger sister the practice of "roots" (I'll explain about roots when I see you).

Nanny Pen worked for Charlotte's parents until Nanny's mother's death, when Charlotte was around age sixteen, after which her father decided to take Charlotte to live permanently in their Charleston home until a suitable marriage could be arranged for her. Apparently, she hasn't seen Nanny Pen since.

Perhaps she hadn't meant to, but once she began talking about Nanny Pen, she couldn't seem to stop. There was a faraway look in her eyes, and she appeared to be in a mild trance while telling me of the close relationship they'd had during her childhood. She said,

"I had no siblings and few playmates. But I didn't need them when I was with her. Nanny Pen taught me the mysteries of life during the many hours we spent together while she worked in the kitchen. She was never idle, and always encouraged me to be as creative as she was. She made cooking an adventure into the healing arts, and I learned secret recipes I had to promise never to share with anyone. She taught me about plants and animals and the importance of having a kinship with nature and the wild.

"You see, Kate, it was Nanny Pen who taught me about roosters and how certain ones have special qualities that can serve you well, particularly when they are separated from the others of their kind. Of course they can be used for bad things too. But then you know that, having saved Henry—and the Morgans, I might add—from the curse put upon them, one which surely would have come to fruition had Joe Morgan shot my poor sacrificial lamb. When I think of how Henry was treated, I could sob. He was meant for more important things. I knew it as soon as I laid eyes on him, even before, when I first heard about the incident. Why his feathers alone . . . "

I must have looked shocked, Dev. I was certainly speechless. Then she abruptly changed the subject to her son, Taylor, who was expected to arrive the next day to spend the summer with her. She went on to tell me about how close they had once been, sharing more intimately than I'd expected, disclosing problems in her marriage, implying that Taylor was caught in the middle. I was still reeling from the rooster story (the part about the curse) and had heard enough. Sensing my discomfort, she suddenly became bright and cheerful again, as though nothing she had said was of any importance, indicating I should forget all of her ramblings and "glory in the day." Of course, before I could leave, we had to return to the garden to say my farewells to "Darling Henry." He actually looked sorry to see me go.

The other news I have concerns Jeff Farley. He stopped by yesterday morning to ask about you, when you'll be back. I invited him in for coffee, and our conversation led to the reason he wants to talk you: a matter concerning the apparent accidental deaths of two local men, Caleb Thompson and Ernest Davis. The deaths occurred as two separate incidents, the bodies found in different locations, with no apparent connection. But he said both bodies were discovered in the forest, and both died of alcohol overdose.

I didn't know Caleb Thompson personally, but knew who he was. The other man, Ernie Davis, I didn't know at all. Jeff knew them and said they had both been heavy drinkers in the past. He is having trouble accepting the notion that either man went so far as to drink to the excessive point of overdose. He also suspects the alcohol may have been toxic, illegally distilled liquor and is concerned about its source. The coroner made a determination of alcohol poisoning, and the deaths were reported accidental. Jeff is not convinced. The medical examiner told him that toxins were not unusual in moonshine whiskey, and there would have to be more evidence to change the cause of death.

Jeff says a detailed screening could be requested, but Jeff is reluctant to push the issue until talking to you. He said he'll probably be accused of making a mountain out of a molehill, or even grandstanding after all the attention he's received since last fall. But you and I know Jeff is not one to jump to conclusions. If something doesn't seem right, he won't let it go until he's completely satisfied, and at present, he's not.

I felt pleased that he trusted me enough to confide, at least in your absence. The three of us *have* been through a lot together. I told him you'd call him as soon as you arrive.

However, he will have to wait until after you are properly welcomed home.

Your loving Kate

CHAPTER TEN

Turn, turn, my wheel! All things must change
To something new, to something strange;
Nothing that is can pause or stay;
The moon will wax, the moon will wane,
The mist and cloud will turn to rain,
The rain to mist and cloud again, To-morrow be to-day.

~ Henry Wadsworth Longfellow

THE SPEEDOMETER READ EIGHTY-FIVE AND climbing. The new BMW sports car raced steadily toward the exit off I-85 toward the mountains. There wasn't a state patrol car in sight, but Taylor Reed wasn't watching for one anyway. That would take all the fun out of the risk. He pressed harder on the gas pedal and then eased off as he approached the exit ramp onto I-74. It would be another long stretch of highway and at least another hour before the mountains came into view. He wasn't in a hurry, and yet continued to push his luck, increasing his speed again and feeling the rush as the mile markers flew by.

The sky had been perfectly clear, a robin's egg blue all day long until late afternoon when an unseen artist, gone mad with his brush, painted bold streaks of white and granite-blue clouds across the sky canvas, outlining them in deep purple, backlit by the glow of an orange-red setting sun. Taylor enjoyed this type of imagery, particularly when on drugs, and felt aroused by the scene and the impending dusk. If he gauged his time right, he could reach a vantage point where he could see the mountains on the horizon before they melded into a blackened moonless sky, a dark-of-the-moon sky.

Suddenly, with this imagery, he felt a different kind of darkness close over him and began to slow down. He'd be there soon enough, and then the eternal weeks would stretch before him like the seemingly endless highway ahead.

He felt his heartbeat slow in accordance with his speed. His recent lifestyle had kept him in a perpetual state of heightened excitement, which he'd supplemented with performance-enhancing drugs and secretive late night activities. He could feel the depletion of adrenaline as his body began to relax and felt the urge to kick himself "back into gear" in the way one would fuel an engine—his fuel being drugs. He resisted the temptation, although he had plenty of supply in a hidden compartment of the car.

He laughed—quietly, sardonically. The car he was driving was top of the line, tricked out with all the bells and whistles, the reward for his undivided loyalty.

He was tired. He'd been tired of it for so long. First his mother, then his father, then both, and now this; he wasn't even angry anymore, just tired. He knew she'd be waiting, had been so happy when he'd called earlier to let her know he was on the way. She'd pull out all the stops, probably had the house redecorated, flowers everywhere, a million plans for their joyous time together, her enthusiasm marred by disappointment regarding his summer job. Always it was there, the division, the inescapable reality of his life, at least for the present.

He'd have rebelled long ago if not for his reliance on them. He reflected on his childhood as a distraction from his nagging urges. There'd been an absence of competition for his loyalty then. There'd been only his mother, who'd catered to his every need while smothering him with her all-consuming love. He had supposed it was due to his father's continual traveling during those years—that is, he'd later supposed it—hadn't really thought about it when he was a boy. He couldn't remember what he'd thought about then, but did remember a desire to be free, to be away from his mother's cloying attention and that of others he mistrusted. He recalled having wished for more time with his father, who'd paid little or no attention to him during that time.

What was the saying? *Be careful what you wish for.* Well he'd gotten his wish, but not his freedom. After his twelfth birthday, when his father's attention miraculously turned toward him, it had felt like a beam of magnetic light on his entire being, energizing his spirit and pulling him out of an abyss of maternal protection into a man's world of new knowledge and adventure. Defiantly, he'd tried to break free of his mother's hold on him. Sadly, he'd found it necessary to turn his back on her to gain his father's favor. Having no avenue of compromise, it had to be one or the other. His emotional survival thereafter depended on suppressing his love for her and any guilt that surfaced.

To ensure his allegiance, his father had showered him with the expensive boy-toys coveted by his peer group. With the means to attract them, he'd gained many friends, not that he believed any of them were true friends. His cynical notion about their ulterior motives became an ever-present source of insecurity. He'd felt more comfortable buying friendships than believing in them. As a result, he'd often felt alone in a crowd, and increasingly lonely when alone. Alcohol and other drugs became the great equalizer.

In time, he'd matured from avoiding his mother, having learned the advantages of appeasing both his parents for his own benefit, to spending time with her in small doses. It was the closest thing to a loving relationship he could muster. He'd also become accustomed to privileges and luxuries and was not about to go without until he could find a way to afford them himself. This summer was going to be an endurance test, but a necessary one.

In comparison, his relationship with his father had developed from a wish granted to a nightmare of pressure and complexity. The man he had once admired—adored really—had bizarre hidden facets to his personality, which had been revealed to him in a series of startling discoveries. The first one came as a shock to his young pubescent mind when he discovered his father's cache of pornography, including intimate photos of nude women, some of whom had visited in their home; one he recognized as the wife of his father's accountant. He'd felt both repelled and excited, feeling sickened by his own arousal. He could never see his father in the same light again and grew more curious about his extra-curricular activities.

Around age fourteen, on the first of what would become their seasonal hunting trips, a lecture ensued about the facts of life and the nature of women. His father had a system for dividing women into categories and explained why the use of women designated to certain categories was a practical and natural custom to adopt for sexual pleasure. During his father's lengthy discourse, Taylor had felt trapped, horribly embarrassed, disgusted, and simultaneously intrigued. Ashamed and agitated, he'd wanted to escape the complicated reality his father presented and return to his idealized fantasies about sex.

He'd had flirtations with girls during middle school. Several of them had made sexual advances. There'd been the typical experimenting, most of it innocent and harmless. He'd had a tendency to resist the more aggressive girls, being drawn to those who had little interest in him and therefore no hidden agenda.

Thinking back, he realized he'd not been ready for such a talk. Perhaps his father had thought him more mature at that age, more like him. But he'd had a romantic imagery more akin to his mother's unrealistic nature and approach to life. As he recalled, the first sexual fantasies of his puberty were rather Byronic—not that he knew who Lord Byron was then. There was always a fair young maiden at the center, a medieval scene, a robust chase, a final seduction, usually on a hillside or in a field of flowers. They were nothing more than sexualized versions of the fairy-tales his mother had read to him as a young boy.

He laughed a little and said to himself, "What a screwed-up kid I was then."

Of course the pornographic images of his father's collection, once discovered, had invaded his puritanical fantasy world like a virus until they mutated into some kind of strange mix he had yet to sort out. He was obviously not as categorical as his father.

His sexual education over a series of hunting trips was followed by an introduction to the real thing, arranged by his father on the momentous occasion of his sixteenth birthday. Per his father's instructions, his dating life was kept separate and above-board, seldom enjoyable, too often boring, and increasingly led to after-hour excursions into a downtown underworld of sexual deviance. By the time he'd entered college, he was a master of the game, more worldly than his freshmen peers, and an accomplice to his father in both public and private life.

Now, having completed his freshman year, he was being asked (the same thing as an order) to spend the summer with his mother, and he had no idea how he was going to get through it. Of course, his father had a purpose for his visit, and his dealings with Rodney Granger were behind it. Taylor had been kept in the dark about the nature of their business but he'd overheard phone conversations and observed topographical maps of the land around Serena in his father's private quarters. He was being encouraged to learn more about the area and reminded that his maternal great-grandfather had thought it a worthy place in which to invest. He'd been told not to mention anything about this to his mother, since she was currently thinking of Serena as her own private haven from the world. It would be better, his father suggested, if she thought he was becoming interested in Serena as a result of his work with Rodney Granger and his mother's love for the area.

Taylor didn't have to be told to keep his father's business separate from his mother. He would have done it on his own. He also suspected his father didn't trust Rodney Granger, or he wouldn't have sent Taylor to work for him for the summer. He'd eventually find out what was going on. He'd had previous assignments of this kind, spying for his father, but none involving his mother. She really believed he was coming to Serena just for her. He almost felt a pang of guilt about allowing his father to use his mother in this way.

He had a sudden revelation, hit the steering wheel for emphasis, and said aloud, "Maybe *thinking* I should feel guilty is a good sign. Maybe my feelings *haven't* been extinguished completely, just simply pushed inward to a reserve tank accessed by some kind of automatic release valve? Maybe if I could access them, I'd feel more human, instead of like a car in overdrive, being driven to the point of no return."

He laughed again, this time loudly, and asked himself, "Why do I keep thinking of myself as a car, a machine, an overworked engine, a fuel-injected auto-man? Is that what I've become? Is that all I am?"

He pressed the gas pedal down to the floor.

CHAPTER ELEVEN

Under the summer roses
When the flagrant crimson
Lurks in the dust
Of the wild red leaves,
Love, with little hands.
Comes and touches you
With a thousand memories,
And asks you
Beautiful unanswerable questions.

~ Carl Sandburg, *Under the Harvest Moon*

CHIEF FARLEY HAD BEEN WORKING at his desk all morning, with only two interruptions. The first was an unsettling phone call from Millie Grayson's brother, Bradford Johnson. Farley tried to picture the man as he ranted on about a crowing rooster disturbing his sleep. He didn't know Johnson but had heard he'd had problems and was currently living in the lower section of Millie's house. He vaguely recalled Aura Lee saying something about the strain this had put on Millie, one of her closest friends. She said Millie had been at her wits' end of late because of her brother's difficult nature and constant complaining. Farley half-listened to his tirade, allowing him to vent his anger, until hearing the name Charlotte Reed.

He had tried, unsuccessfully, not to think about her since her return to Serena. They had a history, a long-ago history, true, but one he had never put to rest. How lovely she had been then, so vivacious and pretty. For a few short months, in the autumn of his seventeenth year, he had thought they would be together for a lifetime.

It was easy for him to remember how awkward he had been: tall and lanky, shirtsleeves and pant legs too short, never enough room for his long legs, even then.

He'd worked as a logger in Pisgah National Forest by his father's side all during the summer months and would have chosen being with him over school had his parents not insisted he become educated. He was in his last year of high school when he met Charlotte, looking as though he belonged in the woods instead of a classroom. He felt like a country hick sitting next to a girl like her. He felt even worse when, on the first day of school, he almost knocked over her desk trying to get out from his own. He could still feel his embarrassment as the memory rose.

Instead of getting upset or laughing at him, she had looked up at him kindly and said, "Why, no big strong boy like you should have to be scrunched up in such a tiny desk."

After gathering her books from the floor, she asked him to carry them to her locker so they could become better acquainted. She had a way of talking that pleased him, like dripping honey. The sound of her voice made him feel warm inside, at ease, less out of place. She talked freely, taking the pressure off of him to think of something to say.

By the time they got to the locker, he learned about her summers in Serena, her mother's chronic illness and confinement in a private sanitarium in Asheville—the reason she had not returned to Charleston to attend school there—and why she felt as out of place in the county high school as he did. He felt surprisingly dismayed to learn she would be returning to Charleston for the second half of the school year, if her mother's health improved.

His interest in school changed for him that day. It was the best time of his life, despite the fact he continued to grow. Charlotte seemed to delight in it and made every effort to build up his ego, always praising him and asking him about the forest and his work with his father. She had a keen interest in nature and an unusual way of speaking about it, as though she could see more in her environment than most. It was odd, because in the classroom, her attention was rarely focused on her studies, while at the same time he was becoming more studious in light of her praise.

He discovered a renewed interest in history, law, and justice, awakened earlier in him by his Uncle Mace, a county deputy sheriff who, when visiting their home, often regaled them with stories about the mountain way of fighting crime. Farley wondered if he might have inherited a penchant for law enforcement and talked to Charlotte about it. She encouraged him and said she could tell he had a clever mind because of his way of knowing about people, even though he was quiet about it. She told him she'd learned a lot about special qualities from her Nanny Pen.

Nanny Pen was her primary caretaker. Her mother had been in and out of residential medical care for years, and her father was away most of the time on business when not attending to his wife. Charlotte seemed very attached to Nanny Pen. Other girls her age would not have mentioned a nanny—not that he knew anyone who had one. Charlotte was childlike in that respect, but he was too smitten to care. In other respects, she was quite intuitive.

Charlotte gave him the incentive to rethink his future. He had the option of entering forestry school upon graduation, but he felt pulled in another direction. Charlotte was too busy socializing to think about the future. She was very popular and always appeared lighthearted. Nevertheless, he felt her need to have him nearby as an anchor in her new environment. He attributed this need to her spontaneous, creative mind, one capable of strange flights of fancy. She didn't seem to have a firm hold on reality; he sensed her insecurity about it and thought it explained her dependence on Nanny Pen.

They did not see each other outside of high school during the month of September. He lived on the outskirts of Serena near the Henderson County line, and she lived on the Warrior Mountain Ridge north of downtown Serena. He had many chores after school, and she had music and dance lessons. At school, she treated him as an equal, although it was becoming clear to him she was on a higher social level. His mother described her family as Serena gentry and warned him about getting too fond of Charlotte. He was sorry he'd told his mother about her.

On the first day of October, Charlotte invited him to her home on a Saturday afternoon to meet Nanny Pen. She said it was a preliminary step he would have to take before escorting her to the Harvest Moon Dance at school. The dance was scheduled for later that month. He'd known about it but hadn't planned to go. Charlotte told him she knew all along she would have to be the one to ask him, explained how important it was to her, how it would be the most wonderful event of the season, and why he simply had to take her.

Charlotte had the dance embellished in her mind into an exaggerated fairy tale in which he was expected to play the role of prince. He sometimes worried about living up to her expectations but found himself striving to do just that. So he talked to his parents about borrowing the pickup truck for his Saturday visit to Charlotte's home. He could see the concern in his mother's eyes and a questioning look in his father's, but neither said a negative word. They instinctively knew it was time to let him make his own choices.

He knew Serena fairly well but had never explored all of the narrow lanes that wound from the center of town up and around the forested ridges surrounding it. He took the Church Street Road from Main Street, driving up the steep hill past the old church house, bearing left at the curve and continuing on, weaving his way toward her lane. He passed a number of small and large summer homes, amazed at the luxury of having an extra house sitting empty most of the year, waiting to be inhabited for the summer. Many were modest and some were elaborate, but none could compare to the place where Charlotte lived. When he pulled into the white-graveled circular driveway at the top of the hill, he kept the engine idling while trying to resist the impulse to drive around the circle and keep on going. Then he heard her voice.

Charlotte ran down the steps of the wide veranda, calling his name and greeting him with all the effusive charm of a Southern belle from days gone by. He almost forgot to be nervous until he noticed the slim, erect figure of a dark-skinned woman standing in the doorway, watching them without expression, as still as a hawk on a fence post, he thought.

Charlotte took his hand and pulled him toward the porch, laughing and tugging at his arm, calling to Nanny Pen. "He's here, Nanny! Isn't he as handsome as I described? Come on, Jeff, don't be shy. Nanny's been waiting to meet you. I know she'll just love you too."

He heard a rooster crow from somewhere in the yard and looked around for chickens. He was also looking for a way out but knew it was hopeless. He wondered if he and Nanny Pen were thinking the same thing. She hadn't moved. As they came closer, he could see that she was much younger than he'd expected, and lighter than his first impression; her skin was the color of caramel, the scarf around her head a bright blue. She came forward in a fluid motion of welcoming grace as she reached her arms out to embrace him. He was taken aback by her warmth and felt pulled into her presence as though being cast in a spell.

He and Charlotte were seated in rocking chairs on the veranda while Nanny Pen went inside for refreshments. She reappeared in minutes with a tall glass of iced tea with lemon slices on the rim and a lace napkin for each of them. A tray of homemade sugar cookies followed, placed on a round table in easy reach of their chairs. Charlotte chatted away while Nanny sat in a third rocker and observed the two of them. When she finally began to talk, she spoke softly, inquiring about his family and interests and hopes for the future. He felt scrutinized but strangely relaxed, and he answered each question as honestly as possible, knowing how much it meant to Charlotte.

The rooster crowed every so often, distracting him from Nanny's inquisition, which continued throughout lunch and ended with dessert.

By that time, he'd become aware of the emptiness of the house, the many rooms, the lack of people, just the two of them living there, Charlotte and Nanny Pen, and realized why they were so close. He understood because he and Charlotte shared one thing in common: being an only child. He thought of how close he felt to his parents, how rarely they needed words to communicate, and observed a similar form of communication between Charlotte and Nanny Pen. He began to feel more at ease, enjoying Charlotte's delight in his presence, and Nanny's Pen's quiet acceptance of him, which was evident by the time he had to leave.

The night of the dance came after more visits and a deepening relationship with Charlotte. For the first time in his life, he'd fallen in love and was spellbound. He thought of her night and day and physically desired her. Their limited alone-time together became intimate, passionate, yet not consummated. His parents had watched him transform from a boy into a man that season, as he sublimated his sexual desire into work, his lean muscular frame hardening, his ambitions formulating, and his confidence growing. He'd discussed a future in law enforcement with his Uncle Mace, who'd agreed to guide him through the process.

He spent the day of the dance washing and polishing the truck, helping his father cut wood for winter, his mother with chores, then dressing in his Sunday best and stopping in town for flowers: a corsage for Charlotte, a bouquet for Nanny Pen.

Charlotte had been too excited to wait in her room, although she had planned to dramatically descend the stairs for an entrance. Instead, she was waiting at the door. Nanny Pen had scolded her for appearing so anxious, but he loved her even more for this and thought she looked as beautiful as a princess. Her dress was white with lace trim and fit her slim curvy figure to perfection. She said Nanny Pen had helped her with her hair and made sure of her accessories. Nanny told her to hush and went to put her flowers in a vase. He pinned the corsage to Charlotte's dress. Her skin glowed with happiness, and he felt proud to be the one taking her to the dance. She'd been right all along about it. It would be a special night for them.

The harvest moon rose outside as he held her in his arms, dance after dance. They were captivated by one another, unaware of the eyes upon them, the envious stares. The evening slipped away like a dream. Time had no meaning. It ended too soon for them to separate. He found a secluded cove down by the Green River bank, where the big yellow moon reflected off deep dark waters. She wouldn't let go of him, and he never wanted to let go of her. The moon began to descend, but they didn't care. The care would come later, but never the regret. They owned this night and took all they could from it. It would have to last them a lifetime because it would never come again. It was as though they knew it, but without the realization.

Farley couldn't remember all that happened afterward: the unexpected arrival of her father, the news of her mother's death, Charlotte's removal from school to be taken back to Charleston for the remainder of the school year, her father's decline in health, and his impossible demands.

His own father had died shortly thereafter in a forest fire. He'd heroically saved two fellow loggers caught in a back draft but became trapped in an attempt to save another. Farley could only recall a daze of grief and an extended time of agony: the separation from Charlotte, the tragic loss of his father, his mother's heartbroken silence, his last months of high school forgotten completely. He'd somehow graduated. Perhaps they'd taken mercy on him and simply awarded him a diploma despite his absence; he couldn't recall. Things were done that way in the mountains then.

There had been letters between the pair of them, passionate at first, expressing love and commitment, but travel was not affordable for him or permissible for her. It was a different time, a different world, unlike today's world of immediate communication: texting, e-mail, and face-to-face interaction by cell phone. They had instead been caught up in a whirlwind of death and loss and responsibility and had no experience with rebellion. He'd also been facing the challenge of deciding what to do with the rest of his life in terms of livelihood. She'd been drawn back into her father's realm of Charleston society with all the expectations of her class.

Forcefully, Uncle Mace had stepped in to take charge for a while, enfolding his mother back into her family clan and their nurturing care. Uncle Mace had recommended Jeff enlist in military service for the training and paid education he would receive in preparation for a career in law enforcement. It was a six-year program requiring active service that would take him overseas for two tours of duty in the Middle East. He'd written to Charlotte before making the decision to enlist. Her reply had been brief, encouraging him to do so with no promise to wait for him or request that he write. It was a letter void of emotion, a subdued Charlotte, her love for him suppressed, perhaps by her father, perhaps by her own feeling of hopelessness, resigned to her situation. His heart had been breaking in stages. The letter broke it in two.

During a leave from his first tour of duty, he'd been surprised to receive another letter from Charlotte. It was a strange, long letter, beginning with familiar terms of endearment, written as though time had not passed and she somehow had to apologize and explain what had happened after leaving Serena.

She wrote of her father's poor health and domineering personality since her mother's death, his discovery of her letters, his outrage at Nanny Pen for allowing her to associate with someone not of her social class. He'd fired Nanny Pen, accusing her of teaching his daughter *Negro* practices and encouraging deviant behavior. She wrote of her mental breakdown over being forbidden to see him and Nanny Pen again. She described being admitted into a private mental health facility for a period of months until a slow and painful recovery resulted in discharge into the waiting arms of her father.

Friends had been told she'd been away at school in Switzerland. Her father had arranged a debutante ball in her honor to welcome her home. She described the event as everything she might have once wished for, before their night together at the Harvest Moon Dance. He could see traces of tears on the page as he read. And then she wrote of her engagement to Jordon Reed, a young man deemed suitable for her by her father. She closed her letter with love, and for a moment as he read the words, he felt her love. Then it faded into the past with the knowledge that Charlotte's future had been arranged for her, not taking into account her unique and fragile spirit.

The following year, he received a newspaper clipping about her marriage to Jordon Reed. Reed was reported to have a bright future in politics, and the photo of him and Charlotte depicted a couple worthy of the society column. She looked different than she had, thinner, more mature, still lovely, but her smile was forced, her posture stiff, her eyes without the luster they once had. His heart felt heavy at the sight of her image. He wondered why she had sent it.

He spent the next several years away from Serena, focusing on his career. After six years of military service and criminal justice education, he was recruited by the FBI into their homeland security investigations training division. He had a solid future laid out for him working for the government, but he could not commit fully. His mother's health had been failing, and his visits home had become more frequent. He'd also met a young woman at one of the many family gatherings hosted by his Uncle Mace. Emma was a friend of one of his cousins and seemed as familiar as family.

Their clans had been friends for generations, and Emma's brothers had jobs all over the county, just like his uncles. These mountain families made up an intricate network of skill and communication as sophisticated as anything he'd experienced in the military or FBI. Jeff began to see his place in the midst of this and set about re-evaluating his future in a way he had not previously considered.

He'd also come to realize that, much like his father had been, he was a solitary man but not a loner. He could relate to people and liked having them around. His mother's extended family had been an important part of his upbringing, and he'd enjoyed their presence in his life. He'd come to understand that he worked best alone within a circumference of support, and therefore needed a job more suitable to his character. Like many born and raised in the mountains who had left, he felt a yearning to return, but wanted to come home with something to offer the people of his birthplace. Having worked this out after some consideration, he had the incentive to move forward with his intentions.

He and Emma were married a year later. He managed a transfer from FBI headquarters to a government radar-tracking station positioned in the high reaches of the Pisgah Forest, an hour-long drive from Serena. They moved into his family home, where Emma lovingly cared for his mother until her death. She also created a home environment much like the one in which he'd been raised. His fervent commitment to her laid the foundation for the love and devotion that grew between them, unlike the burning passion and unfulfilled promise he'd experienced with Charlotte. As a result, he thrived in his occupation, while waiting for the right opportunity to come along. He also kept abreast of news in Serena, renewed his kinfolk relationships, and gathered information about the criminal element in the county and surrounding areas.

More than a decade passed before the opportunity came. He took an early retirement from the FBI and accepted the position as Chief of Police of Serena. Emma lived long enough to see him settled into office. They'd been married twelve years when she was diagnosed with cervical cancer. He'd grieved for her as he had done for his parents and knew he'd been blessed to have had them in his life. They were an integral part of his being.

The persistent ringing of the telephone on his desk pulled him out of the past. He answered on the eighth ring and was momentarily irritated that Aura Lee had not returned from the post office.

"Chief Farley?" the high-pitched voice of Margaret Raney pierced his eardrum. "You've got to come up here to see what's been done to my garden! Must have been a wild hog came in from the woods, tearin' everything to pieces, rootin' out all my potatoes, and wreckin' my bean-poles. There needs to be some huntin' done up here on Piney Ridge, and it need to be done now! Them hogs a-been multiplying like rabbits, and mine's not the only place they've torn up."

"I'll send Travis Ledbetter and his boys up, Miss Margaret, and come take a look myself. I'll get Silas Webber up there too, to help you fix up the garden."

The call ended abruptly, just as Aura Lee returned with the mail.

"Sorry it took so long, Chief. I ran into Martha Wheeler, and you'll never guess what she told me."

"I don't have time to guess, Aura Lee. I've got to leave in a few minutes for Piney Mountain. What's up?"

Aura Lee scurried to her desk and plopped her large, overstuffed purse on it as she sank into her seat. "Well, Chief, Martha told me she heard talk at the Grill about Charlotte Reed's boy, Taylor. Seems he's staying here for the summer and taken a job working for Rodney Granger. He's been seen stopping in the store pretty regular since seeing Willa Mae working in there. Well, no one can blame him, her being so pretty and all. Folks say she's been paying him no mind. If he knows what's good for him, he'll leave her be. But being a Reed, he might think he has a right to do what he pleases, his daddy being a congressman and all.

"Her daddy won't like it a bit, nor will that Cather boy, Raven. Folks up at the inn say Willa's followed him around since they were kids. They're all about the same age; the Reed boy may be a year or two older. Seems like a fiery situation to me. Not that there's been any talk about Willa and Raven being a couple, him not havin' any family except that colored woman who raised him. He's a good-looking boy, no one would dispute that, but looks more Indian than black. You know how pretty some of those mixed breeds are, but wild as the woods he grew up in, and—"

Farley interrupted her, excusing himself to leave, stunned by what he had heard and trying not to let it show.

CHAPTER TWELVE

it was the kind of moon
that I would want to
send back to my ancestors
and gift to my descendants

~ Sanober Khan

FARLEY THOUGHT OF HER ALL the way up Piney Mountain. He hadn't seen Penelope Cather in years because she rarely, if ever, came into town. She'd been a fairly young woman when she'd cared for Charlotte Reed, and he'd never forgotten her quiet acceptance of him, and her dignified reserve. He remembered the power in her serene presence, her watchful gaze, her devoted guardianship of Charlotte. He wondered how she had felt being cast aside as he had been, and regretted not having taken the time to visit her since his return to Serena as Chief of Police. For a brief moment, he hoped she might be proud of him—a curious reaction, he thought, to his memory of her.

The story went that she'd become a widow after a brief marriage, and had taken in a child of a distant relative who had died. There had been some question about a lost birth certificate, an issue never pursued since she'd made the decision to home school the boy and raise him as her own. It was the ways of things in the mountains, some things better left alone.

Penelope Cather's truth was quite different. After losing her husband, she'd been hired as summer cook and winter caretaker at the sprawling

Orchard Oaks Inn, located on the highest point of the southern ridge on the outskirts of Serena. She'd been given living quarters in a cottage located a short distance behind the inn, separate from the rental cottages located near the front area. Her cottage, originally a guest house for visiting family members of the former owners when it was a private residence, afforded her both privacy and the same spectacular view seen from the inn's rear, glass-enclosed veranda. The view was one of its major attractions for summer visitors.

The nearest private property to the cottage and the inn belonged to the Parsons. Their modest farmhouse was located not far from the inn, on the opposite side near the guest cottages and closer to the road leading to town. Frank Parsons supplied the inn with produce from his well-tended garden and greenhouse, and he helped with the landscaping and repairs on the inn.

Although many miles and vast wilderness made up the terrain between Penelope's cottage and Mamma Phoebe's cabin, there existed a visual connection she relied upon. From the high elevation of the cottage, she could see for miles across the undulating ridges to the distinctive rise of Shadow Peak. From the peak, looking downward, where only the treetops were visible, she could pinpoint the spot where her sister resided and see the smoke billowing up whenever she was working at her craft. This would always give her comfort, for she knew the good her sister did for others.

Penelope felt her older sister's presence without word or sign, whether smoke could be seen or not. She worked from sunrise to sunset in her disciplined way and loved the boy her sister had given to her with every ounce of her being. The day he'd been placed in her arms represented a new beginning in her life. He had soothed the heartbreak she'd suffered and gave her a reason to live.

Penelope taught him more than he could have ever learned in the county school, as well as all that she had been taught by her sister, whom she revered. She'd encouraged his wild spirit, markedly noticeable during his infancy, and simultaneously taught him how to restrain it. Her sister had named him

Raven Brook, after the place of his birth. He was to be protected at all cost and educated in the old ways, in the practice of roots, primal and ancient, spiritual and ancestral. He had the look of a dark angel, exotic and angelic, a Raphael cherub as a babe, rose-tinted alabaster skin and thick black hair with a slight bit of curl. A laughing baby, gifted with cheer for some unfathomable reason, considering his birth.

He was so different from her tiny blonde angel, Charlotte, who'd been too sensitive for this world, delicate, in need of protection. She'd worked so hard to prepare her for life, had even chosen the right mate for her: a mountain boy, born and bred, who had courted her with the truest intentions, allowing her fantasies to be expressed, accepting her idiosyncrasies with understanding, and loving her with a deep abiding heart.

Her parents had been absent most of her childhood, her mother in constant need of care, her father using business to escape. They'd been relieved to hand over the raising of their fragile only child to her. How cruel it had been to have her taken away from the boy who genuinely loved her and put on the Charleston society market like a slave being put up for auction. It might have been dressed up as a fancy-ball cotillion, but it was the same thing as far as Penelope was concerned. It had all happened so fast that, despite her formidable powers, she'd been powerless to stop it, fired before she could act, and left as grief-stricken as a mother who had lost a child. She'd grown much wiser since then and vowed it would not happen again, not to her boy—not to her dark angel, Raven.

He was her darling of the rushing stream, her angel of the forest and the Raven Brook Falls, which fell in a torrent from the mouth of the towering Shadow Peak, lavishing its waters upon the swirling pool below and stream that flowed from it. The Cherokees had named the falls Raven Brook because of the blue-black color of rock formations beneath and around them that gave the water its peculiar sapphire color, the color of Raven's eyes. Like a rare gemstone that stands out from the others, its waters differed from other waterfalls in the region because of the unique makeup of the soil and mineral compounds formulated at the source.

The Cherokees had called them "healing waters" and considered them mystical. The waters were Raven's birthright; he'd been borne from the womb into their fluid embrace and then lifted from them away from the lifeless body of his mother, away to the warming fires of her sister's cabin. Mamma Phoebe had known to bring him to her, where he'd be safe and secure, where he'd fill the aching void of her loss, where he'd learn all that Phoebe had taught her.

Mamma Phoebe was her elder sister by almost twenty years and had been more like a mother to her than sister. Their mother had died before Penelope's third birthday, and Phoebe had chosen not to marry, devoting her life to her "calling." Even as a young child, Penelope looked up to her sister with awe, watching the people come and go, observing the reverence given to her by white and black folks alike. They came for healing potions and cross-bone readings and mojo-fixings and conjures and such. She followed Phoebe around like a puppy, a "skirt-hem child," Phoebe called her.

She'd known to stay close and to take in all the learnin', "lifetimes of learnin'," Phoebe would say as she went about her root-doctoring, processing herbs for medicinal and magical purposes, explaining to her "little Pen" how she'd been gifted with spirits residing in her head to guide her in the mixin' and fixin'. Mamma Phoebe was a big woman with skin the color of maple syrup, a wide, handsome face with captivating burnished amber eyes and a commanding voice, both silken and resounding. Pen loved her wide girth and ample bosom and limitless ability to care for those in need. There were times when Pen wished she were the only one in her care, feeling envious of the time Phoebe spent attending to others. Then she'd chide herself for selfish thinking, pushing the bad spirits from her mind and trying to emulate her sister.

Mamma Phoebe had waited until her thirteenth birthday before sending her out to work, explaining that "Doing work for the summer folk is necessary preparation to learn to be self-sufficient, just in case."

Just in case of what? Pen hadn't asked. The summer job had been arranged by one of Mamma Phoebe's regular visitors. This, of course, was never to be mentioned. No white society folks ever admitted going to Mamma Phoebe or taking the trail leading from town to her cabin. It was just one of those unspoken things, like buying moonshine whiskey or poaching on the government land.

Mamma Phoebe knew most of the goings-on around her without ever leaving home. She had a knowing that required no communication from others. Pen had learned this the first day of her job. She'd been scared to death about how she was going to get by without her sister. She needn't have worried, because she'd felt Phoebe's presence from the very beginning, despite the geographical distance between them. Phoebe had made her a little pouch to wear hidden under her blouse and told her it had the power to keep them connected. Sometimes she could feel the pouch grow warm where it nestled between her undeveloped breasts. The warmth kept her fears at bay and her courage strong, for there was no time to go back and forth to the cabin when she was working.

It was the warmth that made her believe in the pouch, and then believe in her sister, until she had total faith in their connection when separated. This carried through into her adult life as she advanced in her hired positions from laundress to maid to cook to eventually becoming Charlotte's trusted nanny, and later, the wife of Joseph Cather. It strengthened her through the loss of Charlotte and then the sudden death of her much older husband after his heart attack. She'd been a widow only six months before being gifted with her beautiful child, during which time she accepted the position at the inn, and began a life completely devoted to him.

He'd since grown tall and strong, and through him, Pen could envision the wild beauty of the mother Phoebe had described to her. His father remained a mystery. Phoebe insisted there was no hint of anyone but Evangeline in Raven's looks or bearing, reminding her that he was a miracle child of the waters, a greater father to him than any man. It had proven to be true because by the time Raven was twelve years old, he was drawn to the falls like a magnet and began moving toward them without her knowledge or permission.

Mamma Phoebe and Pen knew it was only a matter of time before he would have to be told the truth of his birth. Phoebe had warned Pen to remain silent on the subject for the boy's protection and promised her that everything she knew about his family legacy had been written in a signed document she would give to them both upon Raven's eighteenth birthday.

During Raven's childhood, Pen visited Phoebe infrequently, stayed away from town, and kept their lives private, except for her closest neighbors, Frank and Mabel Parsons, and their child, Willa Mae. Pen worked year-round as cook during the spring, summer, and autumn seasons, and as housekeeper during the winter months. The owners of the inn spent their winters in Florida, while she and Frank Parsons were the main caretakers.

The inn was enough distance from the cottage to afford them a life separate from her employers and the guests, although she spent many hours a day working there. She loved coming home to her sanctuary, perched high above an expanse of wilderness that sloped down from her lofty dwelling to the protected watershed over one thousand feet below. She enjoyed this view from her open-railed porch but preferred the one behind her cottage. After putting her son to bed, she would often go out the back door to enjoy the cool evening breeze and gaze into the distance until darkness fell over the Shadow Peak Ridge. Raven would sometimes watch her from his bedroom window, curious about the mysterious place she found so captivating.

Raven had not been permitted to venture deep into the forest during his early childhood, but as adolescence approached, he started creating paths from the cottage that intersected with old Indian trails he discovered and recorded on his daily explorations. Pen realized how much he loved the outdoors and eventually gave him the freedom he desired and the trust she felt he had earned.

Raven was not inclined to explore the trails that wound precariously down the steep grade into South Carolina. He found it more interesting to follow the natural outline of the ridges, where native hunting parties had crossed the upper reaches of the mountain range. Many of these old trails were hidden or worn away, their history marked by carvings on trees or other signs and symbols. He learned how to spot them and understand their meaning. He followed them up and down through hollows and across meadows and streams, steering clear of properties and roads where the trails had been destroyed or paved over. He drew maps, interconnecting the ones he had made with the ones he had found, and eventually added a trail leading to the southeastern ridge. Without being aware of it, his inherent trailblazing skills had been taking him in that direction all along.

Unfortunately, the first time he risked going onto private property to reach a landmark destination, he ran into trouble. He'd been following a trail through a thick wooded area leading to the back side of the McCabe compound, trying to reach the high peak of the ridge that could be seen from his home. He had visited Aunt Phoebe with his mother on several occasions and knew that she lived near this peak. When he'd asked her about it, he was abruptly told that it was part of the McCabe property and off-limits. Aunt Phoebe had warned him about the dangers of trespassing, but he felt young and invincible and determined to find the place his mother had found so fascinating.

The old man came out of the shadow of pines like a ghost appearing out of nowhere. He stood stock still, holding his shotgun low, and staring at him with an expression that alternated between menace and bewilderment. He appeared immobilized, not able to move or lift his gun to aim and shoot. This gave Raven a chance to run—and run he did—through bramble and thicket and thorny berry bushes until he was so out of breath he had to stop. But he didn't stop long and didn't stop again until he made it back home, feeling guilty and stupid and grateful to be alive. His mother was not at home. She was working late at the inn. He went into the bathroom and looked in the mirror and thought about what he had done. Then he thought of Willa Mae.

From childhood into adolescence, they'd always been there for one another, her tagging after him and thinking him so wise, strong, and knowing. He'd been like a big brother, and her father had been grateful to him for watching out for her. He'd grown accustomed to her ways, how she'd wait for his return from hunting or fishing in the forest, pick flowers for him, and share sweets she'd been given at home.

Things changed when they entered their teens. His feelings for her had intensified, and her adoring looks held something extra he couldn't define but found exciting. His mother had sensed it, and so had her parents. Willa Mae had physically matured, and this seemed to put everyone on high alert—everyone but Willa.

Raven felt confused about what to do. They were not blood kin, and she was not his sister. He'd not been able to look at her without feeling disturbed and aroused. She'd wanted to be with him as they had always been, not understanding what was changing.

He'd thought it best to avoid her attentions and stay as busy as possible. In fact, they were both kept very busy by their parents. He began spending more time alone, which led to increased restlessness and risk-taking: going off into the forest, trespassing on forbidden property, ignoring Aunt Phoebe's warnings, and eventually almost getting shot by that crazy old man, creating this predicament.

It would be hard to hide his torn shirt and the scratches and bruises from his mother. It was almost impossible to hide anything from her or Aunt Phoebe. They shared a sixth sense about things. It was almost spooky. Even if he cleaned himself up and hid his shirt, she would know something had happened. He felt trouble brewing.

Sure enough, Pen took Raven to see her sister the next day, no questions asked. Aunt Phoebe talked to him about the nature of the situation and gave him a quieting potion. It seemed normal to Raven, her being a hoodoo doctor (the only doctoring he'd ever known), and it did help him feel less agitated. She told him, "It's time to begin your higher education, Raven, now that you're coming of age."

His mother heartily agreed, speaking with a firm, calm tone he recognized too well. "I've taken your home schooling as far as I can, son. Your Aunt Phoebe will take over my teachings. We believe your curious mind and daily explorations need to go in a safer, more challenging direction."

Raven felt sheepish about her remark, but he knew he had it coming.

After that, things settled down between Willa Mae and Raven, and a schedule was arranged for his lessons. He would stay with Aunt Phoebe several days a week, spending the rest of his time at home or working at the inn. He had learned from his mother to respect his aunt, and he was aware of her wide reputation. He felt somewhat intimidated by her—she was very different from his mother—and he didn't know what to expect. He was surprised to learn they would be spending most of their time outdoors.

He began following her about the property, learning every use of root and herb, every flower and plant, every berry and nut, every seed and grain. She taught him facts about the area. He learned the State of North Carolina is comprised of over six-thousand plant and flower species, each with many varieties, ahead of other states in the number of plants that can be made into medicines, and over one hundred different families of drug plants, each family having one or more species. Three-fourths of the drug plants could be found within the one hundred mile region around them, and eight percent of the crude drugs in the world are produced in North Carolina, some of the most prized being ginseng and gold seal.

She taught him to identify lavender, yellowroot, kalmia, jewel-weed, Joe-Pye weed, toad flax, heart leaf, saxifrage, wild ginger, pipsissewa, lion's tongue, Granddaddy Graybeard, the yellow lady's slipper of the orchid family, rosettes of Adam's Flannel, and the dry stalks of St. Bartholomew's Lamp. He learned the difference between woodland and wetland plants, how to look for crimson urns, Indian Dipper, and the strange pitcher plant, the lid of which closes over the pitcher and traps insects lured there by its fluid, and to look around these plants for the tender green of the ground pine, which are like trees in an elfin forest, and to concentrate on the study of mosses and lichens.

She encouraged him to study the tiniest flower, the smallest plant, and then to gaze at the peaks of the mountains and name them in relation to land and sky, number them as they faded away into the purple mist, see them as part of the oldest geological formation in the world, and then think of the ancient lessons to be learned from them. She had an encyclopedic memory for detail, sectioning her teachings into categories as structured as college coursework. She was a gifted teacher, engaging his curiosity, praising his astute responses, enthralling his mind and senses with new discovery, transforming him with each revelation.

He learned to listen to the wind, to observe the constellations, to understand the phases of the moon in relation to earth and water, and to watch and listen to the birds for signs and portents of things to come. He began to see his world as magical and limitless. She discussed with him the power gained by knowledge, and the consequences of its misuse, recognizing an emergence of confidence in him as she moved through each stage of instruction, leading him toward the mastery of root-doctoring and its ethics.

She taught him over the next three years, in-between work and study, taking up his time and energy, inflaming his mind while soothing his passions. He was about to begin the last and most important stage, not unlike a traditional senior year before graduation. His relationship with Willa Mae had continued with restraint, made easier by their time apart, she at the county high school, and he at the experiential school of Mamma Phoebe. He truly believed he and Willa Mae had a familial bond that held them together in mind and spirit as they prepared for a future they would eventually share.

When Raven turned seventeen, Aunt Phoebe turned his attention from the forests and fields to the waters flowing from the Raven Brook Falls. He'd been with her there many times over the years and had been curious about his name in relation to them. He'd wondered about having been forbidden to go there when he was younger and why he'd felt compelled to go there on his own. His mother had told him little of his birth or the mystery surrounding it. She'd promised to one day reveal everything, imploring him to wait for that day with patience and trust. Waiting had been difficult, but he knew it was pointless to press her or his Aunt Phoebe for information they were not ready to share. They were formidable women, and he instinctively understood he was being prepared for something extraordinary connected to the Raven Brook Falls and Shadow Peak.

He'd noticed a change in his aunt that year, a slower step, a slight limp to her gait, the need to stop and rest during their day-long excursions. If he expressed concern or suggested they return to the cabin, she'd just laugh and say, "I'm getting old bones, boy, and I've got to keep them moving. It's a blessing I have all this teaching to do, and when I'm done, I'll be taking my rest."

Her main source of water at home was a narrow creek tributary, which diverted off from the Raven Brook stream. It ran past the garden patch near her cabin, providing plenty of water to meet her needs. But the crystalline pool beneath the falls was her source for the healing potions and conjures she made for those who came to her. The time had come to share this knowledge with Raven and tell him the secret of the waters. The falls had become a strenuous hike for her, but they'd been going there more frequently, leading up to this special day. There was an unspoken understanding between them, a deadline approaching, a destiny to fulfill.

Sitting beside the stream, beneath the teaming falls, she began:

"There's something magical about these waters, child, but it's not just because of my conjuring. I've done some learnin' myself over the years, some of it from a *real* medical doctor and old friend of mine, Dr. Benjamin Jacobs, who used to come to Serena every summer to visit me regular, just to talk about things. He had a scientific mind but was interested in my root-doctoring work and healing successes.

"We'd sit and talk for hours. He'd taken a liking to me, and I to him. Though if other folks would have seen us,—which nobody did— we'd have seemed as different as night and day. He'd say to me, 'Phoebe, you're the most educated woman I know.' I'd just laugh, him havin' gone to medical school and all. You know, child, he's the only man I ever thought about marrying, I mean in my imaginings. But he had a wife and two children a ways off up north. It just wasn't meant to be; some things you might want real bad just aren't. Of course," she laughed heartily, "I could have put a love spell on him and swayed things in my favor a bit. But I thought too much of the man to do it, and I didn't need to. He told me himself we had chemistry between us. Yes, he surely did. And that was something we *both* knew about.

"You see, he was 'specially interested in the chemistry of atmosphere and its effects on healing. He'd studied about atmospheric conditions around this area, explaining to me about the quality of ozone in the air and how it was unique to this region. He'd been most curious about the formation of Shadow Peak, and how its location was like a terminal of a tube end of two funnels, which are in horizontal position. He drew me a picture, showing how one of the funnels, lying downward in a southerly direction, has its mouth in the South Carolina foothills, while the other lies in a northerly direction, opening into the deep Green River gorge. He explained how ozone is formed in the upper stratosphere of air by the discharge of electricity or by the effect of sunlight and cosmic rays on the air."

She became quiet for a moment, wistful, then continued, "As much as I admired Dr. Ben, I never told him everything about the waters, although I was sorely tempted. But I'll always be grateful to him for helping me to understand a scientific explanation for how and why the ozone-laden air is attracted to the falls in such great quantities by the suction from the funnels and then is dispersed into the water. He said if it weren't for the fortunate junction of the tube ends of those funnels at the altitude of approximately 2200 feet, the falls wouldn't have the invigorating atmosphere and superabundance of the great and powerful oxidizing agent, ozone.

"That's how he would talk to me, child, like we was equals and I was as capable of understanding as he was. He said I had an animistic relationship with the world and an inborn understanding of the organizing principles of the universe. Said his knowing came from books and mine came from being part of nature, not separate from it. I didn't always understand his words, but I understood his meaning, and I've never forgotten. I think he was meant to come into my life so I could teach you better."

She pointed. "Look up there to the peak, Raven. When it rains on the surface above the falls, some of the water sinks into the ground and moves downward until it reaches impermeable rock or soil particles, like clay, through which the water cannot pass. The rock and soil above this clay becomes saturated with water. This water-saturated layer of rock and soil is called a water bearer, and it not only contains water, it allows water to pass through it. The top surface of this water-saturated zone is called a water table. The waterfall cut its bed below this water table and became a permanent stream because water from the zone of saturation flows into it all the time.

"In lower elevations or areas where there are other fluids, the water can be contaminated with chemicals, gasoline or other harmful bacteria. But this is a pristine area. The waters are not only protected, the ozone layer contributes to the oxygen in the water, and the ground base provides the elements to make the water source entirely unique to its surroundings. Look at those lichens, for example. They don't have roots or stems, but see how they cover the black rocks of the falls in those red and green shell-like formations? Did you know they secrete acid that dissolves in the rock? Now look at those flat-lobed leaf-shaped plants that grow alongside them. They're called liverworts. They've got these invisible rootlets which hold their tiny leaves fast to the rocks.

"There's a lot of hoodoo superstition about these plants because they look like a human liver. I've used them for medicinal purposes, healing, and a little magic too. I'll be teaching you more about that when we get back to the cabin. But see how they flourish above, beneath, and around the falls in every crevice of the black rocks upon which the waters flow. See how the crystalline minerals and mica shimmer wherever the rock is exposed, how it shimmers blue, just like the waters."

Mamma Phoebe stopped talking and looked into his eyes, the sapphire blue waters reflected in them, and said, "Raven boy, what I tell you now is held by sacred oath to be true. All of these elements, in concentrated doses, have combined here to produce water more valuable than diamonds or gold, and the responsibility of this secret must be now passed to you to do as you believe right.

"There's people like that too, child, born with a combination of inside atmosphere and elements like those in and around the falls. I guess I'm one of them. The old ones said you could see it in the eyes of the newborn child. That child would be set apart from the others for the *learning*, even kept from marrying, them believing the power would be weakened by such a union. But I was blessed because I had my baby sister, and then you came into my life, like the gift of the waters. And just look at you! You've grown so tall and pretty, and smart too. You've taken in everything I've taught you like you was natural-born to learn it.

"But there's one more thing you must know before we leave here today. Look up again at that old demon rock staring out from under the falls, lookin' all mellow and benign. I've seen the face of that demon when he's showed himself and the evil that happens when he does. Always remember, child, in places and people where there's a mighty force of good, there's a mighty force of evil lurking to muddy the waters. Just like when that old devil moon comes rising just to cause some trouble. There can never be harmony when the demons are restless. The Cherokees had rituals to keep that old demon rock peaceful. I've done my own rituals too. Even my neighbor, Purvis McCabe, who scared you that day in the woods, has his way of appeasing it."

Raven grimaced. "You knew about that, Aunt Phoebe?"

"Boy, I don't miss much that goes on around here."

Suddenly she looked tired and said, "It's time for us both to rest a spell. We don't have much more to do, but it's the last important part of your learning. We'll need a few days in my summer kitchen for herb pressin' and mixin'. I'll need your full attention, so it would be best if you take time to let everything you heard today work around in your mind for a few days. Why it's—" she stopped and laughed again and then started singing, "'*Summertime, and the livin' is easy. Fish are jumping, and the cotton is high.*' Now help me up and let's get on back to the cabin. Then you go on home and when you come back, you'll be fresh for learning the magic. It's almost your time, boy. Now let's get movin' along. I can hear that old rooster of mine crowing. He's been making a fuss since morning. *He's* getting up there in age too."

After Raven went home, Mamma Phoebe felt the weight of worry descend upon her. It had been building up for weeks. Night would soon be falling, and a dim murky devil moon was on the rise. The signs were all around her. There had been two deaths already, and there would be more to come. She had to get Raven to his time and keep him safe. But she'd been growing so tired, and knew *her time* was coming. She needed this break from teaching to concentrate on protecting him. There was much work to do. She wouldn't tell Pen about it just yet, not until she had things sorted out: the goings-on, the warnings she'd seen, and the meaning of them. Then she'd put into action all of the power she could muster.

CHAPTER THIRTEEN

Everyone is the moon, and has a dark side
which he never shows to others.

~ Mark Twain

DEVLIN MCMANUS WAS BUSY GATHERING his fishing gear when the doorbell rang. He smiled when he saw his tall friend from the shoulders down through the oval beveled glass of the front door. Farley's head reached above it, but his lanky frame and casual uniform were unmistakable. Dev had hoped Jeff would go fishing with him sometime but doubted he would have time this morning. Kate had left earlier to make a trip down the mountain to attend a day-long conference at the university. He'd called Jeff after getting in from Denver and left a message but hadn't heard back. And now, here he stood!

The two men greeted each other with a warm handshake. After a few minutes of catching up, Dev asked, "Why not take a few hours off this morning, Jeff, and follow me down to the cove? I've got an extra rod and reel and plenty of bait, and you look like you've got something on your mind. I've found a spot down the river a ways where I've yet to see another soul."

"I'd appreciate a rain check on the fishing, Dev, but I will follow you down to the cove. I can talk to you as easily there as here, and I like it by the river, always find it peaceful. There is something I'd like to run by you. Then I'll leave you to do the fishin' for both of us."

Jeff reached down to pick up Dev's tackle box. "Here, let me give you a hand. I'll help you load up your gear and then meet you at the cove landing."

Half an hour later, after driving around multiple hairpin turns that spiraled down an almost vertical drop to the Green River Cove, they were trekking the worn path from the landing to the banks of the emerald green river. The cove was a launching site for kayakers and rafters heading downstream. Jeff and Dev took the path upstream that edged along the bank deeper into the forest. They eventually came to a place where an assembly of gigantic boulders and fallen trees had formed a partial dam from which small cascading waterfalls fell into a series of pools. Dev chose a spot near one of them. Jeff sat down on a wide, flattened rock and propped his right leg up on a log.

The two men were very different in appearance, but there were commonalities. Jeff's chief of police uniform was understated, his badge worn under the flap of his shirt pocket. He carried the weight of his authority with a laid back demeanor, his long sinewy muscular frame impressively supportive.

Dev was shorter than Jeff, with a solid physique that exuded the strength and vitality of an outdoorsman. It was hard to believe he'd suffered a near-fatal stab wound the previous autumn. His recovery had been nothing short of miraculous. He had the Black-Irish looks and charismatic personality unique to his ancestry, and a charm about him that belied a past marked by tragedy.

After several minutes of comfortable silence, Jeff asked Dev, "What do you make of two cases of alcohol overdose within a matter of weeks? They happened while you were in Denver. I figured in your profession, you must have worked with people with alcohol problems. I need some education on the subject."

"Well, Jeff, I'm far from being an expert, but I have had some professional experience with the problem, as well as personal. How can I help?"

"Thanks. I'll make this brief. The first case was a known heavy drinker, but a hard worker too, and managed to do both on a regular basis. The second case had been known to drink white liquor to excess in the past and then get into trouble, but after he turned thirty, he had cleaned up his act and cut back his drinking considerably. He hasn't had an incident in years. The bodies of both men were discovered in the forest, but in different vicinities within the county. Both had overdosed while drinking white liquor moonshine. The county medical examiner determined the cause of death accidental. I'm not so sure. I've requested a toxicology report.

"There's something about these deaths that doesn't sit right with me, Dev. I've known Caleb Thompson for several years now. He was not a careless drinker, more of a maintenance drinker, if you know what I mean."

Dev nodded. "I do, Jeff. Nevertheless, alcoholism can develop as an insidious progression in some people as the body ages and health factors come into play. Traumatic life events can also impact drinking habits. At a certain stage of the progression, tolerance can be very high and then radically change to low tolerance if the liver becomes damaged and cannot metabolize the alcohol as it had previously. This change can create a form of denial in the person who becomes dependent on alcohol and continues drinking despite increased consequences and loss of control." Dev shifted his weight and continued. "It can be likened to having been on a slow-climbing roller-coaster that reaches the top and then plummets down, never reaching that high peak again. At this stage, blackouts can occur and overdoses are more likely, tolerance being impossible to gauge. Of course, there are many other variables, but typically there are warning signs. From what you have described, you have two different kinds of drinkers who ended up dead, and neither one seems to fit into the category I described. You also have a coincidence of setting and time frame. I don't know, Jeff. Do these men have anything in common at all? Did they know one another?"

Jeff shrugged. "Around here, most folks either know one another or know about one another. The only common thread I found was they had both done work for a local realtor, Rodney Granger. But that's reaching, because they've worked for other people too. Caleb was a good land surveyor who worked primarily for Rodney, while Ernie was an odd-job handyman who worked for Rodney and anyone else who would hire him. I'm sure Caleb and Ernie crossed paths, but according to folks who knew them, they were not friends, nor did they frequent the same places."

"It sounds like you've got another mystery on your hands. Hopefully, it will be cleared up by the toxicology report. I'd be interested in the findings, if you'd care to let me know."

"Sure thing, Dev. And thanks for the input. I've also got some variables to consider. It isn't unusual to find a number of toxins in some of these illegally home-stilled products. It might be hard to prove malicious intent when some contamination is common. The only credible moonshiner around here is Purvis McCabe, who lives way out by the Shadow Peak Ridge. His liquor was once known far and wide as the purest and best quality to be found, back when he was producing on a regular basis. My predecessor let him do his business without interference from law enforcement and suggested I do the same. He told me it wasn't worth getting my head shot off to try to locate his still and arrest him. He told me the old man had practically retired after his wife and daughter died. Said he was nothing but a forgotten legend now and had even gone a bit crazy." Jeff shrugged again. "I've a mind to take a ride over there and try to talk to him. He might have something to say about moonshine, like the kind he makes, killing folks."

CHAPTER FOURTEEN

He made an instrument to know
If the moon shine at full or no.
~ Samuel Butler

PURVIS MCCABE KNEW HE WAS getting senile. Back in his day, that's how folks described what was happening to him when it happened to other people. The signs were all there. Each time he forgot how to do something, he felt angry and confused. He combated these feelings by reminding himself that, on good days, his mind was as sharp as ever and his mastery of the old skills evident in the fine product he produced. It had been the pride of his life, and he'd vowed to protect his secret to the grave. But to his way of thinking, the grave was a long way off and his sturdy constitution and strong will would compensate for the forgetfulness. He'd worked from morning till night for most of his life, unlike his worthless brothers. He'd been stewing about them lately, thinking if something happened to him, they'd probably turn up to make a claim on his property. But, he'd made sure they'd never get it, hadn't he? That old woman knew. She'd make sure.

Being alone so much, he'd get to thinking and then get confused. It was better when he kept moving, kept working. Sometimes, he thought he heard Evangeline singing, like when she was a young'un; always singing, that girl. But that was the mountain way. They were a singing people on his mother's side of the family, Evangeline being the only one in his family like her, which made her all the more special.

He mumbled aloud, "Why do the special ones always have to go their own way?"

She'd gone against him, moved up to the old shack on the stony ridge ledge, broke his heart. Or had he told her to leave? It was all so blurry now, he couldn't remember it right. Her mother would have kept her home, but she'd gone and died and left him to deal with the problem. There'd been a big problem, he was sure of it. Then those no-account brothers of his took off—something about Evangeline—he'd blamed them. They'd been pestering her; that was it! He'd been so busy with the whiskey business he'd not had time to notice such things. But he should have known. They couldn't keep their hands off anything. And she was a "beauty to behold, truth be told." The old saying ran though his mind. He could see her face, his beautiful baby girl, sapphire eyes like the waters, hair the color of a black bird, almost purple.

He shook his head, bent it down in sorrow, and spoke lowly, "She's the one I'd have told about the waters, her being the rightful one, always going there, singin' and gazin' at them, like she belonged to them more than to me."

He'd watched her, when he'd been checking on the still. He could see the falls from there. She'd been a rare sight to behold, one he hadn't forgotten and never would. But he couldn't remember what happened after. The past seemed cloudy and far away. Why had she left him? Why had she died? She'd been trying to tell him; he'd been hearing her voice. And he'd seen that boy again, the boy from years ago, sitting down at the falls with the old woman, her acting like he belonged there. She'd never taken anyone there. They'd made a pact about it, long ago. He was sure of it . . . or was he?

He'd have shot the boy if he hadn't been with *her*. Why hadn't he shot him when he'd caught him on his property? He'd had the right to do it; otherwise, there'd be people trespassing all the time, finding the pick-up places and stealing his jars. Recently, he'd been hearing things and sensing movement, feeling like somebody was up to no good. Must be that blasted bad moon; can't make good liquor under a moon like that, need a shining moon to make the best, shouldn't have put out the jars from that batch, better to make a new batch. Not that anyone'd know the difference. Folks these days didn't know good liquor from bad—not that anything he made was bad—just not as good as usual, not up to his high standards.

Purvis's mind stopped wandering when he grew tired. He hadn't been sleeping well, unusual for him. He wasn't one for sitting and resting, but he had been doing more of it lately, after putting on his beans. He had beans and cornbread for dinner every night, sometimes with pork, sometimes with venison, which he'd take in trade for his liquor. He sat down in the old bentwood rocker with the hand-woven seat. The rocker had been his mother's.

He planned to check on the still later that night to test the remaining liquor to see if it was worth keeping. He hated waste, but sometimes it was necessary. He started to feel drowsy and drifted off into a dream filled with the soothing sound of flowing waters, the sweet song of the rippling brook mingled with the soft and sultry voice of Evangeline. Her face appeared in the dream, hauntingly beautiful, and then slowly, strangely it changed, morphing into the face of the boy.

CHAPTER FIFTEEN

What beck'ning ghost along the moon-light shade
Invites my steps, and points to yonder glade.
~ Alexander Pope

CHIEF FARLEY LINGERED ON THE bank of the Green River longer than he'd planned, postponing his drive to the McCabe compound. After his discussion with Dev regarding the two alcohol-related deaths, he'd felt reluctant to leave the secluded fishing spot. He could see why Dev had chosen it. The banks directly up-river from the cove were too steep in some places and too overgrown in others. But farther along, there were areas of dark brown, wet, sandy beach where uneven mounds of rocks and smooth-surfaced boulders had created perfect platforms for sitting and fishing. The rock formations had partially dammed the river in places, creating a succession of small waterfalls, all of which gently gushed into dark pools where fish liked to gather while heading downstream. He'd felt peaceful there all morning, watching Dev cast his line into the glistening waters where the sun filtered down through the trees.

Dev had opened the door to a more personal discussion when he'd indicated a past problem with alcohol. Perhaps it was the relaxed atmosphere or the hypnotizing effect of the river, its green-glass surface reflecting the lush forest canopy overhead. It could have been their shared affinity for the outdoors, or the fact that they'd shared an experience so horrific each had been irreversibly changed by it.

Dev hadn't waited for Jeff to ask. It seemed right that he should know the truth about his past. He became serious as he talked about his time as a young Catholic priest sent from Ireland to the dismal town of Calvary, Montana. He described the years of frustrating, futile effort, his inevitable fall from grace, the brutal unsolved murder of the woman he had loved there, and his subsequent decline into depression and alcohol-dependence during the depths of his despair. He regained a sense of humor when he reflected on his startling realization that he'd not been suited for the vocation chosen for him as a boy. That knowledge had resulted in the beginning of his recovery, resurrection into his chosen profession, and the miracle of Kate in his life.

Jeff listened with understanding and interest, and then found himself talking about his time with Charlotte, before she'd married Jordon Reed, the difficulty he'd had getting over her, how he'd given his life to the military and FBI—his formal education in human behavior—until his true calling brought him back to the mountains and *his* chosen profession. He talked about the loss of his parents and wife, the adjustment to living alone, and now, the unsettling return of Charlotte Reed.

The early morning passed quickly, but time seemed to stop for a while to allow their friendship to deepen. They shared a common belief that, no matter how good life could be, there would always be an evil force at work to disrupt it. From this point on, there would exist between them a pact of guardianship to unofficially work together to protect their home ground of Serena.

Jeff was almost back to the landing when his beeper went off. He called the station from the cruiser. Aura Lee sounded distraught.

"Chief, I just got a call from State Trooper Corley. The accident reported last night out on the county highway involved Charlie Foster's nephew, Eddie, and his girlfriend, Belinda Riley. They are both in critical condition. They were taken to Mission Ridge Hospital sometime after midnight. Isn't that awful? Trooper Corley said the attending physician is questioning the cause of the accident. Corley told him he should talk to you, Eddie and Belinda being from Serena."

Farley had made it a habit to stay on good terms and in regular communication with the State Highway Patrol and the county Sheriff's Department. Serena was a small town in a large county, and the nearby interstate was a well-traveled route from north to south. He hadn't fallen into the ego trap of territorialism in his position as chief of police; he'd seen enough of that in the FBI. He'd learned from his mountain kinfolk how to build a supportive network. Therefore, he appreciated Corley's recommendation that he be informed and drove with haste to the hospital.

Upon arrival, he talked to an admitting nurse and learned the couple had been transported by ambulance after being extricated from Eddie's pickup truck. They'd been found top-sided in a ditch by Trooper Corley, who'd been patrolling the state road to the county line. Minutes later, a very young-looking doctor came through the emergency room doors and introduced himself as Dr. Paul Stevens. He led Farley into a small anti-room where they could talk in private.

"I was on duty when they were brought in. I initially judged it to be a typical drunk-driving accident," he said forthrightly, "until becoming curious about their symptoms and the nature of their physical injuries. It appeared the young man had lost consciousness prior to the accident, the probable reason he'd lost control of his vehicle. There was also evidence the girl had become violently ill before the crash. The coincidence of both becoming severely ill at the same time suggested the possibility they'd taken a combination of alcohol and drugs. Initial testing, however, indicated no other drugs and a blood-alcohol level, although high, not sufficient to explain the symptoms and scenario. I've ordered detailed toxicology screenings. The boy's parents are in the waiting room. I haven't had time to question them. I'd appreciate it if you could handle that, and if you find out anything that might be helpful, let me know. I'll get back to you as soon as I get the results."

Farley thanked Dr. Stevens, impressed with his keen interest and diagnostic skills, then walked down the hallway to the waiting room and found Eddie's parents. He tried to question without upsetting them too much, and they tried to cooperate. They were not able to shed light on the events leading to the accident. They told him Eddie had been working for his uncle, Charlie Foster, and staying over at his place. They'd been worried about him since he left home but had lost their influence over him, "him thinking himself too big for his britches, racing all over the back roads at night with that wild girl, his uncle setting no rules. And see what's come of it."

They'd had Eddie late in life and said they were "at a loss to know what to do with the boy." Jeff could see the pain in their eyes and felt sympathy for them, knowing their suffering was just beginning. Belinda's mother had not yet arrived, having been difficult to contact. Mrs. Foster expressed disapproval, blaming her for "allowing Belinda to be out all hours, her hardly ever at home."

He left them sitting there, clinging to one another, barely holding back their tears.

After leaving the hospital, Jeff checked in with Aura Lee before deciding to postpone having lunch and instead head over to see Charlie Foster. Charlie ran a combination truck stop, garage, and spare-parts junk shop out near the interstate. He'd not been one to mess with in his early years and was still not an easy man to deal with. He came from a long line of railroad men and would have followed in their tradition . . . had the trains continued to run. When Southern Railways stopped rolling through Serena, he'd lost a planned future and found a new one building a makeshift conglomerate enterprise that remained on the fringe of the Serena business community.

Charlie Foster lived by his own rules and refused to conform to any new zoning regulations or plans for beautifying the route from the interstate to Serena. His truck stop was located beyond the city limits, making it possible for him to defy city officials and their ordinances. It was the first stop off the interstate exit and the most unsightly business in the area.

Farley drove into the pot-holed lot and parked by an open garage door. He entered the dark, cavernous interior, edged around a car raised on lifts, went through a side door and down a paneled hallway to Charlie's office. He was in there working at his desk.

"Hey, Chief. I know why you're here," he said, not bothering to stand. "I was just finishing up, planning to head over to the hospital. Bad news all around. I'd been telling that boy he'd end up dead if he didn't start thinking straight."

"What did happen, Charlie?" Farley carefully lowered himself into a chair that had seen better days. "He's been working for you and staying with you."

Charlie shook his head. "He's not been working worth a damn lately. I was about to send him on his way. But I was fond of the boy, always was. But since he's got tied up with that Riley girl, there's no talking sense to him. She got Eddie drinking and staying out so late he couldn't get up in the morning and was of no use when he did, all hung-over and pale-looking." He held up his hands. "He hasn't been getting his liquor from me, I can tell you that, Chief. I've been sober since Jessie died—everyone knows it." A sigh escaped. "My brother and his wife never did drink, them being church-goin' people an' all. That's why they put their foot down with him. I didn't mind some drinking. A boy his age is going to either drink or smoke weed, and I laid down the law about that, told him he'd be out the next day if he was foolin' with dope. I won't have a pothead working for me. I just figured he'd drink a little with his friends on the weekends, but then that girl came along and things got out of hand."

Farley leaned forward. "Do you have any idea where he'd been getting his liquor, Charlie? This is important, because there might have been something wrong with it."

Charlie pushed back from his desk. "Aw, I don't know. He's friends with those ol' boys who run liquor for local shiners, but I don't know if he got it from them or not. You might want to talk to Harold Morris. He's got a place out on Minneola Road. He's been in the supply and demand business for a long time, liquor being his main product. I'd not be telling you this except for Eddie. If that boy dies because of bad liquor, *someone* is going to pay."

"Let's keep a cool head here, Charlie." Farley stood up. "We don't know anything for sure yet. Let me do my job. You know me. I'll get to the bottom of it. And I hope they're able to save Eddie—and Belinda. I'd better let you go so you can get over there. His momma and daddy need your support."

"To tell you the truth, Chief, I've been ashamed to go, Eddie being in my care and all. That's why I've been putting it off, working here. But you're right." Charlie stood as well. "I'll head on out and face it like a man should. What a mess. I don't want that boy to die, or the girl."

Jeff thought about what he'd learned from Charlie while on his way to see Harold Morris, reflecting on the way things had changed in the mountains over the past fifty years. Used to be, bootlegging was big business, and a network as sophisticated as a beehive spread out in every direction to supply individuals, households, and liquor houses throughout the county, even across the state line. But that was before the sixties, when marijuana was discovered to be more profitable than moonshine and the demand for it was high. Later, a more dangerous cottage industry developed around methamphetamine, as meth labs were created right in people's homes. The old moonshiners lost business, and their numbers eventually dwindled, the customer base grew smaller, and many of them just died off.

There was still money to be made, and guys like Morris knew how to capitalize on a product still in demand. Cutting out the middleman bootleggers, he used runners—who were usually too young to know better—to collect jars of liquor left in specific and ever-changing pick-up places supplied by the moonshiner and then distribute the product in the same manner to known customers who would pay a monthly tab. His runners also brought in new business by selling to friends they could trust, like Eddie. It was a smooth-running, small, illegal, untaxed business that provided extra income to run Morris's small farm, as long as nothing went wrong. This time something did go wrong, and word spreads fast in these circles. When Jeff arrived, the doors were bolted and Morris was nowhere to be found.

Jeff figured he probably took off for South Carolina to avoid arrest. He'd put out an all-points bulletin for Morris, but in the meantime, he'd follow his initial hunch and pay a visit to Purvis McCabe. But first, he needed to stop at the station and then have a late lunch.

Aura Lee was busy at the computer. It was good to see she was focusing on work. But that stopped immediately when she saw Farley.

"Chief, Doctor Stevens just called from the hospital. He said you're to call him back as soon as possible." She referred to her notes. "Trooper Corley said there were two broken jars found in the car and alcohol spilled all over the seats. The doc sent him back for a sample of the contents. The boy, Eddie, is still in critical condition, but the girl's condition is reduced to serious, and it looks like she's going to make it."

Farley called and waited almost five minutes before Stevens came on the line.

"Sorry, Chief, I'm up to my ears today. After you left, I remembered mention of two broken jars found in the pickup truck at the crash scene. I requested a sample and had it tested. I thought you should know that we have a case of poisoning. It might have gone undetected had the victims not been found and transported here so expediently."

Farley sucked in his breath but did not speak, allowing the doctor to continue.

"I've had some experience with cyanide poisoning and recognized the symptoms, but I had to be sure. Had Corley not found the pair so quickly, they would have died at the scene and their symptoms would have not presented. I went ahead and ordered an antidote with my first suspicion because to have waited for the toxicology report would have resulted in their deaths. We administered it, and it had an immediate effect, confirming my initial diagnosis. Their accident-related injuries, while severe in Eddie's case, would not have been fatal.

"However, there is something of a mystery here involving the poisonous substance. Initial test results indicate the presence of cyanogenic glucosides, which produce linamarin. When on hydrolysis, linamarin can release hydrocyanic acid into the bloodstream and—depending on the dosage—can cause instantaneous death. In simpler terms, Chief, the alcohol they were drinking contained cassava, a deadly poisonous compound."

"I'm afraid you'll have to make it simpler than that, Doc."

"Cassava has been known to be used in voodoo potions, but it's not native to this region. I guess it will be your job to find out how it got into the moonshine those two kids were sipping."

Farley thanked him, hung up the phone, and stood there staring into space. Aura Lee was too curious to wait for him to speak.

"What is it, Chief? Bad news?"

He filled her in, told her where he was going, and warned her to keep silent about what she had heard.

She nodded respectfully and asked in a hushed voice, "What do you make of it, Chief? Do you think it was intentional?"

"I don't know, Aura Lee, but it does help to explain the rash of alcohol overdoses happening lately. By the way, were there any other calls?"

"Only that grumpy old neighbor of Charlotte Reed's, complaining about her rooster again."

Farley shook his head and then ducked before going through the doorway. On his way to the Serena Grill, he thought about Charlotte. Why had she returned? Mercifully, the scent of grilled hamburgers took his mind away from her and the information from Dr. Stevens he'd been trying to process.

The lunch crowd had come and gone, with a few stragglers remaining. Farley sat on a stool at the counter and placed an order to go. The Grill was not a fast food restaurant; a half hour would pass before the paper sack containing his burger and fries was ready. While waiting, he noticed that his favorite waitress, Thelma Harper, was busy training a young waitress sporting a coiled snake tattoo on the right side of her neck, the tail of which slithered down beneath the collar of her Harley Davidson T-shirt. Both wore the Grill's cheerful red and white checked aprons, which matched the checkered tablecloths and iconic Coca-Cola décor, but the contrast between the two women got him thinking about another contrast, brought to mind by Dr. Stevens's report.

Shortly thereafter, with stomach growling and brown lunch bag placed aside, Farley bumped along the rough and rutted road until coming to the Y fork. For several more minutes, he sat there eating his lunch while contemplating the properties to the left and right of him. He began to recall stories he'd heard about the two people who owned them, Purvis McCabe and Mamma Phoebe, reflecting on the contrast between them. Every mountain region had its legendary people, but rarely did two infamous legends co-exist as neighbors over a period of decades. To the right, there were stories told of hoodoo and witchcraft, miracle healings and magical cures. To the left, there were stories told of moonshine and mayhem, feuding and mysterious death. But how much was true and how much was fiction? How much was past and how much was present?

As far as Farley knew, old Purvis was almost retired. And despite all the rumors and innuendoes about Purvis being dangerous and Mamma Phoebe being a witch, no one had ever informed on them or issued a complaint to the police. The previous chief had told him not to bother with them because they were part of the natural order of things.

It was intriguing how different they were from one another, yet they had something in common: Purvis was known as the best whiskey-maker in these parts (although no one Farley knew admitted being a customer) and Mamma Phoebe was known as the best healer around (although no one he knew admitted going to her for treatment). It was an odd coincidence, something to consider. In addition, they had no reported history of animosity toward one another or property line disputes over the many years they'd been neighbors. He thought of another common thread beyond their specializations: each had something to offer that people wanted and were willing to go to great lengths to obtain. He wondered if any of these people had grievances of some kind.

Suddenly, he wondered why he'd been giving them so much thought and how long he'd been sitting there. He looked at his watch, surprised at the time. He restarted the cruiser and took the left stem of the Y down the road.

The drive yielded lots of dust and one "No Trespassing" sign after another. He felt relatively safe in his cruiser but knew better than to let his guard down. In the past, he'd seen the deadly work of snipers and knew the danger of being in the scope of a man known to be a good shot.

When the compound appeared in the distance, he took in the scene with an experienced eye. He saw no sign of movement or threat; the place looked like a ghost town. The main structure and outbuildings were of similar construction, unpainted and colorless gray-brown, with tin roofing rusted in spots and along the edges, all set about in a sprawl.

There wasn't a sound, just the perfectly still unsettling silence. No one came out onto the porch. No one appeared to be working outside. Most chores were done by mid-afternoon in the summertime, but then Purvis also worked at night. Farley had arrived much later than planned; it had been that kind of a day.

He inhaled deeply. Something wasn't right. He turned off the engine and eased out of the cruiser, walked a few steps, and called out the old man's name. No reply.

The steps to the porch and the planks of its floorboards creaked loud enough to warn a man hard of hearing, so he approached the front door with caution. He called out once more before knocking on the door. The door had not been latched and swung open before him. A rocking chair lay toppled by the wood stove, and the booted feet of the old man sticking out from under it. Farley hurried forward and lifted the chair off McCabe's body, then knelt down to check for a pulse, knowing it was pointless. He'd been dead for several hours, an expression of pain and outrage carved into his withered features. The strong smell of liquor diverted Farley's attention from the body to a toppled Mason jar lying on the floor by the stove.

CHAPTER SIXTEEN

Even the man who is pure in heart
And says his prayers by night
May become a wolf when the wolfbane blooms
And the Moon is pure and bright.
~ Maria Ouspenskaya's famous lines from *The Wolf Man*

TAYLOR REED PULLED UP IN front of the market and parked the red sports car. He'd been obsessing about Willa Mae for days. She was an angel sent to relieve his misery. What the heck was she doing working at a cash register? He had his pick of the girls at the university, but none could compare to this one. And she didn't seem to know it, which made her even more amazing. Thank goodness there was such a creature here in town; he'd been about to lose his mind. His mother was driving him crazy, and the job for Rodney Granger was a joke. He'd been sent all over the county putting up *For Sale* signs or replacing them with *Sold* signs, taking photos for Rodney's weekly sale/rental advertisements, and trekking over one property after another, checking for vagrants or vandalism. Now some old fart moonshiner had been found dead, and he was supposed to check out his place, way back over the southeastern ridge in the middle of nowhere.

His father had been away on one of his trips out of the country. Now, all of a sudden, he was planning to come to Serena to check on things—what things?—and take a break from his hectic schedule, so he'd said. This had his mother in a state of frenzy. The way she was acting, you'd think his father was invading her territory. She seemed to be on the verge of a nervous collapse. He tried to be attentive but had to get high to do it. He'd have to stay high to deal with the two of them being in the same house. He didn't know how long his father planned to stay, but a week was their usual cohabitation limit.

Maybe he wouldn't need drugs if Willa Mae could be had. He was determined to make it happen, no matter how much time or energy it would take. Naturally, he'd have to be secretive. She was not the kind of girl his father had in mind for his future. He wasn't sure what category she fell into, but his father would put her in one not suitable; he didn't approve of prowling around so close to home (one of his rules about women), even if it was their summer home. But good grief, what was summer for? His parents had almost ruined his. He had to have a diversion to make it through to next semester and a new flock of co-eds. He got out of the car and went inside.

"Hello, Willa Mae," he said in his most sincere and genuine voice. He'd dressed outdoor casual that morning, L.L. Bean from top to bottom, thinking it might make Willa Mae feel more at ease with him. "You're looking at a guy who needs help. I haven't had the chance to make any friends here this summer. Everyone my age seems to be camping, hiking, or kayaking down the river, while I've been slaving away. I've noticed you're in the same boat and wondered . . . if," he stammered slightly, adopting a helpless expression, "well, it's just that you've been so nice to me every time I've come in the store, I thought maybe you could find time to take a break and help me learn a little more about my surroundings. I keep getting switched around on the back roads, and my GPS gets as confused as I do. No guy wants to admit this or ask for directions, and I sure don't want ask my boss. What do you say, my breath of sunshine, will you help?"

Willa looked surprised, as no one had ever asked for that kind of help before. She hesitated, and Taylor worried that his ploy wouldn't work. Just as he opened his mouth to plead his case, a flash of confidence shone in Willa's eyes. She looked directly at Taylor and said, "I'd surely like to help you, if you'd just stop by here before going somewhere you don't know how to get to."

"That's not what I had in mind, Willa Mae." He almost called her "sugar" but didn't want to take the chance of offending her. These mountain people were funny about showing respect, and he didn't want to display any unintended disrespect. "Couldn't you spare just a little time after work to show me around? I've seen you walking past the real estate office on your way home after work. It's quite a distance up to where you live, isn't it?"

"Well . . . "

"If I picked you up where you take that shortcut across the railroad tracks, and then drop you off afterward on the ridge road nearer your home, you wouldn't be late, if that's what has you worried. Why, in a just few days, you could teach me enough to know my way around. How about it, Willa Mae? Take pity on a poor lonesome guy."

He tried to look pitiful and charmingly debonair at the same time, watching her consider his plea. She had the sweetest way of tilting her head to the side while thinking it over. He was pleasantly surprised when she came to a decision so quickly.

"Well, I'll go with you for a little while tomorrow, if you're still of a mind to have my help. But I can't promise more."

"Tomorrow it is, Willa Mae. I'll be down by the railroad tracks at six o'clock, and I promise to have you home by seven."

On his way out, Taylor passed a customer and tried to hide his self-satisfied grin.

CHAPTER SEVENTEEN

If the sun claims it has power over the moon,
let it shine in the night.
~ Central African Proverb

KATE WAS BUSY TENDING TO her finches and white dove, Dewey. He hadn't been the same since the rooster incident and was on the lookout for a similar invasion. He rocked forward and back in some kind of dove wardance ritual in response to every outside noise, cooing his warnings several times a day. The finches chirped cheerfully every time he did this, not a warring bone in their tiny bodies.

The chirping and cooing quieted down as the finches gathered around their replenished seed and water containers. Dewey pecked away at his lunchtime fruit treat while keeping a fierce eye on the window. Kate heard the front door chimes and hurried from the kitchen, thinking Dev might have forgotten his key.

She opened the door to Chief Farley. He apologized for arriving unexpected.

"I'm sorry to bother you Kate, but I need to talk to you or Dev or both of you about something. Do you have a few minutes?"

"Of course, Jeff. Come on in. Dev will be back in about an hour. Would you rather wait and talk to him?"

"No, Kate. I'd rather run it by you, first."

"Come into the kitchen. I'll make a fresh pot of coffee while you get started. I know your time is limited."

She placed a platter of cookies on the table in front of him and went about making the coffee while he chose a cookie.

"Kate, I know this might sound like a crazy question, but what do you know about voodoo? Have you ever come across it in your professional experience? Has the subject ever come up in your psychology classes?"

Kate turned around and looked at him with a smile. "Is this a personal interest, Jeff? Are you thinking of taking up a new religion?"

"I'm not joking, Kate. What do you mean about religion?"

"Sorry, Jeff, I didn't realize you were serious. I do know a little about it from a psychological perspective. For example, how it affects people who believe in it. Voodoo is a Haitian religion that is African in character. Why do you ask?"

"Dev may have told you about the two recent alcohol-related deaths I discussed with him a few days ago." Kate nodded. "They were followed by two more similar near-deaths, followed by the death of an old moonshiner named Purvis McCabe. The first two were thought to be accidental, although I had my suspicions, as Dev probably told you. The second two were discovered as a result of an auto accident; they survived, but one is in critical condition. Tests of the liquor they'd been drinking produced evidence of a toxic substance. In each case, the alcohol was identified as white liquor known as moonshine.

"Purvis McCabe was the best illegal whiskey-maker in the county. I went out to his place two days ago to ask if he knew anything about tainted alcohol being sold or who could be making it. I hadn't considered him a suspect. I found him dead, a spilled jar of liquor by his body." Farley shook his head and sighed. "The contents have been tested, and the same toxic substance was identified."

"Oh my," Kate said, bringing two cups of fresh coffee to the table. "I'd be worried if I was a partaker of moonshine. It sounds like this is getting serious."

"This is where I need your help, Kate," Farley said, accepting his coffee. "The substance identified is a poisonous compound made from the cassava plant-root and is commonly used in voodoo rituals. Strangely enough, Purvis

McCabe's only neighbor is an old woman you may have heard of—a reputed hoodoo doctor called Mamma Phoebe—who some folks refer to as a witch-woman. I knew Mamma Phoebe's sister years ago, a fine person, who spoke highly of her as a miracle healer. Her name is Penelope Cather, and I heard she's working up at the Orchard Lake Inn. I plan to question her after I talk to Mamma Phoebe, but I need to be more informed before I do. I thought if you knew anything about voodoo, you might enlighten me on the subject."

"I'll try, Jeff. First of all, you should know that voodoo and hoodoo aren't the same thing. Hoodoo is an American term, and it refers to African-American folklore practices and beliefs with a considerable mixture of American Indian botanical knowledge and European folklore. Hoodoo is also known as root-work, witchcraft, or conjuring. Hoodoo doctors are a combination of herbalist and folk-magician. Supposedly, a true hoodoo doctor is gifted at birth and carries the signs that can be recognized by other practitioners."

Kate hadn't heard Dev come in, but the birds greeted him with wild enthusiasm, alerting Kate to his presence. The birds loved the sight of him, and so did Kate.

"Sounds like a deep conversation going on in here. Are we about to put a spell on some someone?"

"You're just in time, Dev! Jeff needs information about hoodoo, and I've been straining my brain to remember what I know. You're the expert on folk-lore medicine. I'll get you some coffee while you help Jeff out."

The birds quieted down with due respect while Jeff explained the situation to Dev. When he finished, Dev said, "You were right to be suspicious from the onset, Jeff. It sounds like these incidents are tied together by the cassava root compound, but do you think the poisonings were intentional?"

"That might be hard to prove, but I'm leaning in that direction. Mamma Phoebe may not be connected to this—Kate set me straight about hoodoo being different from voodoo—but I'm curious to know about the roots she uses in her hoodoo potions."

Dev replied, "I can tell you something many people don't know about the word *hoodoo*. For the most part, it's been assumed to be of African origin. However, its earliest usage in America is connected with Irish sailors, not African slaves. In the mid-1800s, ships that had suffered a series of ill-fated voyages and mishaps were called hoodoo ships or were said to have been hoodoo'd. In some accounts, the problems onboard these vessels were attributed to an evil spirit or presence. The word *hoodoo* is a phonetic transliteration of the Irish-Gaelic words that mean dark phantom, evil entity, or spiky ghost.

"The Irish origin for the word hoodoo also explains why a certain type of rock formation across the Americas is called hoodoo—Irish trappers saw these weird objects as personified demons." Farley's eyebrows went up, but he did not interrupt, and Dev continued. "Along the eastern seaboard and even into the Carolinas, the word *witchcraft* became another word for hoodoo in African-American communities. But many who practiced it reserved the word *hoodoo* to refer to harmful magic. They used the phrase "spiritual work" for beneficial magic, which included conjuring love spells and protection magic."

Jeff ran a hand over his face, looked across the table at Dev and Kate, and said, "Whew, and here I am, about to have a sit-down with one of these hoodoo women to find out what she might know about Purvis McCabe's death by moonshine."

The three of them sat for a while longer talking. Kate appreciated the way Jeff valued their thoughts and opinions. She and Dev agreed to find out more about the subject and condense it for him should he need to know more.

After Farley left, Kate looked at Dev and said, "I had no idea there was any Irish connection with hoodoo. You amaze me, Dev. I'm beginning to think you have the hoodoo gift too."

Dev winked. "Come over here to me, my sweet Katie, and let me put a wee hoodoo spell on you right now."

CHAPTER EIGHTEEN

Moping, melancholy, and moonstruck madness.

~ John Milton

CHARLOTTE WAS BESIDE HERSELF, AS the saying goes, but in her case it was literally correct. She could see herself in the mirror as she had been, before the days of her marriage, before the years of unhappiness and heartbreak. She couldn't bear the reality of her reflection and was grateful it had been replaced by her former self. The image raised her spirits. It had been a rough week. Her hopes for the renewed relationship with her son had been dashed, despite her best efforts.

Taylor had been coming home after work later than usual, making excuses, skipping the lovely dinners she'd prepared for him, and taking special pains with his wardrobe, dressing like an outdoorsman instead of his usual GQ style. It had to be a girl. He was like his father in that regard; Jordon's infidelities were a well-known secret. She'd come to the painful conclusion that Taylor was lost to her. And now Jordon was coming to Serena, uninvited, ignoring their agreement, and invading the home she had reclaimed as her own. He and Taylor would once again become a team, trying to make her feel insignificant and unstable. But that was not going to happen. Not this time and never again. She could see rebellion in the face in the mirror, not her present one, but the face of the girl who'd been the belle of the Harvest Moon Dance.

She had to have help. She had to find Nanny Pen.

That same morning in his office in Washington, D.C., Jordon Reed received a call from Rodney Granger. He had jet-lag from his trip and plenty to do before departing for Serena, so he resisted the temptation to leave earlier than planned. He'd have to depend on Rodney to be his front man and move in as quickly as possible. The initial proposal would have to be made before he arrived in Serena. His involvement shouldn't be known until the final deal was in place. He found it difficult to concentrate. His secretary had prepared a three-day agenda of the most necessary meetings and appointments she had scheduled for him. He reviewed it and then made a private call to arrange for his preferred brand of personal pleasure.

It was essential he be in a good frame of mind in order to convince Charlotte that his visit was for her benefit, mending fences as it were, perhaps developing a closer relationship during his stay. He knew she would be skeptical, resistant, wary, but then she'd been so desperate of late, he might have a chance to sway her. He could not afford trouble at home during this crucial time, this chance for a new beginning. He'd need her financial support to close the land deal and develop his new enterprise. She'd probably be glad he was considering retiring from politics after this term if it meant a different future for Taylor.

He thought it ironic that in all his research and meticulous planning, he'd not considered the one factor that could ruin everything. Charlotte had always been so reliable, retreating into fantasy in reaction to his behavior instead of retaliating with affairs or threatening divorce. Raising Taylor had kept her grounded, and playing hostess in Charleston had given her an outlet for her princess daydreams. Perhaps he shouldn't have taken Taylor away from her as he did, but if he had left Taylor with her over-the-top mothering much longer, who knows what he'd have become.

It was almost pathetic to think of her now, trying to make him her little boy again. But he'd have to let her believe it possible, at least for a little while longer. Although he found it worrisome that she'd gone to such lengths, moving to Serena for the summer, abandoning their Charleston home and social life. This odd diversion on her part was a distraction for him. He'd not planned on her being in Serena when the deal went down. He'd not thought about her at all, except in terms of money. Now he had to play the attentive husband and convince Taylor to play the attentive son until financial matters were settled.

Putting Taylor to work for Rodney was the one positive factor. Rodney wasn't exactly trustworthy, and Taylor had proved to have a keen eye for spying. Jordon had trained him well and taught him the value of trusting no one when shared profits were involved. Not that he planned to share much profit with Rodney. He had enough on him to keep him in his place. But the mountain people were a different breed; they didn't hold anyone above themselves and were too independent in their thinking. Plus, Rodney had an underground network that made Jordon's pale in comparison. To make matters worse, they were hidden from sight within a wilderness so vast it was impossible to determine their inner-workings. He would have to rely on Rodney more than he liked, until he was no longer needed.

Penelope Cather had been busy that morning as well. She was worried about her son, and for good reason. She'd never seen him so solemn and perplexed. Raven was such an unusual boy. He'd had the willingness, foresight, and intelligence to know the value of Phoebe's teachings. He had accepted their plan for his education without question, and yet he had his own mind and a confident sense of self, even as a child.

Back then, it had been a struggle for her to restrain him from wandering off too far, exploring too deep into the forest, and venturing off into unknown territory at an age when most children were still tied to their mother's apron strings. There was a pull she could not compete with, a call to the waters she and Phoebe had tried to delay. And yet they both understood the power of the moon and the stars and the spirit world in which they practiced their arts, so there had been an acceptance of his destiny, and they'd prepared for it.

There was also another pull in his life, one he had come to depend on. There was one who had always been there waiting for him when his mother had been busy working at the inn or at home. One who had always loved Raven without question, adoring him since childhood, following him as much as he would allow it, and listening to his adventures with wonder in her eyes and expressed admiration.

Something had changed. Pen realized it as she watched Raven from the window of the cottage. He was standing near the edge of the forest where Willa Mae had always waited for him to come home. She'd watched them many times, smiling at the sight of them, Willa Mae's eager expectation, her delight in his appearance, his reliance on her being there. But now he stood there alone, staring out across the ridge toward the Parsons' homestead. Willa Mae hadn't known Phoebe had given him extra time off, so how could she know he would be there? She had a job now and many more duties at home. Pen wondered if he would seek her out and go the Parsons' to inquire about her. But he just stood there. Pen knew what she had to do.

She'd given Raven plenty of work at the inn to keep him busy that day. Phoebe may have given him a break, but Pen had not, although she had been lenient about his afternoons and evenings. After all, it was summertime.

She put together a basket of preserves she'd been meaning to take to Frank Parson. She'd been doing this since he'd become a widower. It had been weeks since her last visit across the ridge. She called to Raven now to let him know she was leaving.

Frank was outside working in his garden when Pen arrived. She liked the comfortable sturdiness of the man, his polite manner and no-nonsense approach to life. He'd always been a hard worker, a man of many talents, and a fine father to Willa Mae. He was also a generous man with his garden produce and made sure Pen had plenty of beans, greens, tomatoes, and squash for her kitchen. They had an unspoken admiration for one another and had developed a solid friendship over the years. She felt she could ask about Willa Mae without seeming too inquisitive. She waited until after their usual pleasantries.

"You must be proud of Willa Mae, Frank. It's quite a change for her to be in the center of all the goings-on in town, holding her own in her first job. But I do miss seeing her every day."

"Well, Miss Pen, to be honest, I'm not too pleased about her taking that job. There's plenty for her to do around here since her momma passed, rest her soul. Maybe I'm just thinkin' of myself, wanting her safe close by or over to your place where she's accustomed. She says she likes working for Miss Judy and earning a little extra money to put aside for school. Says Raven's been so busy she had to find something to do besides working around the house. That's what she says to keep me from speakin' out negative about her working, no bad meaning about Raven, Miss Pen. You know how she's always been so taken with your boy, him being like a big brother to her an' all."

"I'm sorry, Frank. It's my fault he hasn't been around. I've had him preparing himself for better things. He's a good boy, and I thank you for thinking well of him. He misses Willa Mae too. I've been a-noticing it. Maybe it's good for them to not be so dependent on one another and spread their wings a little."

Frank rubbed his whiskers thoughtfully. "I'm not so sure, Miss Pen. There's something going on I don't like, but I've not had anyone to speak my mind to about it. I might as well tell you."

"What is it, Frank? Is Willa Mae in some kind of trouble?"

"She's been coming home later every day after getting off work. First it was only about a half hour, and I didn't pay it no mind. Then it became an hour, and she said she'd been helping someone new in town find their way around Serena, said she felt sorry for him and wanted to show how friendly folks were here. Said I wasn't to worry, he was the son of that Charlotte Reed, who's come back to town for the summer. Says he's gone to work for Rodney

Granger and needs to learn fast about the back roads and shortcuts to places he has to see about. She said he came into the store and they became friends, but *just* friends, that's all, just like the friends she has at school. Says she's old enough to know her own mind about people, and I should trust her." Frank drew a hand over his eyes, and Pen could feel his frustration. "But, she's never had many friends at school, none that I know of or that she speaks about. She was a bit behind maturity-wise growing up, you know. Her momma had worried about her innocent nature. That's why we always appreciated your boy looking out for her. When she started blossoming the way she did, and her momma got sick and passed during that time, I didn't know what to say to her, just tried to keep her busy at home. I guess I put too much on her. Maybe that's why she wanted the job at the store. I do trust her, Miss Pen. She's a good girl, but I think she's too trusting. I don't want to come down hard on her for fear she might get more stubborn about helping that Reed boy than she already is." He sighed. "I wish her momma were here. She always knew the right thing to say."

Pen could hardly speak. The ground under her feet felt like it was moving sideways. She paused for a moment then tried to find words to say.

"I'm sure the boy is . . . well-intentioned, Frank. There's probably no cause for concern. If you'd like, I'll have a talk with her. Sometimes a girl needs a woman's point of view. Why don't you have her deliver a basket of greens to the inn tomorrow morning? I'll be working in the kitchen, and I do my best advice-giving while cooking. Raven's been summoned back to his aunt's tomorrow. Otherwise, I'd give him time off to spend with her."

"I thank you, Miss Pen. Willa thinks the world of you, and with her momma gone to rest, I don't know who else she'd turn to for such a talk."

Pen could say no more and walked back across the ridge in a daze. Her Charlotte had returned after all these years. There had been no communication between them since she'd been taken away. Pen had heard about her marriage to Jordon Reed, but she had no interest in him or his politics and had closed her mind to thinking about Charlotte since being given the gift of her boy.

She found it hard to believe Charlotte also had a son, one who was around the same age as Raven, and that he was spending the summer in Serena pursuing Willa Mae. Her words to Frank Parson had been well-meaning but untrue. She wasn't sure about the Reed boy's intentions and now understood why Willa Mae had not been coming around and why Raven was so upset. She was sure Raven didn't know about his potential rival, but it wouldn't take long for him to find out. When he did, there would be trouble.

She had to talk to Phoebe as soon as possible, tonight, after dark, when she'd be working at her potions. She'd make some excuse to Raven. She wondered why Phoebe had called him back for the day after giving him a much-needed break. She paused for a moment, alerted to something in the air, the too pungent scent of the mimosa carried on a sudden breeze like an omen. Her footsteps quickened, but there was no reason to hurry. She'd have to wait until nightfall, when the old devil moon would be rising.

CHAPTER NINETEEN

The moon, methinks, looks with a watr'y eye;
And when she weeps, weeps every little flower;
~ William Shakespeare

MAMMA PHOEBE HAD BEEN WORKING most of the night. She laid down to rest and fell into a deep sleep, but her dreams were not restful. She heard "*The bad moon cometh*" repeated in a hauntingly clear refrain, warning her that the time had come for action. In her dream, the demon face of the rock came alive beneath the falls, and poisonous waters flowed from its mouth into the crystalline pool. Fish floated to the surface, bloated and dying, their white bellies turned upward in surrender to death. The ghost of the old man stood watching from his hiding place, the full moon shining down on the still. Its fermenting brew bubbled and frothed and ran over the sides, thick and acrid, eating into the earth, crawling like hot lava downhill toward the stream. The refrain was then spoken by the voice of Evangeline, not singing, but crying out in sorrow, a mournful, heartbreaking wail.

Awakened from the nightmare, grim and resolute, she made haste to get ready. Raven was expected that morning. Somehow, she had known it would come to this, that forces would move against him to take what was rightfully his. He had to have the power to fight them. She had to teach him the recipes and mixings today, or all would be lost. The cry of his mother in her dream told her there was no time to waste.

Raven had also been awake most of the night. The morning was bright and sunny, not a cloud in the sky, but his mind was still troubled. He couldn't let it show. If Aunt Phoebe picked up on it, he'd have to tell her about Willa Mae. He didn't want to talk about her or think about her because he couldn't quite grasp what was happening. He'd expected to see her yesterday and had been greatly disappointed. He'd even waited way past her work time, but she hadn't come. He'd wanted to surprise her, tell her about almost being done, have the talk he'd been planning to have with her, knowing she'd been missing him.

He decided it must be the job taking more of her time. He rarely went into town, although it was no great distance from the cabin. He was solitary by nature and his life was spent in the outdoors when not working. But he loved home too, and had always hoped for a home with Willa Mae like the one he shared with his mother. He never worried about how he would provide for her. He simply trusted that his mother and Aunt Phoebe had a plan for him that would make it possible. He'd also never worried about Willa Mae . . . until now.

Mamma Phoebe put Raven right to work when he arrived. By noontime, he'd memorized the most important basic recipes. She taught him the sacred rites and demonstrated the power of the waters mixed with her roots and herbs and showed him how to create magic in the mixtures. She explained why her ancient knowledge was never written down and only a chosen few were gifted to have it. She said Purvis McCabe had respected her because he knew the special quality of the waters and used it to make his fine whiskey, but McCabe hadn't known how to use the waters to make magic. She talked about the pact they had made years ago and how they had honored it, him making the finest whiskey in the land, and her making her healing potions.

Mamma Phoebe and Raven worked together side-by-side while the sun moved across the sky. Raven absorbed the knowledge and retained it because she taught him in the wisdom-methods of her ancestors: sound-bites of information and visual demonstrations purposefully interconnected and story-told to link associations and trigger recall, like an ancient natural computer program installed into a receptive brain. Raven admired his aunt as never before and saw the magic in her that day.

When they came to the end of it, they sat down to rest, and Mamma Phoebe laid a hand on his arm and said, "Always remember, Raven, the power to heal can also destroy. You must use it wisely. I had hoped you'd not carry the weight of this knowing as I have, me being given the gift at birth. I've passed it to you for your protection, because you're going to need it long after I'm gone. I've given you the power to protect the waters because I can no longer carry the burden. The curse of my gift is being able to see the shadows in life and know when they're gathering around. If you ever see the demon rock shows its evil face, it's a sign they're closing in. You can call on the spirits for help. There is a strong spirit living in the waters. When you call, this spirit will answer, but when the spirit calls you, you must answer too."

Raven's brows met. "What shadows are gathering, Aunt Phoebe? What can I do?"

"Something has happened, my boy. Purvis McCabe was found dead earlier this week, and there are others dead too. There is bad business stirring, and questions will be asked about his moonshinin'. That old man never made a bad batch of whiskey in his life, and they're going to say he did. Next, there'll be intruders coming around. No one knows about your connection to the falls, Raven. We've got to keep it that way for a while. The shadows are moving in closer than ever in my lifetime. The forest no longer protects us the way it did before people started developing the land all over the ridges. Folks who'd have never dared to come back into these woods are getting more bold and hungry to know its secrets.

"This will be our last teachin' day together. I meant to have longer, but it isn't meant to be and I've grown very tired. You must take what I've given you and hold it inside until you have a chosen one to leave it to. The rest of what you must know, I've put pen to paper in a legal document your mamma holds for you. You'll have it on your eighteenth birthday the end of October. I'd hoped to live to see the day. This document is registered at the courthouse in case anybody tries to dispute it."

"You don't mean . . . you're not going to die, are you? Isn't there something we can do?"

"Now help me up and don't you go worryin' about me, boy. You've got the love of your old Aunt Phoebe for always, and I won't be leaving you ever. I got a mighty powerful spirit, and that spirit will always be watching over you. I couldn't love you more if you'd been my own son, and you're a pride to me in every way—and your mother too, who gave you to me for this while."

"Aunt Phoebe—"

"Hush now, boy. There's nothing you need to be saying. There's no more words needed between us."

When he helped her up, she drew him to her. Her eyes brimmed with tears as she hugged him tightly.

CHAPTER TWENTY

I promise to be an excellent husband, but give me a wife who, like the moon, will not appear every day in my life.
~ Anton Chekhov, Letter to A.S. Suvorin (1895)

JORDON REED CRUISED AT A steady seventy miles-per-hour along the same route his son had traveled in early June. It was nearing the end of the month, and his schedule had been cleared for the next two weeks. He felt a remarkable sense of freedom and had just begun to realize how great his life could be if relieved from responsibility, debt, and a wife he had to spend time with. It was strange to be traveling without his usual entourage, but also exhilarating. He was sick of all of them. Everyone in Washington had an agenda, and the intrigues going on right under his nose, as people vied for position and favors, were enough to make anyone paranoid.

Over the years he'd learned two vital lessons from his experience in politics: money wielded more power than anything, and business yielded more money than politics. With enough money, he could settle back and do what he wished, have what he wanted, and not be accountable to anyone but the IRS—and even they could be avoided through loopholes, another lesson he'd learned in Washington.

As the mountains came into view, he thought of the place that would make his dream of great wealth possible. He would have never discovered it had he not married Charlotte and used her family's summer home for a refuge. Unfortunately, unforeseen events had occurred during his stay there, and it hadn't been prudent to pursue his dream until now. He'd had years to plan and imagine the possibilities, to educate himself in all matters related to his vision of the future.

The miles sped by as he considered the necessary actions that had been taken. There would be more obstacles to overcome and he'd have to make a good impression in Serena. Few would remember his visits there years ago, and those who did, wouldn't recall a hint of scandal. He'd been careful then, discreet, unlike recent years. They'd be happy to have a congressman in their midst, gracing their town with his presence, showing his interest in their surroundings, his son working for the summer instead of appearing over-privileged, his wife opening the grand summer home once again. A perfect setup for what was to follow. Nothing and no one was going to stop him.

Charlotte phoned Kate's number and left a message, hoping she might be able to help her find Nanny Pen. She'd tried to recall the names of friends from high school days but realized how few she'd had, despite her popularity. She hadn't maintained contact with any of them and felt reluctant to contact them now. They'd faded from her memory because there had been only two close people in her life then: Nanny Pen and Jeff Farley, both of whom she'd been forced to abandon. Somehow, she knew Nanny Pen lived in the vicinity, although there was no listing for her in the Serena directory. She wondered if her sister was still living. Pen wouldn't have traveled far from Mamma Phoebe.

She couldn't think of Nanny Pen without thinking of Jeff. Her father had called him a childish infatuation, a boy not worthy of her attentions. He'd been callous and cruel and controlling—just like her husband. Why hadn't she rebelled, like others of her generation? She'd been raised during an era of social revolution and yet had allowed her father to bully her into leaving.

Returning to Serena had unlocked a treasure chest of memories, but she needed to focus on the present. Time was running out, and Jordon was expected late that afternoon. The thought of him made her feel sick.

She was startled when the phone rang and answered after the first ring.

"Charlotte, this is Kate Delaney returning your call."

"Oh, thank you, Kate, for getting back to me so quickly." Charlotte paced the length of the hallway. "I've got something rather urgent on my mind and hope you can help me. Do you remember my telling you about my nanny? She had a sister who was a well-known healer in these parts. I was wondering if she is still alive. There is no listing for her. I don't think there ever has been. Since you've lived here for several years, I thought you might have heard of her—Mamma Phoebe."

"It's strange you should ask, Charlotte, but just recently I heard Mamma Phoebe's name mentioned in relation to a sister employed at the Orchard Lake Inn. You might be able to reach her there. I'll look the number up for you. From what you've told me about her, I'm sure she'll be pleased to hear from you."

Charlotte pressed a hand to her heart. "Oh, Kate, thank you! You've helped me again. I only hope she will agree to see me. Do you think it's too late to make amends, when so much time has passed?"

Kate's response was so very kind as she said, "Charlotte, you had a very close relationship with your nanny. The bond of love is stronger than time and distance and holds within it a great capacity for forgiveness."

"I hope you are right, Kate, because I still feel the bond, and I need her more now than ever before."

The desperate tone of Charlotte's last remark left Kate wondering afterward if she was in some kind of trouble. She thought it a remarkable coincidence that she and Dev had just been talking to Jeff Farley about Mamma Phoebe and her sister. She'd learned from Dev and Jeff to be suspicious of coincidences but felt no inclination to investigate further. Charlotte's problems were not her concern. She'd had enough drama to last a lifetime and was too happy in her current life to get involved in something so peculiar.

Penelope Cather had plans to visit her sister that evening. Until then, she had plenty to do to keep her mind occupied, preparing luncheon for guests of the inn and making preparations for the dinner menu. The phone on the desk in the foyer rang and was answered by the new part-time, self-important, and impossibly rude young receptionist.

"I'm sorry, but our kitchen staff is not permitted to accept personal phone calls during working hours. However, I'd be happy to take a message . . . Yes, she is working here but, as I said, it is not permitted—"

The receptionist stopped and glared at the receiver and said, "Of all the nerve."

Thirty minutes later, a slim, attractive, beautifully dressed woman walked into the foyer. The receptionist greeted her with a frozen, practiced smile and asked, "May I help you?"

The woman walked past her desk without stopping, saying pleasantly to no one in particular, "I'd like to look around and get a feel for the setting and atmosphere."

It must have been the air of privilege that exuded from the woman that prevented the receptionist from trying to stop her. The woman disappeared into the dining room. When she didn't return after a few minutes, the receptionist likely assumed she'd run into some of her wealthy friends and joined them for lunch. She was not to know that Charlotte strutted haughtily (something she'd learned from Henry) through the dining room toward the swinging doors to the kitchen and, without hesitation, pushed them open.

Pen heard the swish of the doors and turned. The two women stared at each another for only a few seconds before rushing into an embrace, which swept back the hands of time for both of them.

Charlotte sobbed in relief. Pen comforted her as she would a child, then gently pushed Charlotte away to take a good look at her. The woman before her looked sophisticated, well-tended, bejeweled, and refined. But signs of strain were in her eyes, her body frail and thin. She was still lovely, but far too pale, and her sorrow was palpable.

Pen removed her apron and hung it by the door. She called the bus boy in and gave him instructions for finishing up in the kitchen. She made no excuses for leaving but took Charlotte and a covered dish out the back door and along the path to her cottage. There she made an herbal brew, which she insisted Charlotte drink without talking. She tended to other mixtures in her small kitchen until Charlotte had emptied her mug, and then Pen sat down across from her at the table, ready to listen. Charlotte poured out her story as it had unfolded from the time of their separation.

Pen listened, feeling the weight of Charlotte's sorrow. As she listened, she observed Charlotte closely, understanding her sensibilities. When Charlotte came to the end, Pen got up from the table and went back into her kitchen. Soon thereafter, she sent Charlotte home with verbal instructions, a cloth sack, a covered dish, and a warning not to tell anyone she had been there. She directed her to the side pathway around the inn leading to the lower parking lot and told her to use it for future visits. She was back in Charlotte's life now. Things were going to change.

Pen considered what Charlotte had told her about Taylor's recent behavior, and her suspicions about a new infatuation, comparing him to his father. This made it all the more troublesome, knowing that Willa Mae was the focus of his attentions. Willa Mae was an innocent being stalked by a wolf without Raven's knowledge. His time with Phoebe, although necessary, had led to this unforeseen consequence. Pen now understood what was bothering Raven. He'd picked up the scent of the wolf and would soon know his identity and purpose. He had to be protected from finding out, and Willa Mae had to be protected from Taylor's intentions. Frank would be sending Willa Mae with her delivery of greens in the morning. She'd have a long talk with her and hopefully resolve the situation.

Jordon Reed pulled into the drive shortly after Charlotte returned home. He'd decided to put a smile on his face and act pleased to see her as he approached the steps to the veranda. Before he could take the first step, something came from around the side of the house and startled him. He jumped back and almost lost his balance as the creature lurched forward. The gigantic rooster stopped in his tracks and crowed at him like a maniac, scratching the ground with his talons like a bull preparing to lunge at a red cape. Jordon shouted back, trying to scare the beast but it was unfazed. Then he shouted for Charlotte.

Charlotte appeared on the porch as though making an entrance onto the stage. He was taken aback by her appearance. She looked different. She glided down the steps like a ballet dancer and called sweetly to the screeching bird, "Henry darling, we have a guest. Please don't be upset. He's your adoptive father, the Honorable Congressman Reed, who will be staying with us for a spell. Here you are, my big brave protector; I've a treat for you."

She threw something toward him that looked to Jordon like a piece of filet mignon, which the rooster grabbed with his beak and held there, giving Jordon a malicious sidelong glance to let him know he'd been appeased only for the time being. Jordon noted a hint of threat. Good grief, he'd been there only a few minutes and was already going nuts.

"Where in the world did you get that rooster, Charlotte? You know I need peace and quiet when I have some time off. You'll have to get rid of him." She looked unfazed by his order, and he narrowed his eyes at her. "I mean it! What's the matter with you? When did you start keeping chickens?"

"I'm not keeping chickens, dear," she said sweetly. "Let's not talk about it now. You must be exhausted after your trip. Why don't you sit out on the veranda after taking your things upstairs? I'll make you a drink while you freshen up. Would you like a martini? There is such a nice breeze out here, and it's carrying the scent of mimosa. Isn't it heavenly? I feel so revived in the mountains. And you will too. Before you know it, you'll be a new man."

With that, she sashayed away from him and disappeared through the screen door. He remained where he stood at the bottom of the steps, speechless and dumbstruck. The rooster had also disappeared from his sight.

Jordon remembered about trying to be pleasant and called to Charlotte, "I *could* use a martini," then added quietly, "possibly two, maybe three, and very dry."

CHAPTER TWENTY-ONE

Fly away, pretty moth, to the shade
Of the leaf where you slumbered all day;
And make use of your wings while you may.
But tho' dreams of delight may have dazzled you quite,
They at last found it dangerous play;
Many things of this world that look bright, pretty moth,
Only dazzle to lead us astray.

~ Thomas Haynes Bayly

BY LATE AFTERNOON, RAVEN WAS on his way home, his mind reeling from what he'd learned that day working in Aunt Phoebe's summer kitchen. His memory had retained the basic recipes, ancient rituals, and a litany of invocations preceding or in conjunction with her most powerful spell-casting conjures. The soothing rhythmic sound of her voice describing procedures was like a melody with lyrics playing over and over again in his mind. His natural ear for music had caught the rhythm and tone of her voice and transposed them into a brain destined to accept this knowledge.

He would never forget how feverishly she had worked, the atmosphere in the cabin electrified by her mental energy and spell-binding presence—a sorceress teaching her apprentice. The mysticism of her trade had been in full force as she'd instilled in him her knowledge, revealing the magic of the waters and her elixirs. At day's end, their work done, she'd seemed to shrink back into her age. They'd embraced as though for the last time before she sent him on his way.

On the long walk home, he felt excited and infused with virility instead of being tired. He wasn't ready to go home, although he knew his mother would be waiting with dinner prepared. He should have been ravenous but had no appetite for food. Physically aroused, he felt the blood coursing through his veins and sensed every movement and sound around him. He imagined the forest enveloping him in its leafy grace, creatures scurrying in his wake, wildflowers turning their blooms toward him, the birds singing his praise. Today, he had graduated into manhood, and something more profound than words could explain. He felt proud of his accomplishment and wanted to share it with the one person who would look at him with wonder.

He wouldn't have to explain everything to Willa Mae, or reveal what he could not share. She would understand and be happy he'd returned to her again, for always. He'd make up for all the time he'd been away, knowing she'd felt hurt and abandoned. Things would be as they once were; they had to be. Then he realized she wouldn't be waiting for him up on the ridge. It occurred to him how she must have felt waiting for him and being disappointed. He'd been experiencing it only for a week and found it intolerable.

She'd be getting off from work about now. He decided to change his route home and cut through the lower section of the ridge to meet her coming up the road from town. It would take him another half hour. He hoped he wouldn't miss her. If he did, he'd go to her home and present himself. She'd be very surprised he'd come looking for her, and happy, he knew. His step quickened and his heart sang.

On the road from town, there was a wide curve one-half mile before reaching the Parsons' farmhouse. A quarter-mile before the curve, there was a turn-about on the side of the road. This half-moon shaped extension—common on mountain roads—was carved out of an embankment to widen the narrow road where it steepened, and the embankment dropped off precariously on the other side. White pines and mountain laurel jutted out defiantly from the bulldozed red clay to provide an umbrella of shade for anyone using the space to turn around or to park.

Taylor Reed used the turn-about as a stopping point when driving Willa Mae almost home. He'd picked the spot because it was ideal for semi-privacy and extending their time together before she got out of the car to walk the rest of the way. The hovering trees above the alcove made the late summer afternoons seem like evening there. As he'd expected, she'd been letting him get more familiar each day while guiding him up and down and around an endless maze of roads, including unpaved gravel and dirt roads rarely acknowledged by his GPS. She'd limited their time together, but not his attentions. He was ready to make his move. The occasional passing car or tractor made the turn-about inadequate for his needs. Fortunately, he'd found the perfect place during his recent venture for Rodney into the backwoods.

Taylor was determined to convince Willa to go there with him. He'd have to couch his request in one last plea for help. That approach got her every time. Or maybe he should tell her he had a wonderful place to show her in repayment for all the places she'd shown him. Yes, that was even better. It would come across like he was giving her a present or reward. He'd make a mystery of it, one she couldn't resist. She'd better not. He'd done all the preliminaries and had put up with her tiresome naiveté. Of course, her innocence made the challenge all the more exciting. She would be tempted by a mystery because she had a curious mind, always asking questions about his life at the university and about him personally, wanting to know his views on life and nature and such, acting interested—a new one on him. Most of the girls or women he knew were more interested in his lower region than his mind.

Seated beside him now in the sports car, Willa Mae was unusually silent. Her stomach churned with turmoil; she felt confused and agitated. He'd been acting different, getting a might touchy-feely for her liking, grabbing her arm to help her in and out of the car, reaching around her shoulder to lock it as though she couldn't do it for herself, and then letting his arm rest a bit until she nudged it away. And now he was holding her hand, her not knowing what to do about it, not wanting to be impolite. She'd never experienced this kind of forwardness, and it made her feel uneasy.

At first, it had been exciting to have someone like Taylor need her help and make her feel so important. After all, he was very good-looking, though not beautiful like Raven, but she figured he was popular with the girls at the university and probably had lots of dates. She'd not expected him to think of her as someone to date, him being so worldly and all, and from such an important family. Why, his mamma and daddy probably already had him a wife in mind, one from their social set. So why was he grabbing her hand like this and ruining what had been a helpful gesture on her part? He should be grateful for all the time she'd given him instead of making her feel all queasy inside.

When the car approached the turn-about, Willa Mae moved her hand from under his and placed it back in her lap, curved into a fist.

"I won't be able to stay and talk, Taylor. I promised Daddy I'd be home earlier tonight. It's sure been a pleasure showing you around and getting to know you, but I can't go on staying out after work like this when he's needing me at home. Besides, I've shown you enough for you to get by. The rest you can learn from your car navigator."

Taylor pulled over to park, turned off the engine, and turned toward her.

"Now don't rush off, Willa Mae. You can wait just a few minutes. I've got to go too, so don't worry, I won't keep you. My father should have arrived by now, and I'm already late for dinner. Tomorrow, I'll be acting as his chauffeur. Thanks to you, he'll be impressed with how well I know my way around. And believe me, he is not an easy person to impress." He glanced down for a moment, and then looked up with a smile. "Willa Mae, you must allow me to show you my gratitude. I've discovered the most incredible place, on my own. It's somewhere I'm sure you've never seen. I won't be able to take you there until Friday. I could pick you up after work at the usual time." When she seemed about to decline, he hurriedly continued. "It won't take that long, I promise. It's my way of giving back, and you must give me the chance. You can help your father in the meantime. Surely he would understand if you wanted a little extra time for yourself on Friday. Say yes, Willa Mae. Say yes." He smiled his most heartfelt-appearing, persuasive smile.

Willa Mae didn't know what to say. Taylor seemed so sincere, she thought maybe she had him all wrong. Why, he was behaving fine now, and there *were* things about him she *did* like. At least he knew she was alive, instead of never being around, like Raven. There'd be no harm in letting him repay her kindness. It would be selfish not to. He was just giving her something in keeping with what she'd given him, that's all. It would be the last time she'd go with him, and then they could part friends.

So she said yes and got out of the car. As he drove away, her spirits dropped again. She'd been put on the spot and allowed herself to be persuaded into something she wasn't sure about. She felt disconcerted and tried to remember how genuine his request had seemed. She didn't see the self-satisfied smile on Taylor's face as made his way down the road back to town.

From a cut in the hillside, hidden behind a cluster of laurel and rhododendron, Raven stood watching as the driver of the expensive sports car made his turn and disappeared from view. He'd stopped breathing, and Willa Mae hadn't moved. She turned slowly toward him, as though sensing his presence. He might have spoken then, but did not, could not. She turned away and began her walk home.

Raven's knees buckled, and he took hold of a tree limb to steady himself. His heart felt heavy, weighing him down like a great burden he had to carry home. It was an aching heaviness coupled with a cavernous feeling in his stomach. He wanted to call to her, scream her name, but resisted the impulse. The troubled expression on her face was new to him, but the lost look that followed was a familiar one. He could remember her as a little girl, waiting for him with that look on her face, and how he'd loved to see it evaporate whenever he'd appear.

He knew Willa Mae too well and willed himself to believe in her in that moment. Losing trust in her would shatter everything he believed to be true. There was no one like her. He hadn't traveled the greater world but understood the mountain world and all of its creatures, and he recognized one who stood out among the rest. This stranger had seen it too. Willa Mae was such an innocent, always trying to see the best in people. She couldn't comprehend the evil that existed in this world, the evil his Aunt Phoebe had warned him about.

He straightened himself and stood resolute. He would not confront Willa Mae, who was too kind for her own good. No, he'd go after the predator invading his territory and find out where he'd come from and how he had lured her into his car. Aunt Phoebe had taught him to think before acting, and his mother had taught him restraint. These habitual responses were the only things holding him in place while he thought about what to do next.

It was getting late, and his mother would be worried. He'd go home and share the news of his completion. She probably already knew; she and Aunt Phoebe had a telepathic way of communicating. After dinner, he'd excuse himself. She'd understand his fatigue. He couldn't talk to her about Willa Mae tonight. He had to think, be alone, and sort out the problem. He'd been taught well. This wolf in his fancy sports car didn't know what was about to hit him.

When he arrived home, his problem was solved. A note from his mother lay on the table.

> I've gone to visit Aunt Phoebe and will return later tonight. I borrowed the inn's pickup. Don't worry, I will drive carefully. You'll find a special dinner in the oven. Please go to bed early and don't wait up for me. I'm very proud of you.
>
> Mother

He was so relieved to find her gone he didn't question the why of it. Although he always worried whenever she attempted to drive. She had permission from the inn's owners to use the truck for errands but rarely did. She was not a confident driver. Since obtaining his driver's license, he'd been given the job of driving to the Spartanburg meat and poultry markets on Thursday mornings, but he was not permitted to use the truck otherwise.

Raven assumed she'd been summoned by Aunt Phoebe to discuss his future, their master plan for him almost complete. Her visits to Aunt Phoebe were secretive and always at night. Aunt Phoebe had warned his mother years ago not to put her position at the inn in jeopardy by an association with her. Although respected as a healer by many, she was feared as a witch by others. She'd insisted his mother maintain her distance for that and other reasons he suspected were related to him. Yet he could also see now how intrinsically close they were, despite separation, for the common purpose of his welfare. For this and much more, he loved them deeply. It was about time he put some of what he'd learned from them into practice. The rage he felt burning inside would not be tempered until he did.

Far across the ridges and down into the vale under Shadow Peak, Phoebe and Pen talked until almost midnight. Pen presented the interwoven tale of Willa Mae, Taylor Reed, Charlotte, and Jordon Reed to her sister, and Mamma Phoebe considered the situation with all her insight and wisdom. After a while, she led Pen out into the open field beyond the cabin. Together they stood hand in hand beneath the looming black outline of Shadow Peak, its ominous form palely lit by a silent somber moon, and made their plea.

"The time is near
The time is nigh
Oh water spirit
Hear our cry
The shadows loom
The wolfen roams
The lamb is prey
The loved one moans
The demon wakes
The seeds are sown
We call to you
Protect your own"

CHAPTER TWENTY-TWO

I'd rather be a dog, and bay at the moon,
Than such a Roman.

~ William Shakespeare

JORDAN REED STARTED HIS DAY trying to wake from a nightmare. In the dream, a rooster kept crowing, the angry cacophony driving him nearly insane. He ran down one dark hallway after another to get away from the horrible sound, but it grew louder at every turn. When his eyes opened to the dawn light, he felt momentary relief—until his eardrums were blasted by another *cock-a-doodle-doo. Cock-a-doodle-doo! Cock-a-doodle-doo!* The rooster screeched until Jordon pushed the bedspread away and sat upright. He looked at the clock on the nightstand and cursed. He cursed again as he stood and stretched and almost called to Charlotte. They'd slept in separate bedrooms for years.

He reconsidered and thought it just as well he was up. He had a lot to do today: a meeting with Rodney and then Taylor was going to drive him out to the property. He was eager to get a report from Rodney, as well as one from Taylor during their time alone.

Last night was still a blur. He must have been more exhausted than he'd realized. He had a vague recollection of Taylor apologizing for coming home late and Charlotte fussing over both of them while chattering on and on—about what?—he couldn't remember. His head throbbed slightly from the several martinis he'd put away before dinner. The crowing exacerbated every throb and continued incessantly until Jordon found solace in the shower.

He repeated a mantra while scrubbing his body and rinsing, "That bird is going to die. That bird is going to die. That bird is going to die." Somehow it made him feel better, and by the time he was dressed for the day, the rooster had become silent and Jordon was content to bide his time.

Charlotte, who had risen with the rooster's first crow, had started her day making homemade biscuits and sausage gravy for her "menfolk." She insisted Jordon have breakfast while waiting for Taylor. Taylor, whose drug-induced sleep made him oblivious to the crowing, had been awakened by his father. He could hardly believe his parents were both up and expected him to join them within the hour.

Jordon ended up eating a much too heavy breakfast for summertime while being informed by Charlotte of Taylor's latest infatuation.

"At first I was upset, wanting him all to myself. But now I realize he is no longer my little boy. It's sweet the way he tries to be secretive to spare my feelings, while at the same time dressing like an imitation lumberjack every morning and coming home late every evening. You'll see what I mean when he comes down." Charlotte sipped her morning coffee. "I suspect it's a local girl. We'd always thought he'd find someone more sophisticated. This might be just what our small family needs: a girl without social background or money to simplify the over abundant life we've been leading, someone to bring us down to earth. I've been thinking of a new way of living, myself. And really, dear, you should reconsider your lifestyle too. After all, overindulgence of the senses can lead to an assortment of health problems. I've had the wonderful opportunity here to cleanse my soul of darkness and focus on a process of enlightenment. And my darling Henry has been such a help. I greet each dawn with pleasure when awakened by him, and I spend my mornings reassessing my life. I suggest you do the same while you are here, Jordon. It would do you a world of good."

Trying to hold his temper, Jordon said, "Charlotte, what are you talking about? And what do you mean, he's seeing some girl? Are you serious? Is

Taylor serious? That's impossible. He's supposed to be working. It's probably a minor diversion. I thought you were supposed to be bonding again. Isn't that what this is all about, your coming here for the summer?"

"Well, dear, it may have started out that way in my fondest hopes, but it's not to be and I'm trying to make the best of it. It appears he's been struck by cupid's arrow and would rather be elsewhere. I wouldn't confront him about it, Jordon. Yesterday, I requested he be home early for your arrival, and he still came home late for dinner. Although I must say he looked rather happy when he got here. Perhaps it was the pleasure of seeing you."

Taylor came into the room just as Charlotte whisked away Jordon's plate after refreshing his coffee. She returned with a heaping plate for Taylor, which he wolfed down like a hungry animal. Jordon sat watching Taylor, envying his youth, the wide spread of his shoulders, the toned body and muscular frame accentuated by the tan multi-pocketed wilderness guide vest he was wearing. Could lust be the cause of his ravenous appetite, he wondered? Taylor had Charlotte's fair coloring, but was definitely a Reed in physical bearing and temperament. Jordon could understand his son's need for a diversion, being stuck here for the summer, but he needed Taylor to be focused on Rodney instead of another conquest. Charlotte was, as usual, totally off-base projecting her romantic illusions onto Taylor. Everything she'd said this morning was ridiculous. He couldn't get out of this *looney-bin* soon enough. However, he did take Charlotte's advice about not broaching the subject with Taylor. He'd find out what Taylor was up to soon enough; there were more pressing things on his mind.

After they arrived at Granger Reality, Rodney sent Taylor on a few errands while he and Jordon met privately. Rodney updated him on the police proceedings following the recent deaths and told him there was nothing to worry about. The coroner had ruled Purvis McCabe's death accidental, the toxic alcohol he'd manufactured blamed on his impaired mental state.

Rodney warned they would have to be cautious now that Purvis McCabe's property had been turned over to probate court. A notice had been published within the ten-day limit, allowing thirty days for potential heirs to make claim on the property. As far as Rodney could ascertain, the McCabe brothers had shown no interest in returning to Serena or making a claim. It wasn't unusual for distant relatives to balk at the prospect of assuming ownership and paying taxes, even when entitled, unless they were prepared to take up residence. They could, however, try to make a claim with the aim of putting the property on the market.

Rodney had discreetly and unscrupulously enlisted the aid of a friend in probate court to have Granger Realty appointed realtor agency for the court-ordered sale of the McCabe property. It was common practice for a local realtor to be appointed; his agency would probably have been considered, but he'd made certain it was chosen. This allowed him to have an updated survey done to verify property lines and water rights, and have immediate access to the land under the protection of the court. He'd already sent Taylor there to scope out the area and make sure no one was nosing around.

He'd also checked out the deed on record, which had stipulated the land be passed down from father to eldest son and thereon unless otherwise stipulated, leaving the question of next of kin entitlement unaddressed, as no *Last Will and Testament* had been presented or discovered. Of course, if a claim could not be legitimized, the McCabe brothers would still have the right to make an offer for purchase. So far, they'd shown no interest in the property or knowledge of its value. Purvis McCabe had protected his secret to the grave. If they were to come forward, Rodney was prepared to make them a cash settlement offer, through Jordon's attorney, before they could act. So it was crucial he be notified in order to intervene. If they didn't come forward, his friend at probate would help him obtain a contract for the property before it went to public listing.

Rodney planned to go to the office of deeds and records at the courthouse to do a more thorough deed search dating back generations to look for any loopholes. It wouldn't have been prudent to do this until now. They had tried to cover every unknown, but one concern was the absence of a will. If one did exist, it was probably in a lockbox somewhere, and so far, no one had come forward with a key.

Until now, Rodney hadn't wanted to alert anyone to his interest in the property, other than as a listing agent, so most of his information had been obtained on the sly from his network of courthouse insiders. The purchase would be handled through Granger Realty and Jordon Reed's attorney. Reed's name would be kept out of it until the final papers were drawn. If anyone questioned the expediency of the sale, it would be explained that Jordon had learned from Taylor about the property's potential availability during his visit to Serena. It would seem natural that Taylor had shown his father land investment opportunities, including the McCabe land as one of a number of possibilities, they would say. Therefore, Rodney saw no objection to Jordon's plan to go out there and take a look around, with Taylor as guide. They were simply laying the groundwork for the ultimate goal of ownership.

Taylor returned from his errands by mid-morning and parked in front of Rodney's office instead of in the back lot where he was supposed to park, but he didn't think it mattered. After all, the car wouldn't be there long enough to be in the way of customers. He went inside to find out if his father was ready to go.

An old blue pickup truck idled in the post office parking lot across and down the street. Raven had pulled into the post office lot to turn around. He'd been cruising town since sunrise, looking for the red sports car. Halfway through his turn, the red car caught his eye. He sat and watched his adversary park and enter the realty office and then come back out again with an older man. Raven was running late for his drive to the Spartanburg markets, but that could wait. He eased out of the lot and began following the red car, staying a safe distance behind.

The drive from Rodney's office up the mountain to the road leading back to the McCabe compound turned into a harrowing trip. After almost backending a slow-moving logging truck, Taylor tried to pass it on a blind curve and had to veer off the road to avoid a collision from an oncoming car. A pickup truck came up behind him and had to wait while he maneuvered the car back onto the road in an embarrassment of flying gravel and dust. To make matters worse, the logging truck was still in front of them, going about 20 miles-per-hour up the winding road, but he couldn't risk trying to pass again. He tried to ignore his father's obvious disapproval and firm grip on the door handle.

Fortunately, the truck behind them was not riding his tail as they made their way around several sharp bends until, mercifully, the logging truck turned off on a road leading to another mountain-view project under development. Taylor sighed with relief when the road cleared. He gunned the engine to impress his father with his handling of the roadster. He could no longer see the pickup in his rearview mirror.

After staying back out of sight for several miles, Raven came around the bend just in time to see the car he was following turn onto the road leading to his aunt's cabin. He waited before turning onto the road and drove with caution, letting the dust settle in front of him. He figured they were heading for the McCabe property because they'd come from the realty office. When he finally came to the fork in the road, he could also see a cloud of dust above the rutted driveway leading to McCabe's compound. He turned the truck around and headed back out and down the mountain to Spartanburg. He had the scent of the predator now and would soon find his lair.

Taylor was at a complete loss about his father's intentions. It occurred to him his father was acting like a dog circling around a chosen area, trying to find the perfect spot to do his business. He'd been adamant about examining the compound from the center out and had made his way up to the ledge where the old cabin was located. He'd been up there rummaging around for the last half hour. Taylor was tired of waiting.

Surely he didn't intend to explore the forest this way too. What purpose would there be in traipsing around hundreds of acres? The lower acreage of open pastures hadn't been cultivated in years. Taylor was supposed to be showing his father around instead of being stuck at the compound wondering what was going on.

The place gave him the creeps, a ghostly representation of a way of life foreign to him and a closed clannish culture he shuddered to think about. It was evident old McCabe had tried to keep his main residence functional after losing his family, but the rest had fallen into complete disrepair. His father was probably thinking about gutting the whole place and using it as a central location for a construction site for dividing the land into parcels. But why the interest in the old cabin, or for that matter, the whole parcel of land? Developing it would be an enormously expensive undertaking.

He was also puzzled about being excluded from the meeting between his father and Rodney. What was the big secret? Why had his father decided to come to Serena at this time and insist on seeing the McCabe property so ghoulishly soon after the old man's death? Taylor knew he'd been interested in investing in the area, but why this property? He began to question his role working for Rodney. He was supposed to be the spy but felt like he was being used again, just like he'd been used against his mother.

Why had it taken him so long to see it? When he was younger, he'd desperately wanted his father's attention and was blind to his motives. But now he knew there was something to be gained from everything his father did and every relationship he made. There was always a scheme; Taylor had been his accomplice too many times not to know there was more to this venture than a white elephant investment.

Jordon's commanding voice thundered down as he descended the rocky path from the cliff ledge. "I'm done looking around here, Taylor. Did you find anything of interest when you were checking out the property for Rodney?"

He'd initially wanted to surprise his father after taking him on the long hike to the Raven Brook Falls area but had been put off so long that he proudly blurted out, "I found the location of McCabe's still, Dad, and I can take you there."

"How far is it from here?" Jordon asked. "Do I need hiking boots? How did you find it?"

"It was easy, really," Taylor bragged. "I've been hearing about McCabe and his moonshining days, so I decided to find his still. It would be close to water, and I thought a plateau would be necessary, like the ledge carved out for the cabin you were looking at. That's where I got the idea. A person positioned above could see down below and know if anyone was approaching. The old man had everything set up that way. I sat on the steps of his front porch and could see how he had the land cleared so that anyone approaching the compound couldn't escape his line of vision. No wonder no one dared come here uninvited. I learned a lot about the legend of Purvis McCabe from someone who grew up around here."

Taylor could tell his father was impressed by Taylor's clever initiative in finding the still. He would have been even more impressed with Taylor's plan for seducing Willa Mae. That was right down the old man's alley, Taylor thought sardonically.

Jordon trudged after Taylor, acting as though the hike to the stream and the strenuous climb to the forest landing was not worth the effort, which Taylor had to admit stung a little. His father begrudgingly gave him credit for finding the still but appeared only mildly interested in it when they got there. But Taylor had another surprise in store when he led him to a break in the tree-line. There before them lay a perfect view of Raven Brook Falls and the sparkling pool below it. Taylor assumed his father was stunned by the sight of the falls when he saw the blood drain from his face.

"Isn't it great?" Taylor proudly said. "I couldn't believe it when I found the still and then discovered the view from here. I told you how the old man set things up. He could watch everything from this vantage point without being seen at all. I know because when I was here, an old woman was down there with some black-haired guy about my age, talking and pointing to the falls like she had a story to tell. I watched them for a while but finally had to get back to the office." He paused a moment, but when his father didn't respond, Taylor said, "She must be the owner of the other property. I found out she has a pretty decent tract of land too. Maybe she'd be willing to sell, Dad. It has more possibilities than this property. It's just a thought."

"Let's get back to town, Taylor. I just remembered some important calls I have to make."

Taylor was hurt that his suggestion was ignored. Couldn't his father see that the adjacent property was closer to town than this desolate tract? The old woman owned as much property as the old man had and half of the water rights. He'd studied a topographical map of the area before trying to find the still. The falls were an asset for both properties, but this part of Western North Carolina was known as *The Land of the Waterfalls*—they were everywhere. Of course the water source was a plus, although there were many other properties with falls and running streams that held more potential for profitable return. He couldn't figure it out. He *had* learned something working for Rodney Granger and driving around with Willa Mae.

Thinking of Willa Mae suddenly gave the falls increased value for what he had in mind.

CHAPTER TWENTY-THREE

Three things cannot be hidden long: the sun, the moon, and the truth.

~ Buddha

CHIEF FARLEY TURNED THE STEERING wheel of his cruiser to the right at the fork in the road and bumped along the driveway until the cabin came into sight. There was an impression of serenity about the setting that surprised him. The dark, rough-hewn logs of the cabin were much larger in circumference than those of the newer log homes dotting the ridges. It was a sturdy, well-built structure, at least a century old, crafted by hand and molded by the life of the woman he was about to meet.

When he opened the car door, he heard the crow of a rooster. By the time the rooster crowed again and appeared from around the side of the cabin, Mamma Phoebe came out on the porch and greeted him with a smile.

"Good morning, Chief Farley. It's about time you came round to see me. I've heard about you from folks in town."

"I hope you've been hearing good things, ma'am. I've heard about you too, and hope you don't mind us getting acquainted today."

"As long as I'm not in trouble with the law, I'd be mighty happy to make your acquaintance, Chief. I've always been a law-abiding woman, keepin' to my healing work and trying to do no harm to anyone."

"You're in no trouble," Farley replied. "I'm just gathering information."

"I suppose you've come 'bout poor old Purvis, bless his soul," Mamma Phoebe said. "Sad news when I heard. Him and me's been livin' alongside each other all our lives and respectin' each other's ways. Now before we get to talkin', Chief, you come on up here on the porch and set yourself in that rocker, and I'll get mine from inside."

Directing her attention to the rooster, she said firmly, "Now you settle down." He immediately became quiet and trotted away.

"Ma'am, please," Farley said, "let me carry the rocker out for you." And he did while she poured them two glasses of freshly brewed sweet tea over ice.

After they were seated, he asked, "I'll get right to the point, ma'am. I am here because I'm doing some investigating around the death of Mr. McCabe. Did you communicate with him on a regular basis?"

"No, sir, I didn't, but it wasn't because we were on bad terms. We just minded our own business, and it's always been that way except for a few occasions years ago. Course, if he'd been needing me for anything, I'd have helped him out. But he was such an independent old cuss," she said with a laugh, "he'd have been too proud to ask anyway."

Farley looked down at his tea for a moment. "Ma'am, it's a well-known fact that he's been making moonshine liquor and selling it for decades. I know he's not been in business like he used to be, but he was still active. I guess I should have come out here when I took over as chief, but I didn't, and for that reason I feel partially responsible. The last batch of liquor he made was toxic and may have caused the death of two other people besides Purvis, and the near-death of two others. Knowing him as you did, do you think he was capable of intentionally doing this kind of harm, or senile enough to make such a mistake? I'm asking your personal opinion in confidence. I've been told you are a wise woman, and ma'am, I need the help of a wise woman right about now because there's something about his death that doesn't seem right to me."

Mamma Phoebe looked at him intently and replied after taking time to think for a minute. "I'll tell you this, Chief Farley, and you can take my word on it. That man may have had a lot of faults, contrary as he was. And he'd have thought nothing of shooting a man on sight for trespassing on his land. But he'd never do a thing like you're suggesting, crazy or not. His liquor was like a religion to him, just like my healin'. Things were different when we was comin' up. People didn't look at whiskey-makin' like it was breakin' the law. Why, even the law knew that and just left him to do his business—most of 'em being customers. Not many people could afford store-bought liquor, and there weren't many places to buy it anyway, just like there weren't many doctors around to heal the sick of body and the sick of mind. There were some who shouldn't have been makin' whiskey at all because they made it poorly, and some of it was like poison. There were doctors like that, and healers too, some good and some not so good. But Purvis was the best at his trade and proud of it, and I admit to a bit of pride myself. Folks like that don't change, not in their character or in their actions. He could have made his liquor right just by the scent of it or the color or the texture, even when his other senses were leaving him. No, sir. That was not his doing, and you'd best be finding out why it happened."

"Ma'am, what if I told you that a root compound used in the practice of voodoo was found it the liquor?"

Mamma Phoebe looked ashen and stared at him without blinking. She grasped the enormity of what he said and was rendered speechless. Then she nodded her head up and down and pursed her lips in knowing acceptance. She'd seen it coming but didn't know how it would appear or from what direction. Now that it was clear, she knew what she was up against and could pull her thoughts together. After another minute of pondering, she replied, "Seems as though the finger of blame is starting to point my way, Chief, at least in your mind, since you're the only one thinking along those lines."

"As a matter of fact, ma'am, I'm not thinking along those lines at all. I've come here to ask your advice about a certain root you may have heard about in your healing practice. I'm appealing to your expertise and asking you to trust me enough to share your knowledge with me. I need your help."

Mamma Phoebe rocked back in her chair and stared at him long and hard. She'd seen his kind before, long ago. The mountains had been settled by men like him. He had an inner strength under his tall lean exterior, and there was a glint in his hazel-green eyes hinting he was enjoying her surprise at his asking for her help. Maybe he believed she couldn't do such a thing or maybe not. Fact is, she could do much worse if she had a reason or mind to. His asking for help was his way of saying he'd given her the benefit of the doubt. His telling her the truth told her his true nature.

She said, "Tell me about this root and how you come to know about it."

He proceeded to explain what he'd learned from Dr. Stevens.

"A poisonous substance identified as cassava, produced from the roots of a South American shrub, was identified in trace amounts in white liquor suspected to be part of a batch made by McCabe. I've learned that the roots can be dried to a powder or fermented into alcohol and made into a deadly compound that could be dissolved in water or other forms of alcohol without being detected. By a stroke of luck, it was identified because two recent victims of an auto accident survived. The attending physician, who had worked in South America, recognized the symptoms, suspected cassava poisoning, and had samples of the alcohol they'd been drinking tested for the compound. Had they died before presenting symptoms, the alcohol would probably not have been tested because the deaths would have been attributed to an alcohol-related auto accident. Someone had to have known that bitter roots of cassava can mimic alcohol overdose after death.

"Now, I've looked into your background, ma'am, and I found no history of anything associated with poisoning. But you are known as a healer. Some folks call you a root-doctor, and some call you a hoodoo woman. I understand this is the practice of using herbal remedies and potions, some of which could be used for harm. I don't know anyone else who could help me at this point. And I have to be honest, this is not yet an official investigation. But I must warn you that I'm about to make it one. If cassava is found to be the official cause of death in the cases we are looking at, suspicion might fall on you. I would like to prevent that if possible."

Phoebe looked at him suspiciously and replied, "Why would you want to help an old woman like me? Seems like it would make your job a might easier if you had somebody to blame. It would surely make you look good if you could get this cleared up like you did that last business."

"Well ma'am, it's like this. I knew your sister a long time ago. She took a liking to me and trusted me with someone she held very dear. I got to know her only for a short time, but I never forgot her kindness to me. She was a wise and good woman who, I was told, learned everything from you. I've heard a lot of things about you, ma'am, and I know lots of people come to you without talking about it. So there's always this bit of mystery regarding your reputation. But I knew Miss Pen and because of her, I don't believe you'd be mixed up in anything like I'm looking at in these cases. It's up to you whether you want to help me or not. I won't hold it against you if you don't. Right now, I'm the only one looking at the poison aspect, and I'd like to know more about it before I go any further."

"I'll help you, if I can. I have knowledge of the root you're talkin' about but have never seen it or used it. Thing is, if it was chosen by somebody thinking it couldn't be identified, it wouldn't matter where it came from. But if it was chosen thinking there might be a possibility, it might have been picked because the person who got hold of it happened to be where it was grown and thought maybe us practitioners all used the same roots. People who don't know much about us think voodoo and hoodoo is all the same thing."

Jeff looked at her with chagrin. "I was one of those people . . . until a friend set me straight. So what you're suggesting is, if the person was in an area where voodoo was practiced and learned about the poisonous use of cassava, he or she might have obtained it for two purposes: one, that it might not be discovered, and two, that if it was identified, there would be a likely suspect to blame."

Mamma Phoebe nodded. "Casting blame on an old hoodoo woman like me, whether it could be proved or not, might be all that was intended. Don't you see, Chief? If it was a root substance found in these parts, *anyone* might have used it, but being from somewhere strange, it might seem us hoodoo practitioners have a pipeline to exotic roots other folks would know nothin' about."

Jeff looked at her thoughtfully. What kind of a devious mind could have planned something so convoluted and diabolical? If there was any truth in what Mamma Phoebe suggested, what could the motive be? Who could possibly benefit? The only thing of value he could think of was the McCabe property. Surely it wasn't worth the murder of three people and the attempted murder of two others. He had to give it more thought.

Farley handed his empty glass to Mamma Phoebe as he stood and thanked her for her help. He liked the old woman and was impressed with her mental acuity. Why would anyone want to cast blame on her? Was it a simple setup, or was something more involved?

Approaching the Y fork deep in thought, Farley almost missed seeing the tail-end of a sports car in the far distance ahead. He didn't want to speed up and drive through the dust, so he stayed back until he was sure the car had turned left onto the mountain road heading back to town. He didn't have to catch up to it to know where it had been or who was driving. It was the only red sports car in town. It belonged to Charlotte Reed's son.

Mamma Phoebe sat back down in her rocker and rested a spell. She rocked back and forth, back and forth. The previous night, she and Pen had chanted their protective incantation to the rising new moon. Its pale iridescent color would soon turn yellow to greet the month of July. It would become a full thunder moon at the time of year when new antlers of buck deer pushed out of their foreheads, when thunder roared down the hollows of the mountain, and when bolts of lightning shrieked across a cobalt-blue sky. Like Farley,

Mamma Phoebe had much to consider. She remained preoccupied until twilight fell softly upon her peaceful cabin.

Things were far from tranquil in the Reed home. Charlotte had planned for the family to spend the evening together and had been working in the kitchen all afternoon preparing dinner. She felt almost peaceful now that she understood where she fit into their scheme of things. Her talk with Nanny Pen—she still thought of her that way—had set her straight in her thinking. She'd come to accept, after years of denial and subjugation, that Jordon and Taylor were very much alike in the way *they* thought of her. They really didn't know the Charlotte that Nanny Pen knew. They knew only what she had become since being taken from Serena.

In the few hours she'd spent with Nanny Pen, awash in her forgiveness and loving attentions, listening to her wisdoms and accepting her counsel, Charlotte had begun to regain part of the self she had lost. She felt giddy, light as air, floating on a sea of herbal scents and floral sachets. Nanny had "fixed her up" and then sent her home to look at her situation with clarity and hope for the future, and equipped with recipes and instructions for the days ahead.

Jordon Reed was losing clarity while sipping his second martini, prepared with special care by his wife. He was ruminating about the conversation he'd had with Rodney after returning from the McCabe property. Rodney had denied any knowledge of a boy associated with the old woman. He'd admitted that most of what he knew about Mamma Phoebe stemmed from years of rumor and gossip, some from a drinking buddy who'd went to her once because "he couldn't get it up" and she'd given him something for potency. He'd said there wasn't much talk about her anymore because most people who lived in Serena these days went to the county medical center instead of trailing out to visit a hoodoo doctor, and nobody cared about the old moonshiner *or* the old witch anymore, so how could he know about the boy? Infuriated, Jordon had told him it was his business to know.

With each sip of martini, the question repeated in his mind. What was the old woman doing at the falls with some kid? He had to know because there was too much at stake. He'd ordered Rodney to find out before morning or he would take matters into his own hands. Rodney would get right on it because he was on the hook, salivating about his cut in the profits. He'd already put his head in a noose to become one of the mountain rich with a big new log-home with a view built high on the ridge. He'd be in a frenzy tonight, using his resources to gather information. There was nothing for Jordon to do but relax and wait until morning. He needed a distraction. It was time to ask Taylor about the one he'd been trying to hide.

"Charlotte!" he shouted from the veranda. "I'll have another, and make it extra dry. Is Taylor still upstairs? Call him down to have a drink with me and make a martini for him too. He and I can have a talk before dinner."

Despite having her hands full in the kitchen, Charlotte came out to the stairwell and called up to Taylor. In response to his reply, she called sweetly to Jordon, "He'll be down directly."

Jordon was about to take another sip when his archenemy, the rooster, appeared at the bottom of the porch steps. Jordon could swear he had grown in size. The bird was monstrous and glared at him with hatred. Jordon took a gulp of the martini and stood up. He reached for a pillow from one of the porch chairs, grabbed it, and threw it with full force at the rooster, hitting him with a glancing blow, causing feathers to fly. Charlotte had just come to the screen door with the martinis and witnessed the scene. She and Henry exchanged eye contact, and there was immediate understanding between them. He turned and trotted away.

Seething, Jordon said, "Charlotte, if you don't get rid of that bird, I'll kill it!"

Charlotte sat the drinks down without reply and calmly went back inside. She had herbs simmering on the stove and could not let the mixture come to boil. She stirred, checked the recipe once more, and then added some of it to the pork tenderloin gravy.

Taylor wasn't in the mood to come downstairs. He'd been fantasizing about the soft velvety skin of Willa Mae and wanted to be left alone. He thought if he didn't have some relief soon, he'd go crazy. Having a martini with his father was not going to help. Besides, he hated the drink. But he was hungry and dinner would follow, so down he came.

Thirty minutes later, he felt differently but also incredulous. What had his mother done to make a drink he'd despised taste so good? And what was his father leading up to? He had that conspiratorial look he got when asking for details about Taylor's sexual exploits. Was he crazy? His mother was putting dinner on the table, and his father wanted to talk about sex?

Well, this is one conquest he's not going to share in, Taylor thought. *She's going to be mine alone, at least for a while. I've got to have something separate from him or I'll go nuts, just like my mother. Good grief, is she singing in there, something about a harvest moon?*

"Mother, could I have another martini! And could you make it extra dry?"

CHAPTER TWENTY-FOUR

Lo, the moon ascending
Up from the East, the silvery round moon,
Beautiful over the house-tops, ghastly, phantom moon,
Immense and silent moon.

~ Walt Whitman

CHARLOTTE AWOKE WITH A START. She heard nothing but silence and became suddenly alarmed. She looked at the clock on her nightstand and bolted upright, shocked that it was almost eight o'clock. She darted from her bedroom into the hallway. She checked the other bedrooms and found them empty. Scurrying back into her bedroom, she put on her robe and slippers and almost ran to the landing and then down the stairs and into the kitchen. There was no sign of Jordon or Taylor.

A note on the table read,

> Taylor is driving me to an early appointment down the mountain at the County Seat Courthouse. We let you sleep for a change. Your rooster must be sleeping at the switch.
> Jordon

She gasped. "Oh no! Henry!"

She ran out onto the porch and called from the railing, "Henry! Henry! Where are you? Henry!"

Her frantic calls were met with silence. Charlotte scrambled down the porch steps and out to the garden. She searched every square inch of the yard and then ran out into the road. She looked down the hill and called his name again. Then she ran back into the house, grabbed her car keys, and almost crashed into the mailbox pulling out of the driveway. She drove like a madwoman down the lane and around the bend, speeding along the narrow road and treacherous curves, tears streaming from her eyes, until she came to Church Street and the only friend she had made in town.

"Kate! Kate!" she called as she pushed on the doorbell without letting up.

Kate heard the insistent chiming of the bell and hurried to the door. Charlotte's appearance through the window frightened her. She felt a rush of panic as she opened the door and pulled the robed and slippered woman inside. "What is it, Charlotte? What's happened?"

"He's been kidnapped! Kidnapped! Oh, Kate, please help me. Someone's taken him away. He might even be murdered!"

"Who are you talking about, Charlotte? Has something happened to Taylor?"

"Taylor? Taylor? No, Kate, not him. It's Henry, my Henry. He's gone. You've got to help me! I can't think. I can't breathe. Please help me." She buried her face in her hands.

It took Kate a few seconds to realize Charlotte was talking about the rooster. Her relief was replaced with concern, knowing how Charlotte felt about him. She reached out and drew the woman into the living room.

"Come sit down, Charlotte. I'll call Dev, and we'll begin a search right away. Don't worry. Henry probably wandered off. We'll find him in no time."

"No! No!" Charlotte shook her head. "He'd never wander off. He's my protector! He's been kidnapped! I know it." She gripped Kate's arm. "It had to be Jordon. Jordon hates him. Jordon arranged it like he does everything else. And I'll never be able to prove it. Oh, Kate, please help me. Please."

Kate released herself from Charlotte's grip and retrieved her cell phone to make a call. Dev answered right away. He was sitting across from Jeff Farley in one of the booths at the Serena Grill.

"Dev, you'd better come home. Charlotte Reed is here and has a serious problem. Her rooster is missing, and she believes he's been kidnapped. Could you bring Jeff with you? This might be a matter for the police." Kate made an effort to give Henry the importance Charlotte, who was listening, did.

Dev, on the other hand, looked at Jeff and said, "You're not going to believe this. We have an emergency and are both needed. Charlotte Reed is with Kate. It seems her *rooster* has been kidnapped."

Jeff surprised Dev with his serious and immediate reaction. "Let's go!"

They were up the hill in less than five minutes. Kate met them at the door. Jeff was hesitant as he followed Dev and Kate down the hallway to the double doors leading to the living room. He'd avoided following up on complaints about her rooster—giving the assignment to Deputy Purdy—not wanting to face her over something so absurd. Did she know he was chief of police now?

Charlotte was too distraught to see clearly when Dev and Farley entered the room. The tall figure caught her attention. His face appeared through the blur, and she thought she was dreaming a dream in which the hero arrives out of the blue to save the lady in distress. She willingly entered the dream and ran to him, pretending he was real, saying his name to make it true, believing he had come to stand by her as he had when she was young. If this escape into insanity was the only way she could handle what she was feeling, so be it.

"Oh, Jeff, you've come. You've come. Oh, Jeff."

Jeff held her to him while Kate and Dev watched in bewildered amazement, unable to speak or move, unwilling to interrupt the unexpected reunion.

Jeff gently stroked Charlotte's uncombed hair and let her cry and cry until her tears were spent. She looked up at him, trembling in his arms, saying his name over and over again until reality set in, and she truly believed he was there. His presence calmed her, and his eyes revealed the tenderness he felt for her. He gently led her to the sofa and sat by her side. Dev went to his medical bag for a sedative. When he returned, Kate brought her a glass of water, and Charlotte took the small capsule Dev gave to her.

Kate went back into the kitchen to put coffee on while Charlotte tried to explain to Jeff and Dev what had happened. Her words made little sense becoming disjointed and slurred as the sedative took hold. She asked Jeff to come closer and then whispered in his ear,

"Jeff, you must go to see Nanny Pen. She'll explain. I went to see her. Tell her about Henry, please, Jeff. Tell her he's been taken. Please, Jeff. She's working at the Orchard Lake Inn. Tell her what he's done. I need her, Jeff. And I need you too. I wish I'd never left. Can you ever forgive—"

"There's nothing to forgive, Charlotte."

Jeff held her close until she fell into slumber.

Kate and Dev looked at one another during this exchange and then eased quietly into the kitchen. They were two people in love witnessing something they understood. After Charlotte fell asleep, they re-entered the room, at which time Jeff explained to Kate, as he had to Dev, some of their past history. He went on to tell them of his visit to Mamma Phoebe and her willingness to help him with information pertinent to his investigation, and also about seeing Taylor Reed leaving the McCabe property.

"I'd planned to stop by the realty office to talk to Taylor this morning, then visit Penelope Cather afterward to ask about her relationship with her sister and any concerns she might have about the death of Purvis McCabe. Now I find out that Charlotte's been to see her." Farley rubbed the stubble on his jawline. "There's too many coincidences going on, and I don't believe in coincidences. We've had a lot of complaints about the rooster from Charlotte's neighbor. I'll have Deputy Purdy talk to him. I'd like to have a talk with Jordon Reed." He looked at Kate and Dev in almost humorous disbelief. "She said he threatened to kill it last night."

Kate said, "I don't believe that rooster wandered away or flew over the garden fence, not the way Charlotte takes care of him. I don't know Jordon Reed or if he is capable of such a thing, but I do know something odd is going on in that house. Charlotte is unusually fond of the rooster. If someone wanted to put her over the edge, taking him away would be a good start."

"I don't know, Kate. I need to find out more about Jordon Reed before I go accusing him of anything. Maybe Miss Pen can shed some light on the situation before I talk to him. I'll stop back later to give you an update. I'm not sure if Charlotte should return to her home until we know more."

"Don't worry, Jeff. We'll watch over her."

On the drive down the hill to town, Jeff could still feel the soft caress of Charlotte's delicate hands as she'd held his cheek to hers while whispering to him. He could feel the soft curves of her body as he'd held her close to him, just as he had long ago. He remembered the night of the Harvest Moon Dance and how she had felt in his arms. The later heartbreak seemed a distant memory compared to the memory of that night.

She was married and had a son, Farley told himself. He had no intention of letting his personal feelings interfere with an investigation. He stopped at the office to check in with Aura Lee and tell her about the rooster.

Before he could begin, she said, "You'll never guess who I saw this morning driving through town, Chief. Do you remember my telling you about Charlotte Reed's son, and how he's been talking to that pretty Willa Mae Parsons? Remember what I said about her being kind of bespoken to that wild Cather boy, who no one hardly ever sees? Well, who do you suppose I saw driving an old pickup truck through town this morning, and then when I walked down to the post office to pick up my mail, there he was, parked in the lot watching the real estate office where Taylor Reed works!"

"Is that so?" Farley said noncommittally, knowing Aura Lee had more to say.

"I was hoping he'd be around when you came in, but he's gone." She looked over her shoulder as if someone might be eavesdropping, which caused one corner of Farley's mouth to turn up. "I thought you should know as there might be trouble brewing, Taylor talking to his girl and all. I didn't even know he was old enough to drive, but he sure looks it, and you can't help but notice him with that black hair and being so striking." She shook her head. "He doesn't look anything like his mother, but then who knows, these days, everybody's mixin' together. No one sees her in town hardly ever. Always was private, that one. And Martha Eberly told me—"

Farley raised a hand to signal his secretary to stop. "Okay, Aura Lee, I get the picture. I'm heading out to the Orchard Lake Inn. While I'm gone, have Deputy Purdy be on the lookout for a missing Dominicker rooster. I'll explain later."

For once, Jeff left Aura Lee speechless.

Penelope Cather was busy in the kitchen, preparing courses for an annual luncheon sponsored by the Serena Women's Club. The luncheon was being held in the beautifully decorated dining room. Guests of the inn were being served on the veranda, and extra help had been hired to assist in the kitchen and on the floor as servers. Extravagant floral arrangements had been placed throughout the charming rustic interior, giving the inn an elegant touch and filling the air with lavish, heady fragrance. Members of the Serena Garden Club were also members of the Women's Club, so they shared the event and this year had decided to splurge. The women were dressed as colorfully as the décor. A mixture of designer perfumes, colognes, and scented powders blended with the floral and kitchen aromas.

Farley had already been on sensory overload after leaving Charlotte. When he walked into the inn's foyer his senses were assailed. He felt uncharacteristically dizzy when asking the receptionist if he could speak to Miss Cather.

She looked at him as if he were insane and said, "You certainly cannot! You couldn't have picked a worse time. You'll have to come back when she's off duty. This is a very important luncheon, a most lucrative one for my employers."

"I'm sure it is, young lady, and I will not disrupt it. If you'll direct me to where Miss Cather is working, I won't take much of her time."

The receptionist responded with flirtatious defiance. "Will you arrest me if I don't?"

He walked away from her without comment. As he passed by the dining area, trying to stay out of view, several women turned in their chairs to stare at him. A buzz of conversation erupted just as his shoulder grazed a protrusion of peonies jutting out in from an ornamental vase positioned on a nearby pedestal. He felt the eyes of the receptionist bore into his back and feared he would not make it to the kitchen without a catastrophe. Miraculously, doors swung open to the left of him, and a waitress came out carrying a tray of salads. He stepped aside to let her pass and then went through the doorway without looking back.

Penelope Cather was facing his direction when he entered. She smiled and came toward him with arms extended. When he bent down to embrace her, pink and white peony petals fell from his shoulder onto her baking cap. They both laughed.

"It's been a long time, Jeffrey Farley."

"Too long." Farley returned her smile.

"I have felt your strong presence in my vicinity. What a fine man you've become. Welcome to my kitchen. I'm afraid I don't have time to stop, but know it must be something important to bring you here. I can listen while I work."

Jeff's admiration for her was unchanged and inestimable. Her calming presence soothed him. He marveled at her composure in the midst of such chaos. Having met her much older sister, he could see the influence of genes and similarity between the two, except for the difference in weight.

"Miss Pen, Charlotte sent me. Something happened to upset her and she needs you. Apparently she's formed an attachment to a rooster. When she realized the rooster was missing this morning, she drove in a state of hysteria to a friend's house, wearing only her pajamas and a bathrobe."

"Oh dear," Miss Pen said as she worked.

"She's in good hands. Kate teaches psychology, and Devlin, her fiancé and guest, is also a psychologist. Perhaps you've heard of them? Kate and Dev were at the center of the Serena murder case last year. They are trustworthy." Miss

Pen nodded, so Farley continued. "Charlotte believes her husband had the rooster kidnapped or killed. She wasn't very coherent." He shook his head. "This is the first time I've seen or talked to her since we were young, Miss Pen. I don't know what to make of her accusations, but I know she needs help."

"I can't get away until around two o'clock," Miss Pen told him, "and I can't stay long, as I'll still have work to do here."

"Dev will come to get you and transport you to and from their home. I would take you, but I don't want you to be seen in my cruiser."

Miss Pen nodded. "That's fine. If you need to talk to me again, come to my home early evening. I live behind the inn along the high ridge that wraps around from it." She provided directions to her hidden cottage and then said, "You can tell your friend I will come round to the lot to wait for him."

Farley opened his mouth to thank Miss Pen for her time, but she had more to say.

"Jeff, you should know that Charlotte is very unhappy and has been for many years. She returned to Serena with hopes of rekindling a relationship with her son, Taylor, during his summer visit. But her husband interfered, and Taylor has directed his attentions elsewhere, which is another matter of concern.

"In anticipation of Taylor's arrival, Charlotte adopted the rooster as a good omen, a talisman. Then her husband made an unexpected appearance, and Charlotte believes the rooster's aversion to him allowed her to see his true nature and the irreversible effect he's had on their son. She's suspicious about the purpose of his visit, something to do with his insistence that Taylor work for Rodney Granger. She came to me after this realization and asked for my help. I calmed and reassured her, and she went home feeling better, more confident, but not enough to dispel the effects of years of psychological abuse." She shook her head regretfully. "That's all I can say now, Jeff, except for one thing more. Charlotte's rooster would never have abandoned her!"

The kitchen doors swung open, and a server returned for the main course trays. Jeff thanked Miss Pen and left by the kitchen back door, thankful to have an alternate exit route. He stood outside for a few minutes taking in the extraordinary view and breathing in enough fresh air to steady himself. He had the same feeling he'd had after talking to Mamma Phoebe. Miss Pen had told him enough to help, but not everything she knew. She and her sister were fiercely protective women, and they were hiding something. There were layers upon layers of secrets to uncover and he was determined to peel them back to the core.

CHAPTER TWENTY-FIVE

Feare may force a man to cast beyond the moone.

~ John Heywood

THE MORNING OF THE ROOSTER'S disappearance was an endless one for Taylor Reed. His memory of the night before was like a Fellini movie in which the table was set for a banquet and his parents were all out of focus. He had no recollection of going to bed. Incredibly, his father had risen before the crack of dawn and awakened him out of a dead sleep like a military drill sergeant on acid.

They had breakfast around six o'clock at the Serena Grill with people who apparently did this as a routine. The crowd of regulars was so busy exchanging news and gossip that they didn't pay the homage his father typically expected. The waitress didn't seem to care that Jordon Reed expected his eggs poached to perfection and his coffee brewed fresh. This caused him to be in a sour mood and disgruntled, snapping at the waitress, pushing away his unfinished plate of sausage and grits, and grabbing a previously read morning paper someone had left behind. While he read it, Taylor finished everything on his plate, as well as his father's plate of rejected food.

Outside the Grill, Taylor had to wait while his father made several calls on his cell phone. He then had to drive his father down the mountain to the courthouse where he was supposedly scheduled to meet with the county officials while Rodney Granger, who'd driven separately, spent time in the Office of Records and Deeds.

Biding his time in the busy courthouse lobby, Taylor watched the people come and go, some gathering in groups and milling around, and others with troubled expressions waiting for elevators to take them to floors where the hearings and trials were held. The attorneys were easy to spot. Taylor felt grateful his father had a good one and that he'd never had to make an appearance in court.

Feeling restless, he walked down a flight of stairs to find a restroom less occupied than the one on the main floor. He followed an arrow indicating there was one ahead along the darkened hallway. Before reaching it, he heard two familiar voices in heated discussion. He backed away and slid around a corner in time to be out of sight when the men's room door opened. He overhead Rodney say in menacing sing-song as he passed, "Ding dong, the witch will soon be dead."

He waited until after his father had exited and then found an elevator to carry him back to the main floor, where he melded into the crowd. Something had gone wrong, but what?

When his father found him minutes later, Taylor could see from the steely set of his jaw that he was still fuming. Taylor knew better than to ask questions or even turn on the radio on the drive back up the mountain. So naturally he was surprised when his father suggested they have lunch in town at the Serena Bistro. That was fine with him; he was hungry again, despite his large breakfast. He lucked upon an open space in front of the restaurant and parked.

When they walked inside, Jordon hid his anger like a political pro while responding graciously to the proprietor's warm greeting. After they were seated, she presented them with a complimentary antipasto and suggested a red wine suitable for the occasion of his patronage (her words). She made it a point to let the other customers know a person of importance was in her establishment. As if planned, the mayor and another city official came in for lunch (probably having heard the congressman was there) and stopped by their table. Jordon's disposition improved for real when they told him a special luncheon was being planned in his honor.

While they were talking, Taylor excused himself and called the Serena Market to let Willa Mae know he'd be picking her up at the usual time after work. Much to his dismay, she sounded hesitant and reluctant, but she didn't go back on her word to go with him. She reminded him she had to be home before dark, even though it was a Friday night. He felt exasperated, explosive, like a powder keg inside. Yeah, right, he thought. He'd get her home when he was done with her and not before.

He'd had enough of all of them. Being trapped with his parents and dealing with Willa Mae's curfews was like living in a time warp. He'd have to make some excuse to skip dinner tonight. It would be easier with his mother making martinis around five and his father gulping them down like water. By quarter to six, he'd sneak out of the house before anyone missed him.

Rodney Granger was also feeling explosive. He'd have to take care of the hoodoo witch himself. She was too tricky to turn over to someone else. He'd made a mistake by thinking she was too old to matter. Reed was right; he'd really messed up. He should have remembered about the sister. Most folks didn't associate her with Mamma Phoebe. They were never seen together and appeared to lead separate lives. Folks said the boy was adopted, didn't look like either one of them, and was probably not even kin. Maybe it was all a mistake. Maybe she'd just taken him there one time to look at the falls.

But after finding out about the clause this morning, there was no room for doubt. Purvis McCabe and Mamma Phoebe not only shared the water rights, they'd also had a hidden clause added stipulating a sale of the property by one owner gave full water rights to the owner of the other. But why and when had they agreed upon this legally-binding amendment to the deed? He'd somehow missed it during the deed search by going back generations and mistakenly assuming nothing had been changed to present day. They couldn't have known the real value of the water. If they had, surely they wouldn't have kept their knowledge secret? Why live so poor when they could have been rich? It didn't make sense.

They'd planned to discredit her, and only if necessary. Now she had to go. But there had been too many accidental deaths recently to have another one. He'd have be more creative—use her hoodoo superstitions against her. Unlike Reed, Rodney had been raised in the mountains and knew how superstitious the old-timers were. They followed every phase of the moon and believed in all the astrological signs and legends. They even planted their gardens by the moon. He'd make her beliefs in omens and warnings work for him. He wasn't afraid of her; a person had to believe in hoodoo for it to have power against him, and he didn't believe. It was all smoke and mirrors, just like his business dealings and Reed's politicking. Hoodoo was just another way to bamboozle people.

Penelope Cather tried to stay focused on the luncheon after Farley's visit. The missing rooster was an unexpected twist in the evolving dramas happening around her. Phoebe had warned her that shadows were gathering. It wouldn't be wise for Charlotte to leave Jordon Reed at this time. She had to be close to him to combat him, and Pen knew how to help her get through this. Reed's days of hurting her girl were over.

Thankfully, one problem had been resolved early that morning. Willa Mae had delivered the basket of produce as expected, and Pen had engaged her in a conversation. Thinking she might feel ashamed to talk about Taylor Reed, Pen had put her at ease by serving freshly baked buttermilk biscuits and homemade strawberry preserves instead of probing. She gently told Willa Mae about the discussion with her father. The genuine concern in Pen's voice and manner allowed Willa Mae's pent-up emotions to surface. Her story poured out in a rush of words.

"Miss Pen, you must believe me. I'm not interested in Taylor, except as a friend. I was only trying to help him. I guess I felt flattered by his attention, but that's all it was. Raven being so busy had me feeling left out, like he didn't care. I know that's not true, but I was feeling awful lonely. Then Taylor started being so nice to me and . . . and now, Miss Pen, I wish I'd never agreed to help him at all! But don't you worry none. I've told him I can't anymore, and he's accepted that I can't. Daddy's been so upset, and I've been thinkin' I've let Mamma down by upsetting Daddy."

Miss Pen nodded her approval.

"At first," Willa Mae confessed, "I wanted Raven to know I was getting attention from someone like Taylor, his Daddy being so important and all. But now I feel ashamed. I'm glad he don't know anything about him. And please, Miss Pen, please don't tell him. I told Taylor I'd meet him one more time cause he's got something he wants me to see, a goodbye gift for helping him. His father is here now, and he'll be busy showing him how well he knows his way around the mountain roads. He's thankin' me for that. Turns out, that's all he really wanted from me after all." Willa Mae hugged herself and shook her head. "Oh, Miss Pen, why do I feel so mixed up? You know how I feel about Raven. Maybe I've put too much of my hopes on us being together. Maybe he's changed. I thought I was being smart, like those girls at school with their boyfriends, trying to make him jealous, trying to get his attention again. I wish I'd never had those thoughts or tried to be like those girls."

Pen was so relieved to learn that Willa Mae was not infatuated with Taylor Reed that she saw no harm in her accepting his parting gift. Nevertheless, she couldn't help remembering what Charlotte had told her about Taylor being like his father. An inkling of wariness crept into her thoughts, but she dismissed it in her effort to comfort Willa Mae and dry her tears.

Farley drove into town and checked the front and rear parking lots at Granger Realty for Taylor Reed's car. He thought about going inside to talk to Rodney Granger and checked his designated parking space. It was empty. He drove out of the lot and back onto Main Street and almost missed seeing the sports car because of a long-bed pickup truck parked next to it. He continued down Main Street and parked in his space in front of the police station and checked in with Aura Lee, who had just returned from lunch.

"I haven't heard anything back from Deputy Purdy about that rooster, Chief. Is that the same rooster we've been getting complaints about? If so, I'm not surprised it's gone missing. There's no talk about it at the Grill. They's all talking about the mayor and the congressman meeting down at the Bistro today for lunch. Some people I know splurged and went down there to eat, just to see what was going on! Susie Kindle said she overheard the mayor inviting Congressman Reed to a big party the city is going to have for him, probably paid for with our tax dollars." She rolled her eyes. "She said he and his boy were served an extra special lunch too, with wine from a private stock no one's ever heard of. You should go on down there, Chief. I'm sure he'd like to meet you, you being our town hero, though I know you hate to speak of it. I know he's been in town only a couple of days, but I'd have thought he'd have stopped in here to meet you. I guess he thinks he's more important. That's the way these politicians are, them wanting all the glory, if you know what I mean."

"I think you're right, Aura Lee. I'll just take a walk down there. I haven't had lunch yet, and it's about time I met Jordon Reed."

Aura Lee stared at him as he turned and walked out. "Why, that's not like him at all. Not one bit like him."

By the time Jeff Farley ducked under the doorway and entered the restaurant, Jordon Reed had had his fill of Italian food, although he had to admit the Pasta Raphael was fantastic and the wine extraordinary. He'd also had his fill of local officials. Now he had to deal with the chief of police, who had just been introduced to him by the mayor.

Of course he'd heard of the man; who hadn't? He'd put the tiny town of Serena on the map of notoriety. Jordon wasn't sure this was a good thing in relation to his future product, but who knew? The public was drawn to this sort of publicity, and maybe it could eventually be linked to an advertising campaign. These thoughts, which ran through his mind during the introduction, evaporated when he stood up to shake hands. Jordon, who had always been proud of his stature, found Farley's height unsettling and his reticence disturbing. Furthermore, Farley's handshake had been a little too firm, his eyes a little too cold and questioning, and his deference, nonexistent. What was with this guy?

"Have a seat, Chief Farley. Have you met my son, Taylor?"

"No, I can't say I've had the pleasure." Jeff ignored Taylor and turned to the mayor and said, "If you'll excuse me, I'd like to talk to Congressman Reed and his son alone. I'm here on official business."

The mayor acted embarrassed and said, "Jeff. Have you lost your mind?"

Jordon Reed interjected, "What is this about, Chief?"

"I'm sorry to inform you that your wife reported a missing rooster this morning and is quite upset about it. Do you know anything about the disappearance of this rooster?"

The mayor said, "Jeff, for Pete's sake."

"That's okay, Mayor," Reed said calmly. "My wife is a bit high strung. I'm sure there is a logical explanation. Are you telling me that her rooster is gone? Taylor and I were up and out very early this morning." He tilted his head in thought. "Come to think of it, I didn't hear it crowing before we left but didn't give it much thought, as we are not accustomed to its habits. I know my wife is fond of the rooster, so I understand her alarm. But surely this is not a job for the police. It probably wandered off somewhere. She didn't keep it in a cage."

"She said you hated the rooster and threatened to kill it."

"Any man in his right mind would hate that crazy bird! What are you saying? Are you accusing me of something, Chief Farley? This is ridiculous."

"I'm simply telling you what your wife reported. If you can shed some light on the situation, perhaps I can help with a resolution."

"I don't know anything about that crazy rooster! I'm a very busy man with many responsibilities. I'm here to get some rest, but I also have certain protocols to attend to while here. In fact, Taylor and I spent the morning at the County Seat. I do appreciate your attention to this matter, Chief Farley, but I've nothing more to add, except that my wife has a tendency to over-react to things. I'm sure she has this all blown out of proportion." He turned to Taylor and said, "We'd better go home and see about your mother."

Turning back to Farley, Reed said brusquely, "Excuse me, Chief." He gave a stern look to the mayor as he brushed past him.

The mayor was about to chide Jeff for his actions until he saw the look on his face. Farley seemed oblivious to him and the staring customers as he watched the affronted Jordon Reed and his son leave the restaurant. He'd said nothing to Jordon and Taylor Reed about Charlotte being with Kate and Dev. He'd not mentioned Penelope Cather. There was something about the man he didn't like, and he assumed Reed would seek retribution for being questioned in public. He didn't care. He wouldn't have cared if Reed had been running for president.

Nothing was said during the first few minutes of the short drive from the Bistro to the Reed's summer home. Jordon Reed was outraged. Charlotte had gone too far this time. The woman needed to be institutionalized. The thought somehow calmed him. Yes, that was it! If he could prove she was crazy enough to be committed, it would solve his problem of getting rid of her. Maybe this missing rooster fiasco was a blessing in disguise. He'd have to give this some thought. It would be better to act sympathetic rather than angry when they got home. He'd deal with Farley later.

"Taylor, you've been here longer than I have. Has that rooster ever wandered off before?"

"Are you kidding?" Taylor replied. "Why would he leave a place where he's treated like a king?" Taylor looked at his father with suspicion in his gaze. "Maybe someone did take him."

"It doesn't matter, son. If it wasn't the rooster, it would be something else. Your mother is not well. That's why I agreed to let her come to Serena for a change of scenery. I thought it would help, but I was mistaken. She's gotten worse. Listen, when we get home, I'll talk to her and calm her down. Do you think you could find something to do tonight? Perhaps I haven't been giving her enough attention. Maybe if I spend some special time alone with her, she'll forget about the rooster for a while."

"Sure, Dad."

Taylor couldn't believe his good fortune *or* his father's compassionate reaction. But he was not going to look a gift horse in the mouth. He'd dreaded spending the evening with his parents because of the rooster crisis and having to postpone his date with Willa Mae. That would have driven him over the edge of reason. Today had been bad enough. He'd never seen anyone talk to his father the way Chief Farley had. And now his father was acting like it never happened. Something wasn't kosher, but whatever. He'd been given a reprieve and would make the most of it. He felt like bursting into song—*Willa Mae, Willa Mae, pretty, pretty, pretty Willa Mae.*

Another surprise was in store for them when Taylor pulled into the drive. A sleek black SUV was parked next to his mother's classic Mercedes sedan. He could hear his father cursing under his breath. An attractive woman came out onto the porch and down the steps to greet them.

"Hello, I'm Kate Delaney, a friend of Charlotte's", she said, extending her hand. "My fiancé and I have been waiting for you to arrive. Chief Farley called to let us know you were on the way."

Jordon, remarkably back on his game, smiled warmly at Kate and responded, "Thank you, Miss, or is it Ms. Delaney?"

"It's Dr. Delaney," she said modestly, "but please, call me Kate. I'm a psychologist, not a physician. My fiancé, Devlin McManus, is a retired clinical psychologist. I hope you don't mind that he gave Charlotte a sedative. It's wearing off now, and she's much better. Before we escorted her home, she had a visit from a woman who was once her nanny. This seemed to help her more than the medication. After her visit, Charlotte said she was ready to come home."

"How can I thank you, Kate?" He glanced at Taylor, who had exited the car and come around to join him. "This is my son, Taylor. We've both been concerned about her state of mind. My wife has been under a strain recently, and this latest incident must have upset her greatly. She has a tendency to form irrational attachments, as she has with the rooster. I cannot imagine what happened to it, but I will make every effort to find it or replace it." With another glance at Taylor, he said, "I didn't realize Charlotte had taken time to make friends here. She's been away from Serena for such a long time. How did you meet?"

Kate replied with a lighthearted tone, "Oh, didn't you know? I'm afraid I'm the person responsible for Henry—the rooster. Charlotte adopted him after he was unceremoniously dumped in my neighbor's backyard. It seems he's once again displaced. I suppose that's why she came to my home this morning. She probably associated the rooster with me when she found him missing."

Before Jordon could think of a reply, Dev came out to join them. He extended his hand and introduced himself, "Congressman Reed, Devlin McManus. I hope you don't mind our intrusion into your home. Charlotte is resting upstairs, but awake and quite eager to talk to you. We'll be going now, but please, let us know if we can be of any help. We'll certainly keep an eye out for the rooster."

Their smooth, hasty departure left Jordon livid. He said nothing, but his face revealed a metamorphosis from controlled rage back to caring husband for Taylor's benefit. Taylor wasn't fooled this time and was grateful when his cell phone buzzed. He stepped away to take the call, which ended abruptly.

"That was Rodney, Dad. He needs me back at the office this afternoon for a couple more hours. His secretary had to leave early, and I have to hold down the fort until he returns from showing a property."

"Go ahead. I'll see to your mother. There's really nothing you can do for her. We'll have drinks as usual around five before you go out for the evening. If your mother isn't up to it, I'll make the martinis."

But Charlotte *was* up to it. She'd accepted Jordon's sympathetic attentions, acting as though she believed they were genuine. She'd said nothing about accusing him of being responsible for the rooster's disappearance, nor had he. He had initially expected an afternoon of drama and had been immensely relieved to find her so rational and calm. She'd asked him to allow her to rest until the cocktail hour, freeing him to retreat into his den. After shutting the door and collapsing into his red leather chair, angry and exhausted, he made a call to one of his staff and ordered a background check on Kate Delaney and Devlin McManus.

He'd put off asking Charlotte about the mysterious visiting nanny; Kate hadn't mentioned her name. He knew very little about Charlotte's early life. He'd assumed her parents had servants during her childhood, but not one so significant. He began to wonder about this woman and why she was readily available to rush to Charlotte's side. Who called her and why? Was Kate Delaney simply a well-meaning friend put in an awkward position, or were they interfering busy-bodies? His head ached with vexation. He rubbed his forehead and muttered, "Maybe I'm the one over-reacting."

Then his cell phone dinged with a message accompanied by an e-mail attachment. The first pages were a compilation of the professional bios and curriculum vitae of Devlin McManus and Kate Delaney. Scrolling through the pages, he was impressed and almost convinced they were no threat to him. He was about to close the attachment when a page of newspaper headlines scrolled up. An alarm bell went off in his head as he recalled Serena's notorious murder case. He clicked on the most prominent headline link and read about the couple at the center and their close involvement with Chief Jeff Farley. He slammed his fist hard on his desk in frustration.

"They're in thick as thieves with him!"

He decided there and then things would have to be pushed forward. He dialed Rodney's number.

Jeff Farley was convinced his instincts were right about Jordon Reed. Why was he in Serena? The business about being here for a rest was a lie. Why did he have Taylor working for Rodney, and what had Taylor been doing on the McCabe property? There had been three suspicious deaths and two near-deaths pointing to an old man who'd never poisoned anyone in his long history of whiskey-making. Granted he was getting senile, but according to Mamma Phoebe, making high quality moonshine was second-nature to him. Could Jordon Reed be interested in the McCabe property? If so, why would he want land that other developers hadn't even considered?

With these questions in mind, Farley decided to take a drive down to the county courthouse to find out if Reed had been lying about his reasons for being there. His contact for information was Sheila McPherson, a secretary in the clerk of courts office, who was also a friend of Aura Lee. She took a break to answer his questions.

"Oh, he was here, all right, Chief. There was such a fuss. He hadn't given us much notice about coming down here, so everybody had to stop what they were doing to make over him. Not me, of course. I have my duties to attend to. But I did get a glimpse of him. He looks better in his campaign pictures. Don't they all?"

"I imagine you're right, Sheila," Farley said.

"The congressman visited with Judge Beckman and Commissioner McPherson. They were all closed up in private, so I don't know what that was about. Talk is he came down here to drum up votes. He was barely elected last time out, and word is he'll be defeated next time when he runs against that new fella, Jasper Melrose. As far as I'm concerned, they should replace everyone in Congress, the way they've been voting. I have a sister, lives over in Raleigh, and I could tell you things she's told me—"

"Thank you, Sheila. I'd stay and listen, but I've got to get back up the mountain. Aura Lee will have my head if I don't report back in this afternoon."

"No need to explain, Chief. I know how you depend on her. She'd told me how you couldn't do without her and how she's almost like a deputy instead of a secretary. She told me, in confidence of course, how she helps you solve most of your cases. Course there was that big one last year you handled on your own. Who could forget that? If it wasn't for that case, you wouldn't have had to hire a secretary. Aura Lee sure made herself valuable in a short span of time. Why she told me—"

"Now you understand why I have to get moving and report in. Thanks again, Sheila."

Farley left the courthouse satisfied about Reed's visit there. Although somewhat disappointed, he had learned one useful piece of information; Reed's political future was in jeopardy. Reason enough to be planning a new one.

CHAPTER TWENTY-SIX

Though I am old with wandering
Through hollow lands and hilly lands,
I will find out where she has gone,
And kiss her lips and take her hands;
And walk among long dappled grass,
And pluck till time and times are done
The silver apples of the moon,
The golden apples of the sun.

~ William Butler Yeats

THE ENGINE OF HIS CAR was purring like a sleeping tiger, and he was ready to roll. Willa Mae came walking down the road looking pretty as a picture in her flower-print blouse, blue jeans, and the hiking boots he'd suggested she wear. Thankfully, daylight lasted until around nine o'clock during the summer, giving him plenty of time to get her there and back before dark.

As soon as she got into the car, she asked Taylor where they were going. He told her to wait until they came to the entrance road because he wanted to surprise her. He could sense her apprehension and turned on the charm, explaining about the McCabe property and why he had access to it. By the time they reached the Y fork in the road, she had relaxed.

When Taylor parked the car at the compound, he pointed in the direction of the place they were going. He promised the hike would be worth it. His display of conscientiousness was rewarded with Willa Mae's appreciation.

She'd been cooped up in the store all afternoon, she told him, and it felt good to be outdoors.

The trail eventually led down to a stream, which they followed toward a ridge that rose to a high peak that dominated the area. She mentioned that some called it Shadow Peak. Then she hesitated as if she regretted coming along, and Taylor tugged her forward, leading her toward the sound of rushing water. The surprise was just ahead.

The falls appeared before them, gushing from the mouth of Shadow Peak. Willa Mae gasped at their splendor. The waters were crystalline blue and flowing over black rocks and crevices that shimmered in the fading sunlight. A refreshing mist fell on their faces.

"Thank you for—"

Before Willa Mae could say more, Taylor pulled her forward into a clearing where the height of the falls towered over them. She looked up at the falls, and Taylor saw a shadow of fright cross her face, as if she had seen a demon over his shoulder. Then her gaze met his, and he saw fear in her eyes. He did not realize that she saw the face of a demon replicated in his expression.

A strange sense of power took hold of Taylor. He'd waited long enough and knew she'd be resistant. She was trapped in a secluded paradise and could not escape. He'd played rough before and had become addicted to this type of conquest. His father had explained it as genetic, dating back to the days of cavemen. But up until now, he'd either paid for rough sex or it had been given too freely. This would be so much better, out in the wild where he could release his pent-up aggression.

The fear in her eyes was the most exciting part. Willa Mae was just the type to keep this secret because she'd be so ashamed. But if she did, his father would take care of it, as always, after listening to every detail.

There was nowhere to run, yet she tried to dart past him. He grabbed her arm and swung her around. He pressed against her as she tried to claw his face with her fingernails, but he managed to pull her arms down and pin them behind her while he kissed her face and neck. She struggled, but she didn't have the strength to free herself. Taylor released one hand and yanked at the top of her jeans, but she fought his hand with her freed one. He pushed her to the ground and quickly pinned her there, and then he ripped open the top of her blouse. When she started to scream, he smacked her in the face. The red mark on her cheekbone and tears in her eyes brought a grim smile to Taylor's face.

As abruptly as he had pounced on her, he was hauled off her and hit the ground several yards away. Shock kept him from shielding himself from pounding fists until Willa Mae called out to the unexpected assailant.

"Raven!"

Taylor took advantage of that pause when this Raven person turned toward her. Taylor knocked him to the ground and jumped on him, pummeling him like a madman.

Willa Mae pulled herself up and flung herself on Taylor, trying to stop the fight. Taylor flung her to the side like a rag doll. He heard a hard thud, like she hit her head on a rock. Suddenly Raven's knee violently connected with Taylor's groin, and Taylor doubled over, falling to his knees. Raven ran to Willa Mae and bent over her. Taylor gritted his teeth as he rose to his feet, snatched up a palm-sized river rock, and slammed it into the back of Raven's head.

Taylor left them both lying there, injured, unconscious, or maybe dead. He did not care. He made it back to his car with some difficulty, disoriented as dusk turned into darkness. Driving too fast along the hazardous road out, he skidded into a deep rut with a rocky edge that cut into his right front tire. He didn't notice the slow leak until he turned onto the mountain road. By the time he made it to town, his tire was almost flat. He avoided Main Street, taking the back way home, the rim of his tire slicing into the driveway.

There was no one downstairs to see his bruised face and torn clothing. He crept upstairs. On one end of the hallway, he found his father lying in a stupor in his bedroom. On the other end, his mother was in her bedroom listening to old records. His room was in the middle.

"What a nightmare," he mumbled, standing in the hallway between them.

They weren't even aware he was there, weren't even aware of each other, each in their own world and, fortunately for him, in separate rooms. He had to wake his father and sober him up. But first, he had to think, and he needed the privacy of his bedroom to sort out what had happened and come up with a plausible story.

He collapsed onto the bed, his body racked with pain, and thought about what he'd done. He'd left two injured people without aid in an isolated area. It would be a lucky break if they died. No one would ever know he'd been there. If questioned, he could say Willa Mae had changed her mind about meeting him. That is, if she'd told her father about it, which he doubted. Folks would assume she and the guy went there together and met with an unfortunate accident.

Who is he, anyway? He was the one who'd been with the old woman. Did he live near the falls? Why was he there? He almost had the best of me until she called his name. I'd be the one almost dead now if it wasn't for her. What did she call him—Raven? What kind of a name is that? It's probably some local name, sounds Indian. He could have killed me. I had the strange feeling I was fighting myself, the way he moved. How crazy is that?

No one will find them tonight. Even if by some miracle they make it out, who would believe them? It's my word against theirs. If she dies, he'll be the one looking guilty. If he didn't make it, she probably wouldn't either.

He'd have to wait until tomorrow to find out what he was up against. Her father would be the one to deal with. He'd be out searching for her, asking questions.

Man, I think the guy cracked one of my ribs. Maybe I'd better hold off telling Dad. No, he needs to know in case this needs to be fixed. There will be hell to pay if

I've screwed up his property deal with this fiasco. I'd better let him sleep, and then I'll wake him. I've got to get my story straight first . . . and rest my eyes.

An hour before Taylor closed his eyes, Raven opened his. The side of his face was pressed into damp mud; he could feel pebbles of rock embedded in his cheek. The back of his head felt tight and throbbed with pain. His vision was blurry and mouth dry. He reached out to touch Willa Mae and felt her cold skin under his fingertips. The constant spray of water from the teaming waterfall had dampened her clothing and his. He used his elbows to move closer to her and laid his head on her chest. He could feel a faint heartbeat. Tears welled in his eyes. Her life was his life, and now there was hope.

He could hardly see the wound on her head, a crevice of blood that had coagulated but was no longer runny. He'd have to move her; there was no other choice. He knew where to go and had to find the strength to carry her. He whispered her name in her ear and said it again and again. She had to hear him, had to know he was there, had to fight along with him to survive. She was his love, his reason for being, and if she lived past this night, she would never be left unprotected again.

He lifted her into his scraped, aching arms and looked up at the clouded moon and stars to ask for more light. But he had trouble seeing them. The stream would have to be his guide as he carried her along the dark path. Suddenly, it seemed to brighten, despite the dim moonlight, and turned into a glimmering waterway to light his path. He felt the sensation of water flowing through him. A strange fluidity of motion made him feel at one with the glistening stream as he followed it all the way to the cabin.

Mamma Phoebe was asleep in her rocker when she heard the rooster crow. She awakened, wondering why he crowed. She said, "It can't be morning when I've not got myself to bed yet."

With some effort, she got up from the rocker and put another log on the low fire under her cooking pot. She'd kept it burning that night, doing a slow brew of herbs and spices. She always did her brewing at night, according to the whims of the moon. This brew was a devil moon potion, something she'd been working on since Chief Farley had come to visit.

She shuffled from the fireplace to the door, listening to the rooster's crow of alert. Strange bird he was, getting too old to know morning from night. But then she heard the sound of footsteps on the porch, and then Raven's voice. She opened the door.

Mamma Phoebe wasted no time. The girl was near-death when laid before her, and Raven's eyes told Mamma Phoebe he had suffered a concussion. The evil deed done them was secondary to saving the child and tending to her boy. She gathered a combination of herbs and roots from her summer kitchen and spread them on a high wooden table by the fireplace. She pumiced several mixtures at a time using her soapstone mortar and pestle. She separated one made of angelica root and dragon's blood resin to protect them against negative energies and evil forces. She cut agrimony to use as a wash to increase the effectiveness of her healing and calamus and astragalus roots for energy.

She cut thistle to purify the sacred minerals she added to the purification bathing salts and had Raven prepare balsam fir needles and patchouli for burning into incense to evoke the elements of earth and forest for her rituals and incantations. She mixed cloves, sweet basil, bay leaves, and wax myrtle for strength, beeswax for a salve, and blue cohosh for empowerment. Most importantly, she added jalap root to conquer the situation and washed her hands in an infusion of the herb, placing wild cherry bark around her to increase the potency of her magic.

The yellow-purplish mandrake, with its forked root resembling a human body, was made into a drug. The healing poultices she placed upon their heads were unique to each wound, and were empowered by recitation of biblical psalms and verses long used in hoodoo practice. The words spoken moved through her hands as she massaged Willa Mae's body to extract negative energies and maintain her even breathing. She kept Raven awake by putting him to work stirring her liquid medicines in the cast iron pot. She changed his dressing periodically as the swelling on the back of his head decreased in size and pressure diminished. She moved like a young woman in and out of her summer kitchen and pantry; the smoke from her chimney filled the night air with the scent of rose hips, sassafras, lavender, eucalyptus, and patchouli.

The faded moon turned to yellow in the starry night sky. With Raven at her side, Mamma Phoebe worked tirelessly until the crisis passed. At last, she made him sit. She gave him an herbal draught of liquid she poured from an old barrel. She told him it would relax him without putting him to sleep. Willa Mae rested too, adrift in the twilight of consciousness, a sleep state of oblivion, her breathing regulated and her heartbeat strong.

The old woman sat down in her rocker, the years of age returning now that her work was done. She closed her eyes and concentrated, using all her remaining mental energy, and willed Pen to come.

It was late, and Pen was worried. Though Raven had left a note, he should have been home by now. She opened the cabin door and stepped outside, watching for him from the porch, calling his name into the night. A night-owl echoed each of her calls as though assisting her. She followed his call into the darkness, walking around to the back of the cottage to the place where she stood each evening. The waxing moon cast enough light for her to see the outline of Shadow Peak. Her eyes moved down to the land below it where a relentless stream of smoke swirled and streamed and puffed itself into pinkish yellow vaporous clouds. She hurried back inside to fetch the extra set of truck keys and was startled to hear the loud sound of knocking on the cabin door.

"Miss Pen, Miss Pen! It's me, Frank Parsons."

Pen opened the door to let him in.

"Miss Pen, Willa Mae hasn't come home. I've been out looking for her. She called me from work and said she'd be a little late this evening coming home and I wasn't to worry. She didn't explain, except to say she'd be home before dark. She told me she'd talked to you this morning and everything was okay and I wasn't to worry anymore about anything. I didn't question her because she sounded so different, like she had before all this started. Has she been here? Is Raven here? Has he seen her?"

"Neither one has—"

"I've tried to call her phone, but there is no connection. I know reception is unreliable hereabouts, but why hasn't she called? She could have used a regular phone to let me know where she is."

"Frank, Raven hasn't come home either. I was just about to go out to look for him. I think I might know where he is. Would you like to come with me? If we can't find them, my sister Phoebe will know what to do. Would you mind driving? We can take the pickup truck."

"Let's take mine, Miss Pen. I'm parked up at the inn. My truck's old, but it's in better shape."

Pen convinced Frank to drive directly to Phoebe's and directed him to the access road.

"My sister might know something that will help us save time, Frank. She's a very wise woman. Raven's been spending a lot of time with her lately."

Pen did not tell him of Willa Mae's plan to see Taylor Reed one last time and sorely regretted she had not discouraged her. If that young man was involved in this, she'd never forgive herself. The truck bumped along the perilous road, jolting her insides. She gripped the cracked vinyl armrest to keep herself steady, breathing deeply, preparing for the worst.

Frank Parson had never taken the path or the road to visit Mamma Phoebe, but he knew of those who had. His late wife's aunt had attested to the woman's remarkable gift for healing. She'd spoken of others who'd told her—in secret—about going to Mamma Phoebe for love potions and hoodoo conjures. A local preacher once warned his congregation about such practices and equated them with witchcraft. Old-timers were more accepting, remembering the days when medical treatment of any kind was hard to come by. They'd been grateful for anyone who tended to the sick, whether it be a mind or body affliction. He'd never met her or laid eyes on her, but he understood why Miss Pen had insisted they go there. This woman probably knew more about what was going on in Serena than the townsfolk who lived there.

It was after midnight when the truck pulled up in front of the cabin. The pungent scent of herbs filled Pen's nostrils; it was a sign her sister had been ministering to someone. She felt the first wave of panic she'd known since being separated from her as a young girl. Frank was at the truck door before she could open it and helped her down, holding onto her arm as they rushed forward. The cabin door opened before they could knock. Phoebe took them both in hand and told them what had happened. Pen took Raven into her arms and cried.

Frank sat at Willa Mae's bedside and thanked the Lord she'd been brought to this woman. He vowed revenge on the young man who'd hurt her. He thanked Raven profusely for carrying her to safety in spite of his injuries. He thanked Pen for knowing to come there. He bowed his head in gratitude and spoke to his wife, who he believed was in heaven with Jesus. She'd always talked about Jesus and went to church every Sunday. He thought that might be why he'd been shown mercy, why Willa Mae was still alive—because of his wife's faithfulness. He hadn't been to church in a long time and thought it best to start going back now.

Phoebe and Pen were huddled in deep discussion. Frank Parsons would insist on reporting the incident. They had to convince him to reconsider. They were dealing with the son of a prominent figure. It would be Raven's word against Taylor Reed's. There was no evidence of rape. They knew how the tables could be turned when it came to people like them versus people like Jordon Reed. Pen had learned enough from Charlotte to know what they were dealing with. Raven's future was at stake, and Willa Mae's reputation. Frank might try to take matters into his own hands, and Raven would want to go after Taylor Reed. They couldn't let this happen. But how could they prevent it?

Phoebe told Pen about Farley's visit and how he'd reminded her of times long ago. Pen agreed he could be trusted. They decided to contact him.

CHAPTER TWENTY-SEVEN

Now the hungry lion roars,
And the wolf behowls the moon.
~ William Shakespeare

FARLEY WAS IN BED BUT not yet asleep when the phone rang. He recognized the voice of Miss Pen through the scratchy sound of poor reception. *She must be calling from a cell phone,* he thought, and sat up in bed to listen with effort. Through the static he heard, "I'm calling on Frank Parsons' cell phone . . . you . . . please come out to my sister's place? We have . . . problem. Please come . . . hurry. Don't tell . . . one."

He was dressed and on his way in minutes. The drive up the winding mountain road seemed endless in the dark, and when he turned onto the access road to Mamma Phoebe's, he wanted to speed up instead of slow down. His mind reeled with questions. What was Frank Parsons doing out here in the middle of the night with Miss Pen? Had something happened to Mamma Phoebe? He hoped not. Why the secrecy? Would it be another death on his watch?

He was almost to the cabin when he noticed something or someone up ahead moving quickly from the right side of the road into the woods. He slowed the cruiser but could see nothing through the wall of trees but darkness. When he looked back at the road, the startled black-rimmed eyes of a raccoon stared back at him, caught in the glare of his headlights. His reflexes took over as he swerved to avoid the motionless creature and managed to do it without damage to the tires. He sighed with relief. Thoughts of a shadowy figure were forgotten as the well-lit cabin came into view.

Miss Pen met Farley at the door and briefly described what had happened. She introduced Raven to him as her son. He was struck by the teen's appearance, wounded and pale as a moonstone, yet as strikingly beautiful as a jungle panther. There was no resemblance to Miss Pen whatsoever. Mamma Phoebe assured him of Willa Mae's stable condition and allowed him to peek in on her. He spoke with Frank Parsons and then questioned Raven at length. It became obvious the boy needed to rest after Mamma Phoebe gave him another herbal draught. She said it would quiet him while keeping him awake until the swelling in his head went down completely. She checked his eyes and changed the poultice on his wound and then sent him to sit by Willa Mae's bedside, out of earshot.

Farley, Miss Pen, Mamma Phoebe, and Frank Parsons gathered around the worn-smooth pinewood table where Phoebe had worked only hours before. Farley listened to their concerns and calmed Frank Parsons. He strongly urged them to have Willa Mae and Raven transported to the hospital for admission and treatment as evidence of assault and attempted rape. This action and his report would be necessary to obtain a warrant for Taylor Reed's arrest.

Mamma Phoebe countered by reminding him that Willa Mae had not been raped, and therefore no physical evidence could be collected. She warned him that assault charges against Taylor Reed might be difficult to prove if Taylor chose to deny responsibility and dispute the accusations. Miss Pen shared what she'd learned from Charlotte about Jordon Reed and the conversation with Willa Mae about Taylor, including her guilt about not warning the girl against him. She expressed fear that Willa Mae and Raven might be put in danger by going up against Jordon Reed. She pleaded with Farley to reevaluate how to proceed.

Farley tried to consider the situation from their perspective. Again he wondered what they were hiding and decided not to press them further at this point. He was not about to wait for a warrant before questioning Taylor, and he had no qualms about going up against Jordon Reed himself. He'd done some checking on the congressman earlier that day after returning from the courthouse. His computer search had yielded an abundance of information, enabling Farley to peruse headlines, read articles, and view the photo-file highlights of his political career and its downslide.

Jordon Reed's initial image projected a good-ol'-boy network politician and Washington insider with a multitude of allies and supporters. But on closer examination, a lone wolf personality emerged as evidenced by the ever-changing allegiances he had made over the years; there appeared to have been no loyalty in action or deed to anyone. Consequently, he had lost support from those in positions of power who had helped him at various stages of his climb. This peer abandonment had eventually made its way to his constituency, demonstrated by his near-defeat in the last election.

Farley had come to see Jordon Reed as a man with an uncertain future, which made him both desperate and dangerous. Mamma Phoebe was a wise woman. She wouldn't hold information back without a good reason. Farley wanted to trust her, but he had a job to do and had learned to rely on his own instincts. They were both born and raised in the mountains, where instincts sometimes had to override the rules. By placing his trust in this, he believed the truth would be revealed. It was a faith as strong as religion, the faith in one's self, the result of his upbringing and hers.

He suspected Jordon Reed put his faith in power, trusting in its ability to destroy his opponents or anyone else who got in his way. Farley had read enough about him to know he wielded his power ruthlessly and would no doubt stop at nothing to combat an accusation against his son. But his son had put Reed in a vulnerable position at an inconvenient time, which he would quickly overcome if given the chance. Farley had to use time to his advantage and keep Reed on edge. He'd also read about a recent trip Reed had taken to South America, coincidentally, to the same region where the cassava plant grows.

Long after midnight, Taylor Reed tried to wake his father from his drunken slumber. His face was swollen and bruised, and his ribs hurt so bad he had trouble standing upright, so he sat down on the side of the bed and shook his father's arm. Jordon opened his eyes and moaned.

"What time is it?"

"Dad, I need your help."

"We'll talk about it in the morning." He rolled over and closed his eyes.

Taylor shook his arm again and said, "Dad, please wake up. It's bad. I'm in trouble."

Jordon opened his eyes again, rolled back, and tried to sit up. He reached for the lamp on the nightstand and turned the switch, lighting the bedroom and accentuating the bruises on Taylor's face.

His brows came together and he swore. "What happened?"

Taylor proceeded to give him an altered and abridged version of his altercation. He claimed he'd taken his new friend, Willa Mae Parsons, to the falls because he'd described them to her and she'd begged to see them. Once there, he said she "came on to him" and they started kissing when, from out of nowhere, the black-haired guy he'd seen with the old woman attacked him from behind, knocking Willa Mae to the ground. He said he couldn't help Willa Mae because he had to fight back, claiming he had the upper hand until the guy pulled a knife on him and started lunging. He said he barely got away with his life and had to leave the girl or he'd have been stabbed to death.

"I would have gone back for her," he lied, "but I heard her call him by name before she fell. I thought maybe she'd set me up to make him jealous. I should have never taken her there. I'm sorry, Dad. I guess I really screwed up. I shouldn't have gotten involved with anybody from around here, but I got bored. What should I do?"

Jordon listened to the story with skepticism and alarm. That boy again! Why was he hanging around the falls? Taylor had a right to be there. Maybe nothing would be reported. If the girl was injured, she was the kid's problem. His relationship with the old hoodoo woman could be an advantage. If the witch allowed this maniac to run amuck on her property, she could be held responsible. Maybe she'd been teaching him witchcraft, turning him into some kind of drug-crazed lunatic. He and the girl might be part of her cult. The possibilities were endless. Reed could use this incident to discredit both of them or make it easier for Rodney to finish the job he'd been given.

In the meantime, Reed had to help Taylor get his story straight. Taylor was turning out to be as screwy as his mother. His job had been to check on the McCabe property for security reasons. Instead, he returned to the falls with a girl and ended up getting attacked by the boy he'd seen there and should have been watching out for. It would be pointless to berate him now when they needed to formulate a plan before morning. If possible, they'd have to keep the incident from Charlotte, at least for the time being. He didn't need another hysterical outburst from her.

Taylor sat watching his father consider the situation, as he'd done many times before, dreading his response. He was impressed with his father's ability to look at a problem from every angle and strategize before showing any reaction or speaking a word. Therefore, he was relieved when, instead of a scathing reprimand, his father asked him to repeat his story in detail, after which they sat for another hour creating an offensive plan in case one should be needed. Then both went to bed and slept soundly, Taylor from pure exhaustion, and Jordon with total faith in his own power.

It was almost morning when Farley returned to his office. He'd stayed at the cabin until an ambulance arrived to transport Willa Mae to the hospital. The ambulance driver had been warned ahead of time about the road and had been slow in getting there. Mamma Phoebe had reluctantly agreed that Willa

Mae would be safer in the hospital, with her father kept busy guarding over her. Frank Parsons had agreed with Farley that her condition be treated and verified and the attack reported. Pen was less cooperative and adamant that Raven return home with her and recover there, his condition and statement recorded in Farley's report.

Raven had wanted to go to the hospital to be with Willa Mae, but Mamma Phoebe convinced him otherwise, insisting he had a responsibility to recover from his concussion under the watchful care of his mother. It was obvious to Farley that Raven Cather was strong-willed, yet he had acquiesced to his mother and aunt, just as Farley had, to some degree. Mamma Phoebe reluctantly let them all go. Farley promised to return to check on her and keep her updated, assuring her that he would proceed with caution.

Now, Farley sat at his desk reviewing Raven Cather's statement. He rested his chin on his fists and thought about Charlotte and the effect it would have on her. He felt his legs begin to cramp and turned his swivel chair away from his desk to stretch them out. He turned off the desk lamp and leaned back in his chair. The sun would soon rise, but there in the dark before dawn, he thought of them all, apprehensive Mamma Phoebe and anxious Miss Pen, injured Raven and molested Willa Mae, incensed Frank Parson and fragile Charlotte. How helpless they seemed against the powerful force they were up against. But his suspicions were converging into a force of conviction he would use to protect them. He closed his eyes to rest them, and then fell asleep.

He hadn't slept long when the sounds of a waking town roused him. The Serena Grill had already opened, and a parallel line of new and old cars and pickup trucks were parked along Main Street. Construction workers, carpenters, plumbers, and Jacks of all trades were breakfasting early to be on the job by eight-thirty. Early-rising year-round and summer residents had joined the crowd and anyone else interested in local gossip and being in the know. Social divisions did not exist at the Serena Grill. There was not an empty booth, table, or counter stool by six-thirty when the scent of grilled sausage and bacon filled the air and found its way down the street into Farley's office.

The coffee-maker clicked on—the timer pre-set by Aura Lee—and the scent of brewing coffee reminded Farley of his empty stomach. He thought about going to the Grill for breakfast before going to Granger Realty. He'd decided to question Taylor there instead of at home in the presence of Charlotte. Charlotte would find out soon enough, and he wanted to spare her a surprise visit. Granger Realty opened at nine o'clock. There was plenty of time to grab a bite before Aura Lee arrived at eight-thirty.

He poured a cup of coffee and drank it before going into the back bathroom for a quick wash-up and shave. By the time he walked into the Grill, there were empty places at the counter. He ordered a platter of eggs, sausage, and grits. While waiting for them, he said "hey" to several people and helped himself to his second a cup of coffee.

When he returned to the office, Farley updated Aura Lee and swore her to secrecy. Her reaction was the complete opposite of what he'd expected. She became very quiet and looked upset.

"What's on your mind, Aura Lee?" he asked.

She hesitated and then said, "Chief, I'm worried about you. Are you sure about going after Taylor Reed? How do you know that Cather boy's telling the truth? Nobody knows much about him. He's been seen in town lately, stalking around the real estate office, probably upset about Taylor hanging around Willa Mae. Seems like he's got more to be upset about than Taylor Reed. Then you've got the mayor and commissioners all excited about having a party for his daddy, and you're thinking about maybe arresting his son?"

Farley opened his mouth to respond, but Aura Lee was on a roll and not to be stopped.

"Do you know how powerful that man is?" she asked, her voice rising an octave. "From what I hear, he's got a reputation for ruining people who get in his way. He even ruined a man who helped him get elected! I heard that from my friend down at the courthouse. There's already talk about you getting all high and mighty with him down at the restaurant while he was having his lunch and talkin' to the mayor. Some said you might be getting too big for your britches with all the publicity about you being a hero and how it's gone to your head. Now, you know that's not *my* thinking, but I hear things.

"I'm just saying, when you go asking questions like somebody's already guilty of something, it gets their back up, and do you want that kind of trouble? No one even knows where that Cather boy came from. He sure don't look like his mamma, and no one's ever explained how she came to have him. You might be stirring up a whole mess of bad business, Chief."

"I know you mean well, Aura Lee, but Taylor Reed has to be questioned, and that's what I'm about to do. While I'm out, check with Deputy Purdy and find out if he's learned anything more about the missing rooster."

After he was gone, Aura Lee felt tears well in her eyes and bowed her head in prayer. "Lordy, Lordy, Lord Almighty! He's about to get himself in a heap of trouble, and he's worried about a rooster. He'll be needin' you to look after him 'cause he won't listen to me. I've got to put him in your hands now 'cause he's just helpless, helpless, helpless. I've done all I could, praise be to you."

CHAPTER TWENTY-EIGHT

What may this mean
That thou, dead corpse, again in complete steel
Revisit'st thus glimpses of the moon
Making night hideous, and we fools of nature,
So horridly to shake our disposition
With thoughts beyond the reaches of our souls?
~ William Shakespeare, *Hamlet*

MAMMA PHOEBE'S BODY WAS IN a physical state of exhaustion, but her fertile mind was at work in her dreams. She'd been a sturdy woman all of her life, a woman of strength and substance. In her dream she witnessed her own transformation into a frail old woman, her height and weight diminishing, her ample size shrinking, her vulnerability increasing, and the sight of it was horrifying. The nightmare continued to strip her of her earthly form and external qualities. In the midst of her terror, she was suddenly surrounded by the specter of ghostly apparitions, swaying together in a phantom dance of supremacy, crowding in around her as she weakened in their suffocating presence. She looked up through the only space they had not taken and saw the yellow moon, round and full. A moonbeam streaked down like a bolt of lightning into her being, lighting a spark within that began to glow and flicker. The power of her internal spirit was ignited by this flame, and she spoke the words she had learned as a child, chanting the Hoodoo Candle Spell, using her internal light as the candle.

"Protection comes to me this day. This crossed condition goes away. Protection comes to me this day. The crossed condition goes away."

She said it over and over until the phantoms retreated and the moonlit sky opened around her and filled her spirit with the strength and stamina her body had lost.

She awoke from her dream with the gift of this knowledge, her apprehension gone. The power of her spirit was greater than any evil coming her way. She might be old, but the spirit was everlasting and eternally youthful.

Leaving her bed, she stood and listened to the silence of the morning. It was a gray morning. Storm clouds rolled across a colorless sky. The cotton-print curtains moved, the breeze picking up and blowing through the partially open window. It might have seemed gloomy if not for her revived spirit. Instead, it felt strange, too quiet, too still. Then she heard the warning caw of black crow, too loud, too near, and the soft sound of thumping on her front door. Awareness came over her, and she faced it head on. She'd known it was coming, and now it was here. The dream had been her preparation.

She straightened her back and held her chin high as she opened the door. Swinging gently before her was her rooster, hung with a rope around its neck and tied to a hook above her door, the hook for homemade wreaths at Christmastime.

She had to reach high to take her old friend down. She held him in her arms, ignoring the dried blood and his wrung neck. She laid him on her table and gathered her mortar and pestle. She spoke to him as though he was still alive, promising he would live again in three days' time. A thunder moon was on the rise and, until then, she would need him more than ever. After asking his brutalized corpse permission, she plucked some feathers and sliced a piece of flesh from his remains.

She went to work making a *Paket Kongo,* an onion-shaped, brightly colored, cloth-bound package filled with dragon's blood, five-finger grass, ginger, pine, and hyssop herbs, and the powdered flesh of her sacrificed rooster. She tied a string around it seven times, his large feathers sticking out of the top. The packet would be used to cast a spell and reverse the curse back to the one who did this. It would hang by her fireplace until the night of the full moon.

There was more to be done before then. Her cauldron would boil tonight, sending a curse in the smoke to be taken on the wind, returning to the perpetrator all the negativity being generated. The intention of this curse would be pronounced, beginning with the chant she had used in her dream. "Protection comes to me this day. This crossed condition goes away," followed by her determination to fight the source of the evil:

"Feather of fowl, slaughter and blood,
Root of the mandrake, red clay and mud,
Thunder moon rising, night black as coal,
Screech-owl a hootin', safe in his hole,
Stirrin' and brewin', smoke risin' high,
Curse on the devil, someone will die."

In the cabin across the high ridges, Pen was busy changing the dressing on Raven's head and checking his eyes for clearing and pupils for dilation. The signs of concussion were diminished, but the fury inside him was mounting. Somehow she had to stop him from seeking revenge. He would be ruined if he did. She pleaded with him to listen to her, to resist the temptation to act. She promised to take him to see Willa Mae; they would go together. She didn't want him going anywhere alone and implored him to let Chief Farley handle Taylor Reed.

Raven listened to his mother without response. He knew she was afraid for him. But it didn't matter. The grand plan she and Aunt Phoebe had for him meant nothing to him now. His vision had been blurry all through the night, but the sight of Willa Mae lying stricken upon the jagged rock was as clear in his mind as the sparkling waters of Raven Brook Falls. He could have lost her forever.

He couldn't remember how he'd gotten her to Aunt Phoebe. He'd been useless afterward and had little strength this morning. The concoction Aunt Phoebe had made him drink was still working in his system, keeping him subdued. He suspected his mother would give him more, either in food or drink. That didn't matter either. He was smart enough to know he had to get stronger before going after Taylor Reed. He could use some of what Aunt Phoebe had taught him, but he wasn't confident yet in those practices.

In truth, he wanted retribution on an equal level, because physically they were almost a perfect match. It had to be man-to-man, like a forest primeval battle of equals, if he was to exact utter and complete vengeance. He felt his soul blacken, but he didn't care. Taylor's day of reckoning would come.

The windowless hospital room where Willa Mae lay sleeping was cool, spartan, and sterile. Her father sat dozing after hours of constant vigil. When she opened her eyes, the stark white of her surroundings confused her senses. Her last memory was of lush green foliage and flowing blue waters and an image in the face of the rock. She recalled how it changed into the face of a demon as she stood below it staring, mesmerized. Then, something happened. She felt frightened and shivered under the sheet and light blanket, reaching over to feel the tube strapped to her arm. She tried to turn her head but her neck felt stiff. She tried again, drawn by the blinking light of the monitor.

She tried to speak, but her words came out as a whisper: "Raven."

Her father opened his eyes and said, "I'm here, Willa Mae. It's Daddy. I'm here." He sighed a silent prayer of gratitude and went to her bedside.

"Daddy."

"I'm here, darling."

"Raven?"

"He will be here soon. He had to go home for a little while, but he'll be here."

"What happened, Daddy? Why am I here?"

"Don't you remember? You were hurt, sweetheart. Do you remember what happened?"

Before Willa Mae could answer, the staff nurse came in and took over. She asked Frank to go to the waiting room temporarily. The resident physician came in as he was leaving. Frank wasn't offended. He had tears in his eyes.

Farley wasn't surprised to see the red sports car parked in the back lot of Granger Realty. He parked his cruiser next to it and entered the building through the back entrance. He knew the layout of the offices and bypassed Rodney Granger's office as he walked toward the front. Rodney's office door was closed. Taylor was at his desk in a cubicle near the main entrance. When Farley approached, he looked up at him with an expression of resignation. A square bandage was adhered to his right cheekbone. There was an uncovered scrape above his left eye.

"Good morning, Chief. You're probably not going to believe this, but I was about to call you."

"Is that so, Mr. Reed? Do you have a problem?"

"Maybe you'd better tell me why you're here first."

"I'd like you to come down with me to the station to answer a few questions. We can start with what you were doing last evening between the hours of six and ten o'clock."

Farley heard a door open followed by a loud voice and footsteps thundering down the hall.

"Chief Farley! We were just about to contact you. One of your locals attacked my son and the girl he was with last night."

Farley gazed squarely into Jordon Reed's eyes and raised an eyebrow. "Is that so?"

"I've contacted my attorney, but we're not going to make a public issue about it if you can assure me you will attend to his assailant. The kid is obviously deranged, and Taylor could have been seriously hurt or killed. The girl was apparently in cahoots with the boy—a setup from start to finish. Maybe they thought he was carrying a lot of money. No matter. Taylor had a right to be where he was, doing his job. It was the girl's idea to go there. That maniac was hiding in wait.

"You know, Chief, I came here to get some rest. But I have an interest in this town and I'm a tax-paying property owner. I don't throw my weight around here, never have. This isn't the first time my son has been targeted by an unscrupulous plan to get to me. You wouldn't believe what people will do to be paid off to keep quiet about a situation they've set up to make me look bad. And don't tell me these mountain boys aren't sophisticated enough; they can be as wily as a fox. He knows I hold public office and thinks I'm a target for easy money. He's probably got the girl playing along with him. Taylor says she's been flirting with him every time he goes into the market. Then she practically begged him to take her out to the McCabe property to see the falls. Why? And, what's that kid doing hanging around the McCabe property anyway?"

Farley had expected something like this but was amazed at the sheer audacity and ease with which Jordon Reed spouted his diatribe. Turning the tables on the victim was a common tactic used in the courtroom. Farley had no doubt if he pursued an attempt to arrest Taylor Reed, both Willa Mae and Raven would face a barrage of false accusations and character assassination. But Jordon Reed had made one honest statement in his offensive verbiage. Mountain boys *can* be wily as a fox, and Farley was one, born and raised.

"Then Taylor won't mind coming down to the station with me to make a statement, for the record and for his protection, should this require further action."

Jordon Reed replied, "As long as that's all it is, Chief, a statement. I'll have my attorney here by mid-afternoon if it leads to anything else. If it does, I'll have that kid charged with assault and battery and the girl charged along with him. Then we'll see how long they can afford a court-battle with the Reeds." Jordon Reed shot his son a look. "Taylor, you go with the Chief. I'll expect you back shortly. There are places I need to go by this afternoon. In the meantime, I'm having lunch with the mayor, and as of now, this incident will not be part of our discussion."

Jordon Reed turned and walked down the hall and back into Rodney's office. Taylor stood up and followed Farley out to the cruiser. Rodney watched from his office window and then sat down at his desk across from Jordon Reed and finished reporting on the old woman.

"She's got a sister named Penelope Cather. Most people don't associate the two and, to tell you the truth, neither did I. I found out that she works at the Orchard Lake Inn and lives out back in one of their old cottages. Pretty much stays up there on the ridge. The boy belongs to her, but from what I can gather, she adopted him when he was a baby. I tried to find out more about where he came from but haven't had any luck so far. My sources tell me most folks thought he came from a relative, but he looks more Cherokee than black." He shrugged. "You never know anymore. Anyway, they were all there last night, the Cather woman and the girl's father, Frank Parsons. I know him, but not well. Would you believe it? He was a friend of Caleb Thompson! He lives up on the ridge near the inn. The girl and the boy are practically neighbors.

"His name is Raven Cather. He's a strange bird, been home-school raised and keeps to himself, doesn't have any friends in town and never went to a real school. I don't know why he's been hanging around the old woman, except she's like an aunt of sorts."

Jordon rubbed his jaw and nodded for Rodney to continue.

"I had just gotten there and was close to the cabin when he brought the girl there last night. Carried her from the falls. The other two came later, and then Chief Farley. He almost hit me coming down the road. Luckily, I jumped out of the way. Don't worry. He didn't see me. I waited half the night until they took the girl away in an ambulance." Rodney had reported before Chief Farley arrived that Willa Mae and Raven were alive, that in fact the girl was in the hospital, and the boy had been well enough to return home with his mother. "I stayed around long enough to play a hoodoo trick on the old woman. I imagine will scare some sense into her before she starts thinking about taking action. At her age, a sudden shock could do her in, or at the least, shut her up. Now that we know about her sister, at least we know who we're dealing with. If she cares about that boy, we might have some leverage to keep her quiet."

Jordon shook his head. "Whatever their association, the old woman has to go. I don't need to know what you did last night, but she's got to be put out of the picture. Who knows, she might have a will leaving everything to the sister. You've got to find out. Now that we know about the water rights, we've got to have her property too, but not right away. If the sister tries to claim it, it must seem as though we're doing her a favor by purchasing it. Yeah, maybe then she could afford to send the boy to a real school. If she wants that kid alive or out of prison, she'd better cooperate. But it still bothers me that the old woman and the kid have been hanging around the falls. If she has an inkling of its worth, maybe he does too. That puts a different light on the matter. They might all have to go."

Rodney listened but found it hard to speak. He thought it would be finished when McCabe was found dead. Reed thinking about getting rid of the hoodoo woman's family was a scary proposition to consider. He'd have to play along, or he'd likely be next "to go." It might be better to be a struggling realtor than an almost-rich, dead man. The money was still an incentive, but the stakes were getting too high.

"And another thing," Jordon added, "Chief Farley may be the big fish of the moment around here, strutting around playing John Wayne in his very small pond, but if he doesn't back off and keep my boy's name out of this mess, I'll crush him as easily as stepping on an ant."

Rodney suddenly had a visual image of himself, splattered under Jordon Reed's shoe.

CHAPTER TWENTY-NINE

There is no present or future—
only the past, happening over and over again—now.
~ Eugene O'Neill, *Moon for the Misbegotten*

CHARLOTTE REED REACHED DOWN BENEATH the bodice of her nightgown and felt the amulet Nanny Pen had placed around her neck. It had done its job, calmed her and put her overactive mind at rest. Her heartbreak over Henry's loss would be unbearable if not for its magical effect. It was the not knowing that would have debilitated her, for in his majestic bearing and protective nature, he represented all the strength she had left. How could anyone be so cruel as to take him from her? Yet she knew who could be that cruel. He'd taken her son and corrupted him. He'd broken her heart and then tried to break her spirit by making her feel hopeless and insignificant, and now he was playing the devoted husband in this last despicable act of deception. But he hadn't counted on Nanny Pen, and he certainly hadn't counted on Jeff Farley. Nor had she.

It was a miracle, she thought. The very sight of him had brought it all back. He was the same as he had been, the boy she'd been drawn to when she could have had her choice of many others. But the others hadn't looked at her the way he had. She'd seen it in his eyes, devotion so clearly present and love so deep and true. She'd been happy in his presence, her imagination free and unencumbered, her fairy-tale dreams realized by his efforts and acceptance of her. They were the simple dreams of an innocent girl, but she'd been allowed to have them, culminating into that one night under the harvest moon, when all was bliss and she knew that heaven existed.

She'd been taken away from him into a world of harsh reality, where fairy-tale dreams were mocked and fairy-tale wishes were never granted. But she'd returned, and all the hope taken from her was being given back by those who truly loved her. She'd been forgiven because they were good and kind and noble and strong. She'd have to be strong too, and brave, because if Jordon thought for a minute she was getting help and getting stronger, he would go after the source of her strength, just as he had with Henry. For once she had to think like Jordon instead of being a victim of his nefarious manipulations.

Charlotte was convinced he came to Serena for an unscrupulous business deal with Rodney Granger. He wouldn't have Taylor working for him otherwise. It must have something to do with land investment. She didn't understand why he might want land, but there had to be profit involved. Jordon always needed money. He'd spent a fortune staying in office, most of it hers. He probably would have taken it all had her father not tied a substantial part of her inheritance in a trust that would transfer to Taylor upon her death. Taylor's trust was also sizable, and Jordon had envied his son for this reason, keeping him under his thumb with his eye on the prize. Taylor would inherit a yearly sum for life when he reached age twenty-five. Charlotte had hoped to restore their relationship before then and influence Taylor not to allow Jordon to drain his inheritance by enlisting him in some of his schemes. Maybe his deal with Rodney was meant to tide him over until Taylor came into his money. Or maybe Jordon had bigger plans, something that might pay off big like the lottery.

Charlotte was determined to keep her thinking realistic instead of retreating into an avoidance fantasy world as she had in Charleston. She remembered something Kate's friend, Dev, had shared after they'd brought her home the day of Henry's disappearance. Dev had sat with her for a while until Jordon came home. He'd talked of his life before becoming a psychologist, and what had brought him to make the decision to change it, which had been his salvation. His decision had been influenced by a recovering alcoholic who had asked him, "Do you want to kill yourself, or kill the life you are living?" She realized, as he must have, that she wanted to kill the life she was living.

Jordon Reed had lied when he'd told Farley he would not be discussing the incident with the mayor. He'd talked to his attorney before meeting Mayor Tyler for lunch and was buoyed by the aggressive actions he was prepared to take if given the word. After an hour of small talk and discussion about the upcoming event in his honor, Jordon insisted they continue on a first-name basis.

"Confidentially, Ben, your chief of police is becoming a real thorn in my side. You may have to have a talk with him. My son had a little problem last night with a couple of locals, and he's blowing it out of proportion. I had a rather tense exchange with Farley this morning and afterward contacted my attorney.

"Your chief is putting this town in a bad light. You witnessed how he talked to me the last time we were in here. I let that go, but now he's back with an axe to grind. A man gets some attention, and the next thing you know, he thinks he can throw his weight around to get more, thinks people will be impressed if he stands up to someone like me. It would be in your best interest, Mayor, and the town's, if you do something about him, before I have to."

Mayor Tyler scratched the back of his neck and said, "Could you tell me about the problem your son had? I hadn't heard about it."

Jordon waved off the subject. "That's not important. The issue is being handled. What is important is whether or not you are willing to deal with your chief of police. You and your commissioners hired him, and you can fire him. With his recent reputation, he could find another job with no problem. Wouldn't that be better than my having to go after him with all my power and resources? Think about it, Ben. But don't think too long. Now if you'll excuse me, I have a busy afternoon."

Jordon Reed left the mayor sitting at the table, staring into his cup of cold coffee. He felt sick to his stomach. A memory rose from boyhood of a kid at school who had bullied him relentlessly, making his life a living hell for almost a year. Buddy Johnson was a name he'd never forget. He could see Buddy clearly in his mind's eye, along with his group of friends; they followed him around everywhere, acted tough when with him, and did whatever he told them to do. Buddy taunted him at every opportunity, "Hey, it's Benny Henny the chicken, cluck, cluck, cluck, cluck, cluck, cluck," and then his cohorts would join in and laugh uproariously. It happened daily in the school hallways or anywhere else they happened upon him. They would knock him into the lockers or trip him so he would fall. It happened when he was alone or in front of the other kids, but never when an adult was around.

If he'd have stood up to Buddy, which he hadn't, his gang would have backed Buddy up. There'd been no way to win and nowhere to turn. Snitching then was worse than being afraid, so he'd stayed afraid for months until school was out for the summer. But even during that summer, he'd lived with the dread of returning to school in the fall. It was the same sick feeling he had in his stomach now. Back then he'd been given a reprieve because Buddy hadn't returned to school; his family had moved to another state. His gang disbanded without leadership.

The bullying had stopped, but the constant anxiety stayed with him until junior high when he'd found a place for himself in school leadership. He'd felt empowered when chosen for minor positions, and the fear eventually dissipated when he'd been elected class president his senior year. From school government to small town governing, he'd continued to hold office, and his terms were typically extended. He was judicial and calm, fair-minded and just, didn't throw his weight around, and generally avoided controversy. He didn't aspire to greatness and had no political ambition beyond his role as mayor of Serena. He was happy to be a big fish in a small pond, much like he had been in high school. He hadn't been bullied since—not until now.

Mayor Tyler knew Jeff Farley but didn't know him well. No one did, really. Farley was his own man; his position as chief did not define him. He was friendly but aloof, a man of few words. He wasn't the type to call attention to himself in the way Reed suggested. Besides, the attention he got last year had been well-deserved. The residents of Serena were proud to have such a man as chief of police. He'd noticed no change in the man since, nor had anyone talked about him being big-headed or overstepping his bounds. He had been shocked when Jeff confronted Reed in his presence, but after consideration, the mayor thought he must have had a good reason. The man didn't act without reason, not in the years he'd been chief. *Now I'm supposed to fire him? And what will happen if I don't?* The look in Reed's eyes was a look he remembered well. He'd seen it in the eyes of Buddy Johnson.

Mayor Tyler paid the check and left the restaurant. He casually greeted everyone he met along the way down the street toward the storefront city hall. When he reached the police station next door, he stopped and went in. Aura Lee looked up from her computer and gave him a genuine smile.

"Good afternoon, Aura Lee. Is the chief in?"

"He's with someone in the back office, Mayor. I'd better let him tell you about it. There's been a bit of bad business you may have already heard about. I'll let him know you're here."

The police station was divided into two sections by a wall constructed midway across the long narrow building. The rear section was closed to the public except for visitors to the jail and those being questioned or interviewed. The back area was accessed by an alcove-shaped doorway leading to the interview office, adjacent bathrooms, elevator to the upper floors, and jail cells. Aura Lee called to Chief Farley from the alcove doorway and then motioned to Mayor Tyler to join him.

"Chief, I've come down here to find out what is going on. I just had lunch with Jordon Reed, and he's upset with you, to say the least. He didn't go into detail but said you've been stepping out-of-line and that you're after more publicity. Now, I don't believe that for a minute, but I need you to be straight with me and tell me what this is all about. I was standing right there when you insulted him down at the restaurant. And what's this little problem everyone but me seems to know about? Who were you questioning back here, and why?"

Farley looked up at him and then back down at the report he'd been writing and then made a decision.

"Mayor, let's put my beef with the congressman on hold right now and discuss the problem concerning his son."

"His son! Taylor? Are you going to tell me you had *Taylor* in here for questioning?"

"There was an incident last night, and I was called out to Mamma Phoebe's place, out next to Purvis McCabe's land. It seems Taylor took Willa Mae Parsons out there to show her the falls and allegedly tried to rape her. She fought him and was thrown to the ground and severely injured. Raven Cather came upon this scene and attacked Taylor Reed. During the scuffle, Raven tried to help Willa Mae and was struck from behind by Taylor. Taylor left them both unconscious and went home. Raven Cather regained consciousness and carried Willa Mae to Mamma Phoebe's for help. She tended to both of them before I was called. When I arrived, her sister, Penelope Cather, was there with Frank Parsons. Willa Mae was stable but unconscious, and an ambulance was called to take her to the hospital. I called there this morning, and she is awake but remembers nothing. We have only Raven Cather's word to go on. He is currently at home in his mother's residence recovering from a concussion. Frank Parsons is at the hospital with Willa Mae.

"Taylor Reed has a completely different story. He claims he was enticed by Willa Mae and attacked by Raven Cather. He says Willa Mae got knocked down trying to help Raven. He says he left the scene to save his life and that they are falsely accusing him to get money from his father. Jordon Reed threatens to press charges and has already contacted an attorney. He says he will not pursue this if I see to it that Raven Cather is 'put in his place,' whatever that means.

"Reed said, 'If Cather persists with his absurd accusation, he will be destroyed in the courtroom by my attorneys, along with his girlfriend's reputation.'"

Mayor Tyler sat down and said nothing. Jeff Farley leaned back in his chair and waited for him to digest the information. He was in no hurry to be told to comply with Jordon Reed's wishes. He was not about to, and he knew it could mean the loss of his job.

Mayor Tyler breathed in deeply, cleared his throat, and sat up straight in his chair, giving the impression he was about to say something of grave importance. Farley prepared for the inevitable and was shocked when the mayor said, "Sounds like there's a need for more evidence before an arrest can be made. Do what you need to do, Chief. You have my backing."

He stood up and extended his arm for a handshake. Farley stood up too, in a gesture of surprised respect, and shook hands. Mayor Ben Tyler turned with back straight and head held high and walked out of the room.

A few minutes later, Farley called to Aura Lee. "Would you please get the magistrate on the line for me? Then, check with the medical examiner to find out if the detailed toxicology report I requested is back. When you're done, would you make another pot of coffee? I'm going to need it. Also, send Deputy Purdy back here when he comes in. I want a report on that missing rooster."

Aura Lee rolled her eyes at his last request and then set about her tasks with expediency and efficiency. By early afternoon, Farley had the information he needed and clarity of purpose with which to move forward. But there was one thing he had to do first, and it wouldn't be easy. He had to talk to Charlotte, and he wanted to see her alone.

He called the Reed home, and Charlotte answered the phone. She seemed pleased to hear his voice and was receptive to his request to meet him at Miss Pen's cottage behind the Orchard Lake Inn.

She made no mention of the incident at the falls and didn't sound upset. During questioning, Taylor said he'd gotten home late and told his father about what happened, but not his mother. They had apparently left together this morning without seeing Charlotte or letting her know anything about it. He was glad to have the opportunity to tell her before they did, and hopefully in the presence of Penelope Cather.

Rodney Granger rested in his office, taking no calls. It had been a long night and stressful morning, and he felt the need of a nap. Later, he would pay another visit to Mamma Phoebe's cabin, but in the light of day. After the fright he'd given her, she might be receptive to the idea of selling her property. This would solve everything, including the issue of a will. No harm in asking before taking more drastic steps to ensure her cooperation. He'd give the old witch a chance—it was the least he could do. If it didn't work, Reed would never have to know.

When he drove up to the cabin later that day, he noticed the rooster had been removed from the hook. He approached cautiously and then knocked at her door. She didn't answer. He stared at the blood splatters while waiting, then knocked again. The door opened slowly.

"Hello, ma'am. I hope I'm not disturbing you. My name is Rodney Granger. I'm a local realtor handling the McCabe property. I'd like to ask you a few questions, if you don't mind. It will take only a few minutes of your time."

Mamma Phoebe opened the door all the way. Rodney was startled by her appearance. She was dressed in colorful garb as though to attend a festival. She wore a bright yellow scarf around her head and apple red beads around her throat. Her eyes drew his attention toward them; her gaze was magnetic. He had expected a smaller, frail woman. She was almost his height. She did not invite him in, nor did she speak. He felt awkward and unsure of what to say. She did not look frightened, but instead seemed frightening. He apologized for the intrusion. She said nothing in response. He made himself talk, feeling foolish and ridiculous.

"Miss Phoebe, I've come to inquire about an agreement you might have had with Purvis McCabe. We are under the understanding that the water rights you and he shared are subject to change should the McCabe property be sold. Could you enlighten me about the agreement? At present the land is held under the auspices of probate court, but at some point will be put on the market as there are no apparent heirs interested in making a claim. It's my job to have his land surveyed and have all the proper documentation in place. That's why I'm here. I hope you'll be willing to help me. I understand you've lived here about as long as Purvis McCabe . . . I don't suppose you'd consider selling your land? You know us realtors. We're always looking to handle a sale. This is a unique opportunity you should consider. The sale of both properties would bring a better price, and I have a potential investor."

He kept on talking, the words flowing from his mouth like a waterfall. He couldn't stop or control what he was saying. He was sharing everything he'd planned to avoid mentioning. She had yet to say a word or move an inch from the doorway. He continued to talk as he backed away and almost lost his footing. A large black bird flew overhead, cawing at him, and then another appeared, and another. He felt like a piece of road-kill, except he was still alive. The sound of their cawing pierced his eardrums. He placed his hands over his ears and swayed to and fro in a state of misery and terror. Her eyes bore into his despite the space between them. He tried to turn away, but couldn't.

Then suddenly, mercifully, she let him go. The passenger side of his car was closer so he ran to yank the door open. He jumped in and grasped the steering wheel to pull himself over to the driver's side. The blackbirds swooped down, and one almost got in before he could reach and pull the door shut. His trembling fingers made it difficult to start the car. Mamma Phoebe was no longer in the doorway, but her presence was all around him. He drove like a maniac down the deep rutted road, throwing his vehicle out of alignment and praying to reach the end before his heart gave out. When he turned onto the mountain road, he was shaking all over. He sped around the curves to get as far away as fast as he could. He swore to God he would never step foot on the old woman's property again, the same God he had forsaken when he'd made his pact with the devil—Jordon Reed.

Mamma Phoebe sat down in her rocker and decided the time had come. The will would have to be presented, but not yet. She knew what they were after now, but not why. She would have to trust Chief Farley, and he would have to trust her. In three days' time, under the full thunder moon, she would perform her ritual and set things in motion. He would have to do his part to keep her family safe until then. The demon would be called to his place of revelation, and his end time would come—hopefully before hers.

CHAPTER THIRTY

As the moon is more interested in the earth than in any other thing, there is always some woman more interested in a man's mind than anything else, who is willing to follow it sentence by sentence.

~ George Moore

PENELOPE CATHER WAS BUSY AT work in the kitchen of the inn. She'd left Raven at home resting and was hopeful the draught would allow him to sleep for a while. When she came out into the dining room to check the table settings, the front-desk receptionist, in a manner suggesting great inconvenience, presented her with a phone message. Pen remembered a time when others had mistaken her humility and quiet bearing for meekness and servitude. She thought this girl was simply immature and self-important, perhaps compensating for deeper insecurities. She paid her no mind, having more important problems to consider.

After reading the message, she arranged to be done by mid-afternoon. There was no time for a break before then, with the dining room filling and only one server waiting tables. She was tempted to check on Raven anyway but decided against it. He'd be anxious to visit Willa Mae if awake, and she'd have to convince him all over again to wait until this evening.

Raven *was* awake—and restless—and had to move. Taking the extra set of keys from the drawer, he left the cabin and took the path skirting the inn to the parking lot where the pickup truck was parked off from the guest parking area. His mother would be busy for another three hours, plenty of time to get to the hospital and back and check on the whereabouts of Taylor Reed.

He felt a bit shaky on his feet, but the throbbing in his head had stopped and his vision had cleared. He started the engine and took off down the long descending driveway, thinking it likely the truck would not be missed during that time of day.

This was his first trip to the county hospital, but he found his way with no problem. He had an inherited internal compass with an arrow pointing to Willa Mae this day.

When he found her room, he entered quietly. She looked like a sleeping angel, despite the IV-drip tube in her arm and bandaged head. Her eyes opened to see him standing there. A tear ran down her cheek, and she tried to smile. He took her small hand in his and said her name, softly and tenderly.

Her eyes glistened with tears and she said, "I've been waiting."

"You've been waiting for me for too long. I'm here now, and for always."

He left before her father returned from lunch in the hospital cafeteria. She'd fallen asleep again, a sleep of contentment, with joy in the knowledge he would never abandon her again. She'd been a part of him as long as she could remember. They were outsiders who had been given the gift of each other. Their world was the blue mountain ridges and the land of their heritage. They were as much a part of their natural surroundings as the forest and wildlife and mountain streams.

Raven drove the beat-up pickup into town, knowing it was a mistake and not caring. He passed the police station and Chief Farley's cruiser. He thought about stopping to find out about Taylor, but thought better of it. He drove on to Granger Realty and checked out the back parking lot. There was no red sports car. He wondered if Farley had him locked up in jail. He drove the winding back roads and up the hill to the Reed's summer home. The red car was not in the driveway. He took this to mean he was free and roaming around somewhere. It was useless to try to find him this way. He drove back to the inn and parked the truck. His muscles felt sore, and his head was starting to ache. He went back to the cottage and laid down on his bed. Before long, he fell asleep and began dreaming.

In his dream, Raven was chasing a figure, illusive and obscure. They were in a dark forest. The forest became a maze, and then a roadway. He was in the old pickup, trying to catch the red sports car. He continued to lose ground until the road ahead came to a dead end. The car had disappeared and yet there had been nowhere to exit. He got out of the truck and walked away from it, looking around. He heard the truck engine start and turned to see someone sitting at the steering wheel. He couldn't move. The driver stared at him, and then put the truck in reverse and turned it around and drove away. The driver was Taylor Reed. The dream ended, but Raven did not awaken. The need for rest had overtaken him. He was still asleep when his mother came home.

Pen looked in on her son and then prepared the table for her visitors, setting out teacups and cookies, milk and a half-full honey pot. She lit a low flame under the tea kettle and fussed about the tidy cabin. She left the door open so she could see through the screen door to let them in without waking Raven.

Charlotte arrived first, followed by Jeff Farley. Pen felt grateful to see him again. She closed Raven's bedroom door and let them know he was resting. Farley got right to the point and explained why he had come.

"Miss Pen, I wanted to talk to Charlotte in your presence. I asked her to meet me here because she needs to hear this from both of us. She doesn't know about last night."

Clearly alarmed, Charlotte asked, "What is it, Jeff?"

In a low voice, Farley proceeded to explain, describing the incident as told from both sides. Miss Pen poured the tea while he talked, and then she encouraged Charlotte to take a sip. She did and then held Pen's hand until Farley finished. By then she had finished her tea.

"Charlotte, I know very little about Taylor or Raven. Perhaps each of you could help me understand more about them. I have to investigate the incident and have been asked to use caution. I'm trying to do this now, before I move forward. Please know that I wouldn't hurt either of you if I could help it. But a young woman almost lost her life yesterday, and I can't just let that go or be involved in a cover-up."

Miss Pen answered first. Charlotte's reaction was subdued.

"Charlotte, did you know I have a son? He was the blessing I received after grieving the loss of you and my late husband. He's been a joy to me since, and my life has been built around him. I know you felt the same way about Taylor when he was a child. I don't know what I would have done if someone tried to take Raven away from me the way Jordon took Taylor from you. What I do know is that my boy wouldn't do what Taylor has accused him of, nor would Willa Mae. Why, she's the sweetest child you'd ever meet, and innocent in her ways, too innocent for knowing what she'd gotten herself into. Raven was trying to protect her, I know that. I'm so sorry, Miss Charlotte. You were always like my own child, and I love you. But my boy is the moon and the stars to me, and it isn't in his nature to lie."

Charlotte looked at Pen and then lowered her head in sorrow. "I tried so hard to be a good mother, but I was lost in a world of fantasy. I tried to make Taylor into a little prince in my make-believe kingdom. He was a good boy, a sweet boy, but I made him the center of my life, and no child should be put in that position. I see it now, but I was blind then. At the most impressionable time in a boy's life, he escaped me for the freedom Jordon offered. Now my son has come to this." She looked up again, shaking her head with sorrow in her eyes. "He and his father are probably plotting at this moment; it's what they do. Whenever Taylor gets into trouble, Jordon gets him out so that Taylor will owe him allegiance. He led his son down the road to perdition in order to use and control him, but Jordon also envies his youth, physical prowess, and his inheritance. I've seen it, sensed it, and have been sickened by it."

She gave a laugh that was bereft of humor and said, "For some reason, I thought I had a chance this summer, one last chance to save Taylor. I had Henry to help me and was feeling hopeful. Jordon's coming here was not part of my plan. At first I thought he came because he was afraid I might win Taylor's love again—a delusion on my part. Taylor was aloof from the beginning and found one excuse after another to avoid spending time with me. When his father arrived, they resumed their father and son collusion, from which I was excluded. Henry saw through Jordon right away. He tried to alert me to his evil intent, but I was hesitant to act. Henry was so brave and gallant, confronting Jordon as he did, and it cost my poor darling his life."

"Now, Charlotte. We don't know that for sure." Pen put her arm around Charlotte.

Farley waited, feeling helpless, wanting to comfort her too, and watching Pen with admiration. Once again, he felt pulled into Charlotte's world, just as he had when they'd first met, only now the rooster was the hero instead of him—and a martyred hero at that. He felt mildly jealous and wondered if he was losing his grip. He blamed it on lack of sleep. Purdy had better find out what happened to that bird. Charlotte needed some closure in that area of her life.

The effects of the herbal tea and the warmth of Pen's embrace combined to give Charlotte courage. She looked across the table into the steady green eyes of the man to whom she would entrust her son's future.

No one could stand up to Jordon Reed. He rolled over his accusers like he'd rolled over his political opponents. But if somehow Taylor could face the consequences of his actions, it might be his salvation. She could think of no other way. She felt grateful the girl he had harmed was in stable condition. Maybe there was a chance for him.

She said, "Taylor has done wrong in the past, but nothing like this. I fear he will continue if not stopped. I love my son. I believe he is as much a victim of his father as I have been. The only hope I have for him is a chance at redemption. I had the most enlightening conversation with your friend, Dev. He shared with me how he found redemption from his past by killing the life he'd been leading. My son has been caught in a trap of his father's making, and he needs help to find his a way out. I cannot believe the sweet child he once was is beyond hope. I trust you will do what is right, Jeff."

Before Farley had a chance to respond, Raven Cather opened his bedroom door and walked into the room. Charlotte had her back to him and turned as Pen introduced them. The unexpected sight of him was a shock. She heard herself saying the right words while trying not to stare. There was something in the way he moved as he walked around the table to shake hands with Jeff. She recalled a song by the Beatles, and was struck by its meaning. He was a beautiful young man, primarily his coloring and sapphire blue eyes. But there was something intangible and strangely familiar. Where had he come from, this adversary of her son?

Farley asked Raven if he could have a word with him outside. This gave Charlotte a chance to talk to Pen in private, but she did not question her about Raven. She was concerned about returning home, unsure of her ability to handle the situation there. Jordon would have to tell her about Taylor, and both would expect her to support their story. Pen gave her what she needed, warning her again about dosage and overuse. She praised Charlotte for her courage and warned her to be cautious.

"There is a thunder moon rising, Charlotte. Over the next three days, the spirits will be alive in the winds, and the storm clouds will unsettle the skies. But there will be no cleansing rain until the moon is full and the thunder has its say. It is the night when evil is forced out into the open and revealed in its human form. Be strong, my dear Charlotte, and careful until the moon comes to fullness. My sister is a very powerful woman. She has set things in motion. You have the protection of my amulet and the knowledge I have taught you. It won't be long now."

Farley's conversation with Raven was quite different.

"I'm glad to see you're in better condition today. That was a nasty wallop to your head, and you were pretty much in a daze last night. So imagine my surprise when my secretary told me she saw you driving through town a few hours ago. And don't tell me you were running errands for the inn."

"No, Chief. I won't tell you that. But don't say anything. My mother doesn't know I took the truck. I promised her I'd stay home and rest, but I couldn't. I had to see Willa Mae. I had to know she is all right."

Farley crossed his arms. "You also promised me you'd let me do my job without interference. Do your promises mean anything?"

Raven felt stung by Farley's words and became defensive. "I can't just sit back and let him get away with what he did to her." His gaze became accusatory. "You don't even have him in jail! He left her for dead, and I can't let that go. I've got to settle this with him, in my own way."

"I can understand how you feel, Raven. But you don't know what you're up against. This can be turned back on you. His father has the power to do it. Your mother and aunt know that. If you go after him, you might be the one who ends up in jail. What good would that do anyone? You'd leave Willa Mae unprotected and break your mother's heart. Jordon Reed will not only go after you, he'll go after Willa Mae. He has powerful friends in the justice system. He's already on the muscle, and Taylor Reed is denying everything, accusing you of being the aggressor."

"That scum! How can you expect me to sit back and let him get away with this? It's not natural, not right. You of all people, knowing how it is here, knowing I can't let another man avenge Willa Mae. She's *my* responsibility, Chief, and I already let her down. I should have finished the job while I had my hands on him. I've got to finish it now."

Farley gripped Raven by the shoulders. "Now you listen to me. I'm not asking you, I'm telling you. You've got to hold back. I need time to put together a good case against Taylor *and* his father. There's more going on here than you realize, and some of it involves your Aunt Phoebe. There might be a way you can help me if you can get your mind to thinking straight. But I don't want your mother knowing about it. If you're feeling well enough to be running around in broad daylight, how would you feel about doing a little undercover work for me in your own territory?"

Raven looked at him and held back for a moment, allowing his mind to calm and make sense of what he was hearing. Fatigue followed the aftermath of his outburst. He'd been taught to think before acting, to resist negative impulses, but he'd never been put to the test. He'd seen his mother put to the test many times, and he'd tried to follow her example. But this situation was different, or was it? Either way, he shouldn't be going off half-cocked.

"What do you have in mind, Chief?"

CHAPTER THIRTY-ONE

There are nights when the wolves are silent and only the moon howls.

~ George Carlin

CHARLOTTE ARRIVED HOME IN TIME to prepare for the cocktail hour. She actually enjoyed the process, arranging the martini shaker, taking the Russian vodka from the freezer, stuffing the olives (a specialty she'd learned from Nanny Pen), and arranging the festive napkins on a tray. She was sure Jordon would need a drink before telling her about Taylor, and she was eager to hear his spin on the incident. He probably feared she would have a meltdown—silly man.

Since coming to terms with the truth about herself, she no longer felt intimidated by him. It was up to her to change. She remembered how her father had ruled over her mother. She had to be at his beck and call every minute of the day, until she got sick. Charlotte often wondered if her mother's chronic illness was an unconscious form of escape from him. But Charlotte had been blessed with Nanny Pen, who was just a young girl at the time, yet more independent than her mother could ever hope to be. She didn't blame her mother; she'd been raised to be obedient, and her father had been authoritarian. It was a different time and culture then. But she'd been raised after a social revolution, and after all this time, it was finally kicking in. Jordon Reed was an imposter who had fooled her father, his political supporters, the voters, and his son. But not her, not anymore.

Manny Carlson, Jordon's attorney, had flown in from Charleston that afternoon, rented a car, and met with Jordon and Taylor in Rodney's offices. For some unknown reason, Rodney was a no-show. His secretary had no explanation. Jordon was infuriated by his absence but went ahead with the meeting anyway, discussing Taylor's options and how they should proceed. He was outraged when Taylor told him Chief Farley warned him not to leave town during his ongoing investigation of the assault. Contrary to what he'd told Farley, Jordon didn't want to press charges against Raven Cather unless absolutely necessary. Carlson suggested they wait for Farley to show his hand, citing the lack of evidence in their favor.

But Jordon wasn't persuaded. He wasn't accustomed to being told to wait for a local yokel to dictate his actions. He'd let Manny take care of the legal machinations while he took care of a few other things on his own. He didn't bother to call Charlotte to let her know he was bringing a guest home. He was grateful to have a third party in residence when he had to tell her about Taylor.

Charlotte was indeed surprised, but relieved as well. She feigned shock and distress when Jordon, in the privacy of the den, explained the situation to her and asked for her unconditional support of their son. Of course he lied and minimized the incident, saying it would all be cleared up by their attorney. He asked that she not discuss it with anyone, including Taylor. He told her it would be best if she and Taylor returned to Charleston at the first opportunity, that he and Manny could handle things much better if they were not in Serena. He said their trip would have to wait a few days due to investigative nonsense being conducted by the local chief of police, but there was nothing to worry about. It would give her time to pack and take care of necessities before returning home, where she belonged anyway.

After their conversation, he rejoined Taylor and Manny on the veranda, where he consumed two more martinis before Charlotte served a hastily prepared dinner. Taylor excused himself after eating very little and went to his room. Manny made his apologies and retired to the guest room. Jordon, with slurred speech, requested an after-dinner drink. Charlotte happily obliged him. He took it, staggered into his den, slumped into his oversized leather chair, and began to sip. *The drink tastes like ambrosia,* he thought. *What does she put in this drink to make it taste so good?*

His head began to loll, and a strange sensation took hold of his body. He got up and stumbled to the stairs, bumping the wall and holding onto the banister for support. He made it to his bedroom and shut the door, falling onto the bed and then into oblivion.

In the bedroom down the hall, Taylor wasn't sleeping. He felt sick, but not from the martini (he'd had only one) or the pot he'd smoked in his room. He'd felt sick all day after being questioned by Chief Farley. Farley hadn't believed a word he'd said. He'd felt small in Farley's presence, small and ashamed. He'd been in trouble before, but this time was different. The difference was Farley. He was like something out of a novel. *He's not going to let this go. He's not going to stop, no matter what my father says. I know it. I'm tired. Tired of everything, tired of my life and living on the edge. Dad and Manny think this is nothing but a big game, another fix in their world of countless fixes. They can fix everything but the guilt.*

Farley had made him feel guilty, and that was a bummer. Now he just wanted it to go away. He reached down to the box and took out another joint. After a while, he drifted away to Neverland.

Charlotte finished in the kitchen and went out to the veranda. It was a warm night, a night for crickets and lightning bugs, but she heard not a sound. As Nanny Pen had predicted, there were stirrings in the air. She watched as the clouds moved across the sky, hiding the stars and muting the moon into an opaque luminous orb, eerie and silent. The house was quiet too. She'd seen to that.

She reflected on the evening and the orders she'd been given. *So, he's made his plans for me. I'm to go to Charleston and resume my life there. He doesn't know it yet, but soon will. My life there is dead and buried.*

It was a rough morning for the men in the Reed summer home. They couldn't seem to get moving. Memories of the night before were forgotten. Each assumed he was the only one suffering from malaise, and each made an attempt to appear eager for the day. It was easier for Jordon, who'd received a call from Rodney indicating he had good news. A meeting was scheduled for mid-morning. Jordon told Charlotte not to bother making breakfast for them. They were going to the Serena Grill to put on a good front. If word had gotten out about the accusation against Taylor, he wanted him to project the image of innocence. He'd learned this strategy in Washington.

Charlotte waited until mid-morning to call Kate and ask if she could stop by for a visit. She wanted to thank Kate and Dev personally for their kindness. She had no intention of leaving Serena ever again, and they were the only friends she'd made thus far. They had accepted her without judgment when she must have seemed crazy. She had to let Dev know how much his talk with her had helped. She also wanted to tell them about Taylor and request their professional guidance in helping him at some point.

Rodney Granger was still shaken from the day before as evidenced by a slight tremor at the corner of his mouth and a barely discernible twitch in his right eye. Three cups of coffee had helped. He'd come into his office early after a night of terrifying dreams and a strange new fear of being home alone. When the phone call came from the courthouse, letting him know that a claim had been made on the property, he'd been relieved. But even more so when he learned that one of the McCabe brothers, Marcus, had died two years ago and the other, Virgil, would either claim as entitled next of kin or purchase it to sell from a distance, allowing a local realtor to handle the sale.

Since Purvis died intestate, without leaving a will, the stipulation of father to son would hold and Virgil McCabe would be required to purchase the property in order to sell. Rodney would handle the property assessment. With no other living heirs to come forward, Jordon's offer would be readily accepted by Virgil, who only seemed interested in the money. With Virgil being a family member and being forced to purchase the property, there might be a way to appeal the absurd water rights clause and regain the to-middle-of-stream water rights as part of the purchase agreement and permanently eliminate it before the sale to Jordon Reed. With half the rights, Jordon could do whatever he wanted with the water. He wouldn't need the old woman's property. Preliminaries of purchase could be completed in the meantime and transfer of deed papers signed on the final day of probate control. Jordon could return to Charleston or Washington and let his attorney do the rest.

The only cog in the wheel was Taylor. If Farley didn't lay off, Jordon would go after him, ruining everything. The thought of it gave Rodney chills. Jordon was accustomed to having his way. Maybe the land deal news would calm him down. If not, Rodney thought *he* might have leave town.

Jordon *was* calmed, but deadly calm. The news had an empowering effect on him, and he felt stimulated by it. He instructed Taylor to stay with Rodney and "put in a good day's work." Manny also had his work to do, attending to the Taylor problem and going over the land deal particulars with Rodney. Jordon took the sports car and headed up the road toward the Orchard Lake Inn. He didn't want a driver today, nor did he need Manny's help to have a talk with Penelope Cather about her son. His way of doing things might not appeal to Manny's legal-mind approach to the problem but was usually effective.

Jordon entered the inn alone but with the full authority of his position in persona and attitude. The first person he encountered was the receptionist. He noticed she was young and had the overdone appearance of a girl trying to look older and more sophisticated. Jordon introduced himself and watched the girl's bored expression turn to awe. She was impressed. Her expression changed again when he asked to see Penelope Cather. The girl appeared to be confused.

"She is working here, is she not?"

"Yes, but . . . she's in the kitchen and doesn't have a break coming until after the lunch hour."

"Where is the kitchen?"

"Well, you can't just go back there. The owners aren't here right now or you could talk to them. Could you come back later?"

"Miss, do you know who I am? I will say this to you once. I would like to see Miss Cather right now, and in private. Either direct me to the kitchen or bring her here to me, immediately!"

"Well, I guess if she's in trouble, it's none of my business." She pointed toward the kitchen doors. Her knees were knocking so hard she'd have fallen if she'd attempted to walk across the room in her extremely high heels.

After Congressman Reed disappeared into the kitchen, she mumbled, "First the police chief and now a congressman. She'll probably be arrested next, and then what will this place do for a cook?"

Pen had just placed a large bowl of peeled potatoes on the counter when Jordon Reed came through the swinging doors. She was alone except for him. She said nothing.

He introduced himself and asked, "Is there somewhere we can talk in private?"

She replied, "This is as good a place as any. We can talk over there at the table for a few minutes," gesturing toward a small round table covered with an oilskin tablecloth. "Then I've got to see about lunch for our guests. Would you like a cup of coffee or tea?" She spoke with assuredness and calm.

He declined the offer of a beverage and watched her move from her work station to the table with exceptional ease and grace. When she sat down in the chair opposite the other empty one, she sat up straight as though a natural habit, rather than for his benefit, and waited for him to sit. Jordon resisted being seated on her level. He preferred a dominant position, and it bothered him that her erect posture would put them almost eye to eye. He'd have to make an effort to sit up straight. These thoughts caused him to hesitate. She sat waiting with no apparent apprehension.

He'd dismissed the receptionist's lack of understanding of his status, although she had been impressed. But it was obvious this woman *did* understand and didn't appear to be the least bit impressed by him or alarmed by his unannounced visit. He'd have to turn on the charm. That would take even more effort than sitting up straight in his chair. If that didn't work, he'd have to use intimidation. Once he had his strategy formulated, he sat down.

"Ms. Cather, I've come to see you on an informal basis to see if we can avoid both legal problems and publicity regarding the incident involving your son and his girlfriend. I have no wish to press charges against them and drag the girl's name through the mud. I plan to speak to her father after I leave here, but I wanted to talk to you first. Your son, I believe his name is Raven?"

Pen nodded her head.

"Raven has put himself in a very awkward position by making accusations against my son. Now, Ms. Cather, as you know, boys will be boys. My son is no angel, but he would never have purposely hurt . . . is it Willa Mae? He says your son assaulted him, and Willa Mae was hurt as a result of this attack. I learned this morning from the doctor in charge of her care that she has no memory of the incident. This means it is Taylor's word against Raven's, and there is no evidence to the contrary. Our local chief of police would like to keep things stirred up, but I can see from looking at you that you are a very wise woman. And a very attractive one, I might add."

At this point he leaned forward and gave her his most seductive expression.

"Surely we can come to some agreement. Even if you wish to believe Raven's story, it is useless to press charges in 'he said, she said' cases. Furthermore, I am thinking of investing in some property here in Serena and plan to one day retire from politics. I have no wish to have disagreements with my neighbors. I plan to live a life of peaceful co-existence. I've won enough battles in the world of politics to know what I can do. I don't want to have to use that power to settle what can be settled here at this table, particularly when it involves a person as lovely as you are. I might feel differently, of course, if Taylor had been severely injured or worse. We should both feel fortunate that he suffered no permanent damage, and from what I have learned, Raven and Willa Mae are recovering as well.

"Maybe we could chalk this up to youthful adventure and forget the whole fracas. I will send Taylor back to Charleston with his mother for the remainder of the summer, and perhaps you could influence Raven to reconsider his statement. I know of no other way to keep Chief Farley from interfering with our civil and peaceful negotiation. I would even offer a modest monetary contribution to each party to perhaps calm ruffled feathers and provide an incentive to drop the charges. After all, when passions are aroused in the young, things can easily get out of hand. I'm sure you would agree. I suspect you have had the experience of passion in your youth, and certainly must have aroused the passions of many. You are still a very attractive woman, Ms. Cather."

There it was. All he had to offer crammed into one masterful speech. If he'd have been running for office, he could not have done better, in his mind. Why wasn't she responding? He felt like taking her by the throat. He smiled instead—not a big smile—the one used when trying to appear naïve and eager for approval. That usually worked with women around her age.

Pen realized he hadn't connected her with Charlotte. He would have mentioned it otherwise. He was everything Charlotte had described, but even more devious than she'd expected. She decided this was not the time to reveal her feelings or her disgust. It was enough that she'd taken his power for a while and made him work to convince her of his sincerity. The best thing to do was put him off, and this would make him unhappy. She could tell he liked immediate results, but that was not going to happen.

"I'm afraid you will have to excuse me, Congressman Reed. I must get back to work. I will think about your offer and give it serious consideration."

Jordon stood up and towered over her. A smirk of cruelty that had been hidden behind his flirtatious leer replaced his vanishing smile. "Ms. Cather, I am a busy man. Don't think about it too long. This opportunity will not come again, I can assure you. Your son is in a losing position and could be destroyed by a legal dispute. You are his mother. It is your job to protect him, and you can also save the girl from having her reputation ruined. It took a lot for me to come here. I will not return. I hope to hear from you by tomorrow."

He handed her a card. "My private cell phone number is listed. I'll expect a call."

He strode past the dining room, ignoring the curious stares of guests. The receptionist looked up as he approached and sat very still, hoping he would leave without stopping. He almost did and changed his mind, turning to her.

"I'd advise you, young lady, to find another job."

Jordon was so infuriated, he gunned the engine of the sports car and spun its tires in the parking lot gravel as he was leaving. Along the narrow driveway leading out to the highway, he almost side-swiped an old blue pickup truck turning in. He caught a glimpse of the young driver and almost wrecked the car again.

The boy's face. His coloring. His profile. Had he imagined it, or was it real? He almost turned and went back but then realized who it might be, who it *must* be. No, it couldn't be. That was impossible.

His nerves were getting to him. He'd been seeing things. It was the shadow of the trees, his state of mind, the woman's resistance, those devilish martinis, everything. Thankfully, the deal was almost done, and he could get out of Serena for a while. There was just the matter of Taylor. Surely Penelope Cather would come around.

CHAPTER THIRTY-TWO

The fox went out in a hungry plight
And he begged the moon to give him light,
For he'd many miles to go that night
Before he could reach his den-O.

~ Author Unknown, *The Gray Goose*

IT WAS ALMOST NOON, AND Chief Farley sat deep in thought after completing another Internet search and consolidating his notes. While he didn't have enough evidence to arrest Taylor Reed, he knew he was guilty. There had been a moment during the questioning when he'd sensed a hint of vulnerability in the young man. He thought about Charlotte's description of him as a boy. He'd been her whole world, an innocent captive of her idealism and love. Farley understood the boy's desire at puberty to follow the absent parent who suddenly showered him with paternal attention. What he didn't understand was a parent who had ignored his son prior to this and then set about corrupting him into the young man he'd become.

For Charlotte's sake, he hoped it was not too late to save Taylor. During his time in the FBI, Farley had worked with enough hardened criminals, including white-collar sociopaths, to know that most didn't change. For one reason or another, many of them had gone past the point of no return in terms of rehabilitation, the final recourse left in the hands of their maker. Taylor was not yet in their category, and due to his early formative years with Charlotte, there might be hope. Still, Farley found it hard to feel empathy for him.

He was more interested in the greater picture emerging from Taylor's incident. Central to this picture was Raven Brook Falls. How ironic that the assault took place there. What was it about the falls that drew people? Purvis McCabe, Mamma Phoebe, Taylor Reed, Willa Mae, and Raven Cather. He began to wonder about Raven's name. He'd been raised by Miss Pen in a cabin by the inn, quite a distance from the falls. Raven wasn't a common name. Was there an association? He had to see Mamma Phoebe again and convince her to tell him everything. He had learned from Kate and Dev about the practice of hoodoo, but now he wanted to know more about the woman who practiced it.

Farley looked across the room at his busy secretary and said, "Aura Lee, what do you know about Mamma Phoebe, the old woman who lives out by the McCabe property?"

Aura Lee gave him a stern look. "Now, don't tell me you're thinking about going to her for advice, Chief. I know you're under a lot of pressure, but there's some things best left alone." Farley hid a quick smile as Aura Lee went on. "Why, I heard tales when I was growing up about spells she put on people that made them go crazy! Some folks went to her for healing—still do, I suppose. Janie Parkinson swears she cured her epilepsy, and Selma Franklin told me she cured her husband of his gout. Some I won't mention went to her for love spells and curses—that's the devil's work. Fortunately, I never needed to use a love spell, always had the boys chasing after me. But there were a few I wouldn't have minded putting a curse on. That's not to say I'd have done it. It's been said she's a powerful witch and a few who went trekkin' that path over to her cabin, were sometimes scared witless before they returned."

"Is that so?" Farley said mildly and waited for Aura Lee to share more.

"Years ago, they found Miss Macy Carrington in a state of delirium after going there. Although some said she'd been meeting Thelma Jameson's husband in the back woods and hadn't been to see Mamma Phoebe at all. My late mother, bless her heart, always gave people the benefit of the doubt. She told me Mamma Phoebe did a lot of good and saved lives when there wasn't any doctoring to be had—said I shouldn't believe anything to the contrary. She said anyone who could live out there alone next to the McCabe clan had to be a force to be reckoned with, them being so wild and all."

Farley broke in to ask a question. "What do you know about McCabe's daughter, Aura Lee?"

"Not much, Chief. I'm trying to remember her name. My mother said she was a real beauty, reclusive and rarely seen. You know how those backwoods clans were, keeping to themselves, creating their own environment. They'd put these modern-day survivalists to shame. Why, I saw a program the other day about a bunch out in Utah—"

"Aura Lee, the daughter?"

"Sorry, Chief. They found her drowned out by the falls. Must have slipped and fell. It was a sad time for old Purvis. But he kept on going, tough-minded as he was, until here lately, God rest his soul."

"Thanks, Aura Lee. I'm going to take a ride out there. Don't beep me unless it's an emergency. Oh, and have Deputy Purdy check on Taylor Reed's whereabouts, do a drive-by Granger Realty to see if he's working. Tell the deputy to be obvious. I want Taylor to know he's under surveillance."

"Sure, Chief." Aura Lee pressed her lips together and then let out a sigh. "I hope you know what you're doing. Seems to me you're prodding the little bull to anger the big one. It's up to you, but do you think you want that big bull charging?"

"Just tell him, Aura Lee."

"Yes, sir." She rolled her eyes as soon as his back was turned and said, "Lord, please help that man. He knows not what he's doing."

Charlotte Reed was sitting at the table in Kate Delaney's kitchen having a cup of freshly ground coffee and eating a toasty warm pecan roll. The zebra finches were having quiet time after a morning of community activity, and Dewey was quietly observing Charlotte, with one eye on the breakfast room window. Charlotte felt enveloped in the warmth of Kate's hospitality and the unique atmosphere she'd created in her kitchen.

"Kate, I feel like you are seeing the real me for the first time. Have you ever felt like you've come out of a fog after being lost in it for a long time? It's all so strange and new."

"You are talking to the right girl, Charlotte. I've had my experience with fog so thick I almost didn't find my way out. Thanks to Dev, and a wee dancing fairy, I did."

"A dancing fairy?"

"I'll tell you about it someday. Right now, we're trying to keep you in the real world."

"I'm sorry to have missed Dev because I wanted to thank him too. The talk he had with me the day I came to you for help . . . well, it changed my whole perspective and helped me find my way. I am so grateful. I might need his help again, and yours too, regarding my son." Charlotte proceeded to tell Kate about Taylor and the talk she'd had with Jeff Farley.

"I am sorry to burden you with my problems again, Kate, but I may need guidance and support, should Taylor have to pay the consequences for his actions. Dev made me believe that no one is hopeless, and I wish my son could know him and talk to him as I did. Do you think he would consider seeing Taylor if the opportunity arises? I believe Dev is an extraordinary man. I would not ask you otherwise. You are so dear to have put up with me as you have. I hope to repay your friendship by becoming a person of substance you could come to value as a friend."

"I value you now, Charlotte, and so does Dev. Of course he would be willing to help."

"Thank you, Kate. I'm also very concerned about Jeff—Chief Farley. I'm afraid my husband will try to ruin him if he persists in holding my son accountable."

"Try not to worry about Jeff, Charlotte. He will do what is necessary and cannot do otherwise. The most we can do is support him and let him do his job. He has faced many dangers over the years and will not stand down. He's quite an extraordinary fellow."

For the first time in a long time, Charlotte smiled and blushed. "Yes, I know, Kate. He is."

Farley did not feel the least bit extraordinary driving along the treacherous, bumpy road again. The land surrounding him held all the answers and yet hid them from him. What had really happened to Purvis McCabe's daughter, and was it important? Why had he spontaneously questioned Aura Lee about her, when he'd wanted information about Mamma Phoebe? Was some inner force guiding him? Maybe the bigger question was . . . was there a magnetic force field pulling all of them to some bitter end?

Why did people keep secrets? Wise people kept them for reasons that held weight. Old wise people, like Purvis McCabe and Mamma Phoebe, had a penchant for preserving the past; they were each a product of an ancestry of craft that had come to the end of the line, at least in terms of offspring. Was he trying to unearth a secret better left buried?

Farley knew from his experience in the FBI that secrets were not easy to keep. Crimes had a way of circling round, like murderers who came back to the scene of their crimes. Arsonists would often stand watching their own fires, returning to re-experience the arousal and feel a sense of power otherwise not achieved. Some returned to relive past glories or triumphs, others to correct past mistakes, and some to cover up crimes that might be discovered. A question arose in his mind that caused him to stop the car. Would a person not only revisit the scene of a crime, but try to possess it, going to great lengths to possess it?

Farley shook his head. His thoughts made no sense. He was clutching at straws, trying in vain to connect a group of unrelated incidents. He felt suddenly unsure of himself and drove on. When he approached the Y fork in the road, the sky turned the flat gray color of slate, covering the bright summer sun with a dense, dreary ceiling of gloom. Black crows flew overhead, soundless and circling, but keeping their distance. It was an ominous sign, a weather system in play happening only here, as though created solely for his benefit, to scare him away, erode his confidence, and dampen his mood into depression.

He veered right at the fork and continued on. The feeling grew worse, and he fought it with determination. The silence was disturbing when he reached the cabin. It took him only a few seconds to understand why. The croaking cackling crow of Mamma Phoebe's old rooster was eerily absent. The rooster that had alerted her to every visitor like an aging watchdog was nowhere to be seen.

Farley climbed the steps to the porch slowly. When he reached the top step, he noticed the blood on the door. Standing taller than the door, he had to stoop down to inspect the red-brown splotches, splattered and smeared. A creature had been hung there. He noticed the hook in the center of the doorframe. He felt a surge of anger and hesitated before knocking.

The door opened, and there she stood, dressed in her colorful garb, flamboyant as an exotic bird, headscarf and beads reminiscent of a tropical island, chestnut eyes gleaming with purpose, her age disguised by her wardrobe. Beyond her, Farley could see a cloth sack tied with twine hung by the fireplace, rooster feathers sticking out of the top of it. He felt sick and disgusted. She was an old woman, bravely hiding her fear. He admired her more than he could say.

He asked with concern, "Mamma Phoebe, are you okay?"

"Just set yourself down out there, and I'll bring you some tea. I know why you've come back. It's time we had another talk. I know you've already inspected what's happened here, and this is just the start of it. I guess we'd best be working together."

She disappeared back into the cabin, returning with a tall glass of tea, no ice. The water was refreshingly cool; Farley didn't mind it wasn't cold. He sipped several times and wondered if she'd put something in it. He didn't care. The sky started to brighten, and his mood lifted. He felt her acceptance, and it felt good.

It felt good to her too, to tell him about the waters. She took her time and taught him as she had Raven, a concise and condensed version, but clear. He learned about her family history and what she knew of the McCabes. Through many generations they had kept the secret, even from family members, trusting the eldest child of each clan, male on the McCabe side and female on hers.

When she came to the end of it, she said, "I know the times is a-changing and everything moves faster now. Peoples are moving in closer, and land is being swallowed up by developers all around us. It's harder to protect what was left alone for centuries, and I'm just an old woman, trying to do what's right and what I've been taught. Our family lines have almost dwindled away, and old Purvis is no longer here to help me. Why even up until his death, people had to fear being shot coming onto his land. That helped me considerable.

"Course, I had my own way of keeping people away. Even those who came to me for help knew to stick to the path or the road and not be nosing around." She laughed. "They feared I'd put a hex on them, and I'd have surely done it if it meant keeping the waters safe. Trouble is, there's some as started thinking these lands are up for grabs now that Purvis is gone, and maybe think I'm standing in the way of progress. They's also knowing I'm nearing the end of the line with no one comin' behind me. I've kept myself separate from my little sister 'cause I had a long-ago foreboding things might come to this."

"Do you mean you feared she might come to harm, if something happened to you? Are you planning to leave the land to her, Mamma Phoebe? Were you afraid if someone found out about the waters, she'd be in danger?"

"No, Chief, it was never that. You see, she's not the rightful one."

"But why where you worried? Why did you deprive yourself of her companionship for so many years?"

"It's the boy, Chief Farley. Our boy. The boy I fished from Raven Brook stream and at the moment of his birth held him in my hands and passed the gift to him as if he'd been borned to me. I saw it clear when the waters came alive around him as his mother's spirit passed him to me. I named him for the waters from whence he came. I put him in Pen's care to keep him safe. Now he has all my teachings and must be protected until he comes into his own."

She paused as if reluctant to continue and then bent forward toward him, having made the decision. "He is my only rightful heir, and the only rightful heir to Purvis McCabe's land!"

Farley responded with an astonished expression. And yet he'd known, somehow he'd known.

"His mother was a beauty, as wild as the mountains and forest she loved. I'd watched Evangeline from the time she was a child, playing in the stream, picking flowers by the falls. Always she was drawn there, in the dawn light and the twilight, and sometimes under the light of the full moon. The waters cast their spell on her, as they have the power to do. She held the reflection and color of them in her eyes. She was as different from her family as night and day, seemed a throwback to a different time and place, a native spirit in her blood. She didn't mix with others, except on those occasions of festival when Purvis would give her permission to go into town. He didn't like it, but he knew she was coming of age. He'd have one of his brothers take her and bring her home."

Mamma Phoebe gazed into the distance. "She could dance like a gypsy. I'd seen her dance alone by the falls. It was a sight to see, the way she moved. It was no wonder she caught someone's eye. Most of the local young men kept their distance, fearing Purvis and his brothers. They had put the threat out, so no one dared approach her before he gave the word, which wouldn't have happened until she turned sixteen. And even then, anyone who did would have to deal with the rest of the McCabes, an ordeal most thought best avoided. She didn't seem to mind being over-protected. It was the natural way back then.

"She was happiest when running wild in the forest or sitting and gazing at the falls. I'd hear her singing melodies she'd make up all by herself, real pretty, like the sound of the waters. Sometimes I can still hear her when I'm by the falls, the memory of it so clear, and lately even when I'm here in the cabin.

"She'd see me come to fill my buckets of water. I could carry two full buckets at a time when I was younger, Chief. She'd splash across the shallow section of the stream where I filled them and help me. She'd have carried my load for me if I'd have let her. She was still a child in many ways, but fully developed by age fifteen. I used to shake my head and worry, but I didn't want to over-step my boundaries with Purvis. He knew my ways and respected them, but he wouldn't have wanted me messin' with his kin, even if it was to protect her.

"As I said, I'd see her at the falls but no one could watch her all the time. There was too much work to be done. Then her mother fell ill, sudden-like, and died. Evangeline had to take on all the cooking and house chores, and even some errands in town. That's why she'd steal away to the falls in the early mornings, when I'd be fetching my water, or at night when she'd sit watching them sparkle in the light of the moon. I'd be out too, when the moon was full and bright, working on my healing conjures. Purvis would be up there on the ridge making his liquor under the full moon shine, both of us watching over her. But I figured she must have gone there during the dark of the moon, when she wouldn't have been seen at all.

"Her first signs of showing was in the late fall, so it must have happened about this time of year. I noticed it first but didn't say anything. I thought I shouldn't interfere because it was a family problem. I felt poorly about it later, wished I'd have asked and tried to help her. But back then, you minded your own business in these matters. Purvis wouldn't have taken kindly to my knowing or helping. When he did find out, he almost went out of his mind.

She'd not had a boyfriend anyone knew about. Purvis accused his brothers. They were much younger than him and known to be reckless and wild. They took the suspicion to be unforgivable. Next thing I knew, they were gone.

"Evangeline told Purvis they were not to blame but refused to divulge the identity of the unborn baby's father. Purvis turned his back on her and she, being as stubborn as him, moved out of the main house and up into the old cabin on a ledge above the compound, where she lived in disgrace, alone and forsaken during the remainder of her short life. Purvis could be a hard man, but I believe he was as hurt as a man could be. Evangeline had been as much a pride to him as his whiskey-makin'.

"It was during the early morning hours that I heard her forlorn cry. She'd been there all night, suffering and alone. But she hadn't slipped, and she hadn't fallen by accident. She'd been struck down as sure as I'm sitting here. This girl could skip along the slippery rocks of the stream like a fairy-girl with wings. I found her lying there helpless in a shallow section, the rippling waters gushing over her spread legs like a whirlpool. I held her bloody head next to my breast and tried to comfort her, then tended to condition her as best I could. She made a final moan, a full and mournful cry, and the baby flowed from her into the waters and my hands as she died. It happened as I said, and I lifted him from the rippling stream into my heart.

"After I did what was needed for the baby, I took him to Purvis and told him what'd happened. He was never the same after that day and wanted nothing to do with the child—asked me to take the baby away. I let him have his peace for a few days, but after Evangeline was buried, I went back, and we came to an agreement about the baby's future. I agreed to see to his raising and promised not to reveal to him the identity of his mother until he was full grown, that meaning age eighteen. Evangeline's death was ruled an accident, a result of her head injury."

"Was there anything in the coroner's report indicating a recent childbirth?" Farley asked.

"Not to my knowledge." Mamma Phoebe pursed her lips as she thought back. "The coroner at the time was one of Purvis McCabe's best customers. He was probably told she had a miscarriage and might have agreed to keep quiet about it. Purvis' brothers' had moved to Tennessee. They were the only ones other than Purvis and me who knew of her condition. If they heard about her death, they probably figured the baby died too. They haven't been back since, but they could verify his birthright if they knew the baby survived. There wasn't a chief of police like you then."

The pair sat in silence for a moment before Mamma Phoebe remembered another important detail the police chief needed to know. "I have Purvis McCabe's will and our signed document in a lockbox registered in my sister's name. We were planning to tell Raven the truth about his birthright on his eighteenth birthday, come harvest time. All these years have passed with no one interested in the properties and no one asking questions about the boy. But now the property is in probate, and we have to come forward before his birthday. If someone out there wants that property bad enough, our coming forward could put Raven's life in jeopardy. I need your help, Chief, and I'd never be askin' it for myself."

Farley gazed at Mamma Phoebe solemnly. "I believe there is someone who knows the value of the waters but has not made the connection to Raven. Not yet."

"That's been plaguing my mind too. I've seen the signs, a bad omen of something to come. I've even felt the presence of him closing in. He's been trying to scare me off, killin' my old rooster. Then that realtor man came to me, asking if I'd be wanting to sell my land. I gave him quite a scare, Chief. Got him to tell me more than he wanted to. The only reason they'd be wanting the McCabe land or mine is the water. And if they know about that, we're all in danger. Do you know who's behind this?"

Farley dipped his head in affirmation. "I've got my suspicions, and if they're right, he's been behind several murders leading up to the murder of Purvis

McCabe. So far, he's kept his hands clean, getting others to do his dirty work. If he could be lured into the open, I might have a chance of stopping him."

"I've been working on that luring part and might be able to help you," Mamma Phoebe said. "I might be old, but I can still mix up a powerful conjure, and the full moon is rising. I got my Paket ready for my ritual tomorrow night. They may have killed my old friend, but his spirit is alive and ready to help me fight the demon."

"Listen to me, Mamma Phoebe." Farley put his hands up in a signal to stop. "You've got to leave this to me. You've helped considerably by telling me the truth. I can't have you casting spells under the moonlight trying to catch this man. I don't doubt your skills, but this is a matter for law enforcement. We have our ways of drawing people out of the shadows too. I'd feel much better if you would let me take you to your sister. She's a fine woman, and you'd be safer staying with her."

Mamma Phoebe drew back, stiffening her spine. "Chief Farley, I'm too old for you to be tellin' me what to do. I'll let you do your job, and I'll take to mind what you've said. There's no harm in letting me do my spells and rituals, is there? Some folks don't think they amount to anything anyway. It will keep me busy instead of sitting around frettin' and worryin'."

Farley shook his head. "Somehow, you don't come across to me as the frettin' and worryin' type."

"Oh go on, Chief." Her eyes twinkled with delight. "Don't be tryin' to charm me. Give an old woman some peace and go do your job. Maybe by tomorrow night, you'll have this all settled and won't be needin' my magic at all."

Farley left her feeling better than when he'd arrived but also vulnerable because he cared so much about the people being victimized, including her. He headed back into town, stopping at Granger Realty to give one more prod to big bull Jordon by taking another poke at his son.

Taylor Reed was working at his desk when Farley walked in and surprised him. Rodney Granger and Jordon Reed were not there, nor was the secretary. Farley assumed they were keeping Taylor occupied and in the public eye until getting him out of Serena.

"I've been advised by my attorney not to talk to you anymore, Chief Farley."

"Is that a fact?" Farley said dryly. "I just thought you might like to know that Willa Mae is being released from the hospital today. She won't be able to return to her job for a while, but she is recovering and will most likely be able to remember what happened in time. Her doctor said her memory might even come back in a flash of recollection."

Taylor shrugged. "Dad told me he is getting the matter settled with her father."

"How about you, Taylor? Are you settled about everything? Is this what your life is going to be, a long series of having your father pay to get you out of trouble? A shameful life led at the expense of others, including your mother? Do you think you're the first kid I've seen go down this path? I've seen hundreds before you, many from wealthy and famous backgrounds."

A look of disbelief spread across Taylor's face. "Where would you see anything like that? You're just a hick-town policeman."

Farley gave him a piercing look. "Twenty years in the FBI, son. And make no mistake, I will hold you accountable in one way or another and will not back off. You can tell your father and your attorney what I said. You think about your life in the meantime, and maybe make a decision about it before it's too late."

Farley walked out of Granger Realty in a better mood. Mamma Phoebe had her ways, and he had his.

After the chief left, Taylor Reed felt miserable. He hadn't been sleeping well. His dreams were the stuff of nightmares, and his daydreams were just the opposite, but equally disturbing. He would drift off several times a day into a mind-video replay of Willa Mae, laughing and guiding him as he drove up and down and around and around the never-ending winding county roads.

They were not true memories because in these scenarios, he was laughing too, without false pretense, without sexual motive, but with innocent laughter, the way he had laughed as a child. He'd felt sickened each time he had been jolted out of a daydream by either his father or Rodney issuing some order or sending him somewhere so he wouldn't overhear their conversations. He was sick of them and sick of himself. Farley had shamed him, and he hated him for it. But maybe Farley was right.

The front door opened, and his father came in looking like he'd seen a ghost. He walked right by Taylor without speaking and went back into Rodney's office and shut the door. A few minutes later, Rodney came in and did the same. Taylor pretended to be filling out a form, his head down with his attention on his work. But he knew something was wrong. This time, he was not going to be kept in the background. He crept silently down the hall and put his ear to the door.

Dad had a booming voice when making a speech. Like a trained theater actor, his voice carried even when lowered. Taylor had no problem hearing these words:

"You've got to get rid of the boy, Rodney. I don't care how you do it, but see that it is done. He drives an old truck that shouldn't even be on the road. Make it look like an accident. We can't have any more suspicious deaths. They served their purpose, but this one must be convincingly accidental. I almost wrecked with him myself, driving down from the inn."

"Do you know what you're asking me to do?"

"I'm not asking you, Rodney. You either take care of that kid, or I'll take care of you. You should have told me about him in the first place, and the mother. They've got to be dealt with. No one cares about them anyway, except the old woman, and she'll be next. I'm going to let Manny take care of the girl's father and pay him off. Your job is to take care of this right away. Tonight. Later on, when you're living high on the hill, you'll forget what it took to get there, believe me. Now, get Manny on the phone."

Taylor's legs felt weak as he moved quietly back down the hall, terrified to make a sound, trying to hold his breath until he reached his office. He collapsed into his chair and sat there in a daze, trying to sort out what he'd heard, adding missing pieces to what he knew, remembering the fight with his adversary and what he'd felt, the odd similarities of movement, the sensation of familiarity. Still, his thoughts of late had been so hallucinatory, the daydreams and nightmares, the shifting reality and perspective. He could not grasp the significance of these images, had never taken a drug with this effect. The drugs in his stash had lost their potency, and he'd lost his desire to take them. He had difficulty remembering his evenings, and mornings had become an effort to survive. He drifted once again to Willa Mae's laughter and wanted to stay in the car with her, driving round and round the mountain with no end in sight.

"Taylor. Taylor!" his father's voice boomed. "Finish up, son. It's time to go home. I'll go outside and wait. But hurry up. I could use a martini."

Taylor shuddered and shook himself awake, and then said aloud, though no one could hear, "So could I."

And then he repeated with emphasis, "So could I."

CHAPTER THIRTY-THREE

Yours is the light by which my spirit's born: - you are my sun, my moon, and all my stars.

~ e. e. cummings

THE BIG FAT MISSHAPEN MOON needed only a sliver to make it whole. The atmosphere around the Shadow Peak Ridge was stirring like the herbs in Mamma Phoebe's blackened cauldron, the summer night air churning into a buttery haze under the big yellow moon. The demon face in the rock glowered and came alive in the moonlight, its features made fierce and terrible by the shadows of darkness. The wind swept through the pines, creating a soft purring whine. Mamma Phoebe slept soundly, unaware of her guardian on duty from midnight 'til dawn.

The parking lot at the Orchard Lake Inn was full, but the guests were all sleeping, the help nestled in their quarters. It was one hour past midnight when the dark figure came creeping and the truck was made ready for its next trip to town. The task was a simple one. The truck had its problems: the brakeline was faulty, the gears old and worn. Each problem was worsened; the man took his time. There was no need to hurry, the sabotage refined. He made some adjustments, ensuring results, then slipped away silently into the night.

Penelope Cather woke with a start and looked at her clock. It was an hour before dawn, and the cabin felt empty. She knew Raven was gone before reaching his bedroom. She'd hidden the truck keys so he wouldn't be tempted to take them. She'd hoped Jeff Farley's talk with him, and everything she'd taught him, would keep him from going after Taylor Reed. She admonished herself for expecting him to resist avenging Willa Mae. She wanted to give him the benefit of the doubt, but couldn't. It was almost a full thunder moon and he was a child of the mountains. The primal laws of nature had been set in motion, despite her efforts to calm him. His future was at stake and possibly his life.

Fear took over and once again, she felt the sensation of panic. She ran back into her bedroom and dressed, grabbing the set of keys from a small box she'd placed under her cedar chest. She ran down the path to the inn and then into the parking lot, the truck keys in her hand. She had to find him before he did something rash. He was hurt and angry, on foot and alone. But he could find his way anywhere in daylight or darkness. He knew every shortcut and path through the forest and moved like a cat with stealth and acuity. She had no idea how long he'd been gone. If time was in her favor, she might be able to reach the Reed home before he did, if that was his destination. Charlotte would help her; they would work together to save their sons. If Jordon Reed interfered, he would have his awakening.

She started the engine and pushed down on the gas pedal. The truck jerked forward and then stopped abruptly. She lifted her foot from the pedal, turned the key, pushed down again, and the engine started. She drove down the narrow driveway to the mountain road. The trip from the inn into town was a winding downhill drive with several treacherous curves bordering a steep incline. The moonlight cast shadows on the black tarmac. There were shadows all around.

Pen was an insecure driver who tended to go slow. But the truck kept going faster, and she couldn't slow it down. She pressed her foot on the brake, holding the pedal to the floorboard. The truck gained momentum, careening out of control. She pulled on the emergency brake, but it felt loose in her hand. She turned off the ignition key, but the truck continued on. She reached for her amulet, gripping it tightly. The truck crashed through the guardrail and plunged into darkness. She screamed out Raven's name and then felt the sudden impact. The night turned into blackness and then nothing more.

The Reed house was quiet, but no one was resting. Charlotte was about to get up, an hour before the dawn. Taylor appeared to be sleeping, but his mind was in active torment. Manny was awake and agitated, thinking another of day fixing the endless problems of Jordon Reed and his spoiled rotten son was almost not worth the money . . . almost.

Jordon Reed's brain was on fire. The face of the boy had haunted his intoxicated sleep and awakened him during the night to face the impossible reality of its meaning. He refused to accept it; it simply couldn't be. It was the alcohol. He'd been drinking too much. He feared going back to sleep but was too tired to get up. He lay there in a half-awake stupor, half-drunk, half-sober, the alcohol seemed to be refreshing itself in his body like it had a second or third life, metabolizing slowly through his liver and then reversing back into his bloodstream. What had Charlotte put in those drinks? He didn't care. He needed them. She had him addicted to them.

There was something about Charlotte that wasn't right. She was the same, but not quite. There was something missing, the fantasies and fairy-tale talk, the whimsical faraway look was gone from her eyes. She was more alluring, had always been attractive, but this was more sensual, as though she was coming alive sexually, sensually. What was that about? She hardly ever left the house. She had her groceries delivered and the liquor, which she kept in full supply. He'd even noticed Manny giving her the once-over. He was another one who would have to go when this was over. If Charlotte kept waiting on him like this and looking so good, he might even keep her around for a while, at least until he could get something else lined up: someone who would fit into his new lifestyle, much younger, of course, sexy, but with a touch of class.

Frank Parsons was also awake in his farmhouse, thinking about the call he'd gotten from Jordon Reed's attorney. He'd agreed to a late morning meeting. He'd promised Chief Farley to hold back and discuss everything with him before acting. The attorney had caught him off-guard. Willa Mae was sleeping like an angel in her bedroom. He thanked the Lord again for the blessing of her life and sparing him the pain of another loss. He'd have tried to kill Taylor Reed by now if not for Farley. He knew Raven felt the same and worried about Miss Pen, knowing how she loved that boy. She was a fine woman, best he'd ever known outside his late wife. He'd come to look forward to her visits and enjoyed watching her walk back up and across the ridge carrying his produce in her big straw-woven basket. She'd done a good job raising Raven.

Farley was right about going up against the Reeds. He had to think about Willa Mae, and Miss Pen had to think about Raven. He got up and put on a pot of coffee. It was almost daybreak. He showered, shaved, and dressed in his new blue overalls. He'd be waiting for Farley outside the police station when he arrived. He was not talking to Reed's attorney before talking to Farley.

After two cups of strong black coffee, Frank got into his pickup and headed down the road. He was halfway to town when he noticed the twisted metal of the guardrail. It hadn't been like that yesterday. He pulled to the side of the road and got out, running to the opening where the rail had been ripped apart. When he saw the tail-bed of the inn's blue pickup truck, he ran back to the truck and used his brand new cell phone to call 9-1-1. He returned to the roadside and nearly slid all the way down to the truck, which was lodged midway down the incline, the front smashed into the tree that stopped it. He'd expected to see Raven Cather behind the mangled steering wheel of the wreckage and was stunned to find Miss Pen, sitting there upright, conscious and breathing. She was trapped in the seat, the wheel pressed against her seatbelt and chest area. The belt would have to be cut to remove her, but he was afraid to move anything until help arrived, in case there were internal injuries.

Miss Pen wasn't bleeding anywhere and assured Frank she was in no pain and nothing was broken. She held something tightly in her hand attached to a fine-braid of twine hanging around her neck. She held it up to him and smiled. "It saved me, Frank. And now so have you."

Farley arrived at the scene, along with the Serena Life Squad. Pen was extricated from the truck and examined for injuries. She insisted she had none and refused to be taken to the hospital. When Farley found out why she'd been driving, he felt responsible, thinking he should have told her about Raven's unauthorized secret undercover job. He'd given Raven the assignment to keep him from going after Taylor Reed, and because he was perfectly suited for it. He'd explain to Miss Pen and apologize.

Farley ordered the truck impounded for a thorough inspection. He requested that news of this accident be withheld for 24 hours. The state police officer and life squad paramedic were willing to cooperate when Farley explained he suspected sabotage related to a current investigation. He had earned their respect and willingness to cooperate over the years, although a report would have had to be made if there had been serious injuries or a fatality. The guard rail was removed and an *Under Repair* barrier placed in the gap.

The paramedic diagnosed Miss Pen as miraculously unharmed. While she was being examined, Frank Parsons informed Farley about the call from Reed's attorney and the meeting scheduled for later that morning. Farley instructed him to go ahead with it and play along.

Farley said, "If he makes an offer to settle, Frank, tell him you want to think it over. I need more time, and I need your help. There is more to this than you know. Reed is trying to hush everything up with money and is accustomed to getting his way."

"No need to explain, Chief. It helps me to know I'm helping you. I've got Willa Mae to take care of, and now Miss Pen. If I'd have been paying more attention to both of them, none of this would have happened. Let me do my part, and you take care of that devil and his no-good son, forgive me, Lord, for saying it."

"You're not the one needing forgiveness, Frank. And I don't think the man I'm after deserves any."

On the outskirts of town, in a modest frame house with blue siding, Rodney Granger slept the restless sleep of the guilt-ridden, his mind working overtime. The mechanic he'd hired to do the job was capable and trustworthy, but another loose end. How many people had to die for him to have that house on the hill—that cabin in the sky? He hated the house he lived in. Most realtors he knew managed to live well doing everything by the book, being straight with people and ethical. Somehow, he'd never managed it. Right from the beginning, his deals had been shady. He'd gone through three wives and had no children to show for it. It was just as well. He might have ended up with a kid like Taylor. He didn't believe for a minute Taylor was innocent. But neither was he, not anymore. He'd gone from shady to crooked to jaded during the span of his career, but he never thought of himself as a criminal until this deal with Jordon Reed. How did it get so out of hand? The first two were losers, and the third an old man, but now? *I'm surely going to hell,* he thought, the idea of it bringing him fully awake.

Farley drove back into town and decided to go to the Grill for breakfast. There had been no traffic on that stretch of mountain road while he'd been at the crash site. It had been a fluke Miss Pen was discovered before sun-up. He thought about secrets again, how easily some got out while others stayed hidden for years, decades, sometimes generations. All he needed was another day. He believed Mamma Phoebe's words about the full thunder moon. He could feel it too, pushing him along, like the tide moving into shore.

The weekend was approaching, and the party being held for Reed would be a catalyst, his big-man-in-town moment, swaying public opinion in his favor, winning the crowd. The Serena Grill was buzzing, everyone talking when their chief of police came through the door. A hush of silence crossed the room like a wave as he stood there looking for a place to sit. The stools at the counter were all occupied, and so were the booths.

Farley nodded his head and said, "Good morning." Uncomfortable seconds passed, and then his friend and proprietor, Judy Ward, said, "Morning, Chief. I'll have a place for you in just a minute. Henry, aren't you about done?"

Henry Morgan had been there since the place opened, had finished his breakfast, and had been nursing several re-filled cups of coffee ever since. He reluctantly moved from the stool and paid his check, giving Farley a sideways glance, mumbling, "Morning, Chief," as he passed by him to leave.

Trenton Standish, a fairly new resident, retired business executive, and recently appointed member of Serena's City Council spoke up as if representing the other customers. "I hear you're trying to make a name for yourself by harassing Congressman Reed. He could do a lot of good for this town. We're concerned about your actions, Chief. As a responsible citizen, I feel obligated to speak for the others and ask for an explanation. The mayor has dropped the ball on this one, but we have not."

Farley walked over to the empty stool and sat down. Judy brought him a cup of coffee and asked, "Do you want your regular, Chief?"

"Yes, thank you, Judy."

"Are you ignoring me, Chief?" Standish asked. "We've got a big event planned in his honor, and you've put a damper on it. Your behavior is an embarrassment to the town, and we'd like it to stop."

Farley looked around the room at all the familiar faces. Most were the kind of people he'd been raised around, quiet and unassuming. Some had relocated to Serena from other cities and towns, desiring a simpler life in a small town surrounded by wilderness. The retirees brought with them expertise from numerous professions, and many wanted to do their part to make Serena a better place to live, and for the most part, they did. Residents born and raised in Serena resisted change forced upon them by newcomers, holding on to the old ways and customs, fiercely defending them, proud of their mountain heritage. They knew him better than the rest because they understood him at the core, and this is where he placed his trust.

"Is that how all of you feel? How about you Jeb? And you Miss Sarah?"

Jeb McFarland, his round, cherubic face inflamed to a reddish-pink glow, stood up and said, "Now wait a minute, Standish. You're not speakin' for all of us, and you're sure not speakin' for me. I've known Chief Farley long enough to know he must have a good reason for doing what he's doing, and I'll not be a-questionin' him about it. I, for one, am glad he's here."

Several others spoke forth in agreement. Then Miss Sarah Foster, who'd returned to Serena after serving several decades as a missionary, said, "I've experienced my share of danger during my travels abroad. I came back to the place of my birth to find peace and serenity in my old age. I feel safe and secure here because of Chief Farley. I'm sure the congressman will survive his visit to Serena and enjoy the party you're giving him. I suggest you focus on the event, Mr. Standish, and choose a more appropriate time to discuss your concerns with our chief of police."

Standish lost some of his bluster and replied huffily, "You can be sure I will, madam."

He sat back down. Within minutes, the men sitting with him paid their checks and left. Everyone else went back to their morning ritual, most relieved the confrontation was over. Farley gave Jeb and Miss Sarah a slight nod of gratitude, finished his coffee and breakfast, and left. In the short time it took to reach his office, he reflected on what he'd learned. The scuttlebutt had been limited to his exchanges with Jordon Reed, but there had been no mention of the incident involving Taylor. Frank Parsons had made excuses to Judy Ward for Willa Mae's absence at the store. As far as he knew, there were no rumors floating around about her not being there. And no one had mentioned the wreck involving Miss Pen. He would know for sure after talking to Aura Lee, who was already busy at her desk when he entered the police station.

"Good morning, Chief. I heard you got quite a reception down at the Grill."

"Yes, you could say that," Farley replied as he hung his jacket on the coat rack.

"Jennie Wilson stopped in just now and told me what happened. She heard it from her husband, who'd been sitting in the booth next to Mr. High-and-Mighty Standish. Well, I could have warned you. They're all keyed up about that party and haven't taken kindly to you insulting their guest of honor. Hopefully it's done and forgotten. And I hope you will be more careful in the future."

"Mm-hmm," Farley grunted noncommittally.

"Oh, and speaking of Congressman Reed, Mrs. Reed called asking for you right after I came in. She requested you return her call right away. I guess she wants to put in her two cents too. I'd be even more careful with that one. I don't think she's right in the head, the way she carried on about that rooster." Aura Lee lowered her voice. "You know how these summer society folk are, Chief. Too much high-living causes craziness in my opinion."

"I'll keep that in mind," Farley replied mildly.

"That reminds me. Deputy Purdy called in and said he's picked up some clues about the missing rooster. Said he may have a suspect and is looking into information he got from an informant." Aura Lee shook her head. "He sounded a bit daft to me, like he thinks he's working on an important criminal case. You've got to give him more to do, Chief. Trouble is, we don't have enough crime around here to keep him busy, not counting that business last year, of course. I guess there's no harm in him making a mountain out of a molehill. But really, Chief, I'm worried about him."

Farley excused himself to the back office and made his call from there. Charlotte answered right away. "I need to see you, Jeff. It's important. I'll meet you at Kate's. She knows about the call, and everything else. I'll drive over there now."

Farley waited a few minutes and then drove up the hill to the old church. Charlotte's Mercedes was not parked in front, but Kate's car and Dev's were parked side-by-side in front of the garage doors. Dev was waiting for him outside.

"I took the liberty of putting Charlotte's car in the garage, Jeff. It was her idea. She has updated us on what's been happening. Is there anything I can do?"

"Thanks, Dev. You've both been a great help already. I might need your assistance tonight, but I'm not sure yet. Are you and Kate planning to attend the party being held for Jordon Reed?"

"We hadn't planned to. Kate *did* receive an invitation with the option of bringing a guest. I'm sure she could reverse her RSVP if she calls the person in charge of the event."

"Good," Farley replied.

Charlotte was inside waiting. Kate and Dev went into the kitchen to give them privacy. Charlotte took Jeff by the hand and said, "Jordon wants me to return to Charleston with Taylor. He says it is my duty to protect my son, that he cannot be held here without evidence. I'm expected to attend the party tonight and act as if nothing is wrong and not mention anything about leaving town." She lifted her chin. "I'm not leaving, Jeff, but I haven't told him. I'm trying to be strong for myself and for Taylor. But I'm confused about what to do next. I can't keep running to Nanny Pen every time I become unsure. And I'm not running to you to be saved from my responsibilities. I just need to know how to proceed to help you and to help my son."

"You've been very brave, Charlotte. I need you to be brave one more night." He paused a moment and then gently said, "Miss Pen had an accident this morning."

Charlotte gasped. "Oh no!"

He quickly explained and then assured her, "Miss Pen is in good hands. She sent me a message for you. She said you should trust what you felt during your visit with her."

"What does that mean?"

"I don't know, Charlotte. Maybe it will come to you. How do you feel about attending the party tonight? Can you go through with it? I'd feel better if I knew you were there and not at home alone. Kate and Dev are going too, so you will have their protection. At some point, your husband will be called away, and I'd like you to remain with them, out of harm's way. Please promise you will do this, Charlotte."

"Jeff, don't worry about protecting me. Let me do something to help, please."

"This will be helping me. And I won't let you lose your best quality in all this effort to be realistic. Please don't devalue your vivid imagination. I need you to use it tonight. Dress up tonight in your prettiest dress. Pretend you are going to the Harvest Moon Dance, even though it isn't October and the July moon is dark and stormy. You still have what it takes to keep everyone distracted. Can you do it?"

"Why, Jeffrey Farley," she replied in her most charming drawl, "you must never underestimate a Southern girl. After I arrive at the party tonight, no one will notice the man who escorted me there."

"That's my girl."

Tears welled in her eyes. "Jeff, I've always been your girl."

He took her in his arms.

In the kitchen, Kate whispered to Dev, "Should we go in there?"

Before he could answer, Farley called out, "Kate, sorry I can't stay for coffee. I've got to get back. Dev, could you walk outside with me?"

Charlotte stood back quietly by the long vertical living room windows. Morning sunrays filtered through the silken sheer drapes, highlighting her slightly tilted head as she watched them go. Kate stood in the kitchen doorway watching her, amazed at the transformation. She looked twenty years younger, her pale skin iridescent, her features softened by love.

Charlotte turned toward Kate with a brave expression and said, "Kate, may I have one of your delicious cookies and the cup of the coffee you offered? We must talk about what we are going to wear tonight. Don't bother to call about the RSVP. I'll take care of it. Do you think there will be dancing? When I was a girl, dancing was customary at all the events in Serena."

Kate stopped her and said, "Charlotte, don't ever say again you *hope* to be a woman of substance. You *are* one, and I am proud to call you my friend."

CHAPTER THIRTY-FOUR

The crickets still sing in October. And lilly, she's trying to bloom.
Tho she's resting her head on the shoulder of death,
she still shines by the light of the moon.

~ Kevin Dalton

THE SHIMMERING SUNLIGHT THAT HAD graced the summer morning until noon lost its radiance to a slow-moving weather system moving in from the southwest. It was a subtle change from lightness to darkness as the day progressed, but the atmospheric pressure created by the gathering clouds created a collective tension in those to whom it gave grave significance.

Mamma Phoebe was in rare form, bustling about the cabin, preparing for her midnight adventure. This would be her last hurrah, the culmination of years of experience wrapped up into one great feat of magic. Mamma Phoebe believed her magic was God-given, not the work of the devil. In her way of thinking, it was only the work of the devil if the hoodoo doctor was in league with the devil. She viewed her hoodoo magic as a blessing to be used judiciously and with wise discretion.

She also had what she considered a healthy belief in the devil, recognizing the existence of evil in the world. She had fought evil on many levels as a young woman and had been tempted many times to take a wrong path. But she'd been able to stay strong for several reasons: the gift of her heritage, handed down to her by her maternal ancestors; the gift of the land she'd inherited, a paradise of abundance; the gift of intelligence, necessary to her craft; and the gift of the waters, giving her special power to heal.

But she never drew water at the base of the Raven Brook Falls without seeing the evil in that old demon rock, staring and taunting her, just waiting for a chance to come alive again. He had shown his face once before, witnessing the death of Evangeline. He had seen Raven and Willa Mae struck down with brutal force. He took hold of his disciples whenever they came into his territory, igniting their spirits into violence. She'd warned Raven about the rock, teaching him that evil could be found in certain places as well as in certain people, even in the midst of glorious good and spectacular beauty.

Tonight she would battle that old demon rock and also use it to pull his disciple back into the devil's lair.

Rodney Granger received a phone call shortly before noon that left him sitting in his chair in a state of shock. The call came from his buddy at the courthouse, letting him know that Chief Farley had contacted the probate court officer with news that a claim for rightful ownership of the McCabe property would be forthcoming Monday morning, along with the Last Will and Testament of Purvis McCabe, currently held in a lockbox where it has been stored for almost eighteen years. Farley had not divulged the name of the claimant but assured the court representative of the claimant's validity and McCabe's signature on the document.

Rodney didn't even feel afraid anymore. The old woman had won. The witch had him by the throat, and he knew it. He'd tried to scare her, and she ended up scaring the life out of him. *Let Reed do his own dirty work. I'm done, finished. Everything is finished for me.*

He wrote a note to Jordon Reed and left it on his desk. He told his secretary to take the afternoon off. He turned off his cell phone and walked out of his office for the last time.

Jordon Reed had been lunching in town, enjoying the attention, and expecting to have his business done by mid-afternoon. That would give him time to go home, rest, and get dressed for the party being given in his honor. This would be his last effort to put on a good front for the locals. They had such pride in their little town. They *should* celebrate his greatness. After all, he was about to force them out of the past and into a new era of change and prosperity.

He could see it all: grand hotels dotting the landscape, health advocates from all over the world coming to Serena for the healing waters, an industry created to market the sparkling high-end product, consumers demanding more as the legend grew. He was almost in a good mood. Lunch had been delicious, the cannelloni the best he'd ever tasted.

Taylor had been given a multitude of tasks by Rodney earlier that morning. There were several properties to be checked and signs to be removed and locks to be inspected and so forth, none of it necessary, and all of it a waste of time. Everything hinged on the payoff for his mishap. When that was done, they could leave. He'd been told to have his things packed by the weekend for a return to Charleston with his mother.

It wasn't going to happen, but Taylor didn't as yet have a plan. His mind had been too muddled with confusion, crazy thoughts, and wild dreams. He kept thinking about what he'd heard and the accident his father had ordered Rodney to arrange. For some reason, he wanted to prevent it but didn't have a clue how. Why should he care? But he did, and he felt confused by his feelings. He smoked another joint from his stash in the car and felt nothing except relief about not having to attend the party. He was expected to stay home tonight, out of his father's limelight and out of the way.

After several hours of driving from property to property, Taylor happened along the Orchard Lake Inn entrance on his way back to town. He was almost tempted to turn in, but he decided against it and drove on. Farther along, about two miles down the road, he noticed the repair barricade and slowed down. He parked and got out of the car. He stepped over it, looking down into the ravine where a trail of broken branches and smashed laurel led to a gouged tree. The damage appeared fresh, the underbrush newly disturbed, the missing evidence apparent to his informed view of the scene.

There had been no news of an accident. He would have heard it before leaving town. It had to have happened sometime last night in order for the vehicle to have been removed and towed already. It was too near the inn not to be the one.

Taylor got into his car and turned around, driving back to the entrance of the inn. He felt frightened but kept on going until it came into view, spacious and sprawling, positioned high above and beyond the parking lot. The lot was partially full, with no old truck parked in it. He backed his car away until he found a place to turn around and, feeling a rush of adrenaline, carelessly sped down toward the exit. He had the strange sensation of having done something forbidden, which prompted a desire within him to do it again. He decided to return after dark and check again for the blue pickup; he had to. As he drove past the place where the barricade held sentry, he vowed to find out before nightfall what had happened there. Having altered his route on impulse, he'd taken a pivotal detour in his life.

Raven Cather was standing near the window by the front door of the inn when something caught his eye. He wouldn't have noticed it if not for the color. The gleaming splotch of red stood out from the greenery like a red-headed woodpecker among the pines. He stared through the window, waiting for the car to come forward into the parking lot. It went backwards instead and disappeared from view.

His mother had insisted on coming in to take care of the lunch crowd despite objections from him and Frank Parsons, arguing that she had sustained no injuries nor had felt any after-effects from the accident. She said the two extra servers Friday through Sunday made her job much easier, and the owners were expected to return some time over the weekend; she wanted the inn to be in good order.

She had told Frank to quit fussing and sent him to his garden for a basket of tomatoes and greens. He'd been put to work on the front entrance, sweeping, weeding, and bringing in the moveable planters; she said a storm was coming. From the other side of the inn, a black mass of clouds gathered in the distance.

Raven felt responsible for her accident. She'd downplayed it as a mere fender-bender and had glared at Frank when he'd attempted to disagree, saying she'd been foolish taking the truck out so late. She told Raven that Chief Farley had explained where Raven had been last night and would come by later today to talk to him about tonight. She'd taken the amulet from around her neck and placed it around his, kissing him gently on the cheek. "This will keep you safe from harm."

He wasn't worried about being harmed. It seemed to him they were keeping him busy with one unnecessary task after another, keeping him occupied, keeping him from going after Taylor Reed. Now the truck was gone, taking away the only transportation he had. He envisioned running down the road on foot, chasing the red sports car, being left in the dust. Since when did a truck have to be towed away after a minor fender-bender? No matter. It appeared that Taylor Reed was coming after him. What other reason would he have for sneaking up the driveway, checking out the surroundings? *Either he'll come to me, or I'll go to him. We have a score to settle. It is as inevitable as the rising thunder moon.*

CHAPTER THIRTY-FIVE

Conversion may come under many shapes,
and it may be brought about in many ways.
With some men it needs a cataclysm,
As a stone may be broken to fragments by the fury of a torrent;
but with some it comes gradually,
as a stone may be worn away by the ceaseless fall of a drop of water.
~ W. Somerset Maugham, *The Moon and Sixpence*

CHARLOTTE ASCENDED THE STAIRCASE WITH a large martini glass on a small tray. She hadn't started dressing, but was about to. It was going to be a challenge with Jordon grumbling and grousing at the other end of the hall. He was in a horrible mood, something about not being able to reach Granger. He'd been harping at Taylor ever since they came home and insisted on having a martini while getting ready, knowing it was unwise with a party to attend.

She'd laid out his clothes, formal attire. In Serena that meant casual formal. The ladies were free to dress up or dress down as they desired, so different from Charleston, where the rules of dress were strictly enforced by a bevy of society mavens one dared not offend. That's why Charlotte loved Serena. If she wanted to dress like a princess, she could, or not, and no one would criticize. So she gave Jordon a martini and shut the door to her bedroom.

When she came out and descended the stairs, a vision in lilac chiffon, there were no admirers waiting. Nanny Pen was not there to check her over and attend to every detail. She walked out onto the veranda and looked up at the sky. It seemed too dark for the hour. A gust of wind lifted the skirt of her dress, causing it to billow out. The cool breeze on her legs gave her goose-bumps and sent a shiver up her spine. She heard the faraway rumble of thunder and then another one sounding closer. *I'd better get some kind of wrap,* she thought. Nanny Pen would have thought of it ahead of time.

She wasn't trying to pretend. The long-ago time had been waiting for her outside instead of Jeffrey Farley. The long-ago time would be with her to-night, giving her courage throughout the evening. The long-ago time was her strength and more real to her than the past twenty years. A storm was coming, but tonight she would make the big yellow moon come out and shine.

Jordon was upstairs fuming. He read the note over and over, trying to comprehend its meaning. Granger was nowhere to be found. Calls and mes-sages went unanswered. The note he'd left for Jordon simply read, *"The old witch has won."*

Finally dressed and feeling a slight buzz from his drink, Jordon knocked on Taylor's door and peeked in. Taylor had just flushed his joint down the toilet. It no longer had any effect. Besides, he wanted a clear head tonight. He had plans of his own.

"You'd better be getting your things together, son. Neither you nor your mother has prepared to head back to Charleston yet. It will give you some-thing to do tonight, keep you out of trouble. If Farley comes nosing around, don't answer the door."

"Sure, Dad," Taylor replied without enthusiasm.

Jordon went down the hall and down the stairs and found Charlotte standing there waiting for him. She looked incredible, and it wasn't just the martini. The change in the woman was remarkable. It wasn't the clothes or her makeup. She actually looked happy. How could that be? He'd never known her to be happy. Oh, she'd pretended to be at times, but this time it seemed real. Of course, he'd never tried to make her happy, he'd been too busy, and to be honest, he hadn't really cared if she was or not.

What did his wife have to be happy about now? Taylor had certainly turned out to be a disappointment. Charlotte didn't have any friends. There was that couple, Kate and Devlin. Surely they couldn't be responsible for this sudden onset of bliss. Hmmm. She'd mentioned something about a nanny. With everything else going on, he'd almost forgotten about that. What had Charlotte been doing while he'd been gone all day? He'd assumed she'd been home. He felt suspicious and irritated, adding to the anger and frustration caused by Granger.

"You look nice, Charlotte. Fix me another martini before we go."

"Are you sure you should have another drink, Jordon?"

"The only drinks they serve at these events are wine and beer. I need something stronger to get through it. You know I can hold my liquor. Put it in a paper cup. It's almost time to go."

She made him another one, a special one, light on the vodka. He took a sip, and they left together. He drove the Mercedes one-handed and took another sip from the cup before each curve leading to the outskirts of town.

The parking lot was full when they arrived at the reception hall. Serena's society had turned out for the event. The reception hall had been built years before by a local entrepreneur on a plot of acreage adjacent to his mountain home. It was a large rectangle facility, perched on a knoll, perfect for parties, weddings, and memorial events. The entrance was well-lit and welcoming, the interior knotty-pine from floor to ceiling. Globe-covered chandeliers highlighted the beauty of the wood. The dance floor was varnished and gleaming, and a stage rose above for the band. The bar built into one corner was in harmony with its surroundings, and round tables half-circled the dance floor.

A hostess was waiting to greet and escort them into the main room. Jordon put on his best smile, and he did look impressive. But all eyes were focused on Charlotte.

Jordon was immediately surrounded by local supporters and city officials. Charlotte discreetly stepped aside. Champagne was being served by roaming waiters. When one of the waiters approached her, a very refined older man took a glass from his tray and offered it to her, saying, "For the loveliest lady in the room."

Kate and Dev came forward and embraced her before guiding her to the table at which they were to be seated together, thanks to the call Charlotte made to the event organizer earlier. Kate and Dev's supportive presence gave Charlotte confidence. They understood what she was trying to do and why. Others came forward, both women and men, and she took time with each person, charming them all.

Before long, everyone was seated. Dinner was served, and speeches were made. The mayor's speech was surprisingly brief. Others were far too long. Jordon managed an unimpressive speech of gratitude, but he seemed distracted. It was a blessed relief to all when the band came onto the stage and the dessert plates were removed.

Jordon got up from the table and went to the bar. A small group gathered around him, too small for his liking. The band started playing, and Charlotte was swept onto the dance floor by one admirer after another. Kate and Dev danced too, lost in the love they had for one another, almost, but not quite, forgetting about their charge.

Annoyed by the amount of attention Charlotte was stealing from him, Jordon couldn't concentrate on his conversations, said things that made no sense, and behaved rudely while trying to be engaging. His small group began to disperse. The last thing he wanted to do was dance, but he thought he should before people started talking negatively. He made his way to Charlotte, who had just returned to their table, and asked her to dance.

Jordon wasn't the best dancer and preferred slow songs. Charlotte made him look good and followed his movements gracefully. When had she learned to dance like this? Who had taught her? Just to make small talk, he asked.

Sweetly, she replied, "Why, my Nanny Pen taught me."

"What kind of a name is Pen?" he asked roughly.

"Pen is short for Penelope. Nanny Pen's full name is Penelope Cather."

Jordon almost pushed her away in stunned disbelief. His eyes grew narrow, and he gripped her by the arm and led her away from the floor, past the table, and off to the side.

"Have you been seeing this woman, Charlotte?" he almost hissed.

"Why yes," she said sweetly. "She means a great deal to me. I've even met her son, a beautiful young man. We were both upset about the incident involving our boys. They are quite alike, you know. I noticed it when I met him during my last visit to their home. It was something in the way he moved. Do you remember that song by the Beatles, Jordon? That was what caught my attention, the way he moved so much like Taylor."

"Why didn't you tell me about this?" he asked.

"You didn't ask."

Jordon's head was spinning, and so was the room. "I've got to get out of here. We're leaving."

"You go on, Jordon. I'm having such a wonderful time. Kate and Devlin are here. They will be glad to take me home later."

People were staring. Jordon had to get out of there. He couldn't make a scene, and his wife knew it. He would make her pay later. Right now he had some business to take care of. He turned from her and hurried for the door.

As he strode out, Charlotte explained gaily that he'd been called away to attend to an issue of importance and would return, if possible. With wine flowing and the band playing, few missed the guest of honor, too dazzled by his lovely wife. No one heard the rumblings of thunder rolling and reverberating through the mountain gap toward the southeastern ridge.

Miss Pen had done her duty, sending Raven out into the night. She trusted Jeff Farley and had done everything he'd instructed. Her boy was becoming a man, and he had no better man to follow than Jeff Farley. She thought of all the mothers who'd had to send their sons off to war. There were many types of war, but to those involved, it usually came down to fighting when no other recourse was possible. Without a fight, the evil in this world could take over. Sacrifice had to be made, like the one she was making tonight. She had to send him out into the battle and pray that Farley knew what he was doing.

Mamma Phoebe had walked the distance after dark and all alone. She carried everything she needed in a knapsack strapped to her back and a burlap sack tied to her waistband. When she reached the falls, she found the exact spot to begin. She laid the knapsack down and removed a small bale of twigs bound with twine from it. She took a garden trowel from the burlap sack and dug out a round, shallow hole in a bare sandy area near the stream. She gathered several smooth round rocks from the water and placed them in a circle around the hole. She untied the bale of twigs and formed them into the shape of a teepee in the center of the hole, using the twine to secure them. She searched and found two long, sturdy branches and removed all the small branches from them with her pocket knife. She stuck each one in the ground within the circle on opposite sides of the teepee of twigs, pushing their bases into the soft ground until stabilized. She wrapped twine around the tops of each branch and connected them, pulling the tops together to form an arch over the teepee. She removed the Paket Kongo with the rooster feathers sticking out from the burlap pouch and hung it from the center of the arch.

She looked up to calculate the time. A train of dark clouds were passing in haste over the perfectly round, darkened moon, rolling along like the thunder. The wind swirled the smoke coming from her cabin chimney, creating a big black cauldron in the sky. It was time to light her small fire. It was time to call the evil home. She looked at the demon rock and shuddered. He was watching as surely as the moon up above.

She began chanting:

"Protection come to me this day,
Bring the evil one this way,
Bring him swift and bring him sure
Give me strength and keep me pure.
Bring an end to our despair
Lure him to his devil's lair."

Then she reached down to light the fire. It took her a few tries before it caught. At the moment it did, a clap of thunder shook the ground she was standing on, and she almost toppled over. The flames flickered and cracked and rose higher as she chanted:

"Feather of fowl, slaughter of blood,
Root of the mandrake, red clay and mud,
Yellow moon watching, clouds hanging low,
Thunder a-roarin', nowhere to go,
Horned-owl a-screechin', out of his hole
Lightning a-crackin', chillin' the soul,
Stirrin' the cauldron, high in the sky'
Curse on the devil, someone will die."

Taylor Reed was on the move. He'd arrived at the inn after closing time and hadn't been sure what to do next. There was no sign of the truck. He decided to walk up the steps to the inn and look inside. There were guests sitting about and some out on the veranda, watching for the storm. A tall, slender woman with dark brown hair came to the door and asked if she could help him. It was evident she didn't want to help him at all.

"Oh, I'm sorry. I'm a friend of Raven Cather, and we were supposed to meet up tonight. I—I thought he might still be working. Would you know where I could find him?"

"I'm not in the habit of giving out information to strangers."

"I'm not a stranger, ma'am. I've been working in town all summer—that's how we met. I didn't mean to upset you. It's just that I promised to meet him and ran late and was hoping he might be running late too, but I didn't see his truck in the parking lot."

"Well, first of all, the truck is not his. It was wrecked this morning and is probably totaled, but fortunately no one was injured. Raven is probably home with his mother after the scare she had this morning. If not, she'd be the one to tell you where he is."

She pointed the way and said, "Just take that path round the side of the inn and you'll come to their cottage. But don't creep around peeking in doors and scaring our guests."

"Sorry, ma'am, it won't happen again."

She shut the door in his face.

He followed the path with trepidation, upset by what he had heard. The insidiousness of his father's plan hit him, the reality unbearable. He felt hopeless and alone as thunder pounded into his brain. He fell to his knees on the shadowed path and cried bitter tears of remorse. He was no better than his father and might as well be dead. Was that why he'd come, to meet his deserved end? He didn't know anymore and didn't care. After a few minutes, he got back on his feet and walked on like a condemned man, trudging along until he came to the cottage. He saw candles burning in each window. Odd, he thought, for a summer night. Did it have something to do with the storm, candles on a stormy night? People put candles in windows for someone coming home.

He stood at the front door, unable to knock, unable to leave. She opened the door, took him by the hand and led him inside, and then closed the door behind them. A streak of lightning crossed the sky and knocked out the electricity at the inn. A few seconds later, the thunder shook its foundation. But all was calm in the cottage, and the candles still burned in the windows.

CHAPTER THIRTY-SIX

O love is a crooked thing,
There is nobody wise enough
To find out all that is in it,
For he would be thinking of love
Till the stars had run away
And the shadows had eaten the moon.

~ William Butler Yeats

CHIEF FARLEY SAT WAITING IN his cruiser. He was parked in the town parking lot, back in the corner by a stand of trees, hidden from view. It was Deputy Purdy's favorite spot for catching speeders. During daytime hours, it was almost impossible to speed down Main Street without hitting a pedestrian, a car backing out from one of the slanted slots, a delivery truck stopped for unloading, a mountain biker maneuvering through town, or a retiree driving a golf cart. During evening hours, the rare speeder was easy to catch, hence Aura Lee's suggestion that Farley assign Deputy Purdy additional responsibilities.

He'd followed her suggestion tonight, putting Purdy on surveillance patrol at the inn, beginning at ten o'clock. Their conversation had been brief, and it occurred to Farley that he hadn't taken the time to ask Purdy about his missing rooster investigation. Purdy had been so excited about the surveillance assignment, he must have forgotten to bring it up. If Farley's plan was going to work, he had to make the call now. Dev had agreed to be the catalyst to draw him out.

Farley was about to call when his cell phone buzzed. It was Dev.

"He's on his way. Charlotte said something to him on the dance floor about Miss Pen, and Reed stormed out after she refused to go with him.

"Don't worry, Jeff, we'll take care of her, but you should have seen her tonight. She stole the show! It almost made Reed nuts. Call me if you need any more help tonight. I'm not sure you should be going after him alone."

"Thanks, Dev. I might take you up on your offer."

Farley put the phone back in his shirt pocket and waited. The bull had been prodded enough to make him charge. Farley was ready. Jordon would have to drive back through town from the reception hall to get to the Orchard Lake Inn or the mountain road leading to Mamma Phoebe's access road. He was betting on the latter but wanted to make sure Miss Pen was protected. He could hear thunder on the mountain and hoped the rain would hold off.

He remembered Mamma Phoebe telling him, "The rain will not come until the thunder roars and the old devil moon has his say."

He stuck his head out the open window of the cruiser and looked up at the shadowy full moon. He said aloud as if talking to a friend, "I need your help tonight, buddy."

Just then, Farley saw the headlights and hit his head on the window frame pulling it back inside. The Mercedes glided past, slow and deliberate. Farley started the engine and pulled out of the lot. He held back enough to see the faint glow of tail-lights and followed with caution until the Mercedes turned onto the mountain road. He'd been right. Now he could safely hold back, knowing where the car was headed, being extra careful to stay hidden.

It had taken Jordon Reed's full concentration to get through town without speeding. He was trying not to speed now but couldn't restrain himself. The lines in the road were blurry, his vision impaired by the alcohol and his state of mind. He drove straight through the blind curves, ignoring the dividing lines and the possibility of an oncoming vehicle. "Who would be driving on a night like this anyway?" he muttered angrily.

He pushed down on the gas pedal and made each bend in the road a challenge. He was gearing up for a showdown. He was going to get rid of that old woman if he had to kill her himself, and that was exactly what he proposed to do. It was a perfect night for it. She'd probably scared Granger off with her hoodoo magic, but she wouldn't scare him. He'd show her the magic of *power* and how it could crush anyone, including her uppity sister and her illegitimate boy. He'd tell her that before she croaked. He'd let all of them know it, including his pitiful excuse of a wife. She'd find out the penalty for betrayal. She'd be the last on his list.

An oncoming car came from around the next bend, and he swerved to avoid it. If he'd been farther along at the curve, he'd have hit it head on. The odds were in his favor tonight, a good sign. He was driving so fast he almost missed the access road. It seemed criminal to drive the Mercedes on it, but he had no choice. It was difficult to slow down with his adrenaline rushing ahead. The branches of the trees along the side of the road were swaying in the breeze. His headlights illuminated the gaps and ruts and rocks and fallen branches, but he ignored all obstacles and accelerated his speed, skimming along undeterred until the right front tire hit a deep pothole, throwing the vehicle out of alignment. He swerved to avoid another hole, sending rocks and gravel flying.

The repetitive sound of thunder jarred his nerves, but the occasional jagged streaks of lightning excited him. But when a lightning bolt hit one of the trees on the side of the road ahead of him, he almost jumped out of his seat. He heard the tree split as the top half of its trunk separated and started to fall. He sped up and felt the ground-shaking thud behind him. The tree missed his back bumper by inches. He felt driven to mania by his luck and started laughing. But his laughter soon died when he came to the Y fork in the road and his headlights fell upon a wooden post.

Hanging from it was the carcass of a large, dead rooster, its feathers plucked and parts of its flesh missing. It was bound with twine and decorated with colorful pieces of material. There were thatches of various plants or herbs hanging from its torso and an odd-shaped root attached to one remaining claw. Jordon stared at the root and knew its meaning. He grew serious and vengeful in that moment and took the right fork.

Farley was not far behind but kept his distance. He'd catch up at the fork and move in on him then. When he saw the road blocked, he wasted no time. He had tools in the trunk and was strong enough to get the job done. He got out of the car and went to work. His father had taught him well. A tree trunk this size would not stop a woodsman. But he had to hurry.

There was a light on in Mamma Phoebe's cabin, and smoke billowed from the chimney. Jordon assumed she was in there and likely alone. He turned off his headlights as he approached. He shut off the engine, got out of the car, and crept as silently as he could toward the front porch. The shrill screech of a night-owl announced his presence. He wanted to shoot it dead. It screeched once again and then stopped.

Jordon was on the front porch and pushed on the door. It creaked open. He stepped inside and looked around. She wasn't there. No one was there. There was a huge pot hanging from a hook under the chimney, like something from medieval days. With stealthy movements he crept forward and carefully looked inside. It was bubbling something black and gooey and smelled awful. There were rooster feathers hanging here and there. Glancing around, he saw what appeared to be stains of blood on her table.

He went back outside and went to his car for a flashlight. He found the path and followed it. He'd been on this path before, but long ago and farther along at a place where he'd have to cross the stream. It seemed like yesterday as he thought of it. He stumbled and almost fell, stopping to pause as his memories carried him back.

He'd been married less than a year and was full of ambition then. It was the first summer he'd used the family summer home. His father-in-law had given him the keys and told him to use it whenever he pleased. It was a perfect place for planning campaigns and getting away from the responsibilities of marriage. His typical pattern was to stay for two weeks at a time during the summer to gear up for elections, bringing with him a team of supporters. He didn't mind the company—they were necessary to his future—but needed a break from them too, so he would go into town to get to know some of the local potential voters.

She was sliding out of a pickup truck, the most common vehicle in town. The man driving, he later found out, was her uncle, a mean and wild-looking fellow. She was wild-looking too, in a far different way—sleek, smooth, and sensual—an unbelievable creature. He'd found it hard to breathe watching her. He'd been coming down the street from the post office, and she had stopped him dead in his tracks.

He could tell she was young, too young. Somehow he had to know her, get to her. He watched her go into the market alone. He followed. She had a list she gave to the elderly woman sitting on a stool by the cash register. This old woman knew everyone in the county, allowed people to run tabs, and still did all the calculations in her head. She never forgot a face or how much they owed.

"I've come to pay our tab, Miss Rose," the girl said, "and pick up a few things."

Her voice sounded musical. He listened while standing out of sight behind a row of shelves.

"I'm sorry to hear about your mama, Evangeline. It's been a while since you've been in, and I've been meanin' to send my condolences."

"Thank you, Miss Rose."

Evangeline. Her name was Evangeline. He waited while she did her shopping, meandering around, waiting for the right moment. It came in front of the bread rack behind the second aisle. Miss Rose was hard of hearing, so he wasn't concerned about being overheard, and they were standing where she couldn't see them. He had a brief window of opportunity and made the most of it. With a few words of introduction and his flair for seduction, he captured her attention. He must have seemed as exotic to her as she had to him because the attraction was mutual; he could see it in her eyes. He pleaded with her on the spot to see him again. He told her he would meet her anywhere, anytime, night or day. He drew her toward him and looked deeply into her eyes and told her they were meant to be together.

Evangeline was a child of nature, mature in that respect, despite her inexperience. She ran from him that day, but he knew she would return, and she did. He made an excuse to get away each day around the time they'd met and take a walk by the store and then back again. On the third day, she appeared, driven to town by the same man. Jordon waited until she'd been inside the store for a few minutes before he went in. She passed by him quickly and handed him a note, purchased her items, talked to Miss Rose, and then left.

The map she'd given him was crude and daunting. It would take effort and fortitude to get to her. There were roads and signs and trails and a stream. She'd drawn him a picture that included every detail and landmark. She marked the halfway place where she would meet him and lead him the rest of the way. It had to be very early morning, another challenge put before him. His whole life back then was a challenge, but this would be one he'd enjoy. He had two days left before he had to leave Serena. He was not going to leave without seeing her.

The first time they met was at daybreak, when she'd led him to the falls. The next time, after he knew the way, was during the dark of the moon. It had to be that way because her father worked at his still under the light of the moon and could see the falls from there, and the hoodoo woman came there too, to do her magic, Evangeline had said, as if all of this was normal. He remembered feeling he was in a foreign land with strange inhabitants and she was the exotic bird in the midst.

He'd gone away after their first meeting and thought of nothing else until his return. He returned many times that summer, building his campaign and finding his way to her. He lost his way once and she had to find him, he'd lost his bearings in darkness she could see through as clearly as daylight. He'd have gone through fire to get to her, and the knowledge of her waiting for him almost drove him mad. He'd work in a frenzy, as if ignited by a potent fuel, and delegated limitless tasks to his team until he could steal away in the night.

He remembered now the scent of her, fresh as the waters. He remembered the waters and how they produced their own light, illuminating the pitch black of night when the moon disappeared completely. She'd told him the waters were special and spoke of the Cherokee legend about them. But mostly he remembered the way she gave herself to him, fully, completely, without reservation, without fear, as though it were the most natural thing in the world and she was meant to be his for all time.

He'd even felt that way too, when he wasn't thinking at all and the passion overtook his rational mind, when he had no thought of his life in Charleston, his child on the way, his political ambitions, and his lust for power. The people around him had started to notice things; the scratches and bruises covering his arms, the torn clothing—the result of traipsing through the wild in the middle of the night—and his inability to stay awake during the daytime.

It would be his lust for power that would bring him back to his senses. He had to have it more than he had to have her. It was nothing he could explain; it just had to be. Just as he'd known from the beginning, his time with Evangeline had to come to an end.

However, the end he'd planned had gone terribly wrong. He faltered again on the path and found it hard to move forward as that night came alive in his mind and the thunder roared above him.

He'd been busy for months gearing up for an election and had promised to return to Serena and her as soon as it was over. The break had given him time to assess the distraction she caused in his life. There was too much money at stake, and he couldn't afford to lose Charlotte. His desire for Evangeline was a burning problem he couldn't shake, but he knew he would in time. He'd taken a ten-day reprieve after winning the election, and she would be his reward. He'd see her a few more times to get the need for her out of his system so he could tackle his new office with vigor and full concentration, leaving Serena and Evangeline behind. But tonight, ah tonight, would be heaven. It was the dark of the moon, and she'd be there waiting.

He was not prepared for the shock of her condition. She saw it in his eyes and in every nuance of his expression. The look on her face was devastating . . . or would have been to someone less callous. She begged him to hold her, to kiss her once more, to never leave her, to take her away with him. How could he do that? He had the perfect wife for the life he wanted. What would he do with Evangeline? It was impossible. She was like a child, well, actually, *was* a child chronologically. He hadn't even thought about the consequences of that. Hadn't been thinking at all.

He had to get out of there. The place was giving him the creeps. Even the falls had lost their luster. Had there always been a face in the rock? Maybe Jordon was seeing things, but that face appeared to be smirking at him.

He turned to leave, to run, to get as far away from his mistake as he could, but she clung to him from behind. He turned to push her away. The rock-face was leering, mocking him as she pleaded. He spoke to her harshly. She made the most sorrowful sound, a musical moan. She reached for him and he pushed her again, violent and hard, the rock-face egging him on. She stumbled backwards to the edge of the stream and fell, but started to get up, reaching to him again. In that moment, Jordon saw her as she had appeared the first time he'd come to her there beside the falls.

The ecstasy of her expression was worse than her pleading, and Jordon knew in that moment she would never let him go. He picked up a large rock with both hands and hit her with it, on an angle to the side of her head. He had to stop her, stop everything she could do to him, all that she could ruin, and erase her from his life. She slipped back, halfway into the stream, her head resting on the bank, the red blood running into the sparkling blue water. He placed the rock beside her wound and hurried into the dark woods without looking back.

CHAPTER THIRTY-SEVEN

The wind is rushing after us,
and the clouds are flying after us,
and the moon is plunging after us,
and the whole wild night is in pursuit of us;
but so far we are pursued by nothing else.

~ Charles Dickens

FARLEY MOVED WITH AGILITY AND haste. He'd been a short distance behind Reed before being stopped by the fallen section of the tree. The minutes were flying by as thunder reverberated in the turbulent air and lightning spiked down from the sky. When the road was finally cleared, he raced to the cabin, fearing the worst and denying its possibility. Jordon Reed was not going to hurt Mamma Phoebe; he couldn't let that happen. He almost slammed into Reed's car, left in the shadows on the road a ways back from the cabin. He leapt out of his car and ran to the porch. The front door was wide open.

Jordon Reed had returned to the present and plodded along the path, his rage building with each step. Someone had been screwing with his mind, working against him all along. They were probably all in it together: Charlotte and those friends of hers, the old witch and her sister, maybe even the kid. No wonder he'd been having crazy dreams, feeling like he'd been hit by a truck every morning, and remembering things best left forgotten. Remembering Evangeline.

He'd come back, hadn't he? He'd come back to her and her waters for good. It was ironic how he'd thought about it from the beginning but had focused his ambitions elsewhere, thinking he'd make it rich in politics. What a joke. How was he to know people would end up carrying plastic bottles of water everywhere, buying them by the caseload, spending a fortune on water from the purest sources? Who would have believed the air and water would become so polluted that most of it would not be fit to drink? If he'd have stayed with Evangeline, he'd be rich now instead of just getting started.

The sound of the waterfall gave him pause. There was a faint glimmer of light up ahead. He heard a voice, strong for an old woman. He couldn't make out the words, but she seemed to be chanting. She was probably putting a curse on him. He crept silently along, stooping over to sneak up on her. The rolling, rumbling thunder had grown louder. A bolt of lightning streaked across the sky. He saw her in the distance, standing in front of some makeshift campfire, her arms held high, chanting to the moon. The waters served as backlight, the falls rushing behind her, shimmering, glistening, blue light on blackness. The demonic face beckoned. There was no sneaking up on its evil. It had come alive watching her and waiting for him.

Mamma Phoebe called him out, her words spoken loud and clear.

"Feather of fowl, slaughter and blood
Root of the mandrake, red clay and mud
Thunder moon risen, night black as coal
Screech-owl a hootin', safe in his hole
Thunder is speakin', calling you near
Devil is watchin', knowin' you're here
Devil is weaker, stronger am I
Curse on the devil, someone will die."

She turned to him and called him out again, startling him for a moment. She was dressed like the voodoo woman he'd seen in South America, the one he'd bought the root from. That woman had been small and wiry. This old woman was much larger and wide. She was still no match for him, not even close. He stood up straight and walked toward her.

She stood her ground unafraid. Shadows seemed to move around her, wavy and water-like, a reflection of the shifting waters. She took a burlap bag of some kind and waved it around her. There were feathers sticking out of it, and a putrid scent permeated the air. He felt a bit dizzy and sick to his stomach. The demon face grinned.

"I'll kill you, old woman!" Jordon growled. "I'll kill you where you stand!"

"That might be," she said, her gaze steady. "One of us is going to die tonight."

He lunged for her and yanked the bag from her hand. Rooster feathers flew all around him, and one landed on his head. A powdered dust erupted from the bag and stung his eyes. He rubbed them with his forefingers, and the pain lessened, but his vision was hazy. There appeared to be a shadow standing behind the old witch. She started chanting, and Jordon lunged at her again. The shadow pulled her aside and stood in her place. Jordon couldn't believe it, and neither could she. The boy had come out of nowhere!

Mamma Phoebe cried out his name: Raven.

Jordon tried to make sense of it, stood there and stared. He tried to see past him to the face of the demon, but nothing was there but black rock. He suddenly felt abandoned, alone, and afraid. His eyes began to clear, and he started to back away. Abruptly, stubbornly, he stopped. He'd never backed away in his life and wouldn't now; he had to use his wits.

"You've got me all wrong. I have a right to be here."

Pointing to Mamma Phoebe he continued, "She's been plotting against me to keep me from buying the McCabe land. I have a right to buy any land that is put on the market. She called me here tonight to prevent it! You heard her, using her witch spells to make me come here, to make me crazy." He ran his hands over his head. "Who are you? Why have you been harassing my son? He was lured here too. I'm doing what any father would do to protect his son."

Mamma Phoebe said, "Stop your lies, devil. It will do you no good. That land will never be for sale and never be yours. This boy will own all of it, for it is rightfully his."

Both Jordon and Raven stared at her in confusion.

"Raven is the child of Evangeline McCabe. I birthed him right here in the stream while his mama died at a murderer's hand." She placed a hand on the boy's shoulder. "You might as well know it now, Raven. You would have been told this comin' week, anyway."

She said to Jordon, "You have no right to anything here. If you stay, you will die."

Jordon stared at the boy for a long moment, the incredible realization hitting him and an insidious strategy forming. He lowered his voice to a reasonable level, and with a touch of sincerity said to Raven, "Do you know who I am? I am your father! I loved your mother, back before you were born. The old woman is lying. Evangeline died by accident. I wasn't even here. When I found out, I was devastated. I was told she died in these waters." He gestured toward the stream. "I want the land to be near her again, to be near the stream where she perished. I loved her, son, always, and have grieved for her all these years. Had I known the truth, that my child had lived, I would have returned long ago and raised you, alongside Taylor, who—come to think of it—is your half-brother." He threw out a hand toward the hoodoo woman. "But *they* kept you from me with lies and witchcraft. Now see what's happened? You've been fighting your own brother without even knowing it. You must have a lot in common; you both went after the same girl. But that aside, we could be a family. I'm a powerful man. I could do a lot for you, share everything I have with you."

Raven stood silent, staring at Jordon, watching him talk, listening to his words.

Storm clouds hovered above them. The moon was blue and shadowed, and lightning created havoc in the sky. The lion thunder roared. Jordon felt empowered by the audacity of his story. He glanced once more at the demon rock and saw that it was back, and it was changing.

When he looked back at Raven, Jordon detected a hint of humor in his expression, a slight enigmatic smile. Jordon felt unsettled but tried to continue, "Think of this as a family reunion of sorts." Still Raven did not respond, and Jordon's tenuous hold on his temper slipped, "Except most don't have a witch standing around casting spells and chanting curses at the person trying, in good faith, to reunite."

Mamma Phoebe bent down and picked up a few of the scattered rooster feathers, shook them in Jordon's direction, and started chanting again.

"See what I mean!" Jordon ground out. "Can't you shut her up?"

Raven said nothing.

Jordon couldn't take his eyes from the boy and began to shake with fury. He'd swayed thousands with his speeches. Why wasn't this boy reacting to his words, what was the matter with him? Why was he smiling? What—

The face altered before him into softness, framed with black hair flowing wild and free. Her sapphire eyes glistened with tears that fell like raindrops from the sky. She moved forward, reaching out. Jordon trembled and backed away. She flowed toward him, almost floating, and the fresh scent of water filled his nostrils. He felt as if he were drowning, cried out in terror, and tried to fight back. He closed his eyes and mind and moved toward the apparition. The wood-fire crackled, and he opened his eyes. The kid was standing there unchanged, with the old woman next to him, feathers in hand.

Jordon leaped at her, grabbed her by the throat, and started choking her. Raven was on him in a second, pulling him off and thrusting him aside. Jordon landed by the teepee fire and felt the red-hot cinders burn his hand. He reached for one of the stick-poles and yanked at it fiercely. The structure collapsed as he jumped to his feet. He swung the stick wildly, a hickory weapon, with strength of a madman, the demon inside. He moved back toward her, intending to kill her, but Raven was quicker, and kept him at bay.

Raven felt dizzy, impaired by his head wound, his reflexes slowed, and Jordon landed a blow. He landed another as Raven fought boldly. The man was possessed; it was two against one. The spirit of evil embodied this father, a man who was willing to strike down his own son.

Mamma Phoebe lay helpless, the shadows around her, calling to the moon she could no longer see. Her boy was in danger, and it seemed the demon was winning. She called to the spirit and said one last prayer.

The shot split the night air. Blood spurted from the arm mid-swing. The stick fell to the ground as Jordon cried out and staggered back in agony, expecting another bullet, one that was almost fired.

Farley held him in his gun sight but stopped his angry impulse. He was a man with inner strength. Jordon Reed was done.

Raven knelt by Mamma Phoebe. The shadows had dispersed. Raindrops fell upon her brow as she lay with eyes wide open.

"Guess it's not my time," she said hoarsely. "That thunder moon has had its say."

The rain began to fall in torrents. Farley tried to call for help but couldn't get reception. He bandaged Jordon's arm with a scarf from Mamma Phoebe's wet garment. A wet feather was lodged in his hair. The rain came down hard and fast, and they had no time to spare. Raven insisted he was fine, but Farley suspected he was stretching the truth. Mamma Phoebe was on her feet, but he didn't know how she managed. Jordon Reed was whimpering in pain and mumbling to himself. The waterfall was gushing, and the waters were rising. The path would be flooded if the rain continued to pour. They had to move quickly.

Because of his wounded arm, Farley didn't cuff Jordon but kept him ahead on the path with his gun trained on Jordon's back. Raven offered to carry Mamma Phoebe, but she refused.

With raspy voice she scolded, "Don't be fussing, child. I fought that old demon rock tonight and won. Besides, I'm too big a woman to be carted around. I've got enough power left in me to get myself home."

The stream began to overflow, making wading difficult. They still had a ways to go, and Farley was concerned. Jordon continued talking, the pitch of his voice rising with the water. He was starting to panic and beginning to hallucinate.

"She's coming after me. She's all around me, can't you all see? It's not rain, it's not a downpour. It's her, I tell you, sending the water to bring me back. She's been waiting all these years. I knew she'd never let me go. She'll never let me go!"

Farley was accustomed to the unpredictable behavior of criminals when trapped or caught, but this was one he hadn't encountered. He wasn't sure what to do. He felt tempted to shoot Jordon and put him out of his misery, but he put the thought out of his mind. Raven and Mamma Phoebe were following close behind and were his main concern. He had to get them back to the cabin safely. If the driving rain continued, they could be caught in a flash flood.

At first he thought he was seeing things, but there it was again: a tiny beam of light in the distance. He raised up his flashlight and signaled. The light disappeared for several disheartening seconds, but then appeared again, closer, brighter, and signaling back. Farley urged them on, treading water as they moved toward the light and the familiar voice that called out to them.

Farley had never been so relieved in his life when he saw Dev appear with rain gear, an extra knapsack, and his gun in tow. Dev moved quickly, covering Mamma Phoebe in protection, emptying the knapsack of gear, including a rope to keep everyone connected. Visibility worsened when the wind changed direction. The rain fell sideways when gusts of wind as powerful as a hurricane swept down upon them. Dev instructed them to hold tightly to the rope.

Jordon began to wail. "She's sending them for me! She's sending the wind and the waters! It's hopeless. Hopeless! She won't let you take me away. She's trying to save me! She's saving me from all of you. I see it now. I know it!"

Suddenly, he let go of the rope and veered off the path in the opposite direction, splashing his way back in the direction of Shadow Peak. Farley had miscalculated, believing Jordon's bent for self-preservation would keep him on the path. He yelled to Dev to go on with the others, to get them to safety. Then he went after Jordon.

Farley's long legs gave him an advantage, and he was able to move through the water with the wind at his back. Jordon was not far ahead and was easy to follow because he continued yelling, calling her name.

"Evangeline, Evangeline! I've come back. I understand now. I've come back for good, Evangeline! Evangeline! I'm coming to you. You can drown them, kill them all. But save me, Evangeline! Save me and I will be yours forever!"

The waves of the stream rolled back in reverse motion as the wind blew wildly toward Raven Brook Falls. The water surged from behind Farley, pushing him forward, almost knocking him down and then flowing on. It grew lighter up ahead and strangely turbulent. The wind began swirling, gathering centralized momentum. Farley no longer felt pressure on his lower legs and was able to move quickly toward the odd weather system. Then his instincts took over. He slowed down to listen, proceeding with caution, his senses alert.

Jordon's voice sounded weaker, his cries swallowed up as if eaten by the monstrous storm overtaking the falls and its stream. The wind made a sound like a spinning-top whine, a melodious, mysterious sound, mournful and yet menacing. Branches and leaves flew in every direction as the water continued to be sucked into the vortex. Farley stood watching, waiting, knowing he could not move into the whirling phenomenon rising before him. The relentless humming continued with vengeful tenacity, a moaning whine, angry, sorrowful, almost human.

Suddenly, a terrible gut-wrenching cry rang out and brought everything to a halt. Farley felt the evaporation of wind and water happen as spontaneously as it had started. The water lowered around his feet and he was almost able to run, but not quite. He knew where he was headed, the exact distance from the falls. He had stood there with Mamma Phoebe when she'd shown him the place where Evangeline had died.

Jordon Reed was lying there, half in and out of the water, his head resting near a large wet rock washed almost clean of his blood. Blood gushed from a wide gash along the side of his head, spurting a red stream down his neck and shoulders, mingling with blood running from the wound in his arm. The steady flow of crimson followed its course down to his submerged hand, which closed in a tight grip as he tried to hold onto the life force leaving his body. He was conscious enough to realize the futility of his effort as he watched his life drain into the rushing current of the waters he had so coveted. This vital, tainted substance would no longer fuel his actions, nor would it remain in the sacred place where the evil he had wrought was being eradicated.

Farley reached Jordon in time to see his last expression, one of recognition and then surrender. With his last breath, he uttered, "Evangeline."

The rain had subsided while Farley sat waiting, knowing Dev would return with the help he would need. He was drenched and exhausted, yet looked up in wonder. The moon was as blue as the sparkling waters, the color of sapphire, with the added luster of shimmering starlight and luminous pearls. There was a true calm after the storm. He thought back to the days of his ancestors and the Cherokees who once honored the land under Shadow Peak. He pondered the existence of the spirits and gods they'd believed in, and questioned whether evil could be held within a place where evil had been done.

The Cherokees believed that evil could be purged through the sacrifice of life. Mamma Phoebe had talked of rituals done to appease the spirits, to purify contamination, to rectify wrongs. Had nature responded to some ancient plea? Had the land been washed clean by the waters? Had Evangeline's mournful spirit been appeased? Was she finally at rest? Or had her spirit transformed into a peaceful, ever-present entity, watchful and protective over her beloved falls?

CHAPTER THIRTY-EIGHT

And Fall, with her yeller harvest moon
and the hills growin' brown and golden
under a sinkin' sun.

~ Roy Bean

SUMMER PASSED AND OCTOBER CAME with a full harvest moon on the rise. Farley sat in his office with his chair turned to the side of his desk and his legs stretched out, reflecting on the events of the past few months beginning with that night.

The rains had caused flash-flooding throughout the region. Several people had been caught in the flood, with two other deaths attributed to the thunderstorm. Living on a mountaintop was like living in the sky; during a storm, the sky holds dominance over the earth. Perhaps that is why the old-timers studied the sky and lived by the moon and surrounding constellations. They were as much of part of it as the ground upon which they stood.

He remembered feeling a sense of powerlessness as the sky-waters met with the land-waters and everything around them was changed into something he could not control. They could have been swept away as others had been or shown the mercy they'd been given. Reed had met a fate that spared him the scandal, humiliation, and punishment he deserved, had he lived. Farley had been spared the loss of those he'd come to care for and would always be grateful to Dev for his help that night, and to Miss Pen, who had sent him and had been waiting at the cabin when they'd returned.

Dev had contacted Deputy Purdy, who had been helping the owners and terrified guests at the inn weather the storm without power after the alternate source generator was struck by lightning. He'd had the help of Taylor Reed who, with the encouragement of Miss Pen, had turned himself in to him in the parking lot of the inn minutes before the rain started to fall. Miss Pen had then gone with Dev, who she'd called for a ride after Taylor had revealed what he knew. She'd guided Dev to Mamma Phoebe's cabin and then sent him out into the perilous storm to find Farley and her loved ones.

Jordon Reed's death was ruled an accidental death by drowning while fleeing arrest. The truth would have not been believed. Rodney Granger had been captured and confessed his part in Reed's nefarious plan. The cassava supplied by Jordon Reed was linked to each murder and attempted murder, vindicating his victims.

Taylor Reed volunteered for rehab in Denver, Colorado, where he was in long-term addiction treatment and therapy. Dev had made the arrangement and referral and had flown with him personally in mentorship and support to be admitted into a facility run by Dev's professional colleagues. There had been a stark change in Taylor since his talk with Miss Pen. He had tried to make amends before leaving. Dev had encouraged him to wait until his return. He had made amends to his mother, who was concerned only with his welfare. She assured him she would not be as she had been before and would support him instead of smothering him. She, too, was remarkably changed.

Raven Cather and Willa Mae Parsons had recovered. Raven had a setback of injury from that night and needed rest and rehabilitation. Willa Mae attended to him with love and affection. She never regained memory of the assault. Raven had come to terms with his new reality but had difficulty accepting the reality of a father who'd tried to kill him and who had murdered his mother.

Strangely enough, it was Taylor Reed who had helped him. They'd had one conversation when Taylor, with Pen's permission, shared with Raven how his father had hurt him too, but over a long period of time. The strain between them was not mended, but the animosity Raven felt toward Taylor lessened that day. As Dev had told him, amends is for the person who makes it, and the person who receives has the right to accept or reject it. Raven would over time come to accept it.

The will had been read, and Raven Brook Cather was now an heir to a vast amount of property and the waters of Raven Brook Falls. But Mamma Phoebe was still in charge. They'd decided to wait until he was twenty-one to officially take over. Now that she realized her time had not yet come, her vigor had been restored. She'd even put on weight. But she'd retired from being a hoodoo doctor and decided to take up making elderberry wine. She wanted Miss Pen to retire and help her, maybe start a business so that by the time Raven took over, they'd have a little sideline of their own.

The hero who emerged from all this? Deputy Purdy. He received a citation recommended by the owners and guests of the inn. But his most remarkable feat was capturing the bandit who kidnapped Henry the Eighth from Charlotte. This was one offense Jordon Reed had not been guilty of. Bradford Johnson was arrested for stealing the rooster (it couldn't be called kidnapping on a police report). He admitted sneaking into Charlotte's garden in the middle of the night and netting the rooster, putting him in a sack and driving him to the outskirts of Serena where he was thrown out the window on the interstate highway. His sister had suspected something when she'd found rooster feathers stuck in the lining of his shirt when she was doing his laundry. Being the church-going woman she was, it had preyed on her mind since the rooster's disappearance. But it was the self-satisfied manner of her brother since that night that convinced her he was guilty. He'd always been mean and vindictive, and she was tired of taking care of him.

When Deputy Purdy had come around questioning the neighbors door-to-door the first time, her being the only neighbor, she hadn't said anything. But when he came round again, the day before the storm, she told him her suspicions. Two days after the storm, Purdy questioned Johnson, who denied it until his sister produced the feathers she had saved to prove his guilt. The proof drove him to the breaking point and he confessed with glee, proud of the fact that he'd gotten rid of the rooster for good.

However, because Purdy put out a notice the next day about the sack on the highway, he received a call from a woman who had a small farm near the drop-site. She'd been driving home in the middle of the night after tending to a sick relative. She would have stayed all night had she not had chickens to feed early in the morning. She almost ran over the sack in the road. She stopped just in time, got out of her truck, and heard the incensed crowing of the infuriated rooster. She took him home and released him into her barnyard, where he received an overabundance of admiration and attention from her chickens. He'd been there ever since, a king among many princesses.

Charlotte, of course, had been thrilled to know he was safe and alive and went there to visit. She enjoyed the fact that he was living a fairy-tale existence and didn't have the heart to reclaim him. He did recognize her, and they had an exchange of eye contact in which he let her know he was happy in his new home.

Charlotte was happy too—not what one would call a grieving widow. She'd weathered the scandal in the protection of her Serena environment and its people. Scandal wasn't such a big deal in the mountains. The folks who lived there understood the ways of human nature because they lived in the midst of a wilderness ruled by it. Jordon Reed was a rogue human who'd been taken down and given over to his Lord for judgment. That was the way they saw it, and it was time to move on.

Had Charlotte lived elsewhere, she might have been shunned, left out of lunch or society parties, and rejected by friends and acquaintances who had initially gravitated to her because of her powerful husband. In Serena, they brought her casserole dishes and homemade cookies and cared because she was one of them. She'd returned to the mountains by choice and was enfolded into her village community.

Aura Lee came through the door and brought Chief Farley back to the present.

"You'll never guess what I heard on the way back from the post office. There's a film company planning to come here, wanting to make a movie about Purvis McCabe. Seems he's become a bigger legend since his death. They want to meet with Mamma Phoebe and the Cathers to get their permission. It wouldn't get started until sometime next year, but they say they're going to make it whether they have permission or not, except it would be better if they had the full cooperation of everyone who knew him. There's a famous producer behind this, and it might turn out to be one of those big-budget movies. Maybe they'll be wanting extras on location or here in town! Betsy McClure said she'd like to be one, and Miss Lucy would be perfect for a part. You know, Chief, I've been told I have talent. I was in a play once in elementary school and—"

"Aura Lee, I don't want to think about such a thing right now," Farley said, holding up his hands. "We've finally got a little peace and quiet around here. Think about what would be stirred up by a movie being made here."

"Oh, Chief, you're just being a pessimist. Look on the bright side, like I try to do. They wouldn't be here for long, and they'd be a sight better than those news media crews who go round interviewing with their video cams, and it coming to nothing but a few minutes on the nightly news. They never capture the good parts about life here, like a movie would. Besides, by the time they come, folks will be ready for a little excitement. You know how quiet it gets during wintertime. Why, tonight will probably be the last exciting event 'til next spring.

"Shouldn't you be getting home, Chief, to get ready for the wedding? I have my dress all picked out. You probably won't even recognize me, I'll be so decked out. I'd like to see you out of that old uniform you're wearin'—"

"You're right, Aura Lee. I'd better get going."

The wedding was being held at the Orchard Lake Inn. Charlotte had been in charge of the planning, and Miss Pen in charge of the menu, although she no longer worked at the inn. The Serena Garden Club provided the floral arrangements under Charlotte's supervision. Kate and Dev had wanted a simple affair quietly officiated by local clergy, but they were touched by an appeal from their friends to be involved in their celebration. They really hadn't had much choice.

The wedding had taken on a life of its own. Their honeymoon would be in Ireland, and they were leaving in the morning. They would have their special time of intimacy in the lush green land of their ancestors. But this was the time to share with the living, the friends they had made through hardship and happiness, and accept their acts of kindness and the joy those friends had in giving them.

The inn was decorated in the green, white, and gold of a traditional Irish theme, with vases of long-stem French-cream roses, snowy white chrysanthemums, and ivory-white hydrangeas accented by a lush array of greenery. Fresh white snowberry greens covered the mantels and door-frames. Bouquets of gold-tinted Million Star gypsophila baby's breath tied with green satin ribbons decorated each table of the inn. Charlotte had attended to every detail, including soft light and candles to create a romantic atmosphere, and a hefty, kilted bagpiper to add a touch of Celtic flair to the event.

The guests were decked out in their finest regalia, with many variations of style and dress. It was a Serena custom to dress as one pleased, and so they did with colorful effect. Particularly Mamma Phoebe, who was the picture of robust health for a woman who had only months before been prepared to die. She and Miss Pen were living as a family now, grooming Raven for his role of landowner and entrepreneur. They were getting re-acquainted with their community, gaining acceptance and inclusion.

When the ceremony began, all eyes were on Dev, waiting at the altar for the appearance of his bride. The look on his black-browed masculine face touched everyone. He appeared to be waiting for a miracle. Kate didn't disappoint in her understated Irish-lace dress, the color of antique ivory, his mother's Celtic cross with a small emerald in the center at her throat.

Tears welled in the eyes of many in attendance as their vows were spoken and the Irish Claddagh wedding rings exchanged. The bagpipes were played after they were introduced as man and wife. There were a multitude of champagne toasts before dinner, sparking raucous laughter and poignant tears. After the dinner and wedding cake, decorated with shamrocks made of white and green icing, there was dancing on the open veranda beneath a starry sky.

Farley looked handsome in a suit not worn in ages. Charlotte looked stunning in scarlet chiffon. Farley had watched her throughout the evening, her face aglow with a happiness that resulted from helping make the wedding so special for Kate and Dev. After the honeymoon couple had made their retreat and the guests were departing, Farley took Charlotte into his arms, and they danced in the moonlight. The years fell away as they were transported back in time. He was the tall lanky mountain boy she had chosen above the others. She was his fairy-tale princess, living out her make-believe dream. Their love was awakened, their passion rekindled, and the marigold harvest moon watched from above.

Grateful acknowledgements to retired Detective Ron Chmielewski, a veteran of New Jersey Police Department, Trenton, New Jersey, for sharing his invaluable law enforcement expertise. Realtor Graeton Sellars of Cathy Jackson Realty for sharing his expertise and knowledge of ethical practices and demonstrating, in our small town, the highest quality of the profession and service to the community. Dr. D. Lesesne Smith for his explanation of the unusual atmospheric conditions and ozone abundance in the area upon which the fictional town of Serena is based.

Check Out the Prequel to *Murder in a Moonlit Mason Jar:*

The Strange Case of the Doyle Diary Murders

It's Halloween in the quaint, mountain town of Serena, North Carolina, and Kate Delaney is about to discover a hidden secret long tucked away in the dark corners of her century-old church that she and her husband spent several years renovating into a home before his tragic death.

The old building's previous owner used the sacred edifice to practice spiritualism, and her books and objects remain. One book in particular is the work of none other than Sir Arthur Conan Doyle, who traded-in his most famous detective character to prove that ghosts and fairies exist. Kate also unearths a surprising séance message: "Doyle Diary." An avid Sherlock fan, Kate decides a mysterious force has placed this investigation before her, and she compulsively dives into a case that wakes a sinister adversary with a deadly purpose.

Also By Corinne F. Gerwe:

Blood Runs Cold on the Black Side of the Mountain
The Orchestration of Joy and Suffering

For more information about

Corinne F. Gerwe
and
Murder in a Moonlit Mason Jar
please visit:

www.corinnefgerwe.com
cgerwe@rsnet.org
corinnegerwe7@charter.net
@f_gerwe
www.facebook.com/corinne.f.gerwe
Author's Page: www.facebook.com/cfgerwe

For more information about
AE BOOKS
please visit:

www.ambassador-international.com
@AmbassadorIntl
www.facebook.com/AmbassadorIntl